Penguin Books
The Onion Eaters

J. P. Donleavy was born in New York City in 1926 and educated there and at Trinity College, Dublin. In addition to *The Onion Eaters* his works include four novels, *The Ginger Man*, *A Singular Man*, *The Saddest Summer of Samuel S* and *The Beastly Beatitudes of Balthazar B* (1968); a book of short pieces, *Meet My Maker The Mad Molecule* (all these are available as Penguins); and four plays, *The Ginger Man*, *Fairy Tales of New York*, *A Singular Man* and *The Saddest Summer of Samuel S*.

J. P. Donleavy

The Onion Eaters

Penguin Books
in association with Eyre & Spottiswoode

Penguin Books Ltd, Harmondsworth,
Middlesex, England
Penguin Books Australia, Ringwood,
Victoria, Australia
Penguin Books (N.Z.) Ltd,
182–190 Wairau Road,
Auckland 10, New Zealand

First published by Eyre & Spottiswoode 1971
Published in Penguin Books 1972
Reprinted 1975
Copyright © J. P. Donleavy, 1971

Made and printed in Great Britain by
Hazell Watson & Viney Ltd,
Aylesbury, Bucks
Set in Linotype Georgian

1

A cold misty rain descends streaking the windows down an empty shopping street. The university baleful behind its great iron gates, a light in the porter's lodge, a faint yellow beacon at the end of a street where the massive porticoes of the bank shelter lurking figures on this barren saturday afternoon.

Two orange beaked swans paddling up stream under an iron foot bridge arching over a river's sour green waters. At a black door up three stone steps this grey coated gaunt figure looks east and west along the quays. To the slate roof tops and chimney pots puffing smoke over the city. Where a shaft of sunlight spreads, glistens and disappears.

Push open the door. Go down this dark corridor and knock under a sign. Enquiries. Face moist, toes and hands cold. Damp seeping through my gloves. A girl in a big purple hat and large glad smile looks up from behind a high counter.

'Are you Mr Clementine.'

'Yes.'

'Mr Thorn is waiting for you. I'll show you the way. Up the stairs.'

Her heavy blue blotched and pink legs. She holds open the door. From a dark hallway into a darker room. The floors stacked with bulging beribboned files. A desk overflowing with papers. Book filled glass cabinets along the walls. A stuffed owl on a pedestal by the window. This man standing with blond strands patted back on his head, beads of sweat on his brow. Grinning between red tinged cheeks. He turns his head towards the window and looks out upon the grey late day.

'Mr Clementine, Clayton Claw Cleaver Clementine, is it not.'

'Yes.'

'Illustrious family. Elegant and unique. To say the least. Descended directly in the male line from Clementine of The Three Glands. Please, do sit down. Any stack there, of papers will do. On a quiet saturday such as this one's mind wanders and I was wondering, without wanting to pry, naturally. I know this medical rarity has been fully documented three balls on one man, but I mean to say, can one inherit such an incredible bit extra like that. Good Lord, Miss Jones, be gone, please, Mr Clementine and I will not be long and you can lock up.'

'Yes Mr Thorn.'

'Forgive me Mr Clementine, that was a dreadful slip there. Don't be distressed. Of course no one will believe her spreading that all over the city to every Sylvia, Sue and Cynthia. But now between us. What about that. Is there any substance in this scrotal rumour. If I may coin a phrase. Yes, sit there. Pile of torts will give you more comfort than the defendants, what. I mean you understand one can't hold in one's curiosity. Troubling me for months. You don't raise an eyebrow over the chap with one or, God forbid, none, but how many of your chaps will you meet in a month of tuesdays with the bit extra. I mean do having three give any discomfort.'

'I beg your pardon.'

'Well well, of course, one can't contain one's concern over a thing like that. Ah now where are those papers. I put them down. Wasn't a second before you came in. May I trouble you to stand a moment, Mr Clementine, do please forgive me, in case you're sitting on them. Ah to be sure. Now we're right. The full and necessary are here I believe. Three jewels by God in your mechanism and that's that. Very fitting your taking up where your great aunt left off. She herself is a remarkable creature. Must be nearly ninety now. I believe she's just assumed residence in an hotel midway on another continent across the seas.'

'Yes.'

'Well, well. This is the key case which we are instructed to present to you. Daunting proposition if I may say so. Press simultaneously these both points. Open it comes. The big one for the main portal. Rumour is this was used to slap and slay a rapist by your great great grandmother. You wouldn't be any the better for a clap of this across the rotundity. The other keys are arranged alphabetically down to the bottom tray, six trays in all. A few missing. To minor rooms it would seem. You are now possessed of Charnel Castle and certain lands thereabouts.'

'Thank you.'

'Now as a solicitor to whom matrimonial matters upon occasion do come, has the question of your added item, that is to say, the extra of which you are possessed, ever thrown confusion upon a member of the opposite sex.'

'Yes they go out of their minds counting.'

'To be sure, to be sure. But now to be perfectly frank, is it a case that the extra of which you are possessed has led to a little unbridled proclivity now and again. I'm thinking it must be ruddy marvellous, with one more than is standard. To be afloat as you might say on a sea of turpitude. Ah God nature is very good to the aristocracy. Now there's one last matter I've nearly overlooked. You're to pick up the dog at the station. Down there by the custom house. With the compliments of your aunt.'

'Thank you.'

'I'm glad Mr Clementine, to hear, that three is not a crowd in your case.'

Clayton Clementine stepping out into the moisture again. Search one's head for various phrases to throw back at delving questions. Take a calming vision meaningless beyond belief. But a comfort to know.

> That thrice
> They hang
> Down there.
> Untangled
> In the arse white
> Infinity

2

Up the stone steps of the station. Between two white globes on lamp posts. Into this high grey granite edifice. Musty wide corridors under a roof held by girders. Clayton Clementine stops at a counter and open hatchway along the platform. A group of porters and attendants hovering over something huge and grey on a shelf.

'Excuse me.'

'And what can I do for you sir.'

'I am looking for a dog.'

'Are you now. Would you know it if you saw it.'

'Not exactly, just a dog.'

'Are you able to kill a calf a day.'

'I beg your pardon.'

'If we've got the dog you're looking for you'll need to feed him that at least. He can't walk but eat by God, he'd take your hand, shoe or elbow just to fill space between a hindmost molar.'

'Is that him.'

'It is.'

'Hello woof woof. Big bow wow. Come here. Here doggie.'

'It's no use now. Stand up or walk he will not. Four of us it took to carry him here off the train with him licking the countenances off our faces. Then he gobbled down the station master's dentures, full upper and lower like two bits of candy floss.'

Clementine inhaling a large breath to lean and peer over the counter. A little avenue opening between the porters all smiling to show this large grey shaggy animal who looked up from brown friendly eyes as his long tail beat against the shelf.

'Hello doggie. Bow wow. Woof woof. We'll call you Elmer. What about that.'

Elmer with tail flapping was lifted down the front steps of the station by four porters and placed in a horsecab. Past shops, pubs, cinemas and left across a bridge. Woof woof taking note of the city with his big black nose sticking out the window.

Clementine following Elmer lugged by ten hands to this cosy compartment on the train. The great canine spread across three seats. Two friendly drawling travellers referring to each other as ma and pa, peeking in, opening the door. And rearing backwards into the laden arms of their porter.

'Land sakes alive pa that there creature is alive.'

The steam engine throbbed and tinkled, blew a whistle and clicked down the track. As we ride together all alone. There he sits, huge padded paws draped over the edge of the seat. Grey and soft they are. This woof woof's eyes so full of trust. One day soon he should be able to walk, canter, then trot. He's just eating now to gather up the strength to do so. Must be patient. Ah he likes to lick my shoelaces untied. We'll get on together. And he's getting us both plenty of privacy. One likes that.

Flat strange lands pass in the night. Faint lights in cottage windows. Lonely stations and voices in the dark. Unloading goods from the metropolis. With iron wheels rumbling on the platforms. I was instructed to tell the engine driver to stop in the morning at the Castle Crossroads.

At dawn through an open eye I see him already awake, wagging his tail, banging it against the window, smiling at me. The rumbling and roaring of the train. Through the darkness of a tunnel. Light again. And down there the sea. Good God we go across a bridge. Which is swaying. High over a silver stream down between the rocks. Stone walled little fields. A sandy bay and a purple small mountain. The train is slowing. And stopping. Next to a flattened bit of ground. Where the conductor stands with a green flag in one hand and a big key ring in the other.

'Is this the Castle Crossroads.'

'The very same sir.'

'There's nothing here, not even a road.'

'Ah I wouldn't go so far as to say that. Just the other side of the track now there's this bit of road. Sure it's been known that at various times of the week travellers do be passing. I wouldn't be alarmed now sir.'

'Could anyone help me with my luggage and this animal, who must be assisted.'

'Ah we'll get the engine driver and Micko off the goods van and be giving you a hand with the beast and the bags.'

The conductor, driver and Micko, the three of them tugging, pulling and rearing back their heads from Elmer's long licking tongue. Settling him to rest on the sandy ground where he lays his big head between his paws and gives a long contented groan.

Under a sky of moist tumbling clouds this fresh early morning blew with fragrant winds. Clementine with his faithful Elmer stood among their chattels. The whistle went, the engine puffed and the conductor waved and smiled. Micko the last passing face gave a thumbs up sign. The little train down the track over lands rising to barren brown hillsides.

Purple mountains push up into the white mist. Lacy droplets falling. Elmer sitting, his hind legs crouched. Over there in the western greyness sweeping sheets of rain beating across the tarnished heathers. Coming this way. To soak the silence and emptiness. From which one would like to hide. Between two big mothery thighs for warmth and comfort.

Elmer licks the moisture from his nose. Someday he might spring forward aloft on all fours, ears up instead of down. Good lord which way does one go. This map shows a winding road. And there, a castle and walls, ruined church, cemetery. Boundaries of Charnel Demesne. Cliffs, the sea and fathoms. Feel strange distant rumblings, the ground ashake. Elmer stank out the compartment last night. I doused this morning in eau de cologne. March forward now feeble in the knowledge that I have an axe, matches, tin cup and my ebony ivory inlaid case of toothbrushes. And rhinoceros arse shaped trousers.

Clementine told Elmer not to stir. As when a few yards away doggie attempted to rise only to collapse greyly again over the black gladstone bag. A stony road descending between rumbling walls of granite boulders. Thickets of wintry trees over mossy undergrowth stretching soft green and dark up beyond the shadows of hillsides. A steep hedged lane. A gate with a sign. Lands Poisoned.

The sound of wheels. Rounding a bend by a tall pine, a boy standing in a high sided cart rocking and swaying pulled by a donkey. Leap aside to let the roaring traffic plunge by. Must not let this wheeled invention pass without begging assistance. Boy wears tattered trousers which appear to be the lower part of a morning suit. Donkey's ears twitch and goodness, his darkish private part seems to wag expanded. Amazing how emotions can wax in this chill inclemency.

'Excuse me but I wonder could you help me. I'm stranded. Back there on the road. With luggage and a canine friend.'

The squeaking creaking swaying cart halts. The boy rearing up the donkey who bends his head to tear up some grass. The boy shaking his head up and down. Staring at Clementine.

'Will you help me. Do you speak. You no speakum. I mean to say you can't speak. Well I'm up at the crossroads. I will pay you to take me to a place called Charnel Castle, marked here on this map I have.'

The boy smashing his willow branch down on the arse of the donkey who lifts his head and trots off up the hill. The boy looking back over his shoulder. As if Clementine might have the strength left to give chase, drag him from the cart and deliver boot blows to the ribs accompanied by evil gospels in the ear. One will not again carelessly mention Charnel Castle.

Clementine trudging dripping back down and up the stony lane again to the crossroads. Elmer sitting with a silk cravat hanging from the corners of his mouth. A large hole torn in the side of the steerhide gladstone bag. Tooth-brushes scattered everywhere. Each a different colour and neatly printed with a time and day of the week. This broken chewed one marked Tuesday Morning. And this Monday Noon. O my God he's eaten the keys. Nearly all of them. Except the front door. Which mercifully won't fit down his throat as cavernous as it must be.

Clementine suddenly looking up at a sound of laughter. Pealing out from this empty landscape. And a movement. Behind a boulder some yards away. Beyond a few whorls of mist. Thing to do is put the head down and rummage through the strewn remnants of my itinerant personal furnishings. And now suddenly look up. Ah. There. Something behind that rock. A grey battered hat peeking out. From a good hatter if I am not mistaken. So long ago now it seems that I was waking from sleep in a dry hotel room. Pray heavenwards for this rain to stop. Send dust dear God, send dates and sand accompanied by endless other parched aridities.

'Can I be of help sir.'

Clementine rearing upwards in fright from this voice directly behind. A man attired in elegant cut blue pin stripe suit, the trouser cuffs of which hang in tatters over a pair of bespattered spats. A brown sweat stained fedora, the rim well pulled down and dripping rain fore and aft from his head.

'Holy Christ.'

'He is that.'

'O boy. I mean good day.'

'Good day to you now, a bit of softness there is.'

'Indeed.'

'Are you waiting for the train. It won't be passing till noon tomorrow.'

'I've just got off the train.'

'Welcome then.'

'Thank you.'

'Are you just stopping here a bit.'

'Yes I think I am. In fact I think I'm waiting for the train.'

'Ah wise man, there's not a living thing here save a few sheep and a herd of wild goats.'

'I thought I saw something over there behind that rock.'

'You saw Clarence.'

'I did.'

'You did.'

'Who is Clarence.'

'Well to tell you the truth now nobody knows who Clarence is. Except that he's there. He lives beyond the mountains. In a windowless cottage facing out over the sea. Hasn't been known to speak to a soul since anyone can remember. Comes out like that now and again to see what's going on in the world. He would of course be most interested in your arrival. He'll move along the walls in the near distance popping up every now and again to have a peer at you. He could be a comfort as there do be terrible loneliness out here. Not many would take it into their heads to pass this way if they could pass another.'

'Why.'

'It's the old castle. The years of misfortune haunting it and the lands around for miles.'

'What misfortune.'

'Ah God a long tale of inhuman blood curdling shenanigans and indecent idolatry. Be an affront to burden a stranger's ear with. Sure a poor girl was lost in the old castle and wasn't she found the next day her hair nearly white and she paralysed unable to move. Steer clear of that place if you ever have a mind to head in that direction. You can't miss it. On the side of the hill up there as you go. Blood bespattered dungeons, tunnels leading they don't know where. Built it was by Clementine of The Three Glands. He would have at ten women a night. And feared he was everywhere for his visceral atrocities.'

'Thank you. You've been most helpful.'

'Not at all. Sure I'm the four miles down the road there, the first house you'll come to. Should you ever be passing that way you'd be most welcome. I do be in my spare time an antiquarian. And I see there a lot of interesting equipage.

That animal you have I venture to say would take most of it on his back and nearly yourself as well.'

'He's taking a holiday today.'

'Is that a fact. Well if you have a mind to move, Tim will be coming this way now. You'll hear his boots on the road. Well over the seven feet tall he is and could gather you your beast and all together and carry you in comfort. Listen now. That's him.'

A dark shadow approaching steadily through the mist. Striding a strange gait in the centre of the road. Like great limbs of a tree his long arms swinging. Each step speeding him through the wet. With trousers ending just below his knees and jacket sleeves just below his elbows. His tiny head on top of his great shoulders.

'Ah Tim, would you have a moment. There's a gentleman here needing help with a few of his belongings.'

Tim veering like a ship at sea. Moving towards Clementine and Elmer who moaned and wagged his tail. Tim nodded, his lids closed over his eyes. His hands feeling round on the ground as he picks up the gladstone bags and tucks them up under his arm. And with a great swing he swept up Elmer who draped across his shoulder and licked his nose.

'Now sir if you'll just walk along in front of Tim wherever you're going he'll follow you. He's never been known to open his eyes or speak. He's saving these faculties for when his others might fail. Good luck and God bless.'

Clementine waving thanks. Head off now in the mist. Followed by Tim. Who's already white haired. Maybe not from fear. An ancestor had at ten dolls a night. Might re-establish that great tradition. If one can find ten in this utter bereftness. Take time to work up to that many a night. With constant practice and gentle increases and keeping it soft and long and pliable with lotions, who knows, might even dip into the visceral atrocities as well. In one of the tunnels.

Rounding a sharp corner in the road there was a grunt from the shrubberies. A pink fat pig stepped out. And took up the rear of this procession. Between these brambles overhanging the road. Now narrowing and going upwards. A crushing strange loneliness lurking in the valley of these high hedgerows. Where those behind follow the leader all heading for the haunted castle.

The little group trudging by a high stone wall with mossy abutments, grey, green and yellow lichens on the craggy granite. A great black bird squawked overhead its wings flapping and whirring in the mists. See how the troops are to the rear. The hair along Elmer's back standing up. First thing that dog has done denoting action.

A great barred gate. Set in a high wall. Clementine tugging at a chain. Loosening it as the rusty scales fall into the weeds below. Open up and enter this gloom and circumstance. Had such elaborate plans to live a modern go ahead kind of life. Where everything you want jumps out at you at the press of a button.

The great gate creaking open. The heavy bars with peeling scales of green paint. A potholed roadway. Ahead walls and battlements. And a door of oak if I know my wood. Behind the shelter of which I must get my wet chilled self. Together with Elmer, Tim and this nice fat friendly chap. Who is last of all. And a pig as well. Call him Fred.

Under the dripping ramparts Clementine turns the huge key in the lock and Tim puts his great white hand against the door which swings open. All of us standing in the centre of this cavernous black and white tiled hall. A stone stairway ascending four landings towards a skylight in the distant ceiling. Shadowy portraits of solemn faces and ancient instruments of war, lances, bludgeons, swords, shields and suits of armour.

And
A deep
Entrail
Chilling
Cold

3

With terrifying swiftness the afternoon turned into night. Fred the pig seemed to know his way round the castle. And I followed him. Honking up the stairs, peering into battlements, bedrooms and water closets. Until somewhere on the second floor he rushed off down the hall and out of sight.

I stood in some alarm listening as Tim's great black boots went down the granite steps and away over the stony road. A trembling took me. Standing in a darkened library. Trying to light that candle. So hopeful on the mantel. Each match's flame strangely dimming and going out. A nervous sob floating ceilingwards from between my lips. I was not, I am certain, the only soul in this house.

A faint western glow between the curtains. Covering a great red and green stained glass window. Cabinets stacked with trays covered with pieces of stone. Drawers and drawers of birds' eggs. Mouldering books, bindings hanging off by threads, shelf upon shelf. Rolls of maps, sheaves of mildewed papers scattered across a vast desk. Upon which I may presently dance to improve the gaiety of this joint. Or safer and quicker open the drapes. Wide.

Clayton Clementine reached up to take a tasselled cord between his fingers. Giving it a downward tug. A wall of thick crimson fabric plummeted together with a long heavy brass rail. The first enveloping Clementine who fought like a demon till the latter clonked him unconscious on the skull.

Staggering towards the door into the great hall. Clementine putting out his hands to feel his way. Leaving a trail of plaster debris. Remnants of curtain flowing from his outstretched arms and a billow of dust rolling before him.

Elmer, the five and a half foot length of him not including tail stood up erect on all fours with his ears jutting out murmuring a low growl. The first laugh today.

The big bow wow's tail wagging. Jumps up to lick my face. With relief that I am not a ghost. Two of us can quietly weep. Without witnesses or shame. And later find somewhere to sleep. In the endless stale air and solitude. Every shutter I open a stack of dead flies tumble out. I could cavort in an angry circle, shake the clenched fists around the skull. And maybe with a stroke of good luck knock myself out again. For the night.

A squeak of floorboard and a squeal of spring in a door hinge. Clementine turning around. To face an opening door under the staircase. Beneath an apron of candlelight a liveried foot peeking out. With holes in the hose. Followed by other feet and foots. Five persons lining right up in front of me. In one nice neat row of astonishment. And strange what one's eye sees instead. A giant thistle growing right out from the bottom step of the stairs.

'Ahem sir.'

Three ladies, a boy and a man. The latter with a clear throat has just taken a pace forward. Inclining his head to one side. Folding the biggest hands I have ever seen across his flies. Just beneath a black thin brocaded waistcoat. Two small eyes, a monocle over one. And moisture adhering to the end of a hawked nose.

'Ahem. And excuse me sir. And welcome. We would have had the place tidied up a bit but we had no warning of your arrival sir. May I be so bold as to present Miss Ovary the cook, Ena upstairs maid, Imelda downstairs, and Oscar the boy. I am the footman. But these years since I have been butler. Here be the keys to the wine cellars sir.'

'O boy.'

'He's at your service sir.'

'I mean o boy. O boy o boy.'

'Yes sir, yes sir.'

'I mean who is employing you.'

'Well sir. We have always gone with the place as you might say. We've been waiting this long time for sign of you to come. Every Christmas the table has been set. Miss Ovary has done in the kitchen down there for donkey's years. Oscar the boy is trained by meself. Ena and Imelda are apprenticed parlour maids. There hasn't been much doing here since her ladyship left and no grander lady lived, God bless her. Meantimes we do be putting right the odd dilapidation and keeping the portals locked and the intruders at bay if you follow me sir.'

'I'm afraid I simply cannot afford to employ anyone.'

'Ah now sir, who said a thing about employ, wages or the like. We're content with a roof now and again and a bit of board. When you've got a windfall will be time enough for talk of such a nature.'

'What's your name.'

'Percival sir. I have a wee bit of the staggers in the left leg, but watch now while I do this little jig. Now come on you old feet down there. La dee dee deda. I could tap dance down a rainbow. Would you think now there was a mite wrong in that limb. Would you now.'

'No you wouldn't.'

'Now sir settle your mind. And let me do the worrying. That's a fine animal. Would he be of the horse family.'

'He's Elmer. A dog.'

'You don't say. Didn't I think he was some kind of grass eating beast. Welcome Elmer. We'll scrape up a few of your tasty bits and morsels. He'll take a bit of feeding. Will you reside in the King's room sir.'

'I don't know, where is it.'

'It's the octagonal room in the end of the southwest wing. Traditional for the master of the house. A fine room facing out to the sea. I'll get these bags up there now and give it a wipe around. Sure now Miss Ovary will have a bite to eat ready for your worship. Will you be praying this evening sir.'

'Probably.'

'Ena see the chapel is dusted out and the candles lit for his worship. Now sir, I see you've had an inopportune occurrence. In the library if I'm not mistaken.'

'No you're not mistaken.'

'I'll have a change of clothes out in no time.'

Percival making a little clap of the hands. The three ladies courtesied and Oscar gives a deep nod of the head. Ending this little confrontation of echoing voices here in the candlelight. The door squealing closed under the staircase. And a heavy long sighing moaning murmuring out of various near and distant apertures. Followed by a deep rumble.

'What's that.'

'Ah it do be the waters sir.'

'What waters.'

'The sea waters that come up the tunnels in the high tide into the dungeons. Sends the wind rushing up. On a wild night it's like a war down there. Now sir you'll be wanting some beasts soon. To eat down the grass that's got out of hand. Tim the giant is your man, great with cattle. I do meself keep a patch of a garden and know just that bit about stock rearing. Once we had the light electric in here. But it was forever throwing shocks at you. I threw a pail of water on one of them wires smoking away and didn't a flash come up the water and knock me clear across the room. A candle is your man every time. And take this one sir, to light your way.'

Percival gone. Come Elmer. Just step over here with me and we'll yank out this thistle, god damn it's sharp as well as pale green and awesomely evil. Forgot to ask Percival the way to the King's room. How do you like that. A staff. Trots out from under the stairs. With musical instruments we could have had a recital on the spot. Maybe travel abroad to pick up some change as a dance band in selected watering places. Instead of slowly starving together. In this colossus.

Clementine clearing a little space at the vast desk in the library. Writing down the names on a damp sheet. Keep a record. To share out the windfall when it comes. In the form of plunging plasters, rafters, tapestries and drapes. At least one is not alone with these moans and shudderings. Be frozen now instead of frightened to death. Among vegetations sprouting from the floors. And a nice little group of lethal looking mushrooms in this drawer. Growing out amid more maps and ledgers.

'Excuse me your worship. Your bath is drawn.'

'Eeee. Sorry. You gave me a fright Percival. How did you get over there.'

'It be a passage from the pantry. Sir.'

'In future until I get used to this place perhaps you could approach from the front.'

'Very good sir. Now if you'll follow me I'll show you to your quarters.'

Clementine following. Pulling a wobbling Elmer in the flickering candlelight up the stairs of the great hall. Through a door and down a long corridor. Turning right up steps. Along another hall past doors, mouldering paintings, shelves of stacked books. Through a narrow entrance and up circular stone steps.

'Now in there sir, is what's known as the coffin room.'

'Good lord. That's a coffin.'

'Ah it tis indeed.'

'Is it empty.'

'Ah for the time being I think so sir.'

A tall tapestried bed. Under a vaulted ceiling. Candles aflame in front of a mirror. Steam rising from a copper bath in the middle of the floor. Elmer lapping up a few sups. One's pathetic wardrobe laid out. Tattered kimono. My mauve smoking jacket is about the only thing I possess which might go with this house. Other than my socks holed in heels and toes. When summer comes of course, I'll blast a few tennis balls off a battlement in my jock strap and tennis shorts.

'There sir. You'll be the better for a hot bath and a dry off in front of the fire. I have at your convenient disposal a water can from out of the conservatorium. Handy for a rinse.'

'This is quite splendid.'

'It's nothing. Nothing at all. And now if the whole world was against you you'd come to not a bother here. The chain and pulley there lowers an iron door thick as your fist.'

'You don't think it will come down by accident and lock me in.'

'Ah never. Sure you'd have it raised up in half an hour if you put your back into it.'

'Percival you must know a great deal of the history of the castle.'

'Ah just the bits and pieces I hear tell about. I'm nearly reared in the shadow of the place, the other side of the mountain. You don't want to give a mind now to the shocking scandals that have haunted the castle down through the ages. It was Clementine of The Three Glands himself beheaded sixty traitors in this very chamber. The block is there beyond in the coffin room. A fine thick piece of hawthorne. He must have had a pair of arms on him. The flood of blood must have been something shocking.'

'O God.'

'What's the matter sir.'

'Well Percival, as a matter of fact I'm just that bit apprehensive. I mean I'm new to the place.'

'Ah now you'll sleep like a baby. That's what I was going to tell you. The bed there now.'

'Please. Don't tell me. Perhaps in the morning. And I'm not quite sure I'll want to hear it then either.'

'Very good sir.'

'Is there a piece of soap.'

'Ah soap. The soap. Now the soap. Well let me see now. Soap. You know sir, I don't think there has been much need of it around for a while now.'

'There's no soap.'

'I wouldn't say that now. I'd say that between you wanting soap now and the fact that I might not be able to lay my hand on a bit of it that there would be a gap of time affording discomfort unless sir you might on the spot now convinced yourself you didn't need it at all.'

'What's that.'

'Excuse me sir, I think there must be someone at the main door. It's the big bell that rings down there in the courtyard below. I won't be a minute.'

The comfort to skin, soul and future that this water gives.

To lie back soaking. In the execution room. Ancestor took no shit from anyone. Chopping block's in there to prove it. Just two months ago I stepped down the ladder of a ship. And onto a tender that bumped through the tide to a town of church steeples and bright painted houses along a river's banks. To see the first of this land. Dropped a tear or two looking back up the black hull of the vessel on which out of a few female strangers I had made some new friends. Tossed as we were through the arse of a hurricane across a cold ocean.

'Excuse me sir, there's a gentleman from out of a motor car wanting to see you sir. I couldn't catch the name it being of a foreign sound. It was about accommodation sir. Shall I tell him you are otherwise engaged.'

'No. Tell him to wait.'

'Very good sir.'

Poor Percival huffing and puffing, lungs wheezing chasing up and down the stairs. Keeps fitting the monocle back in his eye. It falls out every time he opens his mouth. Giving him a look of distressed astonishment. A caller at the castle. In this bereft clime resistance to intrusion lowered to nil. On the other hand always nice to flex one's social muscles. Feel the size of this. Ladies.

Candles lit on a balcony chandelier made the great hall darker than ever. Clementine in tennis trousers, mauve smoking jacket with clashing pink cravat and billiard slippers, scuffling down the wide marble steps. Grinding in the mortar dust fallen from inaccessible interstices far above. Elmer following, deliberating, his ears hanging forward either side of his big black nose, reaching the bottom stair and promptly lying down with a weary groan.

A gentleman with sparse light hair on his high domed head stands unshivering. In an open necked shirt, skimpy sleeveless yellow sweater, his feet in green socks and black sandals. Holding his hands stiffly at his sides, he bows deeply.

'Ah good evening, good person.'

'Good evening.'

'May I enquire firstly of your good health.'

'Yes. Currently it's untroubled.'

'I am pleased to hear that. And also, may I comment upon the splendour of this dwelling.'

'By all means.'

'Clearly early christian with its finely cut stone arched construction. Although of a later period the ribbed groined vaulting is of especial refinement. Most interesting that the geometric tracery where minutiae charms with the arabesque is not dwarfed. But permit me. I am Erconwald.'

'How do you do.'

'I am with three friends. We have motored some distance this day. If you could forgive me my unforgivable intrusion upon your esteemed privacy we would be most grateful for a night's accommodation. May I offer you an inhalation. Of dried carefully selected tender parts of hemp.'

'Thank you no, not for the moment.'

'Then will you pardon me.'

'Of course.'

'One matter does trouble. Although the arabesque is not dwarfed it would almost suggest that the geometric tracery was an afterthought.'

'Mr Erconwald.'

'Erconwald. Just Erconwald.'

'I've only just moved in. A matter of hours ago. In fact I've only seen two rooms.'

'Ah. Forgive me. I have troubled and perhaps perplexed you. My most humble apologies. Truly. But of course, I will withdraw. I do most sincerely apologise for my most thoughtless inconveniencing. I am appreciative that you have not chosen to upbraid me.'

'But surely I can help you. Even perhaps accommodate you. Please. Do ask your friends to come in. If not out of the cold at least out of the darkness.'

'Kind person. I am most grateful. And I hearken to your courteous invitation.'

This Erconwald taking three backward steps. Bowing horizontally from the waist and momentarily wrestling with the great door lock to step out into the night. Percival emerging from the shadows flexing his big fingers as he holds up his impassioned hands.

'Your worship I couldn't help overhearing engaged as I was putting a few pieces of peat over there in the grate. When first I came across your man at the door he said a stream of things to me that if I could remember half them I'd have one of the greatest educations in these parts.'

'Have we room Percival.'

'Have we room sir. We'd accommodate them and their ancestors back through time.'

'I mean beds.'

'Beds. Are you asking for beds.'

'Yes I am.'

'Beds is it you want. We could put the contents of every cemetery for fifty miles sleeping up yonder there. And that's a fact.'

'Three beds will do.'

'Very good sir. And will you select the wine.'

'What wine.'

'That do be in the bins sir.'

'No kidding.'

'I would not be given to humbug sir on a serious matter such as that. Being as I have risked life and limb for the safe repose of them cherished liquids. With marauders about here. Her ladyship loved her claret and port.'

The door bell tolling in the courtyard. Percival heading for the door giving one knee a smack of his fist and suddenly going down on the tiles on both.

'Never mind sir, I'm all right. It's a glancing blow that's required. Sometimes I don't aim properly for putting it into joint.'

Percival crawling the remaining distance to the door. Slowly standing and wiping off his britches. Erconwald entering ushering a long haired big breasted girl wearing a thick white sweater and orange dress. Followed by two men, carrying lanterns, one with moustache, the other thin faced under a wild head of bushy hair. Both apparelled in leather patched sports coats, grey flannel trousers and black banker's shoes. Erconwald gently raising a left supplicant hand in the faint light.

'Ah kind person. You are truly charitable. Rose I should like to present, ah, unhappily I have not your name.'

'Clayton Clementine.'

'And this is Rose. Of Rathgar. To my left my associates Franz Decibel Pickle and George Putlog Roulette.'

'How do you do.'

'Esteemed.'

'Charmed.'

'Kind person I fear we put upon you. That you are too easy tempered to say any distressful word to strangers. We should not presume upon your good nature. Arrived as we are without gifts and jellies. You have but to nod your head and we will depart taking with us a comfortable memory of the moments communing here.'

'Depart. Like hell.'

'Ah. Rose. Be of contented heart.'

'Contented. Stuffed in the back seat of that car out there all day. I want a bite to eat.'

Clementine nervously tugging at his cravat, moistening his lips. Rose simultaneously smiling in one direction and sneering in another. Not easy to do. She wears high sharp heels. A certain heft in her legs. Thick lipped and throaty of voice. And quite determined of spirit. Capable of man-handling her companions. Who appear most mild of gentlemen.

'I'd like to suggest that you be my guests. Dinner will be quite shortly. Percival will show you to your rooms.'

'Ah we are most indebted.'

A procession up the stairs. Stepping over Elmer out-stretched at the bottom. Percival with candle lugging a cello case followed by Erconwald carrying a french horn. The rear taken up by the lantern carrying associates the last of whom, Franz, stops to scratch at the stone work with his thumbnail. Turns to see me watching from below, nods his head, smiles briefly and continues upward.

A peat fire glowing in the library. The dust settled and the volume of ancient air scented with a smell of the sea.

Percival, beads of sweat on his brow came jangling his keys carrying his cellar book. I closed a large ledger found in a bottom drawer. With its lists of servants. Four stone-masons. Sixteen gardeners. Three boatmen. Yacht captain, eight deck hands, three engineers. And on one ancient page two dungeon keepers.

'Nicely settled in they are sir. Facing the bay. Madam preferred being a bit off on her own. Didn't she pick the northeast turret. You'd think she was ready for war. Skipped right out on the battlement in her bare feet.'

'Percival I see yacht captain listed here. What is that all about.'

'It's the ship moored down in the boat house sir.'

'Ship.'

'Ah well now you wouldn't call it a boat. Seeing as it has its own lift that will take you up and down the decks. A grand vessel. I seen them sail out on many a summer day of me youth with the guests waving back to the castle and the cannons roaring out the salutes up there off the battlements. Them were great days sir. Locked up it's been these years. Now I don't like to comment sir. But the lady and gentlemen. Now as I say I don't like to comment as it's not my place. But the one of them with the bushy hair. And the musical case I was carrying in particular. Now as I say I don't like to comment. But wasn't there a sign on it with do not open venomous reptiles. I thought it my duty to mention it sir.'

'Christ almighty.'

'Could be nothing but you wouldn't want now to be out leaping a dance of death over the ramparts with them things after you.'

Percival leading the way through the disguised door in the library panelling. At the end of a narrow hall to go descending a circling stone stairway, Percival holding aloft a gilt candelabrum. Which could fetch a price. One will estimate later. If I get a private moment to peruse the hall-mark and contour. The weight too.

Five candles flickering in the damp chill air. Under arched stone ceilings. Past a doorway heaped with ashes.

Another stacked with trunks. Rooms of lead lined sinks. And coming to a crossroads. Of tunnels. From one hear washing gurgling waters and the sound of the sea. Straight on, over the stone slabs. From which a cold rises. Right through the billiard slipper and a pair of sheep socks I bought said to be waterproof and homemade straight off hedgerow briars. Percival stopping. Set in the wall a tombstone chiselled with skull and crossbones beneath a coat of arms of a human hand held up between a stag and lion rampant.

'The tide's out sir. There be times now when the pressure rushing this way could break an ear drum. Now you wouldn't know this was a door would you. It's the entrance to the wine cellars. In former times the catacombs. You'd not get through this in a hurry. Nine inches thick of local granite. But like rocking a baby we move it back and forth and now just push right here.'

The large slab rolling away revealing an oak door. I hold the cellar book and candelabrum. The weight of the latter delights. Percival opening up with three keys. Inside bins stacked upon bins. The air musty and stilled. An oasis of dark purplish glass neatly nestling in straw. Yard after yard. Tier upon tier of clarets, champagne, burgundy, among the magnums, jeroboams, rehoboams and methuselahs. And further on ports, brandies, rum, not to mention madeira and the light green glass of moselle.

'It goes there beyond sir. They say the touch of death did no wine harm. I don't meself know a great deal beyond the pouring and keeping but I know your belly wouldn't ever be screaming with the thirst that your throat was cut. Now sir so long as we're down here in the privacy I'd mention that this Mister Erconwald took me aside and let me on to the fact that the lot of them are vegetarians except the woman and strict adherents to the metric system again excepting the woman. And sir didn't he then lift from his pocket an onion the size of a turnip and take out of it a bite big as your fist and chew as if it were the sweetest apple God ever grew.'

The jeroboam of champagne Percival hefted from the

catacombs was put standing with the gilt serving bowls and sauce boats on the massive mahogany sideboard of the dining room. Which without warning collapses. The champagne cork bursting from its wire cap. To draw my attention to the fine quality of the chandelier into which it shot dislodging a crystal slamming down into my soup. Freely splashing my cravat and smoking jacket lapels. Rose seated not far away on my right managed to quell a satanic grin flickering on her face.

'Ah sir that reminds me I forgot to mention you don't want to step over them chalk lines I've got marked on the floor in various places as you'd go down through faster than the fastest elevator invented.'

'Thank you. Is the wine ruined.'

'Not a bit of it sir, frothing it is with life.'

'I do apologise to you all.'

'Ah good person there is no need.'

Sitting here assembled in much silence. Through the soup course of cabbage leaves and potatoes. A tureen of which was carried by Oscar and ladled out by Percival. Rose making considerable noise shovelling it between her lips. Having declared frequently on the long way to dine.

'I can't wait to get a bite to eat.'

When Percival announced dinner he withdrew. Leaving me leading folks from the library in and out of chambers and corridors trying to reach the dining room. Which I found finally by following Elmer. Whose big black nose fastened to some dog delighting aroma. During the search Erconwald remarked upon the pointed trifoliated arches. Derivative he said of the Khufu pyramid. The influence of which could be seen again in the pointed segmental arch over the mullioned bay windows of the dining room.

A stuffed enormous python hanging extended from a minstrels' gallery, open mouthed down into the room. Made Elmer growl. And raised a subject which had me swallowing amounts of saliva and beeping out farts uncontrollably. Muted by a conveniently located rent in the upholstery into which they sneaked.

Conversation not improving with the appearance of fish.

Large and reptilian buried beneath a white sauce. Coiled on a platter I detect as Meissen. How does one raise the question. What the hell are you doing bringing a bunch of god damn poisonous snakes into my house.

The guests draining their glasses. As quickly as they were refilled by Oscar. Who neatly and swiftly pours from the big bottle. Mr Roulette frequently looks my way, raises his glass, nods and smiles. They all appear far too complicated to be criminals. And I seem to be the only one sizing up the cutlery. Solid silver. With the crest of the hand, lion and stag.

'Erconwald.'

'Good person.'

'I don't seem to have caught what it was you and your associates do.'

'Ah. I am delighted you have enquired. We are humble scientists.'

'O. That's interesting.'

'Franz, if he will permit me to say, is an organic chemist, isolator of some of the world's rarest smells. You are best known for your work Franz on putrefaction.'

'I agree.'

'And George, may I speak for you.'

'Certainly.'

'Ah George, mild and sweet George. Whose ancestor Putlog invented the scaffold. George, good person, is a physicist. As am I. But we are now perusing matters somewhat outside our profession. Which I am not at liberty to comment upon. But good person we tire you with such talk.'

'O no you don't.'

'Ah then there is Rose. Ah Rose. A while ago producing an opera we held a singing contest won by Rose. She is able to reach through six octaves and now has been trained as a baritone. By George. May I be permitted to describe you further Rose.'

'You do what you like.'

'Ah. Rose is ninety two point five centimetres around the chest across the nipples unengorged. At the waist across the navel she is seventy five centimetres. The hips across the apex of the buttocks measure one hundred two and a half centimetres. She displays an unusual and remarkable neoarciform from the waist as it sweeps out to encompass the hip. The upper thighs are smooth, the appearance of hair beginning four inches above the knee and increasing in presence towards the ankles. The feet normal in every other way have webbing between the toes. And you good person, perhaps you would tell us something of yourself.'

'Well, I don't have my measurements handy. But I hail from Chicago.'

'Ah, the Indian name. Means wild onion. A city built on a shallow alluvial basin. Important in trade and industry. But do continue.'

'There's not much else to say.'

Percival taking away the remains of the fish. Which one keeps tasting again and again in the mouth. I called for port. Heaps of it. A jeroboam. As just down the table my eyes lit upon a woven silver gilt dessert basket. Full of potatoes. Sprouting pale green tubers sticking out from wrinkled skins. And through one of which the mouth of Franz presently makes its biting way. Deep into the raw. One is I think quite rightly scared. Be glad to get through dessert and onto the cigars and aged potables. And fathom before it is too late. The insides of the cello case.

'Are any of you interested in zoology.'

'If I may speak Mr Clementine, Franz who is uncircumcised is an amateur herpetologist and all of us have taken an interest in the field.'

'O.'

'No true reptile or animal of a poisonous nature exists here. This has made the natives spiritually overconfident. The resulting blind faith has produced on the roads a phenomena of unlit vehicles colliding in the night. Restoration of the country's caution would be interesting. And could be brought about by exposing the population to a lurking but constant threat of danger both fatal and unfamiliar. Electricity is already treated with carefree disregard. To our attention have come several cases of electricians licking live wires in the same manner as the farmer spits on his palms prior to taking up his shovel. In one case a co-axial cable introduced into an orifice, do forgive me Rose, carried current much in excess of a lethal amount. The subject professed obtaining a frisson from the procedure. Which we did not dispute or discourage. Is that correct Franz.'

'That is correct. Optimum thrill was achieved at thirty seven point nine joules. Over twice the intensity which produced frisson in myself and George using the same method.'

Erconwald's chin raised as he listens. A blond stubble sprouting on his cheeks. He pushes gently at the base of his wine glass. Upon a finger of his right hand an emerald sits the size of a brazil nut set in celtic silver entwinings. He stares at Rose. Who wolfed down three helpings of the haunted fish. And asked Franz to pass the gilt dessert basket. She took a potato, blew the dust from it and plunged in her teeth. She gasped. Spat out the spud. And swept it from the table top. Reaching for the finger bowl she drained it in a gulp. Franz remained quietly chewing his raw root and sipping Cointreau. Fetched up so fast by Percival that uncharitably I thought a supply must be secretly near at hand.

The evening lingers. Blackness and raindrops on the windows. Imelda crouched half the evening in the shadows by the fireplace pumping with a bellows. Raising a flame finally which attracts colder winds seeping into the dining room. An arctic blast presently up my trouser leg. As a pipe goes passing between these three. Upon which they suck two handed with a rather noisome frowning intensity. Always seems to be going out. They relight again. Rose smokes a cigar and between puffs lifts up her lip where she pokes a toothpick, blowing the unearthed particles to her right with a left hand cupped over her mouth. Morsels popped between floor boards will fall down into dungeons. Where the scurryings I've heard make me certain a vast rodent population swarms.

The creak of a chair. Franz rising. Bowing to me and the others at the table. Asking if I would mind his taking away a plateful of food. And all now trooped through the four tattered antique filled state rooms leading to the great hall. Take my leave with Elmer. Hear the voice of Erconwald, George and Rose echoing away in the direction of their chambers. I pass a window of the corridor to the octagonal room. See a lantern light moving towards the front gate. Stopping by a long vehicle. The upstanding shadow of Franz's hair. And the shadow of another figure inside the car. Making a total of two out there.

Churn my feet back and forth down between these sheets. And under Elmer curled asleep. Undressed one had to dress again to get into this bed. Nearly wore the billiard slippers as well. So cold it helps calm my mind. As one's soul hovers above dungeons full of snakes and rats gnawing at electric cables extending from folk's rears. Nice to see them smile as a joule or two goes charging up.

The boom of the sea. Lie and listen. High tide. Candle flickering will soon go out. No mention from the visitors about departing. May be gone before dawn. Rose flashed her eyes at me, licked her lips and went round the hall flaring out her skirt as she perused paintings and armour. I saw her lift up and peek under a steel codpiece. As Erconwald stood continually bowing. Heaping upon me good wishes for the night. Deep sleep, muscles replenished, the soul heartened, I do wish good person, to see you again full of joy upon your rising. Impossible to fit in a word about the god damn snakes. As he slowly backed away. Withdrawing as he put it from your good presence. Faint strains now. Of music. Between the explosions of sea water. An organ. Seems to come from that small window giving on the courtyard. Good God. That was a scream. Of unbelievable octave. Elmer. Wake up. Murder. Somewhere.

Clementine's shuffling billiard slippers descending steps past the coffin room into the main corridor. Screams coming from that way. Just take this spear off the wall. If it is a spear. Can't see a thing. What if they're loose. The snakes. Get back to my room. And close down the iron shutter over the door. What an unspeakable but life saving thing to do. If the god damn snakes are having a field day. Or night.

Clementine, spear first, passing on the balcony over the great hall. Screams stop. Death has stilled the victim. A light and sound of feet behind and ahead. What's this coming. Thundering down the hall. A knee high breeze with an unearthly squeal. And grunt. And has. O my goodness. Hit Percival. Somewhere low. It sounds like. It is.

Fred
The
Pig

Like
The natives
Cruising unlit
In the
Night

4

Oscar woke me in the morning putting a steaming pail of water into the jug on my washstand. Left eye glued shut, the right opening on a sunny day showing a world. Out there of rocks bulging from a meadow sloping upwards into a purple sharp pointed mountain. And north a ragged edge of earth beyond a blue black sea. Little white caps here and there. Poor Percival last night was pole-axed. Rose came hurtling out of the shadows. After Fred. In a tight silk kimono. Her bosoms heaving up and down. Uttering language likely to lead to a breach of the peace. Already badly broken.

After a night of such terror hope rises wearily. Rose took one end and I the other of Percival. Lugged him into the nearest room. Of some splendour with white embellished ceilings. Tapestries and carved four poster bed. A large dressing table with pots and jars, silver hand mirrors and tortoise combs. As I felt his heavy but steady pulse Percival gasped that it was her ladyship's room in which he might breathe his last.

But just as I dry a globule of moisture from an ear lobe this apt morning, Percival comes in. With a tray aloft bearing a great brown pot, a plate covered with rashers, three fried eggs, tomato and stack of brown toast. A jar of marmalade and white bowl of golden butter.

'Good morning sir.'

'Percival are you all right.'

'Fit as a cello. Didn't the pig last night knock the knee back into permanent place.'

'I'm delighted to hear that.'

'Grand as it ever was.'

'I hope our guests haven't departed. I'd like to say good-bye.'

'I would think you would have ample time sir, as I watched them a moment ago carrying in a stream of stuff that would sink a ship. And this morning there are five of them where I would swear there were only four last night. Now how's this little spot for you here by the gun turret. Give you a view of the sea on this fine morning.'

'What's that.'

'What sir.'

'Grazing there, just by the wall.'

'Ah that's Toro.'

'Good Lord. Whose is he.'

'Yours sir by the lack of claimants but I wouldn't ever be nearer him than I'd be to a thick wall you could get over in a hurry.'

'Is he vicious.'

'Ah if he has a few old cows around he's harmless enough. I thought I'd mention sir I took the liberty of opening up an account beyond there at the shop.'

'That's awfully kind Percival but as I've told you I can't really afford.'

'Now sir who said anything about bills or the like. Sure when you're ready is time enough. And if you're not ready it's not time enough.'

'Percival you seem to have confidence in the future.'

'Ah now without the present you wouldn't have a future. And sure the present is busy making the past while the future is waiting. And there's no harm keeping the future waiting while it's not here yet. And when you get there what is it but you're in the present all over again. Will you have milk first or last in the tea.'

'I think last, please.'

'Now I've got Tim giving a hand with the garden. Just beyond the wall there. We'll be having a spud or two before long. With the old gun I'll blast a few of them hares off the heather for dinner tonight. How are you with the rod sir.'

'I beg your pardon.'

'For the fishing.'

'I don't fish.'

'That's a pity now. There's plenty to be had from the deep out there. And now sir I must be gone about my chores.'

Staring out the tiny window of the turret, Clementine biting into the red rashers. Laid gently upon a toasted buttery bread of wheat seed. Crushed sweetly between the back molars. Things not so bad. When you think. There's no harm keeping the future waiting. Meanwhile fish, shoot and look at Toro. And if one is not mistaken this is the basket weave of Sheraton I sit on. Just like the chair in great aunt's room. Where I sat. As Percival snored unconscious. And Rose gave me glances. Felt like a guest in my own house when she invited me to go with her down into the kitchen to make cocoa. But the eyes. Of her. Made one cautious and swiftly drowsy. I hesitated. And dead centre of that pause she said you won't mind if I go myself and have a bite to eat.

Clementine descending the stair into the great hall. A shaft of mid morning sunlight glinting on the display of shields on the north wall. Under which stands Franz Pickle adjusting a surveyor's tripod. As Erconwald enters the front door carrying a small statue and an apparatus.

'Ah good person, let me welcome you on this fine day and say good morning. How are you.'

'Fine thanks.'

'We are I think now sufficiently unloaded. It would not do for unauthorised persons to handle our equipage and we are storing it in a safe place.'

'I see.'

'Ah good person I perceive some flummoxity upon your countenance. It is we have certain sample minerals, udometers, hydrometers, recent and fossil brachiopoda. Microscope. Geiger counter. Volt meter. Plant specimens. And here I carry Brahma, the Omnipresent One. And this is an oriental water pipe. Ah but why trouble you with such trivial paraphernalia this morning. I entrust you have breakfasted well.'

'Yes thank you.'

'And voided with ease that of which you are glad to be rid. Should you have difficulty in your personal cycle, we have a most effective remedy. A herbal infusion in which there is a colloidal suspension of selected finely ground sea weeds. Two spoonfuls of the well shaken mixture will blast waste from the bowel with the splendour of the trumpet blown unrestrained. In fact we suggest this musical accompaniment. But I keep you. Pray let me not do that. With the sun shining.'

'Perhaps you could tell me what your associate Mr Pickle is doing.'

'Ah, but of course. It is unforgivable of us not to have asked your permission but you have been so kind we did not wish to trouble you further. Franz is most excited. But does not want to hop skip nor jump to conclusions. And therefore I would ask your good person if I might withhold for a short time the nature of our enquiry.'

'For how long.'

'Ah. Franz. How long is needed for your investigation.'

'Seventy two hours, provided that I do not have to drill.'

'Ah good person I see that latter word uttered by Franz has wrought again upon your countenance some further flummoxity. Please be reassured. It is core drilling to which he refers. The core withdrawn being easily replaced, although we may have to retain certain portions. May I enquire. You are single.'

'I have three.'

'Ah that is forward looking. And where do you keep your spouses.'

'O wives. No I'm single.'

'Ah. As am I. And George. But Franz has seven daughters. Although we have made numerous arrangements George has not yet had the good fortune to cohabit with the female homosapien. My own occasions of doing so are infrequent. I am uncircumcised. My log book records, I have it here, ah yes. Of human sexual unions. Thirteen. Twelve with harlots. Of bestial cohabitations there have been five. I fail to have erection with women to whom I have paid court. Except in one recent case when I have inhaled the donkey distillate prescribed by Franz when engorgement took place immediately thereafter. Although I had parental consent, the subject was under the statutory legal age for carnal knowledge. And it is with regret that a law case ensued. The three of us possess quite normal penises. Mine being the largest both flaccid and in erection. Ten point seven centimetres and seventeen point four respectively. Ah but I must not delay you.'

'You're staying to lunch.'

'Ah that would be most cordial kind sir.'

'And dinner.'

'We are indeed most grateful.'

Erconwald reaching the ends of his sentences gives a little inclination of the head. He and George appear cleaner than Franz. Although the latter is kept busy brewing up the horny distillate. Been offered the laxative but not the aphrodisiac. Take with me outside the discomforting vision of the bunch of them, snakes entwined around ankles taking craps while they tickle the ceilings with their tools in extensum. Thereupon gouging in the soft plaster suggestive rude motifs.

Charnel Castle's ivied turrets massively silhouetted against the sky. Smoke pouring from four chimney pots. Two great black birds throb wings up into the blue from a battlement, turn, wheel and dive with gleaming wings and zoom up again in the mild air. Bleat of sheep. Call of a lamb. From which Percival if he's a good shot may get a chop. Or a trout may flip out for the breakfast table from a stream flowing by the castle wall. The legs want to churn and run, the arms to flail up hills. The voice to shout. To this gang who have invaded. When the hell are you leaving. Taking with you your ghosts, snakes, tripods and reek of onions.

High on the northeastern battlement. In a bright red dress. Rose standing waving down. Look behind me. No one. Wave back. How do you do. Did you get a bite to eat recently. Wow did you hear that. Rose kidding around skipping over a stack of octaves. Echoing back from hillsides. Across the bay. Beyond the sandy beach and boat house. Where sits the yacht. For which I now have a crew to put aboard. Erconwald as captain. Donkey distillate in the engine to make it go.

Clementine followed by Elmer passing his guest's lengthy motor parked outside the castle wall. Packing two spare wheels on the running boards. Upon one of which my big woof woof pees. Inside a gentleman to whom one has not yet been introduced sitting next to the driver's seat. Staring blankly ahead. Does not even seem to see me. I'll put him down in the engine room. Of the yacht. Where his stoicism can play an important part amid the turbines. Which from what I remember of my naval career are very noisy.

A narrow path descending through a wood of beech, pine and sycamore. Sound of lapping water. In the shadows a great slate roof of a large stone building jutting from the steep hillside out into the bay. A set of steps to a door under eaves. Here we go. Open this padlock. And push. Good Lord. It's got a funnel. Two lifeboats. Be my first command. After all my years of naval training. To the rear march. Step over the bulkhead. Toss your oars. This is your captain speaking, give way together belay abaft and keep your luff. You swabies.

Clementine standing in the semidarkness. Saluting and smiling in the wheelhouse. Putting his fists tight around the helm. Could head this thing out through those doors. Smash slicing through the mountainous swells, sea spray on the face. Castle cannon blasting once more. Setting a route for the unknown. Brave mariner with a few selected female deck hands navigating a calm but titillating course while sunning on the uncluttered foredeck out there. And in here a leather cushioned chair for the captain to relax while one is underway. With some rather risqué marine sauciness.

With lighted matches, Clementine explored the ship. Ninety eight feet overall. Twenty one of your feet across the beam. Giant diesel in the engine room. Packing twelve cylinders. Even a little tool table with wrenches, vise and drill. Elevator an upright coffin with a mirror to comb hair. Could fit two deeply in love. Salt stained portholes of the main saloon. Flowered sofas and stacks of yellow covered geographical magazines. A crapper here and a crapper there. In which Elmer samples the rusty water, and rushes up and down the gangway. Chewing on the carpet, peeing on a stair. Take Rose off the parapet, down a dram of donkey distillate, turn this vessel into a ship of shame.

Clementine tapping a barometer on the mahogany panelling of a large stateroom amidships. A double bed covered with a tattered canvas sail. A cough just to my rear. Making only a small area of hair stand up on the back of my head. As one gets used to the random terrors. And Erconwald. Slowly bowing and taking off a white yachting cap.

'Ah good person forgive me. I did see you disappear in this direction. And I came aboard but to ask a question. Which I hesitatingly do as we have already taken generously of your hospitality and a further imposition is unthinkable but pray, some friends have arrived, both of them people who will please you. And here. Humbly I offer, with the compliments of Franz, myself and George, a vial of the donkey distillate. When Franz has completed his precipitation of essences from reproduction fluids of the mamba, we shall of course, upon its meeting with satisfaction in our tests, put it at your immediate disposal.'

'Thank you. Your friends are they just passing through.'

'Ah. Passing through. Ah. Perhaps that might be answered by a brief description. He is Lead Kindly Light. His wife is a woman of cultivation. They have long involved themselves with kindnesses to those imprisoned. And they are accompanied by three exprisoners. Some women of course prefer to cohabit with the stored up passions of men incarcerated for many years.'

'There are five of them.'

'Ah yes to be sure. But I see dear good person that you are dismayed. I would not want that. Pray say the word and we shall depart. But may I say first that Rose wishes for me to send you her compliments. She discerns good person, as certainly do I, your nobility and your abundant humanity. Of which we, your most humble servants, gratefully partake. I withdraw to await your word.'

Clementine stumbling through the companionway and

up out of the damp mustiness. To climb the steps again of the boathouse. Go out the door into the sunshine and rush back up the hill. In the library, thumbing through the dictionary to the letter m. And listed below mama's boy and above mambo, the word mamba. Any of several tropical venomous snakes attaining a length of twelve feet and dreaded because of its lightning quickness and fearless readiness to inflict its fatal bite.

Clementine leaning heavily upon the edge of the desk. Inlaid diamonds of ivory surrounding a green leather top. Sneak back into the world by the skin of my foreskin, get somewhere to live and one is set hysterically dancing between a lot of slashing fatal fangs. Which strike even if you didn't do a god damn thing to it. Like step on its head. Which you can't do because of its lightning speed. And twelve feet of writhing deadliness waiting to inject into one's tegument.

Voices in the great hall. Where Clementine tiptoes. Franz's tripod erected in a different corner. Leaving in the one he has left four tiles removed and a pile of dug up clay. Percival standing amid a collection of luggage. A man of delicate stature and open necked shirt scratching his privates with one hand and holding a shepherd's staff in the other. Next to him a tall, blonde broad shouldered woman, with a large head and bosoms giving the aspect of cemented masonry. To which one might take a heavy hammer and chisel. And not get anywhere. After a long sweaty battering. Quietly behind them three gentlemen with colourful ties and more of the blue pin striped suits. Faces peacefully composed, each with hands folded, looking up now and again at the distant ceiling.

'Ah good person. These are my friends. Permit me. Mrs Lead Kindly Light and her husband.'

'How do you do.'

'How do you do. You will forgive my husband and I as you can see we are covered with spatterings from the roads. And we have been appallingly misdirected by the natives. We do appreciate your having us like this. My husband picked up Erconwald's morse late last night and we motored directly here. It is quaint. Don't you think so dear. I do like the curve of the staircase. It's quite clearly a later addition.'

'Good person their three friends would prefer not to be introduced. And I took the liberty of suggesting to them that they be guided by your faithful Percival to chambers. I did not wish to disturb your scholarship in which you were engaged when I peeked upon you in the library.'

Nine people to lunch. Franz showing up late due he said to changing a bit in his drill. Rose changed from red to a bright yellow dress. Mr and Mrs Lead Kindly Light kept art books open at their places. The exprisoners inquired politely if I required anything from their end of the table. I asked for the salt. Which was passed. During the three course luncheon of tomato soup, fried bacon and egg and steam pudding, Percival poured away four magnums of claret down the eager throats. I asked after Putlog.

'Ah, he is, if you listen carefully playing the organ. He does so much want to create for you any pleasure and thought music throughout luncheon would meet with your approval.'

'Well thank you.'

Dinner brought the appearance of the apparition in the car. Who sat at the opposite end of the table, said nothing and stared at his plate. Candles were fuming from the alls. Percival nudged me in the ribs in the wine cellar.

'Ah God sir these are like the good old days.'

I struck from the cellar book six magnums of claret to be had with two hares and a sheep Tim had said was so near death on the far hillside that it was a pity not to put her cooked on the table. Guests swept the mutton down leg by leg with a gurgling of claret. Erconwald and Franz partook of their own onions and watercress from the stream. And the exprisoners between helpings heaped small courtesies and flatterings upon Rose. Till Mrs L K L said you do enjoy your food my dear, it's nice to hear hungry jaws at work.

One felt that Rose would get up and put her large hands tightly around the sinewy neck which rooted deeply down into Mrs L K L's bosoms now upright like heaving gun emplacements ready to send out busty salvos. I had the most painful erection under the table. Having merely put the tip of my tongue into the donkey distillate. And I watched as Rose got up, went around the table and put her hands constricting around Mrs L K L's neck.

Percival was serving seconds of the hare. Oscar pausing in the dining room doorway with the remains of the mutton floating in the brown greasy gravy which began to slide as the platter tilted. Erconwald's mouth open. To now receive a quartered onion. Ena pouring wine. Which she was doing down the shoulder of the silent mystery man at the end of the table. Who sat rigidly contemplating an empty area just beyond his plate. It has always embarrassed me to stand up in front of people with a bulge in one's trousers. About to plan as I was some lighthearted repartee. To quell the presently brewing social holocaust. And maybe thereby get round to the price of butter, four pounds of which disappeared at lunch.

Mrs L K L gasped and brought her hands up to grab Rose's wrists. A large purplish vein swelling out on her neck. That, by God, could be the jugular. By which so many of us want to get others. Now a vessel protrudes on her temple. Even in this light she is beginning to turn blue. As her husband turns a page of his book. And the exprisoners rise. A swarthy one to take an arm of Rose. Another attempting a lighthearted headlock and getting promptly butted in the face. The remaining exprisoner is feeling her behind. For hidden strengths. Christ what a crew. All turning as the remaining mound of mutton slips from Oscar's tray. The poor kid's face torn with alarm. Erased suddenly by a victory roar from Rose. Certainly not of Tralee.

'I'll strangle you you fucking bitch.'

Erconwald did not include among his many descriptions of self and associates that they were to a man adherents of the doctrine that it is desirable and possible to settle acrimonious miff and bitter huff by peaceful means. And they moved not a muscle. As Rose contorts in the rather over-familiar grasp of the exprisoners. And giggling now pressing away hands from under her armpits. Music in the distance increased in tempo and crescendo. Only need a stage and box office. One or two ancestors there on the wall might by the rate of their eyeball movement even pay admission.

Percival with a new nimbleness since his midnight collision with Fred the pig, making a flying leap. Towards Mrs L K L raising a small pearl handled pistol taken from a mesh evening purse. Bang bang bang. Lead sprinkling the walls. Sending moths out of the tapestry. Bang bang, two bullets pinging upon an armorial knick knack. Exprisoners painfully levering off Rose's fingers sunk into the neck of Mrs L K L whose mouth's open and tongue out, gasping. One arm outstretched, hand clinging to the gun, her robust sinewy qualities no match for Rose. Who is better at strangling than singing.

Lead Kindly Light the husband perused his book throughout, taking from a side dish thin cross sections of onions upon which he squeezes a liquid from a plastic replica of a lemon. With a delicate flourish of the wrist he puts them in his mouth. And now I see he wears sandals over white socks just visible through the other crouched figures under the table. Must call for port to be followed by cheese and cantos. With demi tasse and desperation in the chapel. Where there is an altar to permit premeditated injury and maim among the guests. And be near the organ music as well.

With my secluded feelings spirited away within me I bid the guests goodnight. Mrs L K L was led sobbing from the dining room escorted by the three exprisoners. When Percival appeared with port I instructed it to be placed by my bedside. The mystery man came up to me and with the saddest face I have ever seen, put out his hand to shake mine. Two enormous scars went down both cheeks under the eyes. And one sensed he was trying to smile. Erconwald kept bowing low as he backed away, feeling with one hand to his rear and I confess I was waiting for him to step backwards over one of those lines drawn by Percival. Which sent the victim downwards.

'Abjectly good person I tender my apologies. No balm hath the calm that I do wish I might anoint you with.'

'I certainly don't want to get bitten by one of your god damn snakes.'

'Ah. You have spoken.'

'You're damn right I've spoken.'

'And I'm saddened to note that you do so with alarm.'

'You bet you do, those things are dangerous just bringing them into someone's house like that. And then digging up the floor. What kind of behaviour is that.'

'I am deeply wounded.'

'With your friends carrying guns. Attacking each other. Turning the castle into a circus, I'm really mad, no kidding.'

'Good person my utmost assurance. I understand your concern. But most of the mambas have had their fangs removed.'

'You've got real live poisonous snakes.'

'Most noble person, there is no need for qualm, only three of the fourteen can inflict a fatal bite. Franz is in complete control, so swift of hand he can grasp a mamba in the act of striking. I had much hoped had not the dinner ended with an unfortunate misunderstanding that Franz assisted by Rose would demonstrate his dominance over one of the most deadly of reptiles.'

'What. Let them loose.'

'Ah please, unburden yourself of misgiving. Quick as the mamba is to anger Franz often inspires moments of tranquillity and upon occasion even strokes the serpent under the chin. Enclosed in their container they are perfectly harmless. Fear not good person.'

'Fear. That's all I've known the last two days.'

'I am grieved. Truly I want for an untroubled stillness to cushion your spirit, where no ravage ruin or thuggism may hatch out chafe or gall upon you. Good person, please. Peace. Perhaps you are not a pagan, as am I.'

'I believe in God.'

'Then you are with peace.'

'I'm scared shitless.'

'Have you tried our laxative.'

'Not on your nelly.'

Erconwald bows. Comes slowly erect. Tears in his eyes.

Which avert downwards to my right. His hands hang lonely, a faint green gleam from his emerald caught in the candle light. The rumpled fabric of his tweed coat and whiteness of his skin at the open neck of his shirt. Forlorn and godless. He stands in this testicle chilling chamber. The great door bolted and pinioned shut. With levers, bars and chains. Locking us all in. With no way out. Unless you want to sail down a dungeon tunnel skidding on a sea of rodents.

'I'm sorry Erconwald I did not mean to upset your feelings.'

'My hope was good person to add pleasure to your life by our presence.'

'With dangerous reptiles, exprisoners and one of your associates digging up the front hall over there. What kind of pleasure is that.'

'Your thrust sir, pierces deep. I undertake to disturb and trouble you no further. Your humble and most obedient servant withdraws.'

'Hey now wait a minute.'

'Sir.'

'I don't want to make anybody cry.'

'I merely weep. In sorrow. Not anguish.'

'Why.'

'Not least of all for news that you might treat as good. Should it come.'

'Now what do you mean by that.'

'Pray, trust me.'

'Trust, my God. I don't even know where my next meal is coming from.'

'That indeed may be the very problem we shall solve.'

'By snake bite. O boy.'

'I ask but to be given the opportunity to prove that our present labours will bear fruit. Already one feels an expectancy.'

He stands with a patience monumental. His calm voice echoing and reasonable face gently saddened. Every few moments he shivers. I feel an icy cold pressing my feet. Tell the bunch of them to go and they could start jeering.

Or digging into the foundations. Even now they may be sifting through the silver plate and planning to throw me out.

'Can I sleep on it.'

'But most certainly good person.'

'Good night.'

'Sleep pleased, good person.'

'Thank you.'

A chunk of red cheese, decanter of port and a stack of tomes from the library on my bedside table. Things look warm but feel cold in the firelight. The stone hot water bottles make damp patches on top of the bed. Only that the chapel is over in their wing I would stop in to pray. Erconwald said Putlog had tuned the organ and cleaned the rat nests from the pipes. He would give a recital anytime I liked. Come to this barren waste and over night it's one cavorting albeit cultured holiday camp.

Winds whining and the sea pounding out there. One might sleepwalk. Off battlements into deeps. Percival said there was a black ice cold bottomless lake just up the mountain side. Full of strange thin fish, some so sharp they could swim through a stone. But at the end of the sea tunnel opening out from the cliffs and down six fathoms was the great conger. Lurking in a cave. Percival said ah now sir I didn't want to worry you with an old eel. But for many years they were dropping off terrible things out the end of the tunnel, the like of heads and thighs and it's said Clementine of The Three Glands was shoving off there his discarded females in one screaming piece. Tim now throws off the odd dead sheep if Miss Ovary isn't in need of one for dinner. That thing down there devours bowels and entrails by the wheel barrow. And I'm telling you now it's thought that that's the way old Clarence's mother and father went as well as Paddy the butcher who wandered off the cliff drunk and none has ever been seen since except that in the bright sunshine pelvic girdles are obvious on the sand below. Rumour has it that the great conger remained mild enough feeding on the odd lad stumbling off the edge and that it never added to the huge creature's viciousness till a protestant rose growing land owner was ate by the conger while trying to fish for him out of a little dingy and was dragged to his doom. The conger has been mean vicious and evil to a degree ever since, demonstrating quite clearly a catholic is sweet to the taste just as a protestant is sour.

A low growl from Elmer. During the fracas downstairs he lay quietly by the fireside. And polished off the mutton before Oscar tugging at one end could get it out of his great grey jaws. Which means he won't need a nightcap of my billiard slippers washed down by a few pairs of socks. He contentedly looks up at me propped shivering in bed. No floor board to squeak in this room. Anyone could tiptoe in a good quality pair of sneakers and get me round the neck. And unless they were mutton Elmer might not mind. That's a knock. On my door.

'Come in.'

'I don't want to disturb you. But could I borrow a toothbrush. I was wandering around this morning and saw your collection.'

'Of course. But all of them are used.'

'That's no bother to me. Can I come in and take one.'

'Please do.'

Rose in her silk kimono. Which is blue embellished with green dragons, mouths spitting orange flame. Hear her high heels. And my heart thumping. Opening up as she does the toothbrush case. And picks and chooses.

'Take any one.'

'All the bristles have dropped out of mine.'

'I'm sorry to hear that.'

'Did you think I was unladylike tonight. I'm not a lady but that one is one of them cultured rich ones with her little puppet husband on a string.'

'I quite understand.'

'Well I didn't want to appear as if I was unladylike.'

'No I can quite see that.'

'How do you come to be living in this castle all to yourself, servants waiting on you hand and foot with not a bother in the world. If you don't mind my asking a personal question.'

'My great grand aunt gave it to me.'

'You're not codding me. Gave it to you.'

'And Elmer there as well.'

'Wish I had an aunt like that. Could give me a decent flat. I'm living in a basement. Flooded it is too. Didn't the three of them come in over a weekend and that Franz start digging in the corner saying that according to his map evidence there was a mineral deposit. There was a spring. That's what there was. Gushing right up into me face. Leaving me living in a foot of water and terrified the landlord would see it.'

'I'm sorry to hear that.'

'In my boots day and night.'

'That's awful.'

'He put stones for me to leap from one to the other. The only good thing about them was he tried it himself and fell flat on his face. Would you ever let me have a glass of that wine there and a bit of cheese.'

'By all means help yourself.'

'What a life with wine and cheese by the bedside reading a book. Grrrrrrr. Grrrrr. It makes me growl.'

'Here take this knife.'

'I like to bite out chunks. It's a relief to be shut of them eegits for a bit. They almost killed me coming cross country. Took out my tonsils. Operating in the back of the car with that maniac Franz driving. Couldn't eat a thing for three days. With them killing chickens and cows around every bend in the road. And one odd gentleman they took his cart donkey and hay rick right from underneath him and the poor old man had ten years put onto his life as he came through the sun roof of the car onto my lap making a mess in his trousers. And that Franz beating on the poor creature with a riding crop for being in his way. And like they do to everybody they hand out that donkey distillate. We got the old man back to his cottage. Seventy four he was and chased his eighty four year old wife all over the place with Erconwald trying to train a film camera on them.

Sure the distillate's a fake, the old man was just knocked out of his senses.'

'Why do you stay with them.'

'They pay me. Outside the city limits I'm on combat remuneration so to speak. With the car stinking of onions and their instruments sticking in my backside. They take my rectal temperature every morning. That's an extra pound a week I get for that lark. With them carrying on all the time about precision.'

'What about your singing.'

'That. Sure the opera they put on was the greatest fiasco in the history of performing arts. Franz back stage was putting out a smoke to make a low fog for an ostrich to walk through with its head sticking out the top of it. He said the authenticity of such a scene would be unforgettable. Well I can tell you this bird nearly eight feet high and three hundred weight gave authenticity aplenty when the thing got off the stage and ran amok in the audience. The three of them have been sued ever since for two broken legs and concussions too numerous to mention with the theatre left like a battlefield. That was the end of me own operatic career. And theirs too I can tell you.'

'It seems to me they are very inconsiderate.'

'Inconsiderate, don't make me laugh. They are dangerous.'

'O God.'

'This is grand wine. Would you mind if I had another little bit of the cheese.'

'No not at all.'

'Are you uneasy.'

'Well I'm sort of settling in. I wasn't expecting guests.'

'Guests you call them. Get that notion out of your mind in a hurry. Inhabitants is the word. Haven't they got a laboratory rigged up in one of your rooms and in another weren't they putting a hole in the floor to make a snakepit of the room below.'

'Holy cow.'

'But I'll tell you one thing. They are the only three honest people I have ever met in this country. Not once was I ever diddled out of a penny. And they keep their word to the letter. Sure at Christmas time they distribute dozens of ducks to the poor and educate little orphan waifs sending them to the best of colleges. They refuse no one a kindness. I've seen Erconwald with me own eyes walk along the Green with a bunch of little scallywags begging pennies and he'd empty his pockets to them. Old women dying up there behind the brewery have them to thank for peaceful last moments on this earth. With their own families trying to cuff them into their graves, you would see Erconwald, Putlog and Franz putting balm on the poor creature's forehead and giving her jelly beans and cream lemon delights to eat. While the savages were drinking outside the door merrymaking in a hurry to get the poor old thing under the sods. Would you mind if I sat down.'

'No please do.'

'You could start a good little business in this place.'

Rose renewing her glass of port. Holding the cheese by the rind as she shaves off the last slivers with her incisors, eyes flashing in the candle light. Dark haunting globes. She fixes them on me. Starts a staring match. Wins after nine seconds. And throws her head back, shakes her hair. Her dimensions all bigger than mine go written around in the inside of my head.

'You don't mind me asking are you queer.'

'I beg your pardon.'

'You heard me. Are you queer.'

'I don't think so.'

'Well I'm waiting.'

'O.'

'You know what I'm talking about. Have you not ever heard the expression give the man in the bed a woman.'

'I don't think so.'

'Well do you want me to get into the bed or don't you.'

'Sure. Do please, get in.'

'I'll take off this old yoke on me.'

'Wow.'

'Ha ha. Grrrrrr. How's that.'

'O boy.'

'I'm freezing too. Move over. Linen sheets and pillow cases with embroidery. You're a plutocrat. Them dungeons down there. Chains and shackles on the walls. Rats running all over the place. You and your predecessors must have had a grand time incarcerating the poor natives, whipping and starving them down there, stealing all the land you could get your greedy bloody hands on. What am I doing in this bed with the likes of you.'

'I didn't do anything to the natives. I just got here.'

'Well it's on your head. You've got the features of a cruel landlord. Written all over you. When the insurgents get here. The likes of you will be made quick work of I can tell you.'

'Insurgents.'

'You bet insurgents. The army of insurrection. Get your elbow out of me tit like that. What do you think this is.'

'I don't know, I'm sure. Obviously there's been a misunderstanding.'

'Have you got more port.'

'The decanter's right there.'

'Well I'll help myself then.'

Clementine adjusting his sky blue skull cap. Keeps away the night air's unfavourable effect upon the roots of the hair. A tuft of which in vigorous black grows under Rose's oxster. Wouldn't stand a chance in combat with her. The biggest exprisoner was lifted right up off his toes trying to choke her with a headlock from behind. Wish fervently this most painful erection one sports would go down in case she decides to wrench it off. Before the insurgents get here. And do it.

'Rose would you mind pouring me a glass as well, please.'

'Take mine why don't you and I'll fill another. Would you mind telling me what them things are up there on the wall.'

'Pulley's for raising and lowering the iron door.'

'The insurgents will make quick work of that.'

'Do you happen to know when they're coming.'

'If I did what would I tell you for. I know the commandant personally.'

'Do you think he will take exception to me.'

'How should I know. But one person in this enormous place. With whole families having to live in one room.'

'At the moment there are about sixteen people here. Not including the dog, the pig and a collection of snakes.'

'Ah I love those mambas.'

'They're deadly snakes.'

'I'm injected against harm from them. Look at me arm. The scars. And soon they'll be more they're breeding to let them loose in the fields. You'll be free of the rats.'

'And out of my mind with mambas.'

'You're a funny sort. Rigged up like that to go to sleep. For myself now I'm fond of nakedness. Been photographed back sides and front by Erconwald. He fancies himself as a photographer. Before I entered the singing contest he followed me all over town. If I was having coffee he would sit at a nearby table taking notes. Finally in the lobby of a hotel he steps out from behind a pillar and introduces himself. I laughed in his face. He says to me, ah madam permit me to make myself known from behind this architectural embellishment. Didn't he leap out at me. With a goatlike delicacy using these light footed floating side steps. Down on one knee he goes. Holding out to me a ring he has in the centre of a little tray. Wasn't everyone in the lobby watching. I nearly fainted backwards with embarrassment. Next I'm staring barefaced at an engraved proposal of marriage. And with not another word out of him he gets up, bows and goes off scribbling in his little book in the corner.'

Rain dripping on the stone sills. Wind growing stronger. Boom of the sea. Down where the great conger lurks. Over his collection of bones. Got my elbow back where it was before. Up against the side of her bulging breast. Fattened further by the last of my cheese. Just push my foot down a little between the damp sheets. Feel if it's true. That she's got webbing between the toes. Mamba venom in the veins. And influence with the insurgents. Who might as well be here already. To take up positions. In the halls. And direct traffic for this carnival.

'Are you constipated, Clementine.'

'No.'

'Well I was. For years. Frozen like concrete. Didn't the doctors have to dig it out of me. Till I took the infusion. After winning the contest the three of them in white coats subjected me to a rude intimate examination with stethoscopes and blood pressure contraptions. Said my breath wasn't what it should be, caused by the inner contamination. Sure I listened to them, I had to, strapped stark naked as I was on my back to an operating table under a big sky light with the clouds going over above right in the best part of town. You never heard such a bunch of high falutin comments. Streaming out of the three of them. Said that the tone of my voice would be sweetened. Well I can tell you I'm thankful to them for that. For the greatest relishment I've been having at the bog of a morning. Sitting there with it coming out two feet long at a time like satin. Franz's donkey distillate may be a hoax. But I'm telling you right now the infusion is a holy miracle.'

'The distillate is ok too.'

'You're not codding me now. Grrrrr. Give us a feel. Ah if that's not good quality granite I've never felt a bit in me life. Maybe they're genuine scientists enough then.'

Rose growling, rearing up on top of Clementine. Elmer's ears cocking. The rusty springs of the lumpy mattress squealing. She's trying to open my pyjamas which are on backwards. But through the arse of which I forged a hole for peeing. By constantly making this mistake each time I had to take a midnight leak on my storm tossed trip across the seas. To reach this land. After a eleven and a half days of nautical horror. Witnessed in silence. At the long end of a nervous decline. Right to the edge of the grave. Kept holding myself back. Not wanting to go just yet. But inching there all the same. Waking each day at dawn. The light cold with death. My great aunt sitting through afternoons down below in her gabled house on a shady street. Where I watched the milkman, mailman and garbage collector come and go. And like Erconwald does with Rose I took my rectal temperature. Measuring the slow combustion of the fatal disease. Taking me around the throat and arse. Parts it seemed to fancy. As my aunt's servants went out my bedroom door shaking their heads. With the trays of untouched food. Seven ounces less I weighed each day. Looking at my white tongue in the mirror. New pains behind eyeballs. Doom fuming up from the outstretched suppliant palms of my hands. Had I known Franz, Erconwald and Putlog then they could have squirted a tonic vapour down my throat and an aeriform serum up my arse. To meet in the belly for a gaseous eruption and blow both hips out of joint forever. Flap round like a puppet buried as I am under Rose's two massive swinging breasts and cascading hair. Growling and biting. What a change from crawling down the last mile. Auntie rolling in my bedroom door in her wheel chair, telling me I was just like my father. He was big and strong. Buried my mother and three more after her. Screwed to death. It was rumoured by doctors who diagnosed an agitation caused by his testicular trinity. An uncontrollable temper kept him in excellent condition. Leaping as he did out at traffic lights to drag some poor unfortunate from another car who had the folly to sneer at him at a previous traffic light. I sat in the front seat. A little boy with curls and enormous sad eyes. Standing up to see as my father used his usual right hook to lay a chap backwards over the engine hood. Climbing to the rear seat to peek out and see the victim cross eagled unconscious. Goodness Rose you are strong. Got me by the wrists. Winds raging outside. Last candle going out on the bedside table. Life tip toes back in. As you wait and never see it. Till a time comes. Just like this. The Charnel Castle cure. New vigorous lethal terrors drive out the stale mouldering ones under which one was smothering. Still begging for mommie. To come back. She left on a sunny day. In an ambulance from the side of a house. Carried out on a stretcher and loaded in the shade of the old coach porch. Pressed my nose to the copper screen. My father said mommie wanted peace and quiet. He would take me to see her soon. We went on a rainy day. Down town. It had snowed in the morning and now the streets were grey with slush. Pipes tingling and throbbing in the hospital. We went up three floors in an elevator and down a long corridor. A little boy pushed by sobbing on a trolley. His own mommie holding his clothes in her arms. We came to a door and I felt chilled. As I stood, my father behind me pushing me in the back, saying go in. See your mother. There she is. Go over to her. A silhouette as she lay on the bed, her long delicate nose, eyes closed and her wavy brown hair spread on the pillow. Out the window the roof of another building covered with pipes and roofed with little grey pebbly stones. The sky darkened, rain falling straight and hard. Old snow tucked in the corners of roof tops. My father standing at the door. My mother's hand was pale. Her nails white at the finger tips. I reached over and touched her. I didn't know what dead was. Until the tears started to come out of my eyes. And when I turned round my father was gone. I looked down the hall and saw him talking with a doctor. A nurse passed me to go into the room. I stood at the door and watched her pull a white cover over my mother's face. And when the nurse came out she said to me who are you little boy. I said I'm not anyone.

> Nor
> Anyone else
> Either
> Who
> Made
> All that
> Sorrow

5

A nightime murmuring and mumbling on towards dawn.
Comes sweeping across the earth making winter bird
choruses and chasing out to sea. Puts light on the waves.
Pushes fish down in the deep. Where their teeth might
miss each other in the dark. And after all these obtuse thurs-
day goings on, would that I sleep. Buried under Rose's
snores.

Clementine rolling his head back and forth under Rose's
hair. Till a great moist nose peeked through followed by
the tongue and paws of Elmer. Who wanted to join the
fun. Pushing his monstrous head between the two of us.
Just as one is tasting the tip top joys again way up inside
Rose. As she sleeps and now wakes roaring. And growling
just like Elmer.

'Ah God it's the dog on us. Is he vicious. Get him away
from me altogether.'

'Out Elmer. Naughty dog. He's only playing.'

'He took a nip out of me.'

'I'm sorry. Down Elmer. He's just lonely.'

'Woof woof.'

'He doesn't understand what I'm telling him.'

'Well fuck off you monster understand that from me.'

'Please don't speak like that to my dog.'

'Would you have him savage me defenceless in the condition we're in.'

'You could easily hurt his feelings.'

'While he takes it into his head to make a horse dover
of one of me appendages.'

Rose is somewhat savoury under the oxsters. Inciting Elmer who according to a mouldering dog reference book
in the library can distinguish more smells than you could

shake a mamba at. He only wants to know what sniffs.
Between the strong muscles in Rose's thighs. Which grip
me with pincers of knob ended knees. What on earth am I
going to do with one unearthly wind ready to break. Right
from the bowels of my conscience. So awkward after one
remonstrates over incivility to a canine. To then unleash a
stench closeted with layers of dank linen and wool, not to
mention an inch thick emblazoned motheaten counterpane.
Under which the two of us are unavoidably heavily breathing. Do please, everybody, get ready. As I ease it out. With
no tune. Don masks. Sneak gas attack. Blame it on Elmer.
I know for a fact he's laid one or two. Fuming up pungent.
Merrily riding down here. In the compartment of the
train.

'What's that for the sacrifice of the saints.'

'What.'

'Is there a dead rat.'

'I beg your pardon.'

'It's in the bed it is.'

'Where.'

'Gassing me.'

'It's Elmer.'

'Get him away the dirty thing.'

'Elmer. Out. Down. Naughty.'

'That dog hasn't a trace of a bit of manners on him.'

Through the narrow window slit slants a sliver of moonlight. Tree branches scratching the walls. Clouds tumble
by. A big boom of sea. A tremble of walls. The fraught fart
fading. Brewed up as it must have been from the gravy.
And further fermented by old cheese and ancient port. The
three master minds when they get a moment free from
making their snake pit in my house could concoct a pill to
purify blasts. That freshly out of the pink expand. And
turn a faceless blue in their beauty. The very latest. Just
pop it down the throat. For your fragances. Of fern, lilac
or heather. Matched pills for perfume. For evening wear.
At one of their operas. Whole audience could come primed
with lily of the valley. Making the authenticity of such
a smell unforgettable. Rising triumphantly in crescendo

from the best bottoms. A unified blast as the curtain comes down. And the clapping hands fan it up to the rafters. One curtain call after another. Could be taken by Rose. Who is growling again. Gyrating and plunging down on me. Way up her as I am. Between the curious intermissions we've been having. Like at the saturday morning movies I used to see. Discontinued till next week with the hero's head on the railway track. And I rushed back with my nickels to see if he would get squashed. As did the noses my father punched. Long after he married a wife who kept coming out of their bedroom wrapped in her kimono telling me to get back down stairs. My father so frequent in rage. Saw him sock a man up against a big grain silo and then put his hand around his throat until the man's face turned blue just like Mrs L K L. Once a month at least he blew up charging through the house breaking everything in sight. Hissing and steaming. Then banging his fist which went through whatever it landed on. I began to like it better than the movies. Watching through some discreet aperture. Dust rising from chairs. Windows shattering. Lamp shades crushed. That latter was my favourite. And if he could find me I was always good for absorbing a few punches. Sending me aloft across the room. Screaming child murder. But I grew to be able to scoot down the cellar stairs and squeeze out a window which was too small for him to fit through. And once when he stood in the basement glaring I emptied a pail of water all over him. Into which I had peed before. The chase went up and down cherry trees, over garage roofs and in and out of his three cars. Till he cornered me in a bathroom in the house. And just as he was breaking down the door, the police came charging in. He knew them by name, Hal, Bob, Dick and gave them beer in the kitchen until they couldn't stand up. All telling me one by one to behave myself and obey my father. Whose next wife thank God liked me and baked apple pies whenever I wanted them. Which was every day. With a bottle of cream. Followed by spoonfuls of cod liver oil. My palate enjoyed variation. I was a thin but healthy little devil. This new mother was nice. And I was hoping my father wouldn't get another.

Servants, all of whom had been frightened away came back to work for us. To get a stifled laugh one sunday dinner when my father's rage weakened chair collapsed beneath him and he got showered with a bowl of boiled potatoes. Which Rose might have preferred to the long gone to seed spud she snapped at in her eager hunger. Needed to feed her frenzied energy she uses to grind it right off me. Hold her steady by the great white rear globes. Smooth as mushrooms. Heaving with the remarkable neoarciform described by Erconwald. On her webbed feet she cruised right in to borrow a toiletry. Now she's calling me Joseph. Might be walking in her sleep. Teeth in my neck. Sinking in. One has that terrible feeling there are eyes in the ceiling. Clarence peeking between the stone vaulting. And yesterday one moment as I turned to go back in a hallway which headed far beyond my curiosity, I thought I saw someone skip into a room. Any door you might open now could be a snakepit. Auntie would have a fit. Even if she is arthritic in the legs. When I graduated from high school she was the only one who came. And when I stood under banners on the gymnasium steps with the wind blowing through my hair, great aunt clapped for me long after everyone else stopped. Till a man said shush and she took her parasol and clonked him one. On childhood sundays she took me in her big car, telling Peter the chauffeur through a microphone which way to turn. To reach my mother's tomb round a lot of curving cemetery roads. Under a great stone canopy she stood. As a big white piece of chiselled marble in long flowing robes. My aunt said my mother was the most beautiful woman in the midwest. That fine fine profile. And you my boy are going to make something of yourself. Take no nonsense from inferiors and less from superiors and count on being surrounded by crass stupidity for most of your life. And I knew she wanted to add, instead of beating the shit out of innocent pedestrians, motorists and bystanders like your father. Rose groans. Long and nearly agonized. Flapping around like a fish. On the end of this pole.

'Ah Joseph, Joseph what is it you've got up in me.'

Do I speak. When I'm not Joseph. Best to wait for recognition. And meanwhile plan tomorrow's events. Lick the place into shape. Before some more of it falls on me. Rose digging in her fingernails. She'll be drawing blood. A little pain drives out the doom. Which after high school, college expulsion, naval training and sales careers, finally closed in on me. My slow suitable decline sent me on a stretcher from auntie's gabled house in the shady street. And for the first time I saw her quiver. Just as the moon faced grandfather clock clanged three over her white head. And I passed by supine attempting the merest contorted grin. I was all she had left. And she was all I had. In the form of a very small weekly allowance. She sent me fresh fruit each day to the hospital. Tightwad as she was she kept me in a ward. In a wing the other side of the grey pebbled roof top where my mother died. Windows looked out over a canal. Two a.m. was the greatest stillness. When we all lay. wondering who was next to go. Wheeled out under a sheet. Before dawn came and gave us another day. Stare up now at the ceiling beaded with moisture. This castle like a vine entwining. Rose is off me and taking a rest. I'm in an awful state of worry. What if she's afflicted with something not nice and catching. Which could send me down again only weeks after I've got up.

Elmer asleep. Big shadowy head curled around on his paws. New fiercer winds are lashing cannon ball raindrops. Rose on her back, hands behind her head and elbows sticking in the air, whistling. Elmer wakes, his ears cocking in all directions.

'I needed that. I fancy you.'

'My name's not Joseph.'

'Ah God that's a scream. When I'm like that I can't get the name Joseph out of me head.'

'You know someone called Joseph.'

'No. I just say the name. It does for everybody. You know I like it here. It's a bit damp. But roomy. I got an itch first time I set eyes on you. You've funny brown peepers with spots in them. What's for breakfast.'

'I don't know. I don't think it's morning yet.'

'I could eat a horse. Would you mind if I went down below and fixed up some bacon and eggs.'

'I don't know if there are any.'

'Sure there's pucks of food. I saw that Percival and a giant, blind as a bat unloading enough food out of a cart to feed an army. You're wealthy.'

'Thank you.'

'Don't thank me. I'm just glad of a bite to eat now and again. Only that the Baron never finishes his food I'd be starving.'

'Who's the Baron.'

'Sure he was sitting across from you tonight down there in the dining room. Like the rest of us he's inhabitating a dungeon back in town. For the moment he's on combat pay with Erconwald. Hardly ever speaks but is a maniac for music. He came down my basement one night when I was rehearsing an aria and stood there at the wall beating his head on it, tears and then blood streaming down his face. Poor man was banished by his family in one of them foreign countries. They send him money once a month to stay away. When it arrives doesn't he have a horse cab call and creep out to it in his pyjamas to be taken to the pawn where he redeems his wardrobe, with the likes of a morning suit, silk shirts and whatever else grand continental gentlemen put on their backs. And he's to be seen for the next week immaculate with hotel porters running after him with tips for the races, lounging as he is in a suite with his long cigarette holder in his mouth sipping champagne as if he had not a bother in the world. When the money's gone, he gets the horse cab back to the pawn, climbs into his pyjamas again and waits till the next cheque from his family. He's delirious with joy here in the castle, just like home it is to him.'

'You think he might stay.'

'Stay, you just try to get him out. Sure I met him in the hall trembling and tearful, a sure sign he couldn't be happier. Erconwald says he is an overflowing spring of compassion. Will you have a rasher and an egg if I fetch them up.'

'Yes please.'

'Right you are.'

Rose throws me a smile in the moonlit shadows. Her breasts aflood on her chest. Great black bush of hair sprouting from her belly. Sit here with my shot gun and pop the pheasants as they break from cover. She pirouettes. And goes into high c. Elmer leaping to his feet and tottering with the sudden effort. As Rose's voice dins the ears.

'EEEEEEEEEEEEEE. I'm feeling great. Stand up now on the bed and let me see a sight of you.'

'I'd rather not.'

'Come on haven't you a sight of me.'

'I'm shy.'

'Come on give us a flash of it.'

'Really I don't think so.'

'I love the sight of them standing out like a stallion, pointing straight at you as if you were accused of wanting to be killed by it. You're a retiring sort of gent then.'

'A little.'

'So I'll be off.'

'You're coming back.'

'Well now that's a thought. I'll not come back unless you stand up there and give me an exhibition.'

'I'm sorry but I won't be threatened.'

'Who's threatening. Have you ever seen a black man's. I hear tell they'd choke you with them. And a yellow man's is no bigger than a snail out of its shell.'

'I'm not really acquainted with either.'

'Well I'm off.'

'Goodbye.'

'So long.'

Rose wrapping up in her kimono. Tying a knot around the waist. Twisting her neck in a circle. And throwing back her hair. She goes. Now stops. In the antechamber. Could just reach there over the bed and clang down would come the iron door. Just as she was walking out. I'd be had up for murder. Which might be quite legal around here. Or God forbid decapitate her toes and tits. Which my resident scientists would painstakingly suture back on. And raise her combat pay.

'I'll come back. I've been without an old fashioned horn up me for over three months.'

'What about the scientists.'

'What about them, I wouldn't let one of them near me with their things. Sure they want to be coming at you with calorimeters, gyroscopes and with a bunch of tubes. It's vexing enough being examined by them that I don't have to let them up me. It wouldn't half fill a book the goings on back there in town testing out the distillate. With the three of them sitting there in a row on a bench one hand pulling away possessed and in the other holding stop watches. Didn't they have an innocent little girl out of a convent as an assistant measuring the amount that jumped out into test tubes. The three disgusting pagans. I'm off for to get the eggs and bacon. Will you have a fried tomato as well.'

'Yes please.'

'Right you are.'

Four weeks ago tomorrow I stepped off the boat. Rode a train up along a strange bereft shore. Click clacking by estuaries, stopping in small towns. Finally to chug along a flat deserted cold grey coast. Past ruined roofless houses and wintry marshlands. Arrived at a station and went down the granite steps between the pillars, a dance hall across the street. Rented a room from a big kindly woman. In which I quietly and politely froze. Sitting by the wall at breakfast shivering under her heavy breathing ministrations. I was a stranger stared at wherever I went. Wandering the grey wet streets. Looking into a future. Dimmed by the months of dying. Watching from my pillow a young man in the centre aisle of the ward with his precise methodical ways as he declined. Visited every day by a mother who fussed and kissed him and wore big fur collars on her coat. The day before he was rolled away under a sheet he smiled and played with a jig saw puzzle. That evening I lay still with my eyes closed. Heard choirs singing. Boys in white cassocks trudging over snows with great flaming candles. Their voices rising up in the blue cold skies strewn with colder stars. Watch them. They walk on the endless white.

Mountains in the distance. Follow them. Run light footed into wonder. Where there may be a hand to lay touching gently my eyes. And whispers wake with words. Lie safely wound in my arms in peace. All I am is your soul. To gather you. Now. And I knew I was going. Hearing voices. Nearby my bed. Yes we're finding it difficult to diagnose, refuses all food, possibly an hysterical condition, he's unconscious now, may go into coma. We don't think he'll last through tonight. I opened up a lid a crack. Could see three white coated figures and a nurse standing a little away from the foot of my bed. They are talking about me. And it's touching and comforting that they are. A little group concerned while I live my final moments. I go and they stay. In this great maw of a hospital. Ward of death where the bodies are wheeled in and out. And sometimes screams echoing down the corridors. Sirens of ambulances and police cars in the night. Next to me a man swathed in bandages, only a hole for his mouth. The black nurse who goes by my bed. Stops and looks at me. Try bravely to smile. She smiles. How are we feeling today. I shake my head. And she would say have you ate anything and I would shake it no again. She said that's not good. You've got to eat. Else you won't be here anymore. I had then the strength only to raise and lower my hands on the sheet. She would pass on shaking her head. And then twenty minutes after midnight which I always knew because a whistle blew on a gasworks across the river canal, the black nurse came, stood over my bed, and looked at me. She said yes that's what they say, you're not going to live one more day. That's not good. That's bad. So I am going to cure you.

Rose coming through the shadows holding a tray of plates and tea pot. A candle making big dark holes out of her eyes. The thump of Elmer's tail on the stone floor. Spreading out this feast in front of us. Packed back in the bed. Grease cooled white on the bacon. Steam rising from the cups of tea. Rose with a slice of bread spread with a slab of butter. Takes up an egg of which there are three on her plate and lays it over the fork and shovels it into her mouth. Followed by the bread and mouthfuls of tea.

'You know this is grand. Like a hotel. I was in one once. As the guest of the Baron. It had a bathroom not twenty feet away down the hall. I took seven baths. One after the other. Went out of there so clean the skin was nearly off me. The Baron never took a liberty with me. Perfect gentleman he is. For the matter of that I don't think the Baron has ever taken a liberty with any woman. If he's got his music he hasn't a care in the world. Aren't you going to eat that.'

'I'm not awfully hungry.'

'Fair enough hand it right over here.'

Rose wiped plates and saucers with a piece of bread soaking up tomato seeds, congealed fat and bacon specks. Laughing and growling after the final mouthfuls. A lively strain of organ music in the lulls of the wind. No dull moment in this place. Not even at dawn. Pigs, snakes, barons, scientists and high heeled pieces of arse come floating down the halls. Someone may even show up called Boris. Who can play parts not yet cast. And star as a rectum. In the final production. And I could end up footing the bill for this original opera.

'I like a snack of an evening. Give us a flash of it. That thing down there. Can't I see it showing signs of raising the bed covers off us.'

'That's my knee.'

'You don't say.'

'Yes I do.'

'Well give us a look at your knee then.'

'There.'

'Ah that's a great scar you've got. What ever did that.'

'My father once when he was chasing me.'

'Poor lad. God help you. Grrrrrrr. I've got holt of it. What's wrong with you you won't let me see it. Sure the scientists testing the distillate prance around their laboratory all day with them sticking out. The whole of the population passing down in the street not a stone's throw away. You'd wonder if they ever tell their sins to God. Such whoppers that the almighty would be sent mental. Hasn't Franz said to me there's no supreme being. Would you believe that.'

66

'Yes.'

'By God the bunch of them have been right enough about a few things, it makes you think. Do you think there's a god.'

'Yes.'

'Ah thank God of that. I'm glad to hear it. That Franz would tell you the sky was green and that you could eat it on tuesdays. He has the craziest horn I've ever seen. Curves upwards at you like a banana. Yours seems straight enough. There's a man in town, now the quietest most elegant well spoken gentleman you could meet, came courting me. Didn't I think I was right once and for all. The good looks of him would make you faint. Doesn't he accept an invitation to come for a little dinner I'm giving him down in the flooded flat. Embarrassed as I am to meet him at the door with a pair of me brother's boots to wear. He was lovely. Sits down without a murmur of discontent his feet bunched up in the boots, the water splashing around us. I had the couch propped up on paving stones. Ready for any delight he cared to bestow. A dozen eggs and a pound of rashers we had between us. Like yourself he was shy. I couldn't let him turn off the electric as it would throw you dead into the water with a blaze of current. He kept saying could we have it dark. So I finally aimed an old stale loaf of bread at the bulb and put us into darkness. I was on the couch. I could hear him wading towards me through the water. And didn't the headlights of a car go by on the street. Well I had a fit when I saw it. He had a thing on him like the prow of a ship. Appropriate at the time. But I said for the love of God you're not going to put the likes of that into me, I'd be kilt. Hadn't the words got out of my mouth before I could stop myself. The poor gentleman was mortified. God he was handsome. Must have happened to him many times before. That he had to get at you in the dark before you could object. Haven't I often wondered had he got at me with it first would I have known. I don't mind them thick or on the long side but when they're the like of that as would plough you in half I'll take celibacy instead of death. Well I can tell you when I came with the news to the three of them

67

weren't they into white coats in a flash, ripping instruments out of the drawers and racing out the laboratory door like they were going to a fire. In no time they had your man housed in the best hotel, giving him the treat of his life while they were at him with the stop watches, weighing and measuring and pouring distillate and copious beers down your man's throat. You wouldn't know but that the bunch of them were turning into homosexuals. You'd hear nothing else out of them but the specifications and performance of your man's tool. All in a special book with a blue ribbon. How long it took to get up, come off, go down, get up again in the various temperatures, times of day and phases of the moon. Till your man broke down in tears and wept, a nervous residue. Now that's a handy size I don't mind saying. Built for comfort. Give us a flash. Go on. Sure as I'm feeling it what harm is it to see it.'

'All right.'

'It must be studded with jewels. Grrrrrr. Ah fondly seen by moonlight. Grrrrrr. You have a beautiful prick. Make a grand dessert.'

Rose is at me. Finishing off her supper with a nibble. And now a mouthful. Of the end of my pole. Take it as a radish, take it as a leek. But by God don't gobble it off altogether and make me a freak. Plough acres around Charnel Castle to keep you fed. Grow a few tons of onions too. For the others. The land raging forth with cabbages and spuds would bring in some revenue. Might make ends meet. Just as easily die here as in the hospital. Fading away in the night when nurse said I am going to cure you. The shadows rearing as she pushed the green screens up around my bed, pulled back the covers and put her hand gently tickling between my legs murmuring man you're in a bad bad way but we're going to cure you starting right now tonight before you do any more of this dying. Do you hear. You come back now walking on that road. You can do it. Her whispers reaching quietly into my ears. From this dark slender girl. A little silver watch on her wrist she watched when she held mine. I felt all those first days she might not like me. Till she said you're a model patient not a request or a complaint. I gave her all my tropical fruit. Just to leave with someone something. If only spat out seeds. Little pips. In memory. I had no visitors but one old school friend who thought I had got strange. And after a few sour fading smiles he walked away with my temperature chart caught on his coat. Which clattered to the floor at the swing door of the ward. And then she came. On duty every night at seven. Her uniform sparkling white. Her big long lashed eyes and flashing teeth. Which were pressing a light touching porcelain on my penis. More lightly and lovely than light or love. Till just after half past twelve my pecker came up. A slow fire from a tiny spark kissed into me. She was called April and wore glasses when she read my thermometer. My heart was thumping. Her lips soft wind blowing. A tune played with music tip toeing up my spine. Carrying little tinkling silver chains. Winding them round in bundles. Attached up to a ship. A naval vessel I once saw ready for launching. The great wooden supports knocked away. Taking the thighs off my hips and banging them on my ears I come awake. Bottle of champagne crashing against the bow. People running scattering through the brain. The ship moves. Slowly. Faster now. Rose please. Not so hard. April blew like a mystery. Never solved in the shadows she sweetly beat into billowing flames. The drag chains on the ship swept away in great clouds of rusty dust. Bells pounding. Sirens blaring. The bulge stern of the vessel flooding out into the water. And I was floating too. April's hand over my mouth as I groaned out with life from all the beds of dying. Where she left me. So tenderly that night. A kiss on my cheek and warm honeyed milk licked from her fingers. Dripping down my throat. Healing. Brought to me by her long slender brown hands. She had a husband. Who had gone off to die. Somewhere along the miles of dirty pavements under the elevated train. She met him every afternoon. Where he sat on a bench waiting. She came with milk, chicken pie, cole slaw and ham. His favourite foods. His face lighting up with a smile and they went to a little park to sit by a tree, throwing crumbs to squirrels and she'd tuck his napkin in and try to bring him back to life. Each time she left him saying goodbye at the bus stop, tears in both their eyes because she knew one time she would come and there'd be no one sitting there. And that saturday came. For five hours she waited and waited. Till it was dark and she was late for duty. That day the next day and next. Sitting the hot afternoon pestered by drunks, a hoarding of a vacant lot behind her, a big hand holding up an enormous glass of beer. She gave the food away to men just able to lift up their heads and say thank you. Each midnight the screens up around the bed she blew me. Fed me more warm milk and honey soaked pieces of bread. Within a week I had the strength to grab but not hold her and she laughed and said this is treatment and you mustn't touch. I wrote out in big letters on a piece of paper.

> Thank you
> For eating me
> The way
> You do

She folded the tidings up and put it in a little pocket over her breast and shook her finger at me. She said you're going to talk again too but comments like that are taboo. I could peel an orange now and chew an apple. Saw green again. Grass and cherry blossoms. Press my hand flat on the earth. Watch flowers grow up between my fingers. The doctors came with raised eyebrows. Shaking their heads up and down. Wondering why I wasn't out there a turning left off the hall and down a long ramp where they put the chilled banked up bodies. Rose I'm coming. Should I call you Josephine. Instead of the April I remember night and day. With her trim legs and the agony simmering in me when I saw her put her hand to another forehead or read another chart or smile at another face. I swore on a clean sheet of paper to her that I would go into a further decline. Unless she took less time visiting the other beds and stayed with me. Rose. I'm coming. In April. When she blew me at midnight and again at dawn. I was eating steak then. She took a piece of paper and wrote in letters I thought far bigger than were necessary.

                              You
                              Are
                              Cured

I wrote back. Like hell I am. And she spoke a shouting
whisper. You are. I left just before Christmas. She tied the
knot of my tie and fixed a hanky in my pocket upon which
she wiped a tear. It was a morning. She was off duty in a
light grey suit, and light blue sweater. I would start dying
again just to touch her breasts. Said she stopped in to see
me go. To make sure I didn't give her another wrestling
match that night. And I went. Out the long dismal green
corridor of haunting chemical smells. And hugged her
goodbye as I got into a taxi. And now I come. In her
memory. Wherever she is. Waiting by the big glass of beer.
Near the train which thunders by. A brown girl who gave
a kiss of white life to me. Coaxed up seed to sow. Some
gone now gruntingly swallowed. By Rose. Strength seeping
out of my legs. Her hand feeling in among my balls. During
inquisition, please take it easy. Spheroids of the utmost delicacy. Not to be tested with a pinch between forefinger and
thumb. Or one held while the other two are squeezed for
authenticity. April specially took out her glasses when perusing that part of my case history. Even though I was dying
I smiled. As Rose comes up for air. Big buxom thing from
under the covers on her hands and knees. Smacking her
lips. Swinging those breasts. Could smother you. Quite pleasantly. As I get reported to the scientists. For having three.
Estimated by Rose. Be invited to an hotel. Disrobe please.
We have with us our adding machine. Just like the guy who
came navigating his stupendous prow into port over the
cellar waters. She is amazed.

   'How many balls do you have. I'm going out of my mind
down there counting.'

                              One
                              Two
                              Three
                              Cheek by jowl

Jaw by jest
It's a trinity
By twixt
And christ
Manifest

6

The grass short and shrubs beaten into hiding behind
mossy stones. The sea's blue slow thundering swells creep
in. And rise up on the cliffs and spread a ribbon of white
foam. Met Toro. Who looked from his grazing the other
side of the fence and gave me a red baleful eye. And shook
a ring in his nose. Watched him chew and then bow his
head down to a patch of clover again. Elmer went up to
sniff. To leap back from a swift hook of Toro's horn. Sunny
and breezy out this morning. Nearly as if last night was
not yet until tomorrow.

Clementine strolling along the headland. On a narrow
path worn by the edge of the steep cliff. Grey rocks jutting
out over the heaving water far below. Look back southeast,
the castle turrets loom stacked up against the distant clouds.
Percival said would he run up the standard now that I was
in residence. I thought what the hell why not. And it
flutters red green brown and gold. The upheld crimson
hand looking particularly well against the sky. Take a little
leap I think in the air. Clang my heels together chirpish
and chipper.

Climbing up the stony hillside to the haunted black lake.
Followed at a parallel distance by Clarence. Who's got
tired crouching and is now standing up sticking out over
that rock as barefaced as he was born if that's how he got
here. This new day starts up the spirit's engines again.
Wave at Clarence. He does nothing. But stare. Send by
semaphore the word ahoy. He turns and gallops away. As
I dip my hand in this water and find it impenetrably black
and deathly cold.

Clementine wandering through what Percival said was
the lady's garden. A sun dial sticking up out of a thicket of

nettles and briar. Through a cloistered passage and beyond an iron gate an orchard, thronged by grey thistle stalks and lichen covered branches wildly sticking in the sky. A great domed glass house out from the castle wall. Inside the shadows of tropical trees, palms and ferns. All locked in combat for space and life. And above, more castle battlements, tiny window slits behind which anything could be happening. When I crossed the landing over the great hall this morning, Erconwald was scurrying across the tiles in a white coat with a stethoscope hanging round his neck. Giving me shudders. And passing out the courtyard door I saw Tim with bulging bags from a laden cart slung over each shoulder heading for the kitchen entrance. I put my hands over my eyes. To cover up the sight of the expense. Suppose they only want to see me have plenty of everything. Then Percival peeking in at breakfast time asked if all was to my satisfaction. It took a moment to answer. As I could still feel the feel of Rose's big pillowy body. And the reddened bruised grip of her teeth on my one eyed snake. She departed late dawn in a fit of coughing. Breasts shaking and nipples bouncing all over her chest. Great rumbles down in the lungs and one of her fits made me back away and trip over my pail of slop water promptly drenching my stockinged feet. While Elmer encouraged by the chaos chewed into the mattress and dug a hole with a pair of churning huge paws distributing clumps of wadding, horsehair and straw over the chamber. To make it look lived in. By a dog.

Moist breeze watering my eyes. Press a hand on the ground. Grass and tiny white sheltering little flowers. A bug goes by. Asked Percival this morning what on earth does one do with all these rooms. He said put them out of your mind, sir. Time enough to think of them if you need one. But watch where I've marked the lines. Tim and I weren't we looking for the pig who'd do grand for tomorrow's table and didn't we think we had him cornered when we find the shape of him gone downwards through the timbers just up the two doors from her ladyship's room. Ah sir we investigated below and hadn't he gone as well clean through the old flower room by the conservatory, helping himself no doubt to the baby rats there, they be a great delicacy for pigs. And Ena now will sew back them stuffings into your bed and you won't miss a wink of sleep. I thought one saw the nod of a smile from Percival. And speak of him and here he comes running.

'Ah sir I've been looking everywhere for you. There's a gentleman and his wife calling. They are from over there beyond. Neighbours as you might say. I said you were out for a stroll.'

I went back with Percival to the great hall. Where the two folks stood. A chunky, blood red haired man slapping a riding crop against his britches. And a tall willowy girl with long brown tresses, a hunting hat in hand knocking it against the side of her black gleaming boot.

'I say I'm sorry old chap to barge in like this but my wife and I were passing, couldn't help but see your flag flying.'

'O.'

'Jolly good. The old place has got some life again. See you've got your man hard at work there. That's the way to shore up those old foundations. Dig down deep. Put it back in shape. This is Gail. I'm Jeffrey.'

'How do you do. I'm Clayton Clementine.'

'By God. Of The Three Glands. Would you believe it. Gail do you know who this man is. You are aren't you, you're flying the flag.'

'What.'

'In the male line, a descendant. Of that old boyo with the three grapes on his stem. By jove this calls for celebration. Your ancestors and my ancestors used to shove spears up each other's arses. We were always out trying to cut the gems off a Clementine, what about that.'

'I know little about the family history. As a matter of fact I've just moved in.'

'Well by God we'll knock glasses together and have some sport. Gail and I just cantered over the hill. I took up the binocs just to see if I could put a bit of a lead up the hole of one of these damn poachers. And there it was. Your flag.

What about that Gail. It's written all over his face by God, the Clementines. Nothing for one of us Macfuggers to lop off the head of a Clementine seeing as that rogue of the three glands creamed us for centuries. But let bygones be bygones, what.'

'Won't you come in and have a drink.'

'Suit us fine. I used to take tea here when I was a whipper snapper. Some old bird claimed a relationship to the Clementines, bloody rich tough old bitch.'

'My grand aunt.'

'O I'm most awfully sorry. You know how people are. By God they'd claim the honour of an uncle being booted up the hole by an earl. I don't mean to belittle your aunt old boy. I say there Gail, look, that's great uncle Bubbly, the whole ruddy hunt. Must be fifty years ago. I say you don't mind my asking a personal question but where do you get all your staff. By God they leap out at you from everywhere. Some of them out of livery of course, but you're just settling in. I saw your veterinary surgeon with his stethoscope at the ready, wish more of these chaps would wear the white coat. Keep up appearances. Too many letting the standards fall down around their soiled ruddy ankles. Had an accident old boy.'

'Yes.'

'Want to watch these old drapes. When I was engaged to Gail here and getting on the good side of the family to get my hands on some of their ruddy millions.'

'Really Jeffrey.'

'It's the truth my dear girl. I didn't have a pot to piss in. And I was at the end of a long reception line, bloody family going through their stuffy formalities. I thought I'd sit down on a chair behind me, roped off it was, well I put aside the rope and sat down, damn chair went to dust beneath me old boy, and I made a grab for a tapestry just behind to save myself from a broken arse. Ruddy big carpet went the whole length of the ballroom wall on a big brass rail. The entire works came down on Gail's whole family in one antique explosion of dust, didn't the tribe of them think the other was trying to kill them, buried as they were the lot of them punching around in the dark, it made me sick with laughter.'

'Really Jeffrey.'

'Got old Gail here in the end worth a packet, aren't you. I supply the lineage she supplies the mullah.'

'What will you have to drink Mrs Macfugger.'

'As a matter of fact old boy it's Lady Macfugger.'

'O.'

'And my dear chap you're a Prince, but we won't stand on ceremony. Just call me Nails. My old army name. Got when I won a bet lying down on a bed of nails this ruddy wog was having up his backside. Got right down there in my birthday suit. Won a fiver. Gail will have a sherry, I'll have a port.'

Percival giving a little nod of the head. Nails perusing among the books. As Gail stands her hands neatly folded over yellow gloves, a smile on her smooth wind tanned features. A gold pin and pearl in the silk white scarf at her throat and a sparkle in her light blue eyes. She lifts her chin and displays a delicate adam's apple. Nails pulls down a book.

'Many's the time as a little chap I went searching in these damn tomes looking for smut. Got my nose into those geographical magazines, the tits on those blacks standing around their camp fires in flagrant ruddy nudity. Couldn't wait to get out of sight of my nannie to have a good beat off.'

'Please Jeffrey.'

'Old Clementine here's a man of the world. Isn't that right.'

'Well I think so.'

'I should ruddy well hope so. We're going to put some life back into this area. By the way, Gail why don't you ask if we can have the hunt ball here in the Charnel. Great place in the past. What about it Clementine.'

'Well I suppose so.'

'That's the boy, by jove that'll be a night to remember. Arrive in the state coach over the mountain. By God we'd get some wenches up in the towers in the old days and let them have it back sides and front. The old dungeons down there were packed solid with wickedness. Even Gail there got a little saucy, pranged her on the way home in the carriage over the back seat.'

'Jeffrey.'

'The horses pounding over the roads, two of us flung about the place, damned thrilling nuisance trying to keep it in, she hasn't been as juicy as that since.'

'I do think Jeffrey you've said quite adequate and if you don't stop I shall put my foot down.'

'Drawers down woman would be damn sight more welcome. Quite amusing I married her for her money and found out she was beautiful later. By God with prices of everything soaring a person can't keep a decent household. Down to four gardeners, eight grooms. Sacked my game keeper ruddy chap tried to shoot me. Took the whip to him, put a few scalds across his arse he won't forget. Whole countryside is crawling with rascals. But by the way just between us, couldn't help seeing three of your men out there nosing around by the old boxwood maze, looked suspicious characters to me.'

'Glad you said that Jeffrey I didn't like the look of them either.'

'They're travellers who requested hospitality.'

'That explains it, transients. Can't be too careful you know. Want to let them have what for straight off, louts and chancers. Catch them shooting my pheasant, taking my salmon. I get out there at dawn with a hamper of breakfast. Blast hell out of them. Anguishing when you think that the time's past when after some early morning sport the attics were full with a bevy of upstairs maids to prang.'

Percival with a tray of glasses and decanters of sherry and port as he soft foots it across the library floor streaked with sunshine. Hear a roar of Toro. Probably looking for a heifer. Lady Macfugger keeps glancing at one's outfit especially at the tennis shoes. And then at my red necker-chief I wear for a little colour. Elmer comes strolling in wagging his tail and nudging about with his big black nose in a rather delicate part of Lady Macfugger's figure.

'Jeffrey isn't he sweet.'

'By George he's a monster, look at the pair of balls on him Gail, sticking out there like two avocados. He knows where to sniff.'

'Why must you always notice things like that.'

'Clementine's going to think I've got a tight arsed wife.'

'If you must know I am quite proud of my arse being tight. And I'm sure Mr Clementine has better things to occupy his mind.'

'There you are, Clementine. I was on my uppers till I collared old Gail, tight arsed but with a loose half a million. But by God I'm not afraid of poverty. Take to the roads if I have to in a tinker's caravan. Good healthy itinerant life. Plenty of wenching and gambling. I spotted the old girl at a cousin's wedding. Standing beside her father, a big red nosed old bastard. I knew he was rotten with it, knew the drink would knock him off, and the whole fortune held in trust for Gail would tumble into my yawning coffers. Never missed the opportunity to nudge the old boy's elbow to help along when he was knocking back a whiskey. All a man needs is a mare to plug and a few grazing beasts and spuds. This is excellent port. You must come and see us. Don't stand on ceremony. In fact why not tonight. Bring your better half with you.'

'I haven't got one.'

'What, no mare. I saw a piece of crumpet dancing across the parapet. Didn't want to enquire after your wife in case she had some unresolved bats in the belfry. When they go off like that some chaps like to keep it quiet. Shove them into a spare dressing room with a doll's house to play with. Bachelor eh. Bet that's leading to some goings on. When you don't have someone sneaking up on your bare backside with a pail of water and crashing the stuff over you when you're busy up some fluff.'

'You deserved every drop of it Jeffrey.'

'What. You could have made me impotent, by God. Tossing a cold bucket of water on the arse like that. Put me right off. By jove I had this little piece of carefree frippery with the neatest little arse you've ever seen, like two acorns, get hold of them like a ball bearings. Giving me the eye she was while peeling the spuds. I gave her pronto what for up the whose it right there in the boot closet. Little liar said it was her first time rogered. I clapped her one across the snout with the back of me hand. Soon had the truth. Every groom in the stable been up her. I mean to say a chap having to have a go after his grooms. Simply not on. Damn layabouts can't get their minds off the subject. I went out there with the good book. I preached to them by jove. Put their filthy thoughts onto something uplifting. Carry on like that can put an estate into bankruptcy. A midget randy groom once got every girl in the household up the pole. I mean you can't sack a girl but what are you going to do with seventeen little bastards bawling all over the place. But Clementine we're keeping you from your chores. You shoot.'

'No.'

'Soon fix that. Nothing like a day's outing over the heather. You'll settle in nicely. Is your chap called Percival.'

'Yes.'

'By God he's aged. Give him a pat on the back for me. Quite a lady's man. Just between you and I in a whisper he's had more dollies in a family way than rain drops in a bucket. Come on Gail. Shake your arse. We'll see you Clementine. Show up at sundown.'

'I don't have any transport.'

'We'll send a four in hand for you by God. With extra pillows so your arse will stay in one piece over the mountain road. Good to be in the old castle again. Needs some sprucing up. Get the old bedsteads out of the hedgerows. Put it there, Clementine. See you tonight.'

Lady Macfugger followed by a strutting Nails with a clatter of boot and jangle of spurs crossing the great hall. Through which the exprisoners were passing carrying a large potted tropical palm. Lady Macfugger raising one eyebrow which lowers as Elmer shoves his big black nose deep between the cheeks of her arse, giving her person a push forwards.

'Stop it Jeffrey.'

'Wasn't me sweetie.'

'O it's him, I thought it was you.'

'There you are Clementine. What a chap does is reprimanded and a dog encouraged.'

'I'm not encouraging.'

'You loved that goose soon as you found it wasn't me. Here's another.'

'Stop.'

'You see how it is Clementine, strange dog's nose preferred to a husband's familiar finger.'

By the castle gates the scientists' motor now standing on blocks without wheels. The Macfuggers mounting two monstrous gleaming black hunters. A rifle and shot gun strapped to Nails Macfugger's saddle. And with hooves clattering and slipping on the stone cobbles, they smile, wave, and thunder off galloping down the roadway.

Percival laid out my clothes, a rather outsize dinner suit belonging to my father, a crumpled silk shirt, evening shoes and a pair of dark green socks. As the Macfuggers left I saw Rose out of the corner of my eye on the great hall landing. She stood glaring her upraised fists clenched. Returning to the castle I heard distant doors slamming. The three exprisoners, the Baron and Mr and Mrs L K L in the library. All bent over tomes. I went searching for some privacy. Found a likely vaulted doorway in the northwest wing at the end of a long passage. I pushed against the heavy oak. Locked. Then opening. And Erconwald confronting me with a bow.

'Ah it is you kind person. I have retreated within here due to the disconcerting number of encounters one has in various chambers and passages.'

'What were the exprisoners doing with that palm tree.'

'Ah we have found many interesting specimens in your conservatory. Indeed there is a selection of orchids. I have taken the liberty of having four put in my bedroom. I did not want to trouble you. And the palm tree, in fact several, have been placed among the mambas. They are now quite content. Would you like to see them, they are through here in an adjoining room.'

'O my God.'

'You mustn't alarm yourself good person.'

'The wheels are off your car.'

'Ah we regret that quantities of air have escaped through leaks in the tyres requiring us to make repairs.'

'How long will that take.'

'The tyres are at the crossroads waiting for the morning train. Franz at the moment is most excited. We may have favourable tidings for you soon.'

'I should like the digging and drilling in the hall to stop.'

'I deeply grieve to hear of your feelings in this matter. May I be bold enough to yet hope that you might reconsider and allow Franz to continue so that we may present you with good news. Indeed I hope you will not think it ill of me to make immediately a temporary amend.'

Erconwald standing his hands folded in front of him. Tears in his eyes. Ledgers open on a great oak table. Walls covered with axes, coils of fire hose and pram like vehicles supporting red water tanks. Erconwald reaching into his trouser pocket. Taking forth a wad of white bank notes. Peeling them off and holding them forth.

'What's this.'

'For the unforgivable inconvenience we have caused you. Pray take it. It is offered merely as the merest of compensations. From the very deepest recess of my heart I ask that you will not refuse this pathetic token.'

Clementine taking the money. Erconwald bowing. The afternoon light fading across the high barred windows smothered in cobwebs. And hanging from the far wall are shackles and chains. An open cupboard with black jackets and leather gaiters.

'I am pleased kind person. It has been unfortunate for me that I have been many times disappointed. In both science and love. One of my very earliest attempts at romance was unhappy. I pursued for three months a young lady whose figure I thought to be quite robust. My desire for her was extremely feverish. And one evening while attaching a flower to her bosom, in my nervousness I pushed the pin deeply into her breast. She did not complain, indeed she smiled, and my most earnest hopes were dashed. Upon, if I may say, the level surface of her chest. And kind sir it does not escape me that Rose looks upon you with favour. I would only humbly ask that if your intentions are not profound that you do not entice her away. And I speak no further. Please. Come here. To this door. With your indulgent permission which we hope to seek, we have made a peep hole. See. There they are.'

'Holy heifer.'

'The one in your palm tree you will see extends its body out more than half its length. Note the exquisite stillness it possesses. Yet in an instant that delicate small green head can bring death. The specimen lying coiled on the right is an older specimen. Unfortunately agitated at the moment and one cannot enter.'

Erconwald's impenetrable courtesy. From a little pocket casket he offers me a cheroot. His white long delicate fingers closed over the dark fibres. His emerald glowing mamba green. He waits ready to administer a kindness wherever the opening yawns. Might be found at any street corner shepherding old ladies in an ever constant stream across the roadway.

'Good person might my associates and I be permitted to examine your testicles.'

'Wait a minute.'

'But of course.'

'I mean wait a minute.'

'Ah I do understand your quite natural hesitation to grant scrutiny of your gonads. But I assure you it will be entirely painless and conducted with every dignity that such an exploration might require.'

'Who told you about my testicles.'

'Ah, it is good person, a rumour we have heard. We merely want to measure and weigh, and should it be necessary, to tabulate as well.'

'I've not even found my feet in this place and you guys are trying to count my balls.'

'Permit me kind sir.'

Erconwald putting aside his sweet scented cheroot and undoing his trousers. Frowning as a button pops off and rolls in a circle on the stone floor to disappear down a drain hole.

'What are you doing.'

'Good person I am displaying to you my own organs of regeneration so that you should not think me unmindful of another's trepidation in doing so.'

'Please stop.'

'Would it not help for you to be made easier in this matter by my presentment.'

'No.'

'I am distressed that I have failed to reassure you.'

Clementine backing towards the door. Erconwald's fly wide open. Might have an apparatus quite out of the ordinary. Coils up and strikes like one of his snakes. Seems like years ago I sat alone cold and damp in the library thumbing through the ledgers. Pages of inventories flashing by, the Porcelain Room, Pump Room, South Cloisters, Verandah and by the look of this one I'm trying to get out of, it must be a combination guard room and fire department. Adjoining what is now the snake pit.

'Please Erconwald don't get upset. I just can't see that anything can be gained by your showing me your privates. I've always been unreasonably shy about exhibiting my own. I think a little girl playmate may have laughed at them once, something like that. But good lord if you feel that way about it, show me.'

'Thank you good person.'

Erconwald undoing his belt. Dropping his trousers and lifting up shirt tails to uncover a large and somewhat engorged copulatory machine and pair of balls. His privates with an athletic quality about them absent from the delicate rest of his person. How long is one required to look. Can't see this gives me the nerve to flash mine.

Clementine turning as the door behind squeaks open. A head peering in. Of a strange female face. A lady of riper years in a thick white wool sweater over a flowered skirt of a dress. Her smooth skin and wet lips. A smile breaking on her face as she looks from Erconwald's privates to the raised eyebrows of Clementine.

'Ooo. I'm awfully sorry. Do carry on. Sorry, I mean to say I was just looking for someone. Who might help me. As I am completely stranded about two miles from here without petrol. But I beg your pardon. Clearly I'm intruding. I must have come in the wrong way. I do believe I'm lost. If someone could just tell me how I get out, I'll go. Instantly. I do apologise.'

Erconwald bowing. Most embarrassing to witness during this stranger's conversation Erconwald's private protuberance horizontally stiffening out and jumping up and down between his stripey green, blue and white shirt tails.

'Well, won't you say something someone. I know this is cruelly embarrassing but good lord I don't know my way out. Please help me. A gallon of petrol would get me to the next town. I'm on my way to visit friends. Please believe me I had no intention of barging in this way. Into what is clearly a very private moment.'

'I'm just being shown his regenerative organs merely to accustom me to showing my own.'

'I beg your pardon, I don't think I quite follow you but surely it doesn't matter. Do you know who the owner of this place is.'

'I am the owner.'

'O. I see. Well would it be possible for me to buy a gallon of petrol. I do apologise most contritely to you and your friend. I know I seem to be persisting here at the door but quite honestly I'm covered in mud and have been scratched with briars in my struggle to get in here at all. I'm really feeling quite wretched.'

'Erconwald would you mind if this lady stepped in and waited while I get Percival.'

'Most surely madam you are deeply welcome.'

'Simply awful to gate crash like this but honestly I am at my wits' end. I tried one door and fell down steps. I heard water below. It quite has frightened me.'

Erconwald attempting to get his penis back into his grey flannel trousers tugging them up and turning away from the visitor. Buttoning above and below the projecting waving organ while stepping backwards and stumbling into a fire apparatus. The lady visitor pushing back on her forehead a wave of greyed blonde hair which keeps falling. I'm going to make a run for it. Taste blood on my lower lip where I have bitten myself.

'I'll be back. Quite quickly. If you feel you're all right madam.'

'Yes, may I just sit down please.'

'Of course. You're all right Erconwald.'

'Yes good person. And ah to you madam my most profound apologies if I have in any way given offence. I don't think it has subsided sufficiently for me to return it as promptly as one might wish into the privacy of my trousers. I will of course deflect my front away from you and do hope you will not think me discourteous if I speak over my shoulder.'

'Quite frankly young man provided that it's not to be used, ha ha, on me, I don't in the least mind. Do for heaven's sake if you are more comfortable, sit down. Honestly I'm quite grown up. I have, ha ha, seen them before.'

'Ah truly madam is most kind, generous and of modern demeanour.'

'Please don't apologise, I am after all a total stranger intruding as well as I believe, trespassing.'

'Well folks, please, I'll just run off now. And be back shortly.'

Clementine heading south along the passage. Towards darkness and a door at the end. Opening out into the great hall. Saw a dangling rope of a clapper to a fire bell one could have pulled. Announcing to the castle a viewing of an erection. Ring in series·of two and continue until assistance arrives. Whole mob could have descended. Upon Erconwald's prick upended. The recent elevation measured by Franz. To fire salvos at a growling Rose dancing in strangling poses among the mambas. As the rest of the household assembles and sambas. And all maybe later to scrimmage awhile.

> For
> The circus
> Continues
> More crazy than cruel
> One of us now
> Will spin like a top
> On the end
> Of his tool

7

Clementine hastily through the door under the grand staircase. Could get lost going down these steps. The air colder. Which way. To the kitchens. Of which according to the ledger there are six. Push open this white door. Explore while one is on the way. Give Erconwald ample time to get it back into his trousers. And out of the sight of that woman who has a rather musical laughter. Which might keep Erconwald's pecker up till the cows come home. Or he gets blown.

A room the walls lined with cupboards from floor to ceiling. Barred windows peeking out on the courtyard. Shelves with earthenware pots. Cloves, cinnamon, bay leaves. A spice room. The scientists could add seasoning to the distillate. Of which Erconwald must slam back a dram for breakfast. Get it to pop up and poke the stranded lady right on the red bump on her nose. Between pretty blue eyes. Which will sparkle throughout the eight or nine years of good screwing she must have left. Tonight my first social engagement. And I'm searching for petrol. To motor a matron out of this menagerie.

Clementine pushing through another door. A large candle lit room, round stone pillars holding an arched ceiling. Cavernous fireplace with iron gears, chains and skewers. Along a wall a vast black cast iron stove. Batteries of pans hanging on racks. A girl catching her breath. As she turns suddenly with a dripping ladle in her hand.

'Lord save us.'

'I'm sorry to barge in. I'm looking for Percival.'

'Sir I do be thinking he is down the tunnel doing a bit of fishing, sir.'

'I don't believe I know who you are.'

'I'm from beyond sir, a friend of Imelda. She asked me to give her a hand and I'm after stirring up the soup for tonight's dinner. A gentleman was down before with the onions to put in the cauldron. We have this hour before been trying to prise the pig loose from the darknesses beyond in the tunnels and into the pot, Imelda and Mary are after him this minute.'

'Fine.'

'Is there anything now I can do for you sir.'

'No thanks.'

'Thank you sir.'

Clementine stopping in the spice room. One comes away from that confrontation trembling in every limb. A girl of flowing dark hair. Slender white arms from the blue rolled up sleeves of her sweater. Go back and ask her name. One more mortal on the staff. An incredible beauty found down in the cellars. Move her higher up in the castle to stardom.

'I'm sorry to trouble you again.'

'Ah it's no trouble.'

'But I don't know your name.'

'Charlene.'

'Ah. That's a nice name.'

'It is after me grandmother's. She worked here in the castle her whole life, died out beyond there in the laundry room by the stables where she lived her last fifteen years, never did she stir out of it till they took her in her coffin, she was fond of the warmth from the few heated pipes. She loved folding the linens and stacking them in the airing cupboards that you would cut your hand on the edge of them.'

'Are you permanently here.'

'I wouldn't know sir. I would be thinking that you would be the one to say sir.'

'I hope you've heard that I may not be able to get around to steady wages but I think I can manage to reimburse you now and again. Would this be enough for the moment.'

Clementine pulling the wad from Erconwald out of his pocket. Charlene wiping her hand on a thick grey skirt and taking the large white bill. Holding it out pinched by her hand, a little dirt under her worn fingernails.

'Sir there's no need to give me this. What use have I for it with pucks to eat and a place to sleep.'

'You're staying in the castle.'

'I am sir. I have my own room above.'

'Ah.'

'It suits me fine. I am crowded with me family with seven little brothers and sisters. We only have the one room and a loft above. It's a nuisance at times to get a night's sleep with the scratchings and kickings.'

Boots and thick brown stockings on Charlene's legs. She smiles when she talks with white teeth which look like her own. A little mole next to her nose. Castle full of surprises. Jammed with arrivals. Those summoned by morse code and others crawling through briars. Wake up out of haunted death throes on one side of the ocean and gallivant with big bosomed ravenous dolls on the other. Charlene's are from the bulges in her sweater of refined proportions.

'The soup smells good.'

'It's only a few old ingredients put boiling in a pot, same as we do at home. I'll be bringing you some fish tomorrow when my father comes in with the boat. Do you like fish sir.'

'Yes.'

'Would you like it fried.'

'That would be nice.'

'Well I'll do that. Miss Ovary was saying she'd like to do a bit of shopping in the town, so I'll fix the fish for you. I'll tidy up around here a bit as well. Have it clean as a stone after the rain.'

'Don't you find it gloomy down here in the dark.'

'Not at all. Sure I've never been fond of the outdoors lashed by the wind and the rain. With the stove going it's nice enough here.'

Clementine taking one last sip of this delicate creature. A tiny figure under the massive stone ceilings. Alone down in these damp endless cellars. Got to save her from that kind of life. And fix up some light duties nearer my apartments.

'I wonder Charlene if you could direct me to the tunnel where Percival is fishing.'

'Surely sir, it'll just require a candle or two. Now if you come this way. Past the spice room and the downstairs pantry.'

Charlene opening a thick oak door into a room. More shackles on the walls. Under an archway and down circling steps. A narrow tunnel at the bottom. A stone alcove with two iron gratings in the floor.

'Down there sir are the dungeons. They be an awful dangerous place. They put them poor creatures down into them on a ladder and you couldn't get out with a lifetime of trying. The sea waters get into the lower ones, full of dead bones. They would shovel the food down to them through the bars there. With them fighting over it among themselves and the rats.'

The tunnel slanting downwards. Wet stones slippery under foot. The walls glistening with beads of moisture. The sound of waters and low whine of the wind. The candles wavering, Charlene's hand up sheltering the flame. Poor Erconwald only wanted to inspect my balls and ends up with his own apparatus on display.

'Now sir, hold tight along here to the rail. There's more steps. There now you can see the bit of daylight ahead.'

A blue expanse of sea. Headlands and coast rising to the north. Westwards an ocean. Downwards the jutting cliff-side, stairs cut from rock, moorings twisted and rusting. No sign of Percival.

'I wouldn't want sir to be causing needless worry but it's a long fall to the sea and it wouldn't be the first time a soul had been dragged into the deep by the monster that lurks down there in the water.'

The wind blowing Charlene's wavy tresses back from her soft white skinned face. A pair of eyes bright blue. She bites lips red and moist. Her hands and wrists pink with chill. She stands on a step gripping an old twisted railing in the rock and leans out to look down.

'There's not a sign of him, you couldn't be at the bottom there in the thrashing of them waves and ever get back up here alive. God forbid that he went into that deep to be torn to pieces by the conger.'

'He could have fallen.'

'Yanked would be the case.'

'We'd better go for help.'

'I wouldn't say Percival would require help sir, all he needs now is a bit of blessing as you would give to any soul of the faithful departed. He was a holy terror in his early days with the ladies but these last few days he's made amends enough. Often I've seen him on the bicycle helter skelter to do his spiritual duty. As the years edge them closer to the hammer and tongs of God they soon enough get down on their knees and make friends with the on high, offering him cigarettes, mea culpas, hiccups, coughs and greasy pennies.'

'I see.'

'Sure if he was injured we'd see him impaled below. And if he's been made a meal of by the conger you can forget attending to the remains.'

Charlene leads Clementine back in the tunnel. Past the dungeons, up the spiral stairs, through the pantry and kitchens and by a back passage and servants' hallway to a narrow door opening into the antechamber of the Octagonal Room. Put hands up over eyes and lie next to the evening clothes neatly arranged by Percival. Dead out there on the water. Charlene said she would search through the castle. With Miss Ovary and Oscar and Imelda. One waits. Momentarily out of the castle traffic. And where is Elmer. Someone pounding on the door.

'Come in.'

'Excuse me sir but so far there isn't a sign of Percival. But we've come upon goings on that would make the devil himself blush with shame. Sure God there is the old fire department in flames you might say with impurity. A gentleman in no fit state to be seen. Inviting us in he did. The manners on him would make you think he was asking us to a ball. Miss Ovary has run out sir beyond screaming she'd have nothing to do with the likes of the goings on. Said she did that snakes had landed upon us. I'd say she suffered hallucinations brought on by your man not taking a proper attention to his dress. Can I get you anything now.'

'No thank you.'

'Sir do you mind if I say something.'

'Please do.'

'Well if Miss Ovary does not come back as she was saying, is it in order if I take over in the kitchens. She'll have nothing to do with men and we are besieged down there by gentlemen jumping out at us from behind the pillars and waiting in the scullery. Would it be proper for me to tell them to hop it.'

'Yes of course.'

'Now sir I believe in speaking me mind. The bunch here are eating you out of house and home and not one of them lifting a finger to so much as pour their own tea. Sure one of them a beast of a woman was down there in the kitchen the middle of the night frying up rashers and eggs enough for an army, ordering me out of the way when I was trying to get the morning fires going. Are you all right sir. Is your head bothering you.'

'Just a little pain behind my eyes.'

'We'll attend to that. Here now, let me put this wet cloth to you.'

Charlene putting a compress on Clementine's forehead. Smell the moist thick wool of her skirt. Hear a clatter of wheels out over the countryside. One lies still with the lids down to receive this tender attention. Far off tomorrows. Please come. Without servants drowning. Our guests whipping out their tools. Haven't the fortitude to go back down there and tell this lady there's no sign of Percival never mind petrol. One's head about to explode. Must stop myself sliding into decline. Already stretched out on a bed. Always a bad moment. When the first compresses get put to the brow. Just what I did in auntie's house, the pale light out those three windows overlooking the street. The squeal of the post box on the telephone pole at night when someone mailed a letter. Sending hello through midnight hands, stamped and sealed, tucked in cubby holes, sliding down chutes, speeding over land. Please do not bend. A loving thought is inside.

'Charlene does Percival have next of kin.'

'Not a soul sir as far as I know is belonging to him.'

'If we find his body there will have to be a funeral.'

'No problem. Sean the blacksmith in the town will knock up a box. Sure you have your own cemetery out there ready for him. Wash him down with a few bottles of whiskey. There's an awful chill here now. I'll light up these few pieces of turf and put some warmth into things. Sir, it's the bell in the courtyard someone must be at the front door, shall I see to it.'

'Please.'

To stare up at the ceiling where a black beetle crawls. Could feel Charlene's breath on my face, sweet and warm. Read in an etiquette book that cohabitation with servants breeds insolence leading to the eating of the master's smoked salmon and the liberal downing of his potables. And even to shot gun blasts. Dare the squire wet his wick where masters should fear to dip. Wanted to reach up and drag Charlene down. I am enamoured of your eyes. Globes of one sort leading to globes of another. Arse white as the cheeks of her face. Like two lamps lit outside auntie's house. The bugs bombarded all night. When terror went crouching through the streets. Citizens shot dead on lawns for wallets. And when I could walk faster after I was cured I packed the gladstone bags. Booked on a steamship line and took the train to the coast. Nearly ran on the thick echoing boards down the pier shed. Auntie for six months of every year for five years lived on a ship. Said she liked the routine. Man in a little green kiosk stamped my passport. Seagulls wheeling and screeching overhead. Sailors lifting hawsers off capstans. Ship gave a whistle blast. Auntie said it's the kind of world which will suit you over there. Give you something to fight for. Keep up your standards. They were serving tea in the garden verandah on D deck, all second class passengers welcome. An ancient ship with narrow bows. I sat alone at a table. Saw a girl with blond curly hair and powdery blue eyes who smiled. I thought my

God this is going to be swell. And never saw her again. She lay deathly sea sick down in the bowels of the ship the whole voyage. Three hours out we were hit by a hurricane. The seas rose up black watery moutains in the darkness. The stern where I clutched looking out through the lashing spray went up and down like an elevator. Giant propellers rising from the water, shaking and trembling the vessel. I stood bundled in my racoon skin coat. Death finished stalking me on land. Now dancing with it up and down the ocean waves. Two potted palms stood either side of the restaurant entrance. A sandy haired gentleman sat across from me at my table, seating fourteen. Passengers one by one making runs for the nearest bucket. One little boy heaving right out on the table. Twelve bewildered ashen green faces hurrying away. Leaving this man and myself. He had an appetite. Polished off twelve plates of smoked salmon. Giving me a shy smile and bow of the head as he swept another helping on his plate. I wrote him a short note explaining that I had temporarily lost my voice. He again nodded and smiled. Asked if I played chess. He was an impetuous player, overflowing with confidence. Slowly with a positioning of knights and bishops I annihilated him. Prior to some final moments in these blood baths he would leap to his feet and pace the decks outside to revive his strategy with fresh sea air. His aggressiveness in early moves always decided me to not let him win. The few passengers who could still walk on the tilting ship crowded round. Amateur chess masters gave him advice from an elbow. Still the slaughter continued. Still he rose and raced to the fresh air outside, slapping his cheeks and shaking his head. To return and with grimaces preceded by indulgent smiles he'd move his queen into the attack. Caboom. My knight merrily shoved a spear right up the personal interior of his bishop. And his fists would clench and whiten. At one moment I thought he was going to reach across and take my silent neck into his hands and prevent me from ever taking up residence in auntie's castle. Instead he leaped to his feet and gavotted in silent hysterics across the room. Later in the second class lounge up by the ship's smokestacks he became a sympathetic companion happily quaffing pints of bitter beer. He said he had tried his luck in the new world and been bested. Wore his shoes out looking for work. Stuffed newspapers to stop the soles of his feet from burning on the hot pavements. He said everyone aboard the ship had been bested by the new world. And were now being thrown deathly ill to the decks vomiting. Half the crew were out of action. And the captain put into port. While we waited below a town once levelled by an explosion. A fort up on a hill overlooking the harbour. I went ashore with this gentleman. In an old wooden church we attended sunday services. He borrowed a coin from me to put in the passing collection tray. Some strange sadness took me and I felt tears running down my face. World so lonely. Voices in song. Raised in thanksgiving. Off key I croaked out a note or two. In transit between lands. Tiptoeing between the gouging, testicle kicking greed. Had I but just a house and lawn. Sit in during the snowy winters. Lie out in a hammock by summers. But when I came out of the navy the dirty bastards said they had an opening in the stock exchange. Running messages. And something in my father came out in me. I stood up from my seat at the interview and said come on you god damn pen pusher put up your dukes. Mr Clementine he said, are you out of your senses. He wore glasses, his hair cut short and sticking up all over his head. He was no shoulders and all hips. I felt sure violence would upset him. He said it is quite clear from our interview that you are unsuitable for the position. That summer I spent at the beach. Sifting the sand through my toes. Clocking in at an hotel along the shore. To drink tinkling glasses amid dreams of how the world should always be. Told in words brave. Agreed with nods solemn. And fairness for patrons of this bar above all. Not a bad guy here. The piano player is really president of a big corporation. What can you do but just play along. With the graft. Down down the steps to the lonely boarding house room. But hope to die first at a cotillion in the last second of a treasured moment caught at the end of an elegant woman's voice, isn't he, that man, the masterful one, isn't he the cat's whiskers. Madam not only that but I have three balls to chime. Should you like. To hear bells. Or just feel. Balls.

'Sir it's a four in hand to take you to Mr and Lady Macfuggers'.'

'Thank you, Charlene.'

The lady out of petrol standing in the great hall at the edge of Franz's excavation in the corner. Turns with a girlish twirl at the sound of my footsteps. Charlene kept her eyes averted and retreated to the antchamber as I dressed. Pumped galloping flames into the fire with a long handled bellows. Steamed my socks with the heat. Cooled again when put over my ice cold feet. A little elegance upon the person buoys the spirit. Needed to face the lady out of petrol. Last confronted across the pale pole of Erconwald.

'I'm awfully sorry but my man Percival is missing. We fear the worst.'

'O that's quite all right. As a matter of fact it is rather a strange coincidence. I understand you are on your way to the Macfuggers. Actually it's precisely where I was going. And if you wouldn't mind, perhaps I could come along and pick up my car later. My name's Veronica as a matter of fact.'

Two coachmen in shiny black top hats and green coats. Gleaming windows of the carriage. Clementine climbing aboard after this woman who had a rather musky smell. The darkening day and Rose standing glaring from a parapet. Poor Elmer downcast as I closed the door against his big black nose. Pall of doom. Percival gone.

'As a matter of fact I'm an old friend of the Macfuggers. But apropos of nothing at all do you mind if I ask, who are you.'

'Me red skin.'

'What.'

'Me from tribe.'

'I don't think I follow you.'

'Me brave.'

'Are you having me on. Good lord this contraption is rather uncomfortable. Driver, you out there, do please be more careful.'

'Yes madam.'

'They are the limit you know, these natives. Impossible to impart manners to. Several louts standing about in a village refused to push my car to get it started. Of course I do enjoy it when I see them pounding each other's faces in the pubs. At least they keep each other down. Sexually of course they are extremely interesting. I quite like the ring of sun around farm labourers' necks. It does more for me than I can say. But you appear to be inclined towards having your little games with male companions. As a matter of fact our brief encounter today is the very type of thing I most fancy, I hope I don't embarrass you, but that's an awfully cute penis on your friend. I wanted to photograph it for my album. He was so pleased. Said he has a laboratory back in town with details concerning a gentleman's organ quite outsize. One always hears of these men but never meets them. Why don't they come knocking on my door. I'm divorced from my first husband. He was in the Colonial Service. We often went on elephants up into the hills. What whoppers they've got. But they're a far more comfortable journey than this.'

Mountains rising up purple in the evening sky. Clouds pressing darkly from the sea. Horses' hooves clattering on the stony rutted road. Brown bog lands. Heather and gorse. Tiny spots of yellow flowers. Spring lies somewhere. Hiding butterflies who will skip over the countryside. Rain streaks the carriage glass. Breezes blow up through the floor. My chess playing friend aboard the ship had a gallon of wine in his cabin. He often asked who I was. Said he suspected me of being a deposed monarch and that I would not speak again until I got back on my throne. I grew to like him and chalked in his name as victor of the ping pong competition. He won by default as no one could stand up to play. Tug boats guided us through the channel when we set sail out of the port to ride the great swells of the sea. Still lashed by the tail of the hurricane. And down went the passengers into their bunks again.

'I hope you'll pardon my saying so, but you are a very presentable young man. I like young men. I'd be less than frank not admitting to nearly getting hysterical with desire back there in your fire department or whatever you call it. I think my body might amaze you. Sorry if I'm being tactless. I'm simply mad about pricks. You rich young men are all alike. I hope you're not sitting there being smug. While I just go on talking. You've hardly said a word. I think you're awfully pretentious. Me red skin, me from tribe, me brave. How dare you. I'm not attacking you. But I suppose you spend your time with all those lovely young innocent things who've never had a cock in their mouths in their lives. Precious little buttercups shepherded by their mothers. How dare you own that marvellous castle. How dare you.'

'Madam I've just got out of hospital. My great aunt gave me the castle to recuperate in. I'm trying to make a new life for myself.'

'I'm sorry, I had no idea you were an invalid.'

'I'm not.'

'I love cats you know. I detest your dog. That great ugly monster.'

'I don't mind what you say about me but please don't insult my dog.'

'The very wrong people are getting the upper hand these days. I think it's an affront that you have that castle. When my class are suffering such indignity. Do you know that my ancestors have been officers in the Colonial Service for more than three generations.'

'I'm sorry I didn't know.'

'It's not that I need it known, I'll have you know.'

Rocking swaying and bouncing, horses churning hooves as the carriage mounts these hills. Galloping around turns, crashing over ruts. By barren bog lands. Sheep running from the path of the rumbling vehicle. Veronica with her legs crossed. A strong pair of hands folded in her lap. A sweet perfume she wears. Offers me the rug to put over my knees. Gold embroidered coat of arms, a boar with a sabre in its mouth. Veronica tucking herself in. The cold gripping tight around one's bones. Past a broken roofless stone ruin of a cottage. Mounds marking old boundaries on hillsides. Bracken withered. I went to the library and studied books about this land. Flora fauna and climate. The grass full of frogs. Holds the world's record for loneliness and rainfall. Out there the spirit would dissolve on the wind swept granite. Streams cutting down the hillsides spilling brown water. Fading light. Sea out of sight. Something interfering in the area of my lap. The hand of Veronica. Wonder if my eyeballs are oscillating. Cleverly she has penetrated the fly buttons. The backwards on underwear will bedevil her. Goodness she's got through it. With the dexterity of a seamstress. Her haughty profile as she looks out her window. Just about old enough to be my mother. Whom she resembles. Somehow folk on this side of the ocean seem not to stand on ceremony. By God her hand is cold.

'Do you mind awfully. Helps ha ha keep my hand warm. And I'd quite like to get to know you better. You dear boy. You've such brazen nerve to fly a flag on top of your castle. How dare you. I think you're devilishly sweet if you really want to know.'

Heading downwards, horses sliding as they dig in. Sparks from the brakes. Veronica is pulling away on it possessed. Auntie said life over there will give you backbone. When I asked for an increase in my allowance she decreased it. Said strength comes from struggle. Formulate a code to live by. Stand on your principles. They make money. Find a young woman who's not afraid to get the gloves on her hands dirty with a little gardening. And never marry a woman dear boy who's not fond of flowers. Even better if you can find one who likes to grow vegetables. You bring the girl to me and then we'll see about an increased allowance.

Dark shadows of trees sheltering up narrow glens. A high wall. Smell of steaming horses. The carriage turning between two high stone piers topped with bronze falcons' wings outstretched shining in the moonlight. A candle flickering in the window of the gate lodge. The road descending and bending through a tunnel of rhododendrons. Great boughs twining up into a thatch of leaves. Scent of mouldering wood. Hooves and wheels becoming loud. And fainter across a level road between sloping parkland pastures of grazing beasts. Over a bridge and up again to turn before a sprawling granite mansion.

Lights electric go on. Faintly and slowly growing brighter. Wide stone steps. Four tall pillars. Nails Macfugger evening clothed grinning legs astride. And coming down the steps. Hand held out. Coachman opening door.

'Veronica dear girl. Began to wonder what happened to you. Ah. By God. There you are Clementine. Damn good of you to come. You two not up to any tricks together. Veronica old girl can take it like a trooper in any damn orifice you care to elect or if you fancy, all of them at once and still hum the west's awake. We'll have a disgustingly filthy night of it. Come on in. I say Gail, they've arrived together. And give the men some beer.'

Into a long hall flanked by two roaring fires. Stand full of bull whips on the black and white tiles. Lady Macfugger embracing Veronica. A kiss lingering between their lips.

'Stop that this instant in my house you god damn lesbians.'

'Jeffrey shut up we were only kissing.'

'I damn well know what you were doing. Won't have any flagrancy in my front hall. This is no bawdy house. Now I'll tell you Clementine, you know how Ballsbridge came to be a name. Giant built a bridge who did not want to get his testicles wet crossing the canal. Maybe that's not damn funny but by God it made me laugh. Now is everybody ready for sherry. Knock the chill for six.'

'Veronica would like to change, Jeffrey.'

'Take it off, that's a change.'

'Please Jeffrey.'

'You know Clementine I got back here today. I say to the Mrs let's rip off a piece, I had her by a haunch and she was up there clinging to the banister and she says why don't you take your dirty wants to whores once in a while. Come on we'll go in here while they powder their arses.'

Large white kid skin sofas. Stuffed with swan's down. A room of glass cabinets filled with china. White thick rugs on gleaming mahogany floors. Heaped turf fire glowing and a scented sweet air of smoke. Faces round the walls, some chubby cheeked and fair like Macfugger. Others of thin faced women.

'Ah you see the ancestors do you. Interesting lot. All the damn Macfugger men fat faced fortune hunters. And there they are, the victims. One narrow arsed bitch after another. By God if I don't think I'm carrying on the tradition. Had a cable just as we got back today. Ruddy aunt of Gail's dropped us sixty thousand right out of the sky just as God was lifting her into heaven. Smack into my lap dear boy. Doesn't half give one hope for the future. Man must have a pot to piss in, be it ever so humble as imitation jade. Now tell me did Veronica grab it on you.'

'I beg your pardon.'

'Nonsense, she must have tried to get hold of it.'

'She ran out of petrol for her car. I went searching for Percival to get some. He couldn't be found. He was fishing and might have been drowned.'

'What a dashed nuisance. Lose a good servant like that. You know, let me tell you something boy, that woman has the finest physique I've ever seen. Summers she goes swimming down there in the lough. Never seen anything like it. The whole stable was down there lurking in the shrubbery watching just like myself. Had me they did, couldn't tell them to bugger off or we'd give the whole show away. And she's a ruddy glutton for it. Had a black man back in her flat and the poor chap crawled away in tears after four days.'

'Good lord.'

'Damn right good lord. Wouldn't be surprised if there weren't a queue of chaps waiting outside her door. Now come, this way. Into my little pub. Had it built in the middle of this ten foot thick wall. Come in here when I'm down in spirits, enjoy to get behind the bar and make myself a drink. You know chaps like us ought to stick together. By jove. Louts trying to take over the country. Army of insurrection. By God I'm ready for them.'

Nails with radiant shirt cuffs joined by pea size rubies,

putting two tumblers on the gleaming mahogany bar. With a key on a long gold chain across his cummerbund he unlocks a cut glass cabinet full of bottles.

'Now what will it be. Whiskey.'

'Fine.'

'Dear boy here's to the Macfuggers and Clementines. There are no little Macfuggers yet but by God I'll have Gail up the pole before the winter's out.'

Lady Macfugger entering the salon in black. Her shoulders graceful and spare. Veronica in white, her hair up. A pair of strong shapely arms. Blue little veins over the biceps. A glittering diamond brooch at the division of her breasts. Nails forced out from behind the bar of his pub. A butler appearing called Bonaparte. A thin man in an outsize suit. Nails declaring he had caught the bugger tippling and now having put all the drink under lock and key the man had lost an incredible amount of weight. In this cushiony sweet opulence. Sparkling chandeliers, glowing Meissen and Dresden. Lady Macfugger's lingering smile across her splendid teeth. Each line of her face a smooth fleshed contour. Nourished by titbits from banquets. Makes her elegantly radiant. From my spirit damp cobwebs lift. Shutters closed over great windows. Hidden in here cosy and warm from a wintry stormy night. Among saved up treasures gathered over the years. To make and keep everything nice for the eye, nose and ear. And maybe even other parts as well.

'By God Clementine stay over night.'

'Thank you but I think I'd better get back.'

'Get back, by God, you haven't learned the rules of country living. The grass goes on growing whether you're there or not. Ruddy beasts go on grazing, the bull is nosing around plunging it into every heifer in heat. I mean to say we'll get out there after dinner in the black knickerbockers and play havoc with the poachers. Gail's got a room all ready.'

'Yes please, why don't you stay Mr Clementine, do, it's so seldom we have anyone we can socialize with.'

'Ha Clementine, listen to that. She means I've insulted all her friends. Not a ruddy one of them save good old

Veronica here will set foot in this house and I'm damn glad of it.'

'Jeffrey there is no need to elaborate.'

'Who's elaborating. Bunch of prigs.'

'Prigs. You call people priggish objecting when their host opens his trousers and confronts a mixed party by peeing upon the carpet in front of them.'

'I say there Gail, that's an aspersion. Cast if I may say so without warrant upon my person. Bonaparte was holding my pewter piss pot, peed in by Macfuggers over the centuries. Not my fault it had a hole in it. By God no gentleman worth his salt leaves his guests to take a pee.'

'You had a distinct erection.'

'It was not distinct. It was quite partial. And even pale if I may say so. Clementine knows you can't pee through a full erection.'

'Well let's stop this sordid talk.'

'Clementine don't take on the marriage vows. I had to myself because I needed the mullah. Otherwise be sitting in here without a roof on the place with an open camp fire against the wall. But by God that will suit me fine if the day comes. What the hell, healthy air and if you can get a good feed into you once a day. Now there's my girl Veronica, keeps a ruddy photograph album. Gail here didn't want my appendage included. Of course her former husband you know used to invite his old public school friends home to bed, isn't that right Veronica.'

'Yes, quite correct. But you know Jeffrey I feel you're still in your celluloid penis stage. You're a bit of a bottom pincher, you know.'

'Easy girl, by God, no Macfugger has ever shrunk from his stud duty.'

'You and your grooms skulking in the bushes while I'm swimming in the lough.'

'By God Veronica, that's quite below the belt you know. I mean say what you like about me but don't cast unparliamentary deeds upon my grooms. I think it's immediately time we attached dinner hooks to wrists and scratched a plate or two. Are you on Clementine. Come ladies. I think I'm dashed hurt. Of course I was in the bushes. You've got a pair of boobs my dear girl should be immortalized in the wax museum. Never seen a set like them Clementine. I was stunned. Fell backwards into the mud. Take my hat off to you Veronica when it comes to the body beautiful.'

'Thank you Jeffrey, you are a deliberate little charmer you know.'

'Ah God exactly what my regimental sergeant major would say to me. Only he would add sir.'

Bonaparte bowing his head as Lady Macfugger passed on the arm of Clementine. Under a carved walnut arch festooned with lances crossed above another boar grasping a sabre in its mouth while sporting a rather prominent penis and balls. A candle lit banquet hall. Voices echoing. Upwards between the smoky rafters. Hung with army pennants. Vast sideboard of gilt sauce boats, tureens and candelabra. The sweet green smell of ham and cabbage. Two black haired black uniformed girls standing the far end of the room, white lace caps on heads and eyes downcast on their white lace aprons.

Winds howling outside. Bonaparte pouring three champagnes sidling up to an elbow and growling a grunt to make known his presence. The pink mellow grains of ham laid across the gleaming white plates decorated with blue leaves and melons. Dark green buttery leaves of cabbage. Where do all the terrors run and hide. When washed away by wine and strange vast rooms glowing with the fighting spirit of Macfugger. Who lifts great slabs of meat on his plate. And raises his glass with a roar.

'Clementine. To us. Two last princes of the west. I thought you lot were all finished down over there at the Charnel. But by God we join forces tonight. Our flags will fly together into battle. Are you with me.'

'Well yes I think so.'

'Think so. That's no answer for a Clementine with the three grapes dangling from his vine. These ruddy upstarts have got to be put in their place. Back down where they belong. Nobody is going to dislodge this Macfugger without a fight I can bloody well tell you. One of my grooms will make a good sergeant major. Three of the gardeners can man a mortar, in this kind of terrain it's a ruddy must.'

Nails Macfugger pounded his fist on the ancient oak table. Her ladyship pursing her lips and peering down her nose to take a corner of her napkin to wipe near her wine glass and raise an eyebrow.

'Jeffrey I do think you're troubling Mr Clementine who after all has only just moved in.'

'My dear girl I have right here in my pocket a threatening letter. By God there may be a lot of damn archbishops among my ancestors but we've had our share of admirals and generals, who took not shit from wog nor native. Just listen to this Clementine, the absolute swinish, impertinence. Addressed to me from general headquarters, western army, dear sir I am in receipt of orders from G H Q of the army of insurrection dedicated to driving out the invader, to occupy and hold according to such orders as issued by said G H Q, lands known as ragwort meadows adjoining the river brownwater including the bridge over same and therefore inform you by this present instrument that such lands extending to five hundred and forty six acres, four roods and three perches or thereabouts are as of this letter in the possession and occupation of troops under my command. No person or beast belonging to you will be harmed provided no interference is given while the said armies are on manoeuvres in pursuit of their lawful commands. We require access to hygienic facilities of the manor house and for that purpose a right of way is now declared existing from ragwort meadows along the road marked x y on the ordnance survey map. Upon the overthrow of the present illegal regime you will be made a member of the Legion of the Shamrock, and will be decorated with the third degree of the green rosette. Yours faithfully up the republic, Sean Macdurex, Commandant, fourth tank division western army, of the army of insurrection. By God, that's simply not on. Five hundred acres of some of my best grazing. The first foot put on my land will be writing long distance letters to its ankle. And by God hygienic facilities. Pee and shit in the nobly flower decorated pottery of Macfugger House. Never.'

'Jeffrey surely they're joking.'

'Joking, they'll wish they were when I'm finished with them.'

'It's all so tiresome. But they do say Jeffrey you'll be made a member of the Legion of the Shamrock.'

'I should ruddy well hope so.'

Bonaparte whipping up crêpes suzette on a sideboard in a flurry of flame and clanging plates and spoons. Aroma of brandy and sweet sauce in the night air. Gnarled branches of trees across this countryside swept leaning eastwards by a western wind. Veronica snaps her head and takes a sniff of air. All the land empty, save of beasts and glowering rain. And maybe the insurrecting armies. Ready to mount an attack.

'By God Clementine after port we'll have a go. Pick a few pubic hairs off them with a suitable calibre. Now you ladies out you get, while Clementine and I have a man to man followed by uninterrupted peeing into the pewter.'

Silver chalices filled with purple port poured by Bonaparte who shuffles loudly in his big shoes up to one's elbow. A wine sweet and soft. Ladies gone. Face Macfugger at the head of the table. A smile on his lips. Clipping off an end of cigar. Lighting it from a candle. Blowing out a volume of smoke and quaffing cheekfuls of port.

'Now Clementine here's a little sample answer I've got worked out for this Macdurex. Tell me what you think. Dear Commandant, if you don't get your flying columns, motorised infantry, donkey drawn howitzers, sten guns, heavy as well as medium tanks, the fuck out of my meadows I'll send a shower of withering crossfired shit upon the lot of ye as well as set my hounds to chew off your balls and other extenuating appurtenances. As for your declaration of a right of way to hygienic facilities, anyone of your troops putting a foot in the direction of my water closets will have same decorated with forty five calibre indentations in the shape of a shamrock. How's that. Signed Macfugger.'

'Might that incite to a breach of the peace.'

'Breach of the peace, man. By God, of course. Only way to deal with them. Strap on my two forty fives and I tell you if there are any rich shop keepers among them I'll have his gold fillings splashing around inside his head. I've got this map. Now the plan is I want you to take and occupy this ridge. I'll be at this point here, ideal for entrenchment and we'll pick the buggers off, best time is when they're crouched for a crap. Not a shred of shelter in that area. Pair of balls dangling between the cheeks of the arse makes a marvellous target.'

Macfugger puffing on his cigar, his brows furrowed, a stubby finger pressing the parchment map. A low chuckle as he lefthandedly removes a large black automatic from inside his dinner jacket and clanks it on the oak table.

'Buggers might be climbing the drains out there. Handy to have what for at an elbow to whistle a few blobs of lead about their hair follicles. You let me know as soon as you have your chaps in decent order. If they can follow a few commands, shoulder arms and that sort of thing. Make some use of that armour you've got at the Charnel. Shame about Percival, I think he served. Make you a good sergeant. Be sparing about handing out rank. In that lot of ruddy insurgents every other trooper is commandant. In fact I wouldn't appoint rank above lieutenant. My old ruddy rank was captain, but I was acting major. Of course as of tonight we're both raging field marshals. For starters we'll use my special tactic, barrage various. Casualties will be heavy.'

With a contented growl Macfugger pistol in one hand penis in the other peeing into his pewter pot held by Bonaparte. And leading the way to join the ladies. Gently sitting over tiny glasses of crème de menthe. Take a trip to a new land to rebuild the dignity and fortitude and wake up in the middle of a war. As Macfugger takes us now through a dimly lit passage down stone steps and along a corridor. Outside a door, the key refusing to turn in the lock. Nails aiming the big black automatic. A loud report and the door slumping open. A cackle from Macfugger as he switches on a light flooding over a large billiard table.

'Nice shooting if I do say so myself.'

'Jeffrey what is Mr Clementine to think.'

'Think. By God he'd better think about fighting for his life. This is war. There he is on that wall, the one Macfugger who made field marshal before the drink rotted his brains out. Clementine get yourself a cue. Billiards is excellent practice for the ricochet. Come on you pair of saucy bitches. Just lean over there Veronica and I'll pot one down your cleavage.'

Bonaparte entering with the chalices of port and liqueurs. He bends in his big baggy black suit to light fires in cavernous grates either end of the damp room. Goes from window to window closing and bolting iron bars across the shutters. Winds rustle ivy leaves out in the night. Portraits of military men in red, black and blue tunics around the walls. Bonaparte brushing flecks from the green felt. The fires blaze. Down in a warm belly the foods lie sweetly. A carnival marching through the brain. Led by Macfugger strutting cue stick in hand. Wielding it mightily in this fight commencing soon for liberty. Bonaparte refilling one's chalice. As quickly as one takes pleasure in emptying it. Go swinging now through war torn heathers over granite outcroppings hanging by my strengthened thread of life. Far away from that world where they did incredibly mean things to me. Not knowing I was a prince from way back. Faces turned aside when they thought I was going down. One or two even trying to push. As I was beckoned by the pale hand. Come hither. Out of the office where I worked a short while. And stood staring out my corner window. Steam throbbing in the radiator. They said my salary with the years would rise. To where when elderly and nervous and loaded down with all the years of faithful service one gets nudged off into the abyss. Wrote a letter. Dear auntie, you will be glad to hear I am now moving up in the corporation. Our product is doing extremely well. I don't have the latest figures but it really is taking off. My boss Mr Addenda has been extremely kind and understanding and it is for his sake in trying to keep up my appearance that I have perhaps charged too much to my clothing account for the month of September. There was one football game where I simply couldn't be seen wearing anything remotely resembling what I wore last year. And while styles have been getting rather tight about the waist and hips, I know you will approve my resisting this trend. I was tempted to add but did not, about the extra looseness I required in the area of the crotch.

'Your shot Clementine. By God it's storming up out there. Must stay the night. Can't let you out over the mountain road in that.'

Macfugger said it was too wild to ferret out poachers. And our little group sat finally to an assortment of nougatine, marzipan and bitter chocolate coated peppermints. Macfugger golfing down the sweetmeats and macaroons, Lady Macfugger the winner at billiards, performed on the harpsichord. She said I had a marvellously straight nose in profile. And I went reeling off following Bonaparte to my room on an undertow of apricot brandy.

Mine was a lacy four poster bed. Whiskey and mineral water on the bedside table. A great marble wash basin on gleaming brass standards tucked underneath fatly with towels. Soaps of fern and sandalwood. Dry smooth sheets. Feather pillows pushing up cosily about one's head. I could become a permanent inhabitant of Macfugger House. Like Erconwald at the Charnel. Unshifted entrenched and emitting no offence.

Clementine folding a book closed. Called A World History Of The Pox. Lie nude between the sheets. Linens touching first cool now warm. Pink and blue prints on the walls. Custom House and sail ships thronged along a river quay. Grey elevations of town houses, one of a jail. Reach for the little button on a wire to press off the light. The door slowly opening. Curtains billow out letting in a darkness on the wind. And Veronica a ghost under a gay striped parasol. Breasts bouncing nakedly. Gliding on high laced black shoed roller skates. Rumbling over the floor.

Here in
This hinterland
Lonely sad and black
There's a midnight skater
Figure eighting
And that's
A fact

8

Four days spent bouncing in Macfugger's strange armoured estate car. Lying in soggy heathers blasting at pheasant. Nails standing with his binocs briefing me as to strategic positions to be manned in case of attack from the army of insurrection. The sun shone this noon with a blue sky rising from the west.

Lady Macfugger retiring mid morning with a demi-tasse and long cheroot which she smoked in the porcelain room. Remarking once more as I happened in there, upon my remarkable profile. She sat in a long satin gown and said she did an hour's private thinking here each day. Tabulating the thieving of foodstuffs and drink by servants. Her chin high she spoke with a fluttering of eye lids. Picking up her pearls when asking a question and dropping them back and forth on her chest listening to an answer.

My arse and legs ached as Macfugger brought me galloping up into the hills. From where the sea lay distantly blue black. At a canter he blasted innocent rabbits. With each hit reining up his horse, forelegs churning in the sky as he laughed and shook his rifle over his head. The soft moist breezes blowing. Down through wizened oak forests stretching along a valley. Visions of Veronica. Standing muscles rippling across her slim waisted belly. Hands on her hips. Loose hair streaked grey over her shoulders. Long muscles on her thighs. My dear boy she said I am impoverished. You've got that commodious castle. Won't you let me be your housekeeper, I'm cramped in my flat back in town. You're so young and innocent it makes me cry. I so want to corrupt you. She executed a backwards semi circle on her skates. I lay there terrified by the world history of the pox.

And asked as she unlaced her wheeled footwear and put her parasol propped on the dresser, if she had by any chance a communicable disease. She lit up like a floodlight. The easy measured tones. Would you mind repeating that question just in case I heard you wrongly the first time. I tried to point to the volume. Said it's in there. All about it.

'Whatever do you mean.'

'I mean I've just been reading about it.'

'About what.'

'The pox.'

'How dare you. Are you lying there accusing me of having a venereal disease. Are you.'

'I'm only recently out of the hospital.'

'You've already said that but are you now telling me you have a disease.'

'No. I wondered if you had it.'

'How absolutely dare you. I could slap your face. In fact I will slap your face.'

It stung and I saw stars. Hard as one could I slapped back. Her next blow nearly sent me out of the bed. I raised the bed covers up in front of my face.

'Hit a woman would you.'

'You hit me. Twice.'

'I should think so suggesting I might have VD. What kind of person do you think I am.'

'It said in the book anyone could have it.'

'And you blithely would go to bed with anyone.'

'I was just going to sleep when you sailed in on your roller skates.'

'Well forgive me. I'll sail out just as quickly if you don't mind. I happen to be long and close friends of the Macfuggers. Lady Gail Macfugger also happens to be the daughter of a marquess. And I have two close relatives Commanders of the Bath.'

The storm lashing outside. Veronica sitting back on her hands. The way one does at the beach. I commented upon the colourful parasol. And she blew a noisy breath down her nose, swept back the covers, reached to pick up her roller skates, trod on one and spun in the air landing with a shuddering crash on the floor at the foot of the bed. Silence and now low agonizing groans.

'Are you all right.'

'O God.'

Out of bed. Picking one's way in the half light. She lay on her side holding a hand to her back. Standing over this stricken human being. A large corn on her little toe which seemed crushed together with the others on her foot.

'My ankle is twisted. O God how I hate pain.'

'Should I help you back on the bed.'

'Of course can't you see I'm in agony.'

Bending and reaching behind her arm pits. Lifting her to a sitting position. With a wince and wail. Her breasts wagging forward. Crash aging her ten years. Inappropriate my penis is up but no spiritual admonishment presently shouted all over my brain keeps it down, save for foreskin at half mast.

'If you don't mind, just let me rest sitting a moment to catch my breath.'

'O no I don't mind, please do.'

'I think I have crushed my vertebrae. What am I going to do. I've just been accepted representative for a sanitary napkin company. I can't possibly start work, injured as I am.'

'I'm sure you'll be all right.'

'You're erected, shows how much you care. O God I will be weeks in a cast, I know it.'

'You mustn't worry.'

'What do you know about worry. Where your next meal is coming from. How it is to be a middle aged woman on her own in a cruel and horrid world of gossip and ingratitude. You don't know what it is.'

'Sure I do.'

'Indeed. Accused as I was of having a disease. Hand me my parasol please. I actually think that may be slander.'

'I didn't mean it.'

'Please pick me up. Very carefully. And don't touch me with that thing.'

'I can't lift you then.'

'Make it go down.'

'I can't.'

'As I lie here in agony you stand there frivolously waving that in my face. It's quite an adequate specimen but how contemptible. I have half a mind to ring for Bonaparte. This is the most insulting moment of my entire life. It means nothing to you that I may have lost a good job. Will you make that go down. Grossly impertinent at a moment like this.'

'I'm trying. Why don't you just let me lift you up.'

'I'm shivering now. Take the parasol and cover yourself. I don't want to witness another moment of your public exhibition showing off in that fashion.'

'No.'

'O lift me up then, my God.'

Clementine lifting. The lady with the parasol. Tugging under the arms. She hobbles on a left foot. Support her under the right shoulder. Move forward. Feel the side of her silky breast. Just another few feet. Make out hexagonals pink and yellow and green on the rug. Each one encircled by a chain of arrows and eggs.

'O no no.'

Veronica crying out. Clementine digging in fingers under her shoulder as he stepped, slipped and fell. With another brief ride on a roller skate. Her body landing a heapful in his lap.

'You incredible clot you're trying to kill me.'

'I am not I'm hurt now too.'

'Why can't you watch where you're going when assisting someone injured.'

'Please the skate wheels are sticking in my back. If you just shift a little.'

'I think that this is the last straw.'

'I'm trying to do my best. Please just roll a tiny bit to the side.'

Clementine untangling a leg. Feel this pair of spine splintering wheels. One still spinning attached by a sole to soft kid skin uppers. Showing her shins to advantage. When she locomoted in. A little puffiness and dimples on the knees. Glorious contours about the thorax. A word I heard when doctors tapped me there. Got a quick feel of hers. Along with a stinging slap across the face. She takes to being an invalid. Would lift the lot of her up on the bed. But damaged something quite bizarre at the end of my spine.

'Just slide off me Veronica.'

'I am incapacitated can't you see.'

'I've broken my arse.'

'Serves you right.'

'Just roll.'

'Roll. With my vertebrae crushed. You're less hurt than I am with that thing most rudely sticking in my back.'

'We'll be here on the floor all night.'

'You can easily pull yourself out from under. I absolutely and firmly refuse to jeopardise my vertebrae by movement.'

The curtain billowing into the room. The white lining catching spare moonlight cutting through low rushing clouds. Moist wild smells. The sea will be pounding and foaming up the tunnels of Charnel Castle. Tumbling along the body of Percival. A first night away from my new home. Locked in rigid eternity with a ladies' sanitary representative. Yet to get her first order.

Stiff and sore from that night's gavotte I wore a pillow behind my arse in the saddle. Riding a massive grey hunter up a stony trail to the top of a steep hill. Following Macfugger's big black arsed stallion as he outlined his campaign. Surveying the sprawling house and demesne from a high outcropping with the ever ready binocs round his neck, two automatics bulging under a riding coat. With a map in his lap, pointing with his riding whip.

'Now Clementine defensive positions can be established right along here behind this ridge of granite. Excellent observation, good cover and we'll rain down mortar fire on the wretched buggers. Of course they'll move at night. But our trip wires laid will send up flares. We have an impregnable natural defence barrier. Position the sten guns there and there. When they withdraw for a wound licking reorganization and rest we'll make their little acreage rather unpleasant. Strum their vocal cords with sniper fire.'

In Macfugger House courtyard, grooms lined up shouldering shot guns carbines and rifles. One gardener with a pitch fork another with a scythe and two more standing over a pair of rusty mortars. I lurked near the open door of the hay barn as Macfugger strutted back and forth on the wet grey cobbles shouting out commands, a sten gun resting across his arm.

'We're outnumbered just about five to one. But manoeuvreability and observation is the key to the modern land battle. I know you will all be a lot of good chaps and that treachery will never cross your minds. Not because you would get your fucking heads blown off personally by me but because the name Macfugger has echoed in these hills and valleys since the beginning of time and no bunch of vagrants is going to creep in around here where fuckers for centuries have feared to snoop. Attention. To the right shoulder. Arms. About face. To the left flank. March. Come on you cunts. Left flank.'

Macfugger counting cadence slapping his riding crop against his boot. The dark clothed group of troops, coats held closed with bits of string, battered fedoras on heads, knocked off and picked up as they collided and recollided in the blaze of commands from Captain Macfugger. Who took wild swipes at the chickens scattering between the confused legs of his platoon.

'Halt. For God's sake halt. Wipe that grin off your face Kelly. Now listen to me. To move a force efficiently takes coordination. That means keeping in step. And marching in the same direction. An about face is executed on the ball of the right foot. Not the left with half of you slapping each other's face with rifle barrels. Murphy take three paces forward and get rid of that scythe. Now then. Fall in. Attention. Left face. Forward. March.'

Back and forth across the stable courtyard. Macfugger flanking his troops, stamping his feet. The sun breaking through. Rain puddles glinting. My own parade grounds were dry and dusty. Pounding in tight sweaty leggings.

Staring at the back of the neck ahead. Wondering when the Christ this mad drudgery would ever end. I was best as an overall strategist. The bold winning stroke delivered without warning with overwhelming superiority. Making an enemy run for his life. Clutching his backside. But they forced me to train to one day be an admiral chained to charts down in the bowels of a ship, sipping and chewing freshly made coffee and biscuits.

Macfugger dismissing his troops. Striding with shoulders back across the courtyard. Stopping and confronting a rooster fluttering its wings and taking little threatening leaps at him in the air. A black boot swiftly coming upwards into the white fluffed feathers of its breast. The bird arcing up into the air landing ten yards away where it lay gasping through its open beak for air.

'Did you see that Clementine that god damn bird attacking me. Damn nuisance when things don't know who's boss. Well I'm getting that lot into shape. Drill some soldiering into them yet. Produce a battle classic of the few against the many. They need a little gung ho. Their strongest feature as troops is of course, their natural greed for destruction. Especially polished antiques. My ruddy arm's broken holding this sten gun. Puts the fear of God into them. When I gave them a demonstration. Six bottles blasted out of the sky with my forty fives, three shots each from the left and right hand, they stood around thunderstruck for ten minutes. Think it's time now for tea.'

Veronica arriving on the arm of Bonaparte. Carried as she was to safety that first evening by wheelchair pushed by Macfugger. Who upon confronting our two piled up prostrate contorted bodies doubled into paroxysms of laughter and promptly fell sideways against the bedside table knocking whiskey and mineral water upon us. Later, recounting the story to me which he did every couple of hours, he accompanied the telling by crippling slaps on the back, loudly saying by God there was your opportunity with the female form sublime.

Seated to China tea and watercress sandwiches. Silver bowls of bon bons. Veronica festooned in chiffon scarves throwing back her head and sniffing in the air. Trying to shake something out of her mind. Macfugger smiling into his cup. One wants to streak away over the rocky mountain road towards home. Before it is reduced to ashes or turned into a mine or oil well. With mambas entwining loose about the drilling rig.

'By God a house full of cripples. Like my grandfather in his wheelchair. Never put foot outside Macfugger House during the last twenty five years of his life. Except once when there was a fire in a chimney. Even then he refused to budge off the front porch. Only exercise he got was picking his false teeth out of the soup each day. Always took a spoonful that was too hot and spit the whole thing out teeth and all. Kept a pincers to lift out his dripping bicuspids.'

Late grey afternoon I took my leave from the pillared front and granite steps of Macfugger House. Her ladyship and Nails waving from the doorway. The four in hand rumbling up the drive, turning left, through a village of pub and shop. Past a blacksmith shoeing a horse's hoof over his thick leather apron in the doorway. Up a winding gorse lined road and across the lonely windswept hills. In my hand a letter slipped me by a maid. Opening it as the sprawling fields and parklands of Macfugger House lay distantly behind.

Dear Mr Clementine,
    Although I hope we can still be friends in the future this is just to say that your callous indifference has left me feeling quite ill. I hope you don't think it was intentional to enter a gentleman's bedchambers. I had an irresistible schoolgirl urge to try the skates. I used to ice skate in my youth on the canals of Holland. However it is irrelevant to the purpose of this letter which is to ask if you would pose for some photographs. I expect to be picking up my car in two days.
                                                                    Veronica

The dark grey tall walls of Charnel Castle. First evening star above a black cloud moving in from the sea. Soft salty wind. Waves splash up on the steep coastal cliffs and spread out on the sandy beach of the bay. Strange terrors out there bobbing on the waters. Goodbye to the Macfugger grooms. Hello to the Charnel dwellers.

Clementine crossing the tiles of the great hall. Through the stray boulders surrounding a large pile of rubble. A yellow lamp glow illuminating where a bent head examines a hole perforating a stone arch. Franz. Kneeling and picking away rocks and soil, poking his finger through the little circle of blackness as he suddenly looks up.

'I have unfortunately miscalculated. The excavation should have started perhaps another two yards to the east. There will not be much difficulty beginning a new digging.'

'You're breaking into the cellars.'

'It was a mistake. But all my important discoveries have originated from blunders.'

'I want the whole bunch of you out of here and the holes filled in and the tiles replaced.'

Franz slowly shrugging his shoulders. Holds the pick handle aside and dislodges clay from the rusty cutting edges. Looking back up and scratching his head.

'Mr Clementine you do try my patience. It will be most difficult to reach conclusions on our explorations here if you take that attitude.'

'I don't want your conclusions. And where are those mambas.'

'My colleague Erconwald was of the opinion that they should be released in the surrounding countryside.'

Clementine swiftly ascending the great staircase. Along the corridors. Up past the coffin chamber to the lofty fortified confines of the octagonal room. Change out of Nails Macfugger's borrowed rather loose fitting shooting garments. Nice bone buttons on the flies. A letter on my bedside table. All in the chamber neat and tidy. No Elmer to greet me. Check under the bed for snakes. Open this letter. Addressed to owner or occupier.

> GHQ
> The Crossroads
>
> Dear Sir,
>
> The Army of Insurrection hereby informs you of a requisition order made for the partial use of Charnel Castle during the

present emergency. The north wing of the said premises including the northeast and west towers will be required for the housing of troops under this command. Should you desire further information concerning this requisition please contact above.

Sean Macdurex
Officer Commanding
Fourth Tank Division Western Army

Clementine seating himself. Taking up pen and crested paper. Reply to this first sign of hostilities. With a short résumé of casual internal impediments.

Sean Macdurex
Officer Commanding
GHQ
The Crossroads

Dear Sir,
This castle is already chock full of inhabitants, not to mention poisonous reptiles. Some of these inmates have been violent and others teeter on the verge and therefore I cannot vouch for the safety of your troops. Interior excavations are also being conducted making it dangerous to wander inside here. I note that you do not mention any decorations awarded.

Yours faithfully,
Clayton Claw Cleaver Clementine
Of The Three Glands

A knock. Someone standing in the shadows. A scouting party for the insurrectionists. Creeping to subdue me in my partial state of undress. To punch me under the oxsters. Thunder boots against my free swinging glands. Sell them later to the highest bidding pawnbroker, nothing like three gilded real ones to bring in the customers. While I hang ball less from the ramparts.

'Ah am I disturbing you my dear Clementine. I have just come to say how glad I am to see you. To welcome you back. To indeed say all I can in humble greeting. It was with great excitement this morning that I witnessed ranunculous peeking with its yellow dewy flower just above the blades of graminea to afford itself the rays of a friendly sun. May I inquire had you a pleasant stay with your friends. I trust you slept well with no ill images troubling you. And that the gods of pleasant inconsequentials made your eyelids quiver with all that is joyful in slumber. May nymphs diaphanously clothed anoint you. And might I trouble you to ask for a further moment of your time.'

'It's you.'

'Ah. To be sure. Yes, it is I. I have been busy with equations and can state quite firmly now that the eta meson when discovered will reveal three new particles called pions. As we speak, low dark clouds tumble upon us from the sea. As we breathe new winds are born.'

'Erconwald would you mind just cutting out the shit.'

'Ah good person perchance you are aggrieved.'

'Yes I am.'

'But may I then kind sir hope that from a panorama of absurdities I might seek from you one harmless indulgence.'

'What.'

'Merely to request your gracious presence to dine tonight with me. And be forgiven that I must for this purpose avail myself of the appurtenances of your household. In this connection perhaps you might tell me of the whereabouts of the wine cellar.'

I took a solitary walk in the rear cloister darknesses of the Charnel. Where a growling Toro suddenly thundered past the other side of a wall in the bramble undergrowth. Seagulls sliding up and down purple hillsides of sky. One so quickly gets hungry alone and cold. Out here there may be creeping horrors unseen in the night. Collect up little outposts of hope. High in towers instead of low down in dungeons. Where I showed Erconwald in the doorway of the wine cellar. And stretched out on a bed of straw laid across a shelf of champagne bottles, the prostrate bodies of Percival and Miss Ovary side by side, garments disarrayed indelicately. Elmer on the floor licking up a puddle of port and thumping his tail as he nuzzles his big black guilty drunken nose at my shoe.

The dining room lit with candles. A bleary eyed Percival

bowing each time dropping his monocle and slightly lurching beside the door. Guests standing at their places. Two new ones. A sallow fat sweaty faced man whose name was whispered Bligh. And is it. Yes. My goodness, the sandy haired smoked salmon eating gentleman off the ship. All clapping as I entered. Followed by Percival to the head of the table where he seated me. My throat swallowing. Hold back the tears. What a terribly kind thing of Erconwald to do. With my dishes, food, servants and wine.

A fire throwing a gigantic turf glow into the room. Erconwald mid way down the table between the largest of the exprisoners and the Baron. Rose to my right. Mrs L K L at the opposite end flanked by newcomers. Franz on my left nods his head. And gives me a little shy smile. Erconwald standing.

'Ladies and gentlemen I propose and I am sure you will second a toast to our most noble host.'

Charlene peeking from the serving door. A worried look across her face. As one stared down into the iced bowl of large and most perfect grains of beluga gutted from some sturgeon royal and far away. Sip this champagne bubbling palest gold. A tang of grape across the tongue. Rose smiling a big mouthful of teeth and growls as she packs the caviar on her shovel of toast and throws it back into the maw. My sandy haired friend nods and grins rejoicing in the unteetotal happiness.

A triumphant procession. Of Fred the pig. Roasted. His ears looking especially sad on his head decorated with holly leaves and berries. His poor trotter sticking up in the air from a platter lugged by Ena and Imelda. Trays of steaming pheasant and wild rice. Percival pouring magnums of champagne. Auntie see me now. The toast of this group. No one ever singled me out for a little flattery before. It's nice.

Clementine excusing himself from table. Standing in the adjoining state room near a large doll's house in the darkness. Tears tumble. Good to cry. All pours out. Trickles from the floods of terror. A signal switches the track when you head out to die. Slowly roll there. On the heavy hopeless wheels. Till a kiss tugs you back to the teeming rails of life. A sound behind me. A figure. The lumpy shadow of Percival.

'Ah God sir, it's a grand evening. I've never come across the likes of such as that Mr Erconwald. A more kindly gentleman never trod earth. It was a surprise for you sir we had planned these few days. Wasn't I down there below looking for the grandest of the vintages. Trying me best to tell the great from the grand and the grand from the great. Didn't the struggle befuddle me. Took a good jolt of brandy to sharpen me senses. And didn't both meself and Miss Ovary find ourselves prostrate in the line of duty. If it wasn't for Elmer we'd been kilt by the rats.'

Turf smoke gently lowering from the ceiling. Clementine returning to table as the Baron raises his glass. His monocle flashing in the candle light. He smiles the saddest smile to me and bows his head. Must start some conversation. Just to slow the jaws grinding up the food and knives sawing on the plates. Commandeer Mrs L K L's pistol for defence against the insurgents. Who when they advance stealthily towards the castle walls will have the shit bit out of them by mambas.

On come glacé apricots, shortbreads and gooseberry fool. Putlog Roulette grinning over every mouthful and nodding at Rose. Bottles pouring a golden Sauterne. Which widened a continuous smile on my sandy haired friend. And downed by other faces grim and silent. Putlog waving arms madly to encourage merriment. Where one could not even with hammer and chisel cut gladness on these faces. They glower and murmur as Erconwald rises. Knocks his knuckles against the mahogany.

'Good people gathered here tonight pray may I beg a moment. It is with the greatest pleasure that I bring at this time a tiding to our most gracious, noble and esteemed host who has borne grave inconvenience with indulgent patience. Franz has found material within the confines of Charnel Castle containing valuable metallic constituents.'

Backs stiffening up and down the table. Franz bowing his head. Putlog shaking his face with yeses. The exprisoners looking at one another and clutching at their cutlery. My sandy haired friend clapping discreetly. Mrs L K L sneezing and taking a hanky from her evening purse from which clatters her pistol into her finger bowl. Rose jumping to her feet. Raising an accusing finger down the table.

'That cunt's got her gun.'

'Pray people, peace.'

'Peace of my arse.'

'Who said that.'

'I said that.'

'Is it a beating you want to make enough sauce out of you to add an inch to the seas.'

'Beseech you good people. Bring clarity to this situation before we are haggard with broken clavicles.'

'What is clarity.'

'By God clarity is that force given to a fist sent in the direction of a face that when hit has no trouble seeing stars.'

'Is that so. Well right now I'll give you a sight of the universe.'

Erconwald went down under the avalanche. His pale hands raised to ward off the advancing bodies. Oscar the boy standing grinning ear to ear wiping the blade of a knife over and over again. A voice threatening the breakage of an ulna. Rose heading for Mrs L K L. The Baron holding the gun high over his head from grasping hands. One's athlete's foot is playing havoc between my toes otherwise I'd sort them out in a hurry. Bunch of them breaking my plates, skidding ruts across my mahogany, delighted with the demolition.

'It's ugsome in the Urals is it. You whore.'

'For the love of God please restrain the aspersions.'

Lead Kindly Light himself standing up on his place mat. Shod in sandals, wielding a skewer thrusting it ceilingwards as his wife lowered her head and charged bovine like at the advancing Rose. Many enemies must have been made in my absence. Putlog undoing Lead Kindly Light's sandal straps. Unsporting manoeuvres afoot aplenty. Only the Baron smiles with his pistol pointing at the ceiling and his cheese fork implanted in a chunk of cheddar.

'It's a woolling you want and it's a woolling you'll get.'

'Stop the clarity.

'By God the stars have only begun to be seen.'

Rose and Mrs L K L locked head on, each with hands buried deep in the other's hair. Shaking and pulling. Erconwald on his back underneath the table his feet kicking out at the hands of the exprisoners. Franz with stethoscope pressed over his heart, thumping his free fist methodically into the ear hole of Bligh as the fat new arrival bends to separate the wrestling women. Percival with a lance in front of Clementine.

'Nobody's to lay a finger on the master of this house or he gets this where he'd rather have a lubricant.'

Lead Kindly Light aloft on the table raising a vial of liquid. Waving it slowly back and forth. The protagonists stilled. Desisting from their scratching, biting and kicking. All heed paid to L K L stocking footed on the mahogany among the finger bowls. Amid gruntings from the ladies. Thumping haymakers deep into each other's haggis with one hand and removing handfuls of hair with the other.

'Boors unbeseeming. All of you. Stop. Instantly. As it would be most disagreeable for me to have to detonate this glycerine treated recently with a cold mixture of concentrated nitric and sulphuric acids. Such pointless concussion will only result in a festoonery of entrails about the etruscan trancepts and much needless splattering of fresh blobs on the rare pink glass of the windows. All line up.'

Erconwald brushing himself off. The fighting females holding tight to each other's hair. The three exprisoners sheepish and shy in front of the explosive. Lead Kindly Light one handedly undoing and dropping his trousers. From under which flared out a grass skirt. Percival whispering.

'Your man's out of his mind sir, somewhere in the south seas.'

'Gavotte. Gavotte or I blow you up.'

The gathering danced. Crooked footed and very slow at first. A loose flopping up and down of ankles. Later a thundering of heels, the floor heaving. And a rending crash as Oscar the boy plummeted through the floor boards on his first caper. Standing waist high in a corner. Eyes big globes of fear. As L K L sniffs his vial held up to a nostril and scratches himself under his skirt.

'Idolators. Pagans. Repent. I am the yodeller of the deeps. I have walked in the Prado. And peed in both the gents and ladies conveniences of the British Museum. One more aura of discourtesy and I will impart this titanic turbulence. That'll make Krakatoa seem like a tar blister on the road.'

'Sir that's the ravings of a lunatic, would I be having your permission to slide the shaft of this yoke into him.'

'Dance. Drop that spear you. Radicals. Dandruff makers. I am your comeuppance, Lead Kindly Light of the atomic sloth. You who fester your lives on wine women and perverted tetrahedrons. Who dare question the periodic table. And use ugly demeaning words of me. Lead Kindly Light the less of the backside contorted is it. Take a look now. At me buttocks smiling. Do any of you see baggyness about the arse parts. Fatless I am. Devoid of sinister flesh overlappings. Able to strum upon my spare ribs. The castle evil here is an affront to the cultural interests accumulated by my wife and I abroad. An explosion of this will soon perk up posterity's ears. Shut up you dirty little eegit there in the corner.'

'Help.'

Oscar hip deep in the floor. Lifting one knee up to gain a foothold. Crashing down again through the powdery wood. Landing perched as he must be on a supporting wall. The gathering hushed under the vial aloft. A pale glow of fear over the faces. Mrs L K L and Rose shifting foot positions. L K L's whitened small fist gyrating round his head. And now vibrating in front of his face.

'Fornicators.'

Erconwald raising his slender hand. Tranquil abider. Inclining his head. A prisoner loudly clearing his throat. All eyes on the vial. L K L's skirt sprouting outwards as he twirls. Oscar on his knees hands joined in prayer, his round white face raised towards the ceiling.

'Ah Lead Kindly I entreat to be heard. I offer a solution

to our distraught posture. May I suggest the laying aside of the vial.'

L K L holding the explosive ampoule high in the air. Erconwald hunching his shoulders in prelude to the detonation. Other beholders raising hands to block the blast. L K L screaming.

'I will not have the profundities of posterity tampered with by whoremongers who have not gasped in awe at mystical revelations achieved by long navel gazing.'

'My good Lead Kindly Light. Your sentiments are honoured most humbly by your obedient servant.'

'Haven't I told you my nannies walked me around the green so that I could drink the nobilities of the passing architecture.'

'Pray my good, my very good Lead Kindly Light. All of us will go around the green quite soon to taste of its sombre elegances. Meanwhile may I not say just a few private words to our host who stands most disturbed and anguished there. To perhaps explain the reasonable nature of your remarks and your justifiable consternation. I would hope that you would agree to save him sufferment of further trepidation.'

'You will be allowed fifty seconds.'

'Ah I am most thankful and grateful to you my good, my very good Lead Kindly Light.'

Erconwald stepping around the table with the utmost of ceremonial delicacies. His tongue lightly licking through his lips. This thin throated man of soft voice and rippling kindliness. Eyes closed he nears Clementine.

'Ah good person I am indeed most contrite that this unhappy situation has arisen. L K L is a yodeller of uncommon ability. We are ancient friends. Occasioned first in the capital city during childhood upon our both swimming summers in the canal. Later we launched him upon his singing career. Many months spent abroad perfecting his yodelling made him impatient with his slow recognition upon his return. The blaze of maximum publicity we attempted to achieve by his riding our ostrich down the street failed upon the bird's unrehearsed entry through the plate

glass of a display window full of undraped plastic manne-
quins. The mayhem therein permanently grieved us all.
His wife is a woman of wealth and culture. Her photograph
has been in news periodicals. Although minor misunder-
standings have saddened each of us in turn, where singing
or scientific progress was at stake we worked as one. Pray be
disturbed no longer.'

'Thank you Erconwald.'

Lead Kindly Light throwing the vial with a sweep of his
arm. Hands flashing over faces in the sign of a cross. Bodies
hurtling away from the fireplace where the slender tube
plunged into the flames. A shattering blast. A bright orange
ball of fire. Plaster falling from the ceilings. The twin
chandeliers swinging. Night air streaming through the
broken windows. Outside sparks falling from the sky. Distant booming echoes. And inside, scattered turf embers
smouldering over the room. Lead Kindly Light his grass
skirt up around his throat prostrate on the table, both knees
twitching. Blood pouring out the nose of one of the exprisoners. Rose and Mrs L K L flat on their backs, faces
covered in plaster specks, still engripped in each other's
hair. Above me the face of Charlene. In whose hands lies
my head.

'O dear God have mercy on you Mr Clementine. Yours
is the first good honest face to enter this district for donkey's years. Taken now from us without warning.'

'I'm alive.'

'God so you are. Thanks be to St Anastasia for that.'

'Light the candles.'

'I will sir but are you all right.'

'Yes.'

'O lord listen to the moans. The injuries will need the
doctor in a hurry. Tim's the fastest to the town. I'll send
him sir.'

The candles extinguished relit by Charlene. A ghostly
smoke rising from the debris. The Baron seated propped
against the wall, an ancestor's fallen portrait beside him to
which he nods greeting and to whom he offers a glass.
Percival holding his knee.

'Ah God sir this is out of joint again. It'll take a worse blast than that one now to put it back right again.'

An exprisoner limping slowly round the room his tie hanging down his back, levelling the portraits hanging askew. The holocaust awakening sensitivities. Amid the scattered and tattered clothing. And grunts as the fighting ladies reentrench their grips loosened by the blast. A voice humming a tune. As Elmer now with his huge shaggy grey head sniffs and licks the downed faces. Percival sweeping up the smoking embers of turf. A donkey honks out across the fields. A sweet moist air of night breezing through broken windows.

Sound of an engine and headlights of a car shooting up in the sky. Erconwald, shirt in tatters sitting elbows on the table and head in hands. The large door of the dining hall opening. Tim towering behind a small rotund man in waistcoat carrying a black bag. Pausing in the doorway. The doctor. Donning spectacles. Surveying the scene. His hand slowly reaching up and covering his heart. He sways. He totters. And crashes forward on the floor.

> Another
> Sad stillness
> This night
> Lies prone
> One more clarity
> In the middle
> Of a
> Moan

9

Morning beams blue and sunny after the blast and blame of the boisterous night. Charnel Castle inhabitants crawling away to bedrooms. Those who could. The doctor treated on the dining room table for heart attack. Erconwald and Franz wearing arm bands with a red cross as they danced attendance upon the injured.

I take an early morning pee and stare down from the high walls and see a gossamer webbing on the grass. Spun in the dark to make a waving sea of white. Charlene and Percival lugging me to bed. Mildly concussed I dreamt I dwelt in an igloo. Lots of folk kept arriving across the tundra. An enormous craps game developed on the packed snow over the north pole. I lost my shirt and woke up sweating. To see Elmer playfully on the floor eating the last of my precious money from Erconwald. Who lastly whispered as I was led away.

'Good person although the optical refinements of the dining hall are quite good the moment is now opportune to remove the more sombre expressions and over lavish use of the baroque.'

Lead Kindly Light of the backside contorted was last seen, a suit of armour over his grass skirt, making headway on hands and knees across the great hall and up on the mound of rubble where he attempted to stand and shake a mailed fist before falling backwards into the excavation. His voice heard down amid the material containing minerals.

'I am a legionnaire. I march tonight. Upon the idolatrous and heathen to give them a fright. Those who have dared suggest a breech of impurity by calling me Lead Kindly Light of the held open kimono shall suffer.'

The battling women left abandoned gripped in each other's hair. The Baron seen solitary in a glow of candle light in the library reading the biography of an international swindler, a box of chocolates open on his lap and a bottle and a glass at his side. Offer this place for sale. Containing unusual assortment of permanent inhabitants. Unrepeatable bargain. To include faithful servants, silver hash dishes, bread baskets, toast racks and crumb scoops. Suitable for continuance as an institution. Ideal for those afflicted with constant digging or snake charming. Or just needing to clank casually about in armour.

The doctor infused with an emulsion of Erconwald's donkey distillate, brandy and honey, rose revived after a peaceful night's sleep and was aided with black bag and a broken gold watch to his car. He looked quickly back up at the ramparts and accelerated his two toned blue vehicle down the road.

Clementine reclining on his bedroom chaise longue, a green and blue striped cravat at his throat. Charlene entering followed by the sandy haired gentleman. To place a tray of breakfast, rashers, fried tomato, eggs, pucks of bread and butter and steaming tea. This man his face shiny and pink, smiles so delightedly to see me. Lying here in the slim rays of sunshine. Potentate, landowner and blast victim.

'I am glad to see you alive after last night. An ember burned through my suit but I am all right. You have such interesting friends and way of life. You have recovered your voice.'

'Yes.'

'Well I nearly lost mine. I have been outwitted by the whole human race. I hitch hiked when I got off the boat. My luggage was lost or stolen or sent somewhere without me. I ended up with bowler hat faded light blue and a warped cane. Wet and frozen I started to walk and met a little group on the road. I asked their spokesman what was going on. They said they were in search of the truth in this latter day. I asked where they got the money to support this search as I was interested to search with them. They said it would take some time to get me accredited but meanwhile they would make me a temporary prophet and handed me a map of this area. I met your remarkable friend Erconwald up at the crossroads.'

Pouring a cup of tea for this man called Bloodmourn. Whose face and smile cheers one over breakfast. One regrets not ever having let him win at chess. He asks for my bacon rinds. Laid out on a long piece of toasted soda bread. He sits chewing with seafaring blue eyes. A naval man just like myself.

Percival arriving. To take orders for the day. Can't think of a thing except to have meals in future served right here behind my iron door. Mount Oscar to stand guard. On a spot where he won't plummet through the floor. And search all visitors for combustibles.

'Sorry sir, I shall come back. I didn't know you were engaged.'

Bloodmourn standing. Nervously brushing off his crumbs. His shoe leather grey blotched and wrinkled. A thin orange tweed tie holding the neck of his shirt together. A thick brown sweater under his jacket.

'Please. I'm just leaving. I would like to walk outside in the garden.'

Bloodmourn bowing and backing out the door. Percival picking up a remnant of a bank note. Looks at Elmer peering up out of his dark eyes. Shakes his finger. Elmer burying his head under his paws and claws.

'Ah that was a night last night, wasn't it sir. Now mind you if most of the blast hadn't gone up the chimney we'd have been kilt dead. Are you enjoying your breakfast of them tomatoes.'

'Yes.'

'Never eat them meself. Didn't someone give me a tomato as a little feller telling me it was an apple and I bit into it and it dripped what I thought was blood and I've never been able to bite into an apple or tomato since.'

'Percival what's been going on here.'

'Sir it would take an army of mathematicians playing finger and toe symphonies on abacuses to figure that out.

Mr Erconwald himself and the Baron are at the minute in the dining hall repairing windows. This L K L is some kind of dangerous eejit. He should be locked up. Going round he was making a holy commotion in armour boasting of his sexual knowledge after calling us fornicators. Your man Clarence there now beyond who they say keeps his trap shut as well as his trousers, has the very latest in sexual knowledge. Never is he without his handbook of marital technique adjacent in his coat pocket for immediate reference. Now I wouldn't want to presume upon you sir, but he says sure success comes from varying the stance. Clarence will give you a stream of frank commentary concerning the movements and the caresses, have no doubt about that. Tell you in a matter of seconds what would take a lifetime of hopeless cohabitation to achieve. But sure, sexual ecstasy has no chance in this country with the rain.'

Throughout the late morning and noontime, guests sneaking to the kitchens for snacks. A scent of frying bacon and eggs up staircases and through halls. Bloodmourn with me on a tour of castle grounds. Down moist mouldy tunnels of rhododendrons. Along overgrown paths of boxwood hedges. Traces of springtime. Primroses peeking yellow from sheltery hedgerows. Bracken and heathers faintly growing green. Peering down the sheer cliff sides to the grey boulders and thrashing sea below. Warm sun, air salty and fresh.

Walking along a narrow path over a bramble choked road. Leading back from the meadows to a tall brown entrance. Clementine smashing briars down with a walking stick. Bloodmourn helping to shift the rusted levers and push open the heavy oak gates into the castle courtyard. Behind, the sound of throbbing thunder coming up underfoot. A massive white curly head and pair of yellowing horns smashing aside the undergrowth. And pounding straight for us.

'Let me handle this Clementine.'

Two footed I ran for my life into the castle courtyard. Bloodmourn taking off his jacket, slipping out of his sweater.

Just in time to throw the latter over Toro's massive head now lowered like a plough skimming over the courtyard stones heading for the slender figure of this rapidly retreating man. Muscles rippling over the expanse of haunch, blood and bulk of this animal.

'Keep out of the way Clementine I'm in control.'

Clementine jumping, both hands caught on a roof gutter, feet dangling over the ground. Toro blazing forward blindly under the sweater. And sailing through a closed stable door with a splintering and shattering of wood. Bloodmourn practising a cape movement in the hiatus. Slowly a state coach emerging driven forward by Toro no longer with the sweater over his eyes. With a neat hook of the head half the spokes of a rear wheel ripped out. Bloodmourn grabbing Toro by the tail as he reduces the coach to matchwood for ladies matches. This splendid vehicle demolished before I even knew I owned it.

'Everyone stay where you are. I'm closing the gates. I know how to handle him.'

Toro warming up. Tearing round the confines. Removing two gutter pipes one after the other with a nuzzle of the horn. Arcing a full rain barrel up in the air to crash in watery pieces. Toro now centre courtyard roaring, snorting, pawing the stones. Bloodmourn advancing slowly as he stamps his feet.

'Bloodmourn please, don't.'

'You must show them you're not afraid. This roaring and pawing is mostly bluff. Get me an umbrella.'

A familiar voice from a rampart. Macfugger his dark red hair combed back, smilingly waving his cap down into the arena.

'I say there Clementine, just popped in. See you've got a spot of bother.'

More faces at the turrets. Heads jutting over the ramparts. Some chewing on sandwiches. High up a hawk quivering. A tightly rolled umbrella landing. Bloodmourn side stepping in a crouch to pick it up. Legs astride unfurling the black folds, he presses the gleaming silk canopy open. Stamping a left foot he advances. With the same implacable daring with which he loses at chess. Toro backing up. His big ivory hooves splayed open over the stones. Bloodmourn's coat suspended from the end of the umbrella as he advances.

'A little softening in the throwing muscle, then we'll cut this animal down a little somewhat. Tut Tut Toro.'

A gasp from the crowd. Erconwald, Putlog and Franz seated together feet dangling over the parapet. The Baron behind them with binoculars. Bloodmourn pausing. Bending to tighten his shoe laces. Just belay my own now and I can just make it up out of harm's way on these slates. Bloodmourn upright again, lips thin and grim, eyes steely and hard. Toro still backing away, his tail switching over his big curly back. Macfugger cupping his hands to his mouth.

'He'll put a horn up your hole.'

'Toro tut tut.'

This beast crushing the drainpipe on the cobbles, casually turning, hooks it up and flicks it sailing across the yard smashing against a wall. Bloodmourn advancing. Calf muscles twitching through a torn trouser. Footwork must be his secret. Because if it isn't he'll never play chess again.

'Gad man, keep your feet together, that stance is madness.'

Bloodmourn closing up his feet. Macfugger must know a thing or two about bull fighting. Just as he knows the luxury of crapping beneath matured rhododendrons with a cool fresh wind fanning the bottom after a wipe of a carefully selected leaf. Veins at Bloodmourn's temples expanded and throbbing. Toro charges. Bloodmourn umbrella at the ready, nipping smartly out of the way as this four footed lethality goes thundering past getting a dig of the umbrella spike in the neck. The grass between the cobbles flattening under the blasts of Toro's snorts. As he stops, turns and attacks again. One hears that man looks a hundred times bigger than he really is in a bull's eyes. Which could really scare the bull. But gives him a big target hard to miss.

Faces turning towards the open kitchen doorway. Hands clapping. L K L in armour. Stepping from the castle. Out on the field of valour. A lance held forth. Someone said amid a flurry of mumbled remarks before the blast that ignominy was L K L's friend faithful and true. Ready to stick with him now that Toro's great head and bloodshot eyes face his small gleaming metallic figure slowly stumbling forward. Bloodmourn raising an admonishing hand.

'Get him the hell out of the ring.'

Rain falling. Sudden crystal dollops. From swift clouds passing overhead. Hay and pine scented air. Sun in and out. Cobbles glistening. Shimmering rays of a rainbow arcing upwards out of the sea and down into the bleak mountainside. L K L wobbling. The lance dipping downwards. Toro lowering his head. Front hoof striking up sparks as he crushes stone against stone. And charges.

Bloodmourn making violent movements. With much hand wagging at the end of the wrist. Toro gathering speed. L K L's helmet slipped down on his head. Mercifully make him blind to his catastrophe. He totters leftwards. Small stones now landing previously hoof tossed by Toro into the sky. Large one clanking on L K L. Macfugger frantic waving a large cigar.

'Joust him one you stupid cunt. Joust him.'

Toro's head gliding low. Hanging from the small mountain of a neck behind his horns. Someone fainting up on the ramparts. Flesh meeting stone. Familiar sound hereabouts. Bloodmourn standing impatiently dry under his umbrella. Toro skidding on a mossy patch. Going down on his white thick knees and bumping over the cobbles. Macfugger commanding from the rampart.

'Get him. Dig him with the lance. Now's your chance. He's confused. He's down. For God's sake then tweak his fucking nose.'

Clementine perched watching from the peak of a barn roof. Carefully shifting and tugging to better and safely view this bull fight. Things slippery up here. Whoops. I'm sliding down the slates. A mad grab for the rain gutter. Got it. Yanked out of its moorings. And crashing on me with clarity. With a crowning of rotting leaves and rain water. Good for the scalp.

'By God I say there you bloody galoots, save the prince.'

L K L missing with a lunge of the lance, stumbling over Toro. Who rises grunting, tail slashing and shaking himself. One ton of beast peering round slowly for a victim. Be hours of back breaking labour clearing up remains. In moments of terror stay still as a statue. With the maddest of visions. From a more civilized clime. Of an elegant couple one July evening in a park standing at a tiny distance silent in their beige summer clothes eyes reverently directed at their beige elderly dog as he doubled his woolly body near a tree and earnestly and lengthily crapped beige.

Household pillows plopping into the courtyard. Voices shouting get them on to his horns. Toro boring into the white fluffiness. By hoof and horn ripping them asunder. Dismantling embroidered crests in a whirlwind of feathers. Some sucked up Toro's nose. Bloodmourn ramrod stiff, cape held out. Toro bewildered by the floating whiteness. A throbbing organ dirge from the castle. Putlog gone from the audience. Everyone doing their bit. And a voice now inside the armour.

'God fuck them and keep them down always.'

Bloodmourn running through a repertoire of passes. Furling jacket. Spinning umbrella. Now still. Waiting. The snow of feathers settling. A mazurka from the organ. Rose waving a red handkerchief. The Baron taking a swig from a flask. On this almighty day. A vine grown up a rake leaning against the wall. Start me out farming. In some peaceful little field. Dig over a sod. Pop in the onion seed. Get cows grazing. So the milk as Percival says can leap up at you out of the tall green grass and buttercups while you stand there with your mouth open and your teeth enjoying a bit of sunshine. He suggested as well I ought to marry. That great wine and good food add confidence to life and a good woman adds everything else. And would stop two wifeless chaps getting down on the same straw together of an evening and feeling around in the dark. Only natural to tug on anything that might come to hand.

Bloodmourn, his shirt tails fluttering in the breeze. Toro backing up a few hoof paces. Feathers blasting out his nose holes. Ears twitching. Bloodmourn with chin raised turning to face Toro over a left shoulder. A stamp of his right foot. A flutter of coat. And comes the onslaught of rippling steel tendons of beef. Hoofs clattering over the stones. Six inmates should be enough to carry Bloodmourn to the cemetery. Choose a coffin to fit from the household supply.

Bloodmourn passing the horn high up across the breast. Shirt torn from his back. Motionless he stands, every inch a sportsman. Again Toro descending. Bloodmourn taking him round and round, closer and closer with the cape. The great beast hobbling down to its knees. Macfugger slowly taking cigar out of his mouth.

'By jove man, that's deft. Exquisite. Courageous.'

Bloodmourn smiling. Bowing. Toro rising befuddled, wobbling centre yard. Pushing his head into the black gleaming remains of the coach. Just to make sure it was there. Time for me to make for these half open doors. To get inside. And up on this stack of turf. While Toro's standing staring, giant ribs heaving in and out. And blood dripping from Bloodmourn's chest as he advances.

'Tut tut, Toro.'

Toro backing up two paces. Great pink scrotum wagging between back legs. This matador advancing closer. Tiptoeing now over the horns. A finger pressing down on the curly flat surface between Toro's eyes and giving him a prod on his moist nose. As the massive head slowly lowers. Bloodmourn dropping his cape, casting aside his umbrella. And raising his hand for silence.

'Ladies and gentlemen. I would like to dedicate this brave but confused bull to my host Mr Clementine. If someone will throw me a sword I will dispatch him.'

'Impostor. Backslider.'

L K L shouting out of his metal casing. As he encounters a lonely area of wall. Punching his mailed fist against the grey blocks of granite. Rose sporting bald patches across her head throwing a hanky fluttering down. The clink of coins on the cobbles. Bloodmourn stepping back from this quietened beast. Picking up Rose's red cloth and wiping blood from his breast. To tie the fluttering rag around his throat. Standing baring a slender concave chest, nobbly shoulders and thin white arms. Macfugger leans out over the parapet.

'I'll fetch the proper blade to you my good man.'

Toro making wee wee. Big splash out of his big hose. Toro moving. Low slung balls trembling from his undercarriage. It did not take him long to reach Bloodmourn. At the height of his popularity. Attended now by gasps. At the overt staggering horror. Bloodmourn caught neatly mid arse mid horn. Lobbed upwards. Blocking a momentary ray of sunshine. And landing with a clatter of broken slates flat faced on the roof above me. Down which he slides. To thump into my mound of turf fallen out the door. The man called Bligh strutting obesely into the arena, bellowing at the crumpled Bloodmourn.

'For the love of God man the least you should do is let the picadors weaken the throwing muscle with a few pikes before you try a cup der grace.'

Toro pausing. Head swinging. Moaning out low tremorous growls. Bligh heading for an open shed. Nips in and out again with a hay fork. Toro surveying the ring. As this new nuisance approaches menacing two rusty prongs, sleeves rolled up and a sneer across the face.

'Now how would you like this fork a foot deep in your carcass.'

Toro stretching out legs and twisting his neck back to lick a rear haunch. Bligh advancing. Macfugger in riding breeches and boots at the kitchen entrance with a sword. Bloodmourn rising unsteadily on the turf pile. A dirge thundering from the organ deep inside the castle. Putlog must be watching through a periscope. Toro's tail standing out stiffly. A plop plop on the cobbles from his rear. The horned head lowering. Bligh throwing the fork. Hitting Toro mid shoulder.

'That'll teach you.'

The beast rearing up with a roar. Bligh crouching, bulging legs astride and arms held out. Hay fork shaken with a shrug from Toro's shoulder. As he gathers his thousands of muscles together and commences them towards Bligh. Who abandons the wrestlers stance, turns and runs, fists churning and knees pumping high. Lickety split over the stones. Toro gaining. Breathing down on the Bligh arse bouncing ahead. Now caught and elevated between Toro's long white lashed brown eyes.

Bligh aloft travelling towards the rust coloured kitchen door just closing. As this pair of combatants come hurtling towards it. Laughter erupting inside. The impact of Bligh shuddering through the castle. A wasp's nest falls from under the eaves. Toro rounding on Macfugger who dips a sword tip into Toro's hide. Bligh struggling up holding his head between hands. Bellowing as he slowly turns in a circle of rage.

'Who did that. Closed that door. Could have killed me. I'll find out. If it takes till I'm lying waiting for him in heaven he'll have the shit kicked out of him soon as he strolls in the gates.'

Macfugger backing nimbly away poking his sword at Toro's nose. Bligh beating his fists against the kitchen door. L K L half sitting propped against the well pump. Sunlight bright. A lark rising singing into the sky. On the rampart a black hunting hat, Lady Macfugger yellow gloved peering down into the arena. Wind blowing back her long hair. Her finely knuckled hands when she poured tea. Dreamt of her smiling. Taking off her coat. The pin out of her silk white scarf at her throat. Her shirt off. Her lips and teeth coming near me. Her breasts. Her belly. Her husband. Is out there. Making a declaration to the audience.

'You chaps simply don't have the poise for this kind of thing. Must keep high on the toes. Belly tucked in. Balls too. Easy Toro. Ha Toro. Of course you ruddy must make sure he knows he's dominated.'

Macfugger zigzagging backwards. Toro's snarls of high pitched rage. The beast's beige nose lowered to the cobbles hooking left and right pricked by Nails' sword point. Lady Macfugger blowing her nose with a white hanky. We met in my dream by accident at a lonely airport. She stepped out of a small yellow airplane on the pale green grass.

Strode up to me as I stood in a draughty shed. She said, I think we have something to talk about. At an inn in a brightly coloured suit she ordered lunch. Of asparagus, lobster, salad, hock, raspberries and cream. Across a lawn and roadway there was a row of clipped round poplar trees lining entrance gates to a castle with turrets peeking up behind greenery. After lunch her hand touched mine as we went down the flower carpeted stairs. To a dark back bar of the hotel. My heart thumping we sat on stools sipping port. She ordered four one after the other. Her teeth in the darkness. Gently slapping her riding crop against her thigh. Under the black of her jacket the white of her shirt and lace of an undergarment, her breasts. She said I would enjoy to get to know you better, I like your mind. I smiled she smiled. Her husband out there now where he might get killed. She said she liked men to assert themselves. My God Macfugger is cornered. Toro backing him up against the bars of a cellar window.

Erconwald from a rampart lowering a small black ball suspended from the end of a long bamboo pole. Holding it swaying between Macfugger and Toro. The beast lifting it's head sniffing, opening it's sneering mouth and breathing in and out between its teeth and nosing after the bobbing sphere. As Macfugger looks up the castle wall.

'My God, damn sporting of you to save my life like that.'

Toro mute and lightly lacerated. His massive waddling walk as he follows Erconwald descending from the battlements. Out the yard gates beneath the archway and down the bramble path. Beyond somewhere to calm pastures. Charnel Castle inhabitants chewing the last of lunch watching after this magic display. Nails snatched from death by the hole making horns. Lady Macfugger might have become a widow. Playful and free.

> For
> Yours truly
> To ponder
> What one could do

Up yonder
In figments fiendish
And much more
Foolish
With glee

10

Southwestwards from the octagonal room I watched on clear days the distant dark cycling dot of the postman approaching on the road. In sight on the hills, out of sight down dales. Spring bringing faint green to the wind stunted hawthorne trees. Sit over my tray of breakfast of coffee brewed from beans left each morning by the train at the crossroads. Dispatched with six loaves of bread and succulent barmbracks from an oriental café back in the capital. And charged by Percival to my staggering account.

Midmorning's activity stirred in the castle corridors with inhabitants groping in search of cigarettes. Franz raged back and forth across the great hall for two hours when Charlene threw away his jam jar of butts carefully collected from ash trays and grates from which he rolled new cigarettes of narcotic richness. Puffed while Erconwald awaited shipment of their usual asiatic herb. Charlene standing laughing as she told me the tale.

'Sir he has the holy pictures gone and charts tacked up with writings and scribblings all over the walls. Gauges you wouldn't know what they were to measure and ould lumps of rocks and hammers. When I found the jars of fag ends for decency's sake I got rid of them. They had a smell that would knock you over. He's in bed there of a morning and you couldn't see him for the smoke with big maps propped up on his knees. I had to tell him what he could do with himself when he suggested a familiarity.'

Mrs L K L's concussion received fainting upon the ramparts gave her attacks of nightmare. During one of which she recovered sufficiently to cover her husband's arse with weals from a malacca cane. But now lain for weeks abed corresponding with her solicitors. Who in turn addressed me concerning the spiritual disfigurement and moral maim resulting from her fall. Each morning waiting through the desperation. The slow approach of letters heading across the countryside. Agony creeping up the bowel. Just as spring is bringing breezes balmy.

2 Culpability Buildings,
Inns of Tort

Charnel Castle

Dear sir,

We are in receipt of your attempt to sidetrack the issue of the injury done to our client by libelling our client's husband with the groundless accusation of 'attempting murder by the unlawful detonation of an explosive substance'. It is perfectly clear to us that the force of such a blast described would kill any witnesses present, therefore any such event if it did take place would be by its very nature without corroboration.

We are aware of course that there are certain mitigations in the matter of damages and that you have provided food and lodging to our client and her husband. The sum asked in settlement is in our view trifling when one considers the cultural defacement of our client's personality occasioned by her concussion. She can no longer recall paintings seen at some expense in the great museums.

We regret to be informed that poisonous reptiles are kept at Charnel Castle and we would be obliged to hear at the earliest what measures are in force to protect our client. And there is further the serious matter of an attack by one of your guests in which lumps of scalp and hair were removed from our client's head like divots from a golf course. We await your reply to these matters.

Yours faithfully
Bottomless Diddle
Blameworthy and Dawn

And one noontime a blue and red blanket over my lap and legs facing the fire as I nibbled cold lobster caught by Percival and sat uneasily over a castle account book, when he handed me a brown envelope from which I took a piece of wrapping paper scrawled with black crayon.

From
An abode
Of decency
In the district

Dear sir or Occupier of the Castle,

You are wondering why I write. Recently the goings on were much more than just filthy habits of idolators giving way to base motives of which the authorities (and medical officer of the County Council) would like to be informed. Did you know that you are being watched. Miss Ovary and that harlot Charlene have been long known whorers in the district having lifted aside clothing normally protecting morality and allowed disgusting favours to be indulged to the hilt by every impudent young cur in the district wandering crazed by impure desires. Do not think that it will be long before this wicked trespass on the path of virtue is brought to the attention of solicitors and others in the know who have the power.

Well wisher In The Name Of Holy Purity

P.S. And while the gentleman is at large who would defeat clean living by his carnal knowledge of barnyard fowl no chicken will roost in peace.

'Now sir I wouldn't want to be impertinent but there's alarm all over your face.'

'This letter Percival.'

'Let us have a scrutiny. Ah now. What's this. It do be a touch of the poison pen. There's one writing in the area. Wellwisher is it. In the name of the Holy Purity is it. Take no notice sir. Miss Ovary and Charlene are ladies of the highest credentials. But now there is a lout loose beyond of the name of Padrick, to whom I'd say the P.S. refers. Saw him crouched not a minute ago under the willows near the cloisters there by the stream. In between the weeds he is waiting to take a slice off you with a hook. Carve up his granny by moonlight he would. Kick a beast to death. Or laugh shoving a crowbar in the eye of a wren. He keeps in trim smashing butterflies with a sledge. Didn't he drive a team of horses up on an altar of a church smashing every type and shape of ecclesiastical object in sight. Ah but God sir he's afraid of dogs. Sure you get one ankle high that would make him run for his life. And he's an awful man for the women. Now sir I wouldn't mention this save for the airing of it in the letter from the wellwisher. But it's a fact that if he can't have a ewe or a heifer he'll have at a chicken. Sure everyone knows it for miles around. Now if you've a second I could show him to you in the flesh.'

Down through stairwells and out a back passage to the cloisters. Percival leading a way through clumps of brambles and over black watery earth sprouting dock and nettles. That's Clarence's head bobbing high up along the stone wall. And dancing from tree to tree through the orchard. A misty rain falling. Glistening moistures on leaves and grass. Puffy light clouds cruising in from sea.

'We should be in luck sir. If Padrick's about Clarence is never far away. Adding I'd say first hand to his sexual knowledge.'

Percival staying Clementine on the arm. A little incline and grassy mound surrounded by hawthorne, brambles and fuchsia. The sound of water. The boulder strewn brook. Percival crouching low beckoning. Pointing with a finger. A man big eared and dark haired leaning against a birch tree. Bushy brows over small glittering dark eyes. Sound of a female voice. Percival touching my arm.

'Ah God sir I never thought I'd live to see this day. That's Imelda. Poor unfortunate innocence. Having to do with the scurrilous likes of that impudence. Trespassing right into the castle. Be extra quiet now. Just over here we can get a good look without being seen or there'd be wild ructions and I'd be forced to give your man there a taste of me shod foot.'

Imelda seated on a rock. Hob nailed boots peeking from under a long brown skirt. Percival and Clementine crouched hushed. Padrick legs crossed a long stalk of grass curving down from his smiling mouth. Battered hat pushed back on his head. A crescent of whiteness below his black hair above a weather tanned face. Imelda wrapped in a black shawl, teeth flashing as she giggled. Padrick pursing lips and frowning.

'Ah now Imelda sure you know what a revelation is.'

147

'I do.'

'And is it now you think I can't give you one.'

'That's what I think. Sure that's God's business.'

'Ah then suppose now instead of a revelation we call it a bit of hocus pocus.'

'All tall talk.'

'I will make an unveiling to you Imelda that you've never seen the likes of before. I have a tool upon me as can do tricks.'

'Sure I know them fake tricks you see at the fair.'

'Ah but it is a tool put upon me by the holy ghost.'

'Sure what have the likes of you Padrick got to show me that the holy ghost wouldn't show me if I asked in me prayers.'

'Praying would get you no where now I'm telling you to see the likes of this thing on me as can change it's size.'

'Go on.'

''Tis true enough.'

'More of your tall stories while the damp's coming up through me from this rock.'

'Wait till I show you now. Look away out there at the willow.'

Imelda turning her head away. Her reddened cheeks and long black hair. Padrick unbuttoning his trousers. Putting in a big hand and taking out a long rigid white penis. A squawk of rooks flying low overhead and chatter of a pheasant away in the bush. Percival adjusting his monocle and staying Clementine on the arm.

Imelda frowning. Staring back at Padrick hands on hips his tool twitching up and down. Sudden sunlight flashing pale across the grass.

'What's that thing atall coming out of you there.'

'This is the thing Imelda as can do tricks and change its size.'

'Is it.'

'It is.'

'I am waiting then.'

'It has got big now like this from being very small.'

'You could tell me next now if I'd listen that you could grow the likes of that out of your ears.'

'I haven't shown it to you soon enough.'

'You're showing it to me now, isn't that soon enough and where now are you changing the size. It looks the same size to me for the last minute.'

'Put your hand there to it now for awhile and then it will change its size.'

'Why would I put my hand to it, weren't you changing its size yourself.'

'Have you ever seen one of these before me Imelda.'

'I have not.'

'Then it is news to you.'

'Sure it's not news to me at all. What news would it be if I saw a pole sticking out of a hay cock.'

'I can make it spit.'

'Can you now. And maybe you can make it say the rosary too. '

'Mind now don't mention religion.'

'Where's its tricks. I've got to be back inside the kitchen or they'll wonder where I'm gone.'

'Ah now Imelda come here. Give it a pet. Coax it along and it will be spitting a white salty milk.'

'What would I be wanting to pet it for. Can't you make it spit. Wasn't it you who said it could do tricks and me watching. It's the same size now as it was when it was first staring at me.'

'Sure as God will strike me dead if you give it a little pull like as you would a cow's teat and there will come milk out of it. '

'Next you will ask me to pull the handle of a shovel to get gold.'

'Here now come closer. A bit more. So's you can see the little shawl it's got. Pulled over its head like a glove. Pull the shawl back like so and there now it is with its little pink head smooth as an eyeball. I could put it into you.'

'Where would you be putting it into me. What kind of talk is that. Where would I have a thing like that put into me.'

'Ah Imelda you have seven holes on you.'

'And haven't you got eight then yourself counting the one the holy ghost made in the top of your head to take your brains out.'

'Put your hand to it. '

'Why should I now. Is that all the trick you can show me.'

Percival holding his finger across his lips for silence. Pulling Clementine back down as he tries to stand up. Moisture drops dripping from leaves and branches. Padrick with thumbs stuck under armpits swaggering forward tool wagging. A donkey braying. Across barren bog lands and muddy ditches. Imelda reaching out giggling touching the tip end of Padrick's tool.

'It's rubber is it.'

'The nature is confidential till you give this magician a chance and grab holt with a wrap around of your fingers there.'

'It has veins.'

'Hair at the roots as well. Take a good solid grip of it there now.'

'How did you get that on you like the feel of warm flesh and blood.'

'It would fool you wouldn't it.'

'Next you'll be asking me to put a bit of salt on it and have it for me dinner.'

'It'd do you no harm nicely nestled now between a couple of spuds. Would you eat it with salt Imelda. Would you be hungry enough to do that now. It's a long time till tea. Go on there now. That's your man. Pull away now.'

'It's a funny enough yoke all right. You're not codding me now, will it spit.'

'Will it spit. Ah God. Will it spit. The faster you pull there now the faster it will spit.'

'Why don't you pull.'

'It wouldn't be the same as a fair hand such as you've got nicely at it. Leaving me free to give full heed to the trick. Ah now. God. Pull. There. Pull. The trick is coming. Ah God Imelda don't let go.'

'It's spitting. Messy white stuff.'

'Keep holt.'

'I will not. Sure it smells of something from down there by the sea.'

'O bejabbers. Bejabbers.'

'What's wrong with you going on like you were fainting in a fit.'

'Ah God Imelda to do a trick like that takes a lot of strength. I'm dizzy with it. Same as a man leaving you tottering after giving you a blow of a hammer in the back of the kneecaps.'

'I think you're a mental case. I've got some of it on me shawl.'

'You'll not breathe a word of the trick to a living soul now will you Imelda.'

'Sure if it was so special wouldn't the likes of a layabout like you be showing off in a circus for prize money.'

'Now if I tell you the trick was revealed to me by the holy ghost appearing from right there up out of the mound. He said by God keep it to yourself Padrick. He was a fine build of a feller. In a vision of disturbing beauty.'

'That was no vision I was pulling and it was no holy water coming out of it either.'

'O God you'll have me ruined. Ruined.'

'Will you stop dancing now like you were barefoot in purgatory. What's wrong with you. And the size of your trick has shrunk.'

'Keep your eyes off that.'

'Only a minute ago you were panting telling me to pull on it. '

'What's that laughing.'

'It's not me I can assure you.'

'I heard something. Over there beyond in the orchard.'

'It'd be some old beast having a cough from worms.'

'That's laughter now. That I'm hearing. By God I'll fix that.'

Padrick buttoning and hitching up trousers. Tying tight the twine around his coat. Heading out crashing through the briars and up over the wall. The shadow of Clarence loping like a kangaroo beyond the trees. And speedily upwards into the grey veils of mist hanging on the mountainside. Pursued by Padrick roaring.

'I'll break every last bone in your body youse.'

Two figures hurtling away feet throbbing on the rabbit clipped grass. Imelda spitting on her shawl and wiping the white stain with her knuckles. A grey blue sad beaked heron flaps up into the sky. Flying somewhere to spear up more fish. Away from the roars of this recent holy ghost.

Amuck
 Now in the heathers
Footpoundals ablast
Wagging
His whopper
Softly
At last

11

Moist balmy sea winds and stray sunshine. Pastures exploding green and the brown dark mountain turning blue. Cobwebs wiped from the library windows. Mushrooms removed from desk drawers. Newly sharpened pencils in an old caviar jar. And often one referred to the pair of terrestrial and celestial globes standing gleamingly polished between the windows. To find out where in god's name I am.

Behind these locked library doors letters drafted to stave off evil demands for money. An inventory made of candelabra, fancy cushions, figurines, enamelled glass sweetmeat jars, copper cooking moulds, crystal goblets and silver tureens. And a gentleman called. Shown in by Percival. Kept folding his hands across his waistcoat and rocking gently on his heels.

'Naturally we won't know their value until we've had much of this examined by experts. But of course should you like to sell straight off unburdening yourself as it were of unwanted gewgaws and leaving the risk to us, we'd present to you a round figure.'

Percival following us through the state rooms past the worm eaten Sheraton, Chippendale and fading tattered tapestries. Under the crystal chandeliers of anterooms, over the thread worn carpets, cabinets, bureaus and stools. Past carved chimney pieces, panelling and galleries hung with paintings. A clock chimes mid morning another late afternoon.

'Of course it is very difficult to separate the better imitations from the outright fakes. But again if you'd rather get shut of the stuff, in a heap so to speak, and leave the risk to us, we would quote you a round sum.'

The gentleman sour and superior appraising the armour, crossbows, spears and shields in the great hall and raising his eyebrows over Franz's excavation out of which a most sulphurous smell arose. He put his notes carefully in an inside pocket and regarding my tennis sneakers with some disdain, lifted his chin and lofted out the vowels.

'Of course you know were you titled that would help considerably.'

Erconwald feeding frogs to the mambas saw us passing through to the servants' hall and beyond to the stables and harness room to examine brass and leathers once resplendent on the now demolished state coach mouldering in the courtyard. He came knocking on my locked door after the gentleman's departure. Moisture welling in the eyes.

'Ah good person. My word is humble but I hope no less listened to for that. I could not help but overhear a discussion concerning the sale of some of the treasures adorning this ancient historic residence.'

'I'm cleaned out financially Erconwald. And I'm up to my skull top in debt. And I've got to sell.'

'Noble kind sir, debt is merely a token of another's early esteem bestowed upon the promise of later riches which I know deservingly will come your way. I exhort you not to sell.'

'Erconwald. There is a constant cascade of whole meal bread, barmbrack, bacon, ham, eggs and mineral waters into this castle which as soon as it arrives is descended upon by the inmates with an agility which one can only describe as disheartening. The staff are going out of their minds finding hiding places. Half way up to my room Charlene left my breakfast tray in the corridor to investigate a strange noise and a minute later when she got back it was gone.'

Erconwald slowly bowing his head. Knitting hands in front of him. Eyes cast down on sandals. Sported with bright orange socks. Which. Good Lord. Are mine.

'Words you speak, good person, are both true and sad.'

'And I see, soon as you have the tyres back on your car Franz has taken out the engine and dismantled the entire thing all over the grass out there.'

'He is restoring some missing horsepower. And please, perhaps while that is being done might you not forsake your timidity regarding our enquiries relative to your gonadal uniqueness. Had these been blown from your good person by the dining hall blast or sent up into the peritoneum by your bull Toro we should have been forever deprived of a marvel of nature.'

And in the gloom of that late afternoon Erconwald further suggested that I avail myself of the Baron who would be glad to undertake social duties if allowed to sit and read in the library. Where Percival at intervals of the day came bearing news of the latest in the castle. And to see if there was still an outside world I sent him off to the town for a paper. Which arrived back with a month old outside sheet covering pages inside of two years ago.

'Sure what does it matter sir, news is news no matter the date it comes. But up to the minute now, there's a man waiting to see you. Won't disclose his business, he says it's urgent and confidential. Shall I show him in sir.'

A curly headed man in a raincoat, hair parted down the middle. Blue eyed under a great broad expanse of brow. A stub of cigarette smoking from a long sleeve at his side. Moving smoothly across the floor and glancing back over his shoulder at Percival and at the Baron seated studying moves at the chess table. Nervously putting forth his hand as I reach to shake his soft one. A yellow sweater and grey jacket under his open coat, a tie just peeking from a rumpled white collar.

'Are we alone, Mr Clementine.'

'Yes. The Baron is my aide de camp.'

'I understand. I am commandant Macdurex of the fourth tank division Western Army. I am here in furtherance of my orders issued by the supreme command of which you were notified in my letter. I am also in receipt of your letter in reply to mine. This is an institution of some sort.'

'Won't you sit down.'

'I will thank you.'

'Can I offer you something to drink.'

'I would thank you but I'm on official business.'

'Would you mind if I had a drink.'

'Lower away. Quite a place you've got here.'

'Yes it is.'

'Must take a lot of looking after.'

'Yes it does.'

'Now I am bound to inform you that we have kept a precautionary watch on this premises and the intelligence report which has come to hand is not conclusive. I would appreciate your help. Are you a doctor.'

'No.'

'I take it there is a residential staff to look after the patients.'

'No.'

Adjusting his monocle, the Baron looking up from his chess game. The bell of the courtyard clock gonging out eight o'clock. The commandant looking at his watch and taking a last puff from his stump of cigarette.

'Is there not some risk seeing as you've had a blast here already.'

'There are three scientists but not medically qualified. The occupants are guests.'

'Voluntarily committed are they.'

'I wouldn't quite put it that way but certainly none of them have shown any signs of voluntarily leaving.'

'Is that so. Most of your asylums, around this neck of the woods anyway, have a devil of a time to keep the inmates in. But if as you say they are content here, that's all that matters. A little violence is to be expected. My troops could lend a hand.'

'Commandant, I should be quite pleased if your troops drove the whole bunch of them right out.'

The monocle dropping from the Baron's eye. Scars down his cheeks in the light. Courtyard clock now gonging three. Commandant Macdurex again regarding his wrist watch. Percival said that when he had the clock fixed it would be grand to have a time of day ready at your finger tips.

'Mr Clementine I'm sure your patience must be tried

now and again but I could not take the responsibility of putting violent lunatics loose on the roads. Keeping them subdued inside the premises is one thing but chasing them every which way out over the countryside is another. One was seen running loose from here a while back hurdling stone walls chased by another going through the walls. Now that kind of antic would occupy a platoon of troops. But I am quite prepared to station men to quell uprising and the like.'

'I would like that Commandant. How long will your troops be staying.'

'Just the time it takes to rout out a foreigner over the hills there. A ferocious piece of work he is too. For security reasons I can't discuss it at the moment. But I'll have a drink now official business is done.'

The Baron pouring glass fulls from a decanter of malt. The wheaty aroma cutting through the damp smells. The commandant sitting back in his chair looking up at the high windows, across the book cases and panelled walls.

'I'd say this would be an old place.'

'Yes.'

'And cold in the winter.'

'And in the springtime too.'

'Well a sup of this keeps down the chill. Nice to have books around. In my spare time I am a bit of a poet.'

'Ah.'

'Make an odd verse out of my everyday experience as you might say.'

'I'd like to read one and I'm sure the Baron would too.'

'Well while I'm stationed in this area and going into the town of a Saturday night the verse I have here on this little bit of envelope came to mind. It is called closing time.'

The commandant handing over an envelope. On one side an address, Colonel Sean Macdurex, GHQ, The Bivouac, The Crossroads and on the other a poem scrawled in a small tight hand.

> The street
> Was empty
> The street was sad
> And then by God
> The pubs shut
> And the street was mad

'That's very nice.'

'It was instant inspiration. I was changing pubs at the time. After the unholy upheaval out on the road with fists and boots flying I went into the hotel to get a little bit of peace among some decent law abiding foreign visitors having a game of bridge. I wasn't a minute there before this ignorant lout with a pair of ears on him big enough he could flap and fly comes in. He charges straight across the lounge. Picks up the bridge table and slams it upside down on the floor just as your woman is bidding two no trumps. I thought to myself what kind of tales are those poor unfortunate travellers going to take with them back to their homelands. It was three good blows on the back of his spine with a piano stool before he was subdued. Meanwhile he'd pulled every picture down off the wall, put out every window with his fist and flung these respectable people's drinks in their faces. Padrick he was called. Never a word did he say. This verse here was appropriately composed upon that occasion.'

> When insult
> Is not added
> To injury
> While the night's not sane
> By God then
> Expect from your man
> More maim

Commandant Macdurex downed two large whiskies and suddenly stood up, clicking rubber heels with a thud and smartly saluting. The Baron jumping from his chair to attention and bowing. In the middle of this military departure my hand slipping where I was leaning on the desk.

The commandant spinning round swiftly reaching in under his coat. Towards a bulge. As I straightened up again a smile came over his lips and he gave a little nod of the head.

'Mr Clementine we will be keeping in touch.'

The Baron in cut away coat and striped trousers, black shoe tips gleaming, opening the library door. The commandant falling into step as they clicked across the great hall. The Baron on his return said the commandant had challenged him to a game of chess.

Three days of sun in a row I spent bird watching from my turret. Thrilled by nature on the wing. While Bloodmourn could he heard passing along corridors with a crutch thumping on the floor. Rumours reaching one of body contact between himself and Rose. Percival said the exprisoners were standing guard outside Mrs L K L's door, bringing in her food and bearing out her wastes. Bligh had locally collected children together and was teaching them folk songs gathered around a fire on the beach at night where they sang. He said he wanted to rehearse them to give a rendering in the chapel.

Charlene each morning stayed chatting longer and longer when she brought breakfast. Blue eyes smiling. Relating the castle backbiting, food thefts, slander and lies of the night before. Sleeves rolled back. Muscles flexing on her narrow white arms. And once as I told her to sit down she sat on the bed, her back towards me as she spoke over her shoulder. I reached out and her face flushed as I touched the little hard nobs up and down her spine. Next morning she came to sit again. And I put my hand up under her sweater and passed over each little vertebrae bumping under the smooth soft skin.

'I like you doing that. It sends shivers and tingles all over me.'

'I'm glad.'

'So am I and you know what I heard. Imelda the other day. She was bent up double in the old kitchen against the pig curing trough and I thought she would fall in dying laughing. Took me the time it would take to cook an ox to get the story out of her. Seems as she was larking about with two boys beyond telling them of a wondrous trick that a certain Padrick did do with his tool. And they said they could do the trick as well. With their own tool they said they had. Imelda goes back to Padrick and said ah so, it's no trick you've been doing with that thing you have on you for every man in the parish is able to do the same trick as yourself. And Padrick says isn't the trick easy enough to learn after someone sees you doing it and wasn't the whole countryside watching the day he did it. It wasn't till I told Imelda what it was Padrick showed her that she knew and she's still down there in the kitchen not able to stop laughing. Dropped a whole pot of potatoes peeled for tonight. Said everytime she thinks of it she's convulsed. That big blabber mouth's chased me home over the fields many a time.'

'Did he ever catch you.'

'Not on your life I'm as fast as a deer. That is not to say that I haven't had my experiences. Which maybe I'll tell you sometime. I really look forward to our chats like this in the morning. It's over stepping my place. When I'm only a servant.'

'Unpaid.'

'I'm not complaining. I won't mention names but I can tell you that a lot goes on here that would make the devil himself green with envy.'

Hold Charlene's ribs from the side pinched between my hand. Her tongue out licking over her lips. Doing a wondrous trick with my own tool. Pushing up the tray. Topple the teacup. She sits arms forward, reddened hands stilled in her lap which take up buckets of water, wash over floors, make my bed, tug the entrails from chickens. Unlucky enough to go clucking in this castle. Where one did once streaking out of the pantry passage, flying across the library and scratching up along the shelves of books. Chased by Elmer's clacking great grey hungering jaws. Charlene caught it. And said if you kill it I'll cook it. And I stood out in the yard clutching the feathery thing to my chest near the rain water barrel turning my head away as

I plunged it in. Tough to drown a chicken. It bounced up out the water squawking blue murder. Out came a laughing Charlene catching up the dripping cornered bird by the legs, plopping its head on a block and with one swipe of her cleaver taking off its head. The bird's neck spurting blood as it flapped around the cobbles. Had to keep myself from putting hands up to cover my eyes. Next morning at breakfast Charlene was brisk and busy. Till I said I was no chicken killer. And a soft grin grew across her face, lashes of her eyes flickered and I wanted to touch the blue vein on her neck. She sits there now, eyes cast down, my hand moving up under her sweater. Under there these smooth white things with hardened little tips under the matted wool.

'Mr Clementine. I want to ask you a question.'

'Yes.'

'Do you fancy me.'

'Yes.'

'You won't mind if I ask you something else personal.'

'No.'

'Do you fancy Lady Macfugger. I saw you staring at her during the bull fight. I guess she's very grand and rich. And can have anything she wants. And you've heard stories about me, haven't you.'

'I had a letter.'

'It was about me, wasn't it. The dirty filthy pigs. What did it say.'

'Just a general letter about the historic nature of the surroundings. It did mention though that livestock morals were loose in the district and the department of agriculture were investigating.'

'Before you hear any more lies I'll tell you the truth. While I was just an impressionable little lass I'd rise to the bait of any little flattery flung me way. A business man in the town had a car and gave me rides. Before I knew what was happening I'd given myself to him. To tell you the truth I was just like Imelda. Only that lecherous old bastard told me he was putting in his thermometer to get my temperature. He owned the chemist's shop and I believed him. Grey haired and precise he was. As mean as God ever made anyone. Had a little book. He'd say you've been a very good girl today your temperature was ninety eight point seven degrees. He had a pair of brown shoes with the leather soles so thin he had only to step out of his car and they were worn out. I'd hide at the end of the town in behind a wall. He'd pick me up and we'd drive with me crouching down in the back till we got here to the castle, rumoured as it was to be filled with ghosts and terrors where no one would venture. Which I suppose is true enough. My grandmother had stories aplenty to tell. We came to a bedroom just above off the great hall. After a few occasions of taking my temperature he then one evening left me. After he'd asked me to do something to him that five minutes later he said was unnatural. Stood shaking his finger at me in a bit of moonlight shining into the great hall. I was quaking there terrified. Told me to find my own way back alone to town in the dark. O God I'll never forget it. I wet myself with fright. I got lost. Listening to the rats I just must have finally fainted and they found me paralysed and my hair turning white the next afternoon. Then the dirty bastard wanted me to marry him. When I wouldn't he spread stories. That I was here in the castle giving out to a queue of farmers' sons and itinerants. The man spread filth and evil about me everywhere. And later when I was going with a nice young boy he poisoned him against me. Maybe it was as well for me the young lad died. Pneumonia suddenly came on him and he was destroyed. One evening he was passing down the road with a load of turf kneeling up in a cart and the next he was up on his next of kin's shoulders in his coffin. Not a thing left but a few ould stones on top of where he lies. All I know is if there's no heaven there's sure enough been plenty of hell. They preach to you that God is good and generous. I think he must be a scoundrel. If he accepts worship from the diseased hypocrites of that town. Not a soul here you can trust. From the moment they lay eyes on you their little brains are scheming how to get the better of you. A back turned is a back stabbed. Do you think I'm out of my mind.'

'No.'

'I do. You've got such beautiful teeth. I've lost two behind here. Not one in your head is missing. Open. God that's pure radiant gold in the middle of your back molars. You've got a mouth like a tabernacle. You'd be at risk asleep with it open. Some of them would have that precious metal out of your head and into the pawn. I don't know but that it wouldn't be a relief to be ugly and know that the world will never like you anyway. With teeth or without. Don't look at my hands. I've got the fingernails bit down to me elbows. I'd better be on my way about me chores or I'll get fired.'

'Don't go.'

'Your man Percival will be arriving any moment. He's a one full of his authority. Thinks he has forty parlour maids and a dozen cooks when the few of us are standing down there in front of him in the kitchen of a morning. Telling us the boss wants this done the boss wants that. It's Mrs L K L who never lets up. Yanking on the servants' bell. You can hear the wires twinging in the walls. Propped up on the pillows as if she owned the place. She says in that high toned way of hers, I say you're late with my tea. Then she wants me to stay and pour it out for her in the cup. I said you're no cripple. She said how dare you. I hope you don't mind but I told her she was an interloper, I wouldn't know what that was but it sounded good. Some of the people you have staying here would bleed you white. I guess I better keep my place and keep my trap shut. I just don't think it's right that a kind and generous person like yourself should be put upon.'

Percival rapping with his door key. Charlene leaping up off the bed. Quickly pulling down her sweater which I slowly pulled up. She sails a cloth back and forth across the marble wash stand. And clanks a shovel full of light brown turf ash in a bucket. She backs away as Percival enters. Three ledgers stacked in the crook of his arm.

'Good morning your worship. I trust you slept well.'

'Yes thank you Percival.'

'There have been I am sorry to report sir, shocking

depredations in the wine cellars. A person or persons unknown have entered without authority and removed quantities of spirits. I have my suspicions who it was. I've taken precautions to stop further ravages. Elmer has downed two chickens. He was with me out in the yard looking mild as you please when four of them struts by. I turn my back to answer a call of nature and two are left. It would be as well if we put them wild ones remaining in a coop.'

'But good news too sir. Tim is turning a few sods up there in the old kitchen garden sowing spuds and cabbages. He's come across the old rhubarb beds, gooseberry and raspberry bushes. In no time crops will be pouring out into the markets.'

'Percival I don't think I can hold out that long.'

'Sir aren't you sitting on a mountain of priceless personal chattels, sure in the new world over there they go wild over the genuine worm holes.'

'The worm holes may be authentic but we've been told the rest is imitation and fake.'

'Ah now I know a thing or two meself about fine art. Sure your man missed the date of the mahogany davenport by twenty five years. It's Mr Erconwald who I'd say knows a thing or two. Didn't he tell me that the figurines in the Etruscan room alone would keep you supplied with cars and yachts for a lifetime. The broken bits glued here and there on them, the chips smoothed over and no one would be the wiser.'

'Keep your eye on them anyway won't you Percival.'

'My eye, haven't I got my foot knee and chin on them. Only the place is rumoured full of ghosts and mad dogs there wouldn't be a thing left in it. Porcelain puts into a man such a thirst for destruction he'd cuff his own mother out of the way so he could break it into smithereens. And if he can get his hands on any living thing of beauty he will destroy it or kill himself trying. There was a little cherry tree miraculously up there in a bit of shelter, didn't one of your bog men come along when it had blossoms and rip it from the ground. He flings it away and wipes his hands and says that's that. I said to him that's what. He says that's that, that's what what is, it's that's that. Now what could I say to that but that your man was a pig. It's like life and breath to them to roar and ravage over the countryside, anything to get their hands on a sapling and tear it roots and all from the earth. Now to commissary matters. I thought with the bread we'd be all right keeping on with the fourteen loaves a day. Only five pounds of butter went yesterday. But it's the bacon and eggs. Eighty two of your good sized hen's eggs in the twenty four hours with nearly ten pounds of bacon. Your man above in the shop is lunatic trying to keep up the supply.'

'O God.'

'Now sir, don't worry. We're ready and able to carry on. In your ladyship's day they'd go through three hundred eggs and twenty pounds of butter a day and three quarters of it would be left to be gobbled up by the pigs at night. And there's a suggestion now. Pigs. There's money in them. And a beast or two out there on the grass would not hurt you either.'

'How much land have we Percival.'

'Well now that might be a little difficult to figure straight off. With an exact figure that is. But you'd have a fair bit now on that mountain. I'd not be far amiss to say there'd be seven hundred acres. The demesne would have another nearly three hundred. There'd be fifty or sixty more down to the beach. And out that way on the headland you could reckon a hundred and seventy.'

'If we tried farming.'

'By God then you'd be right. Sure we've got Toro out there who'd have any heifer you'd bring near him in calf in no time. Sheep would be your man for the mountain. In springtime we'd have the lambs leaping and kicking across the meadows.'

'All right Percival, we'll look into it.'

'Sir let me say I'm glad you said that.'

Days floating by while Bloodmourn played the Baron in chess. And I waited to play the winner. Paging through great leather tomes, standing by the table throughout the afternoons. The Baron shaking his cuffs down before he delicately lifted and placed a piece. Bloodmourn first leaning over the board then straightening and rising in his seat. Pouncing when he could capture. Rapidly sweeping up the Baron's bishop or knight. To get from the Baron three rare slowly made words.

'Ah is dat so.'

Putlog and Erconwald arriving in the library to frown, murmur and shake their heads. Bloodmourn and the Baron fighting bitterly to three consecutive draws. Franz entering, a miner's lamp attached to his head, greasy clay sods from his boots wiped on the rug recently made presentable by Charlene. Smoke rising from cigars and cigarettes. The fourth match brooding on through the night. Percival opening the shutters next morning as the two seated figures still sat heads in hands.

Mrs L K L came out of hibernation. Carried by the three prisoners and Lead Kindly Light in a sedan chair unearthed from somewhere. The group approaching one down the hall with slow measured steps. I nipped smartly into the nearest room. Ear held to the door till it went by. One of her solicitor's recent letters had a change of tone. Suggesting that perhaps a solution could be reached should a meeting be convened at the site of the various ugsome complaints.

And one casually calm night Bligh came up the stony little pathway from the beach leading his chorus of voices each carrying a candle. Making a glittering winding snake slowly crawling across the hillside in the dark. High on the ramparts, castle inmates waiting. A soft still evening of sparkling stars. Through the gates, front door and across the great hall they came. Up the grand staircase and along the corridor to the chapel. Percival nudging my elbow.

'Sir the Charnel has never seen the likes of this before I can tell you.'

I sat left of the aisle. Erconwald and Franz first row on the right. Bloodmourn and the Baron sitting together. Taking time out from the library where they sat locked in their sixteenth game. After fifteen draws. The Macfuggers came. Nails bright eyed at the sight of three young blue eyed big bosomed singing sisters. Chaperoned by a big bosomed blue eyed mother. A cheerful gathering meek and mild.

Rose heard above the choruses roaring her head off. Percival with four of the staff kneeling at the rail in the loft where Putlog sweats over the keys and foot pedals of the organ. Tim keeping candles lit. Mrs L K L blocking the aisle with exprisoners and sedan chair behind which stood Lead Kindly Light in full armour. And the little voices raised in song.

> Down in the valley
> Up in the sky
> Our voices singing
> The armies marching by

At this verse Clementine turning to look behind. Might be the signal for the insurgents. Catch Macfugger red haired and handed. Standing much too close to the big bosomed mother. And Charlene by the stone font at the chapel doorway, a black lace mantle on her hair. Concave jowls of these children singing. Out through teeth missing here and there. Eyes wide and roving. Staring at the strange shrouded figure in the sedan chair. That little boy's folded hands trembling. All their faces scrubbed red cheeked and clean. My brown skinned nurse April who said you are cured. See her face smiling up against the altar there. Death could come now. In the middle of this recital. Unnoticed. Take me to lay under sods beyond the granite walls. Out on the headlands. Waves white along the coast. The wild loneliness. And a moist wind wetting the soul.

After the singing the gladdened assemblage descending to the first state room off the great hall set for tea. Cakes and sandwiches spread on a table. Honeycombs and damson jam. Bloodmourn and the Baron rubbing their eyes. Whiskey poured. Bligh smiling to his congratulations. Tightly entwining his hands and nodding his head.

'It was very impressive.'

'Thank you Mr Clementine, I had a lot of work to do on them. I'm glad it showed results.'

'Yes indeed.'

'Now I wonder is there a little favour I could ask of you. I promised the kids one of these days a bit of an outing. There's a row boat down there in the boat house. Could I borrow it to take the kids out on a row one day if it's fine.'

'Certainly. If it's seaworthy most certainly.'

'Thanks a lot. I'm a brewer by trade. I'm sorry now I haven't had much time to talk to you. You feel kind of awkward in a stranger's house. More than once I thought of leaving. But could never find you to say goodbye. With so many guests on your hands I thought it was best I keep well out of the way. I'd like to make amends for not being able to handle that bull. I'd always been told I had the strength to throw one.'

Lead Kindly Light clanking up in his armour. Standing between Bligh and Clementine as he pops sunflower seeds in the opening of his helmet now sporting purple plumes.

'I am a seed eater. Abstainer from red meat. And Mr Clementine you awaken in me deep pangs of sympathy that you have around you so many ruffian flesh eaters. The onion gives one a long life free from heart congestion. Reducing eye wobbling, staggers and diarrhoea. The garlic clove benefits bowel movement, aids penoid erection, ball resiliency and eye whiteness. I am encouraged that since the blast, scurrility, blaspheming and fornication have noticeably abated. I clank here I clank there, I clank everywhere. I would like to clank through the Prado.'

'Ah now L K L Mr Clementine here doesn't want to listen to that kind of talk. Having heard an evening of singing from innocent young voices can't we now hear something uplifting.'

Long silence in the armour. Mrs L K L taking titbits in her portable enclosure. Rose the opposite end of the room smiling worshipfully at Bloodmourn. Good lord it could lead to another blast. With whipped cream splattered from floor to ceiling. Bligh nervously enfolding his hands.

Sweat on his upper lip. L K L's armoured hand rising, pointing at Bligh.

'I know your kind, like Erconwald you dream of fucking Rose over the flying kilometre. I could for your delectation measure the true distance with my calipers so you'd know to a millimetre when you'd had enough. But I won't. Because you are bogus. An uncultured maker of beer.'

'That's a lousy thing to say L K L. That's really lousy.'

'I am firbolg.'

'You're a little fucking trouble maker that's what you are.'

'Down with you Bligh into the monk's passage. I challenge you to the ball tug of the firbolg. And the worsened shall be flung from the tunnel into the sea.'

'Don't make me laugh I could bend you up into a Christmas decoration and sell you by the gross.'

'Bligh, big idolator.'

'I'm a fucking sight more religious than you and your wife will ever be selling your piss filled relics back in town to tourists. O Jesus forgive me the language Mr Clementine. But the likes of him there makes me see red.'

'I challenge you to meet me in the monk's passage you big cunt.'

'By God. That the ears of the little lovely innocents should have to hear the likes of that. Now everybody knows I warned him. Warned him good and proper.'

The big bosomed blue eyed mother teacup and saucer in hand smiling bravely through the use of the language vile. Unfit for youth or ladies. Percival pouring madeira. Oscar stuffing cake in his mouth and swilling back bottle dregs just inside the door of the next room. Charlene and Imelda taking trays between the guests. Lady Macfugger tapping ash from her cigarette as she watches the proceedings open mouthed. Asked me if she could take a tour through the castle. To see the heraldic glass and plaster work. And maybe the rumoured Meissen piss pot adorned with a daisy chain of threesomed testicles.

Lead Kindly Light the Gladiator clanking from the state room out into the great hall followed by Bligh pressing a piece of damson covered barmbrack between his lips and draining a glass of madeira. The two figures pausing by the excavation. Bligh blessing himself hands moving swiftly in the sign of a cross. L K L raising an accusing arm. The voice from the helmet.

'Jump down into that you fat eegit.'

'You jump.'

'Blessing yourself thinking religion will help you now. Are you ready for the pain. You big tub of ugliness.'

'Say what you like about me but leave religion out of it. And I'm warning you by God don't you mention the blessed virgin.'

'The blessed virgin.'

'You did it. You did it. Just do it once more and that will be the end of you.'

'The blessed virgin.'

'You did it again. I'm warning you. I love her. She is to me of the most purest gold.'

'Would you kiss her arse.'

'Blasphemy. Pure deliberate blasphemy. God above will strike. With a lightning that will curl your toe nails to a crisp.'

'You big buffoon. Can't you see I'm enclosed in armour. The bolt will pass harmlessly down around me into the tiles of the hall and further into the molten bowels of the earth where the uncouth likes of you should be undergoing fission.'

'I'll kill you. Even though we are here in the home of a respectable man. I'll kill you. You and your wife conducting disgraceful jubilee gatherings back in town with lascivious grass skirt dancing. Dear God above be merciful to this wretched person here before us. Were I of the church militant you'd be getting measured for your coffin right now. But I am of the church mystic.'

'You'll be of the church crippled.'

'Right then. You won't be satisfied till I knot your bloody little limbs around your neck.'

Nails Macfugger's arm tight about the azure eyed ample bosomed woman laughing from her big blushing face.

Imelda's passing eyes on one's flies. I'm desperate to do a trick with my tool. A nice big erection loose in the castle would lend itself well to the floral grandeur. Palm trees sixty feet high in the great hall. Where people of taste and refinement could find spiritual refreshment. Instead of the generous serving up of multiple contusions that were rumoured going on giving members of the medical profession heart attacks in their tracks.

Erconwald holding up a hand at the doorway under the stair. Staying those who were following Bligh and L K L descending to the monk's tunnel to have it out.

'Ah good people. Wait. One regrets that the nature of the contest is not suitable for the eyes and ears of mixed company. But those of you who are sticklers for fair play be assured that the Gaelic struggle to be engaged in below shall abide by the custom of the firbolg.'

Lady Gail Allouise Trudy Magfugger raising her glass. Swaying slightly in a long black clinging garment. Her hair swept in a bun at the back of her head. Three strands of pearls about her slender neck. Charlene narrow eyed, glowering. Nails Macfugger tap dancing the chaperoning mother in circles around the great hall. One more gathering slowly getting out of hand. Drifting towards turmoil. On a lubricant of madeira.

Down in the tunnel. Candles glowing in storm lanterns. Franz dismantling the lower parts of L K L's armour. Body odour behold. Putlog behind Bligh with his trousers down. Legs bulging with immense muscles and veins. A small white arrow down the side of his socks. Erconwald whispering.

'Now good person be not alarmed. Great kings and chiefs have fought thus before. Each partakes of a grip upon the other's gonads. A signal is given of two slate stones clapped together. And the adversaries twist. Slowly inducing pain. A match of any other kind would be unequal due to Bligh's great strength. The vanquished is he who can stand the torment no longer. Do take two of these wax ear plugs. The screaming will be otherwise unforgettable.'

The tunnel ceiling dripping moisture from matted

corrugations. Erconwald said the vaulting was made squeezing in the propped up stones with a mixture of mortar, bulls blood and hair. Growing stronger with the years. A grey canopy for the light shining on the greasy cobbles. I could have settled in a small apartment. With a view out over the lake. Clocked in every five p.m. for cocktails and piano music. To just say hi to folks hanging around the hotel bar. What kind of a day did you have. I'm having a night of the firbolg thank you.

'Pray good person. Watch. The buttocks of the opponents join and each reaches backwards between his legs to grasp his hold. They are ready. I give the signal. The seconds scrutinize for irregularities. Twisting must be anti clockwise. Yanking or fast twirling is an unfair manoeuvre. Bligh fights in honour of the Madonna of the Spud. Ah the screaming has commenced.'

'Eak. I'll twist your balls off.'

'Ouch. I'll twist yours off.'

Bent double sweating under oxsters, scapulars trembling, the antagonists swaying on the wet stones. L K L up and down bouncing against the vast arse of Bligh. A breeze blowing. The ocean thumps. Candles flicker behind the lantern glass. Up the tunnel a shadow. Lady Macfugger. Allouise come to view the bell ringing. For men only. And hear the agonised roars of pain.

'You little bastard you've greased yours. I declare a foul.'

'You big electro magnetic despicability you'll have a cunt for sure when I'm finished.'

'I give up I give up. Foul.'

Bligh holding his trousers, tears in his eyes, led past Lady Macfugger. A sad small voice from his lips.

'You'll excuse the exposure and I'm sorry to have been of inconvenience to you madam.'

'Sweet of you to apologize but I am tight enough not to mind.'

Hair ashimmer she leans against the wall sweet of breath. Lanterns go shadowy up the stone steps. Between us darkness. Her face close. Could touch it with my hand. Touch it. Along the jaw line. It bends up under her ear. By a cold lobe. The smoothest softest of skin. Press Kiss.

'Careful you might spill my drink. But ah Mr Clementine you do amuse don't you. All quite startling. I do believe that genitalia were on display.'

> In all their
> Glory
> As well
> As a tricky
> Pair
> In all their
> Grease

12

That night. By a back stairs. Clementine holding the long fingered cold knuckled hand of Lady Trudy Macfugger. Stumbling upwards in darkness. To somewhere. A room hoped unknown to the many uninvited who might come foaming in. Dragging someone else. And them tugging others. To a jamboree of holy ecstasy. Of mouths over other mouths and over anything.

We lay on damp tattered eiderdowns. Proceedings here by smell. Like Elmer. Who went by having a doggy time tail wagging between the firbolg. Inside the door I fell over him. Lady Macfugger fell over me. He licked our faces. With a long lapping tongue. Recent events blind one to new dangers. One wet and one warm. Elmer peed on us both.

Lady Macfugger wrestling for release. From my arms around her. Made Elmer bark and growl. Never likes to be left out of the action. We were nearly having. On the wide floor boards softened with the bedcovers various.

'My God I am an animal lover Mr Clementine but really this is not on. Haven't you got that dog house trained.'

'Only in four rooms.'

'I'm wet.'

'I'm sorry.'

'I must be sponged off. Immediately.'

'Please don't go. This is the first civilized moment I've had. I'm desperate.'

'Civilized. When I've been peed on. Good lord.'

'So have I, went all over my leg.'

'Well, it's all over my lap. The wretched stink. I happen to be another man's wife.'

'You gave my hand a reassuring squeeze.'

'I most certainly did not. My grip was quite loose. I'll admit I was intrigued. Naturally one's lower feelings are aroused. By such savagery. But I can scarcely believe it. Two grown men pulling each other by their organs.'

'You said you wanted to see my balls.'

'I did not.'

'Yes you did.'

'I merely asked if you would think it awfully rude of me to ask to see them. I did not in fact ask. Good lord I can see my own husband's any time I want.'

'That's good.'

'Yes it is, isn't it. And if I did encourage you it was because I just happened to be out of humour with Jeffrey. I don't pretend to enjoy standing around while he amuses himself in front of me with a woman twenty years my senior and of quite another class. I know why he does it. He's fond of big tits and mine are quite small. We all have our ulterior motives. I perhaps was ever so slightly interested in your testicles. Simply because Jeffrey, and I wish you wouldn't call him Nails, can never stop talking about them. Does that satisfy you. What a particularly horrid awful smell your dog's pee has.'

'He can't help it. It's his big kidneys.'

'You do seem to invite awkwardnesses. For no earthly reason you accused Veronica of having the pox. When the poor woman had merely gone to your room to borrow a book.'

'She was stark naked on roller skates under a parasol.'

'What a distressingly ungallant thing to say.'

Elmer chewing something in the corner. His favourite is tortoiseshell toiletries. Hear distant outcries. Long moaning calls. Of man or beast. Or the tunnel to the sea. Percival said that when certain doors were open in the castle a wind blew. And once sent someone flying out and down into the deeps. A titbit for the great conger.

'The wool of my dress makes the smell even worse.'

'Take it off.'

'I don't think so.'

'Please.'

'Is it to get rid of the smell or are you carnally intended.'

175

'A little of each.'

'What is it about me that fascinates you.'

'It's all of you.'

'How disappointing. I'd hoped it might be something special, my eyes or lips or something. But how dreary, the whole of me.'

The ammonia smell. Paining the nostrils. A thump thump passing the door. Could be Bloodmourn on his crutch. Might ask him to help. To keep tabs on the castle. Said he has experience in accountancy. Bankrupted three companies with his book keeping. But now he knows for sure how to avoid the pitfalls. Elmer growls. Maybe at a mamba long green and motionless unseen in the dark. Ready to sink fangs. As I get a whiff of Trudy's scent pressing my nose behind her ear. Seems years ago I climbed down steps in a moist fresh early morning breeze to the ship's tender waiting in the harbour. Taking me ashore bumping on the tide. To this land. Full of grumbling hunched figures scurrying through streets. Children thronged dirty faced and barefooted in the doorways. Women huddled in shawls whispering. Great swarms of bicycles stopped by a white gloved policeman. Out of side-streets and into nowhere a female pipe and drum band paraded by. Passing away down between the dark buildings. The music gone. The world wet and grey. And me agog with wonder.

'Apropos of nothing at all. What were you just thinking about.'

'You.'

'I've got to get out of this dress. Do you mind.'

'I'd like it.'

'Naughty. But my God what will Jeffrey think. He'll wonder how I got peed on.'

'Elmer can pee that high.'

'Can he.'

'Certainly.'

'O good. Can we be found here.'

'Only if someone comes up that staircase from the kitchens. And tries forty doors.'

'Who is that dark haired girl with the blue eyes.'

'Charlene, she helps cook.'

'She doesn't know how to keep her place. Distinctly felt her giving me hostile glances. There I am bare.'

'No you're not.'

'Well nearly. It's chilly. It's as far as I'm going to go for the moment anyway. Until you say something flattering.'

'I like your voice. It's beautiful in the dark.'

'Is it.'

'Yes.'

'One gets so tired of the word beautiful. Couldn't you say my timbre makes you tremble.'

'Everything in this place does that to me.'

'Since I don't then perhaps I'd better leave.'

'Don't. Please. It's the truth. Every morning I wake the blood starts pumping into my brain and my temples begin to throb. Imagining some new disaster. Someone plummeting stepping over one of Percival's danger lines. Solicitor's letters, poison pen letters. Bills.'

'But you're awfully rich Jeffrey says.'

'I have exactly four pounds and some odd shillings.'

'How can you afford to keep this huge place with a large staff and an endless stream of guests.'

'Everything's on tick.'

'What about wages.'

'They said not to worry. They like it here.'

'Good lord. Well that's all right. Very sporting. But do be careful, you may find things missing, silver and so on. After all the smiling is over they can be a supremely tiresome people. Would you mind awfully. I can't find the entrance to your privates. Good lord how many pairs of underwear have you got on.'

'Four.'

'Why.'

'I'm cold.'

'I've got them. Are these them.'

'Yes.'

'They're quite warm. How wonderful. After two you know three are so much more interesting.'

Elmer's claws scrabbling. Somewhere behind something. Lady Gail Allouise has sharp elbows. And long fingernails. Weighing up the hidden treasure. Six and a half ounces. Nails might come blasting in any moment behind twin forty fives just as she has them balanced. Wasn't all that bad in that world back there over the seas. Maybe a tiny apartment only having a corner window over the lake. My own tropical fish bubbling in the foyer. A girl friend who comes and cooks on friday nights. Both lie in bed with big mugs of coffee on saturday morning. Each might own little doggies. Walk them together. Sit and listen to music. One's life handy sized and tidy. Hot water throbbing through pipes. Splashing warmly. Instead of this pee cooling coldly.

'A photograph of these would be marvellous for Veronica's scrapbook. You'd have a place of honour. There's genitalia page after page. You wonder who they belong to. Quite amazing to find out. Men who are otherwise quite robust with little ones. She did Jeffrey in colour. I was aghast. No one could mistake him with his red hair. Good lord one doesn't want others to imagine what one is getting from one's husband. It makes you feel good when I hold them like this. Men love comfort. So does dear Jeffrey. I quite find myself forgiving him anything. Upon our first introduction he said in quite ringing tones, heard by my aunts who make honey in the country, here's a good old cow's arse. He took no notice except to give me a pinch now and again. What excited him was my money, which he discovered I had before I did. He's so awfully frightened by poverty. Gets really quite hysterical about it, rampaging all over the house. Once fired all the grooms and game-keepers. When I hired them back he stood in the hall totally rigged out in mountain climbing equipment, a pack on his back. I said Jeffrey whatever are you doing. He was shaking his fist saying by God we'll live on the roadside as itinerants if we have to. And all because one of my maiden aunts had just left me two hundred and sixty thousand pounds instead of three hundred and ten which poor old Jeffrey had counted on. He is a dear one. I've talked quite a lot haven't I. But you know I somehow was raised that not to make conversation with someone right next to you was rude.'

A shout through the castle. Voices raised. A commotion. Sound of Erconwald. Calling out. Good person. Good person. Distress. Distress.

'Lady Macfugger do you hear what I hear.'

'I think so.'

'Someone is shouting distress.'

'Yes. What could it be.'

'The possibilities are encyclopaedic.'

'Good lord you're not going. Leaving me in a state of dishabille.'

'I've got to. Someone might have fallen in a well.'

'At least have the courtesy to embrace me before leaving.'

'Certainly.'

'O God I'm a failed woman. Hold me please. You've simply got to seduce me. Couldn't we just do it quickly. Jeffrey says I'm cold. I don't really in the least care what went on with you and Veronica. I know she caught you with another gentleman who was, to put it in my school girl Latin, in puris naturalibus.'

'I beg your pardon. He was not quite.'

'Honestly I don't mind. Jeffrey has always said that buggery with a beautiful man was quite bestirring.'

'Now wait a minute.'

'O let's not please bandy words. Take me.'

'God there's another cry, someone must be in mortal peril.'

'They'll last somehow. People always come crawling up out of wells. I'm all ready.'

'I'm not.'

'It was hard a second ago.'

'Gail. May I call you Gail.'

'I wish you would.'

'Gail in the nervous state I'm in. I don't think I could manage a quick one. Couldn't I come back when I see what's wrong.'

'And leave me here in the dark. Peed on. Chilled.'

'O God. For Christ's sake I can't stand this whole shit and caboodle any longer. God damn it. This place is driving me out of my mind.'

'What are you doing.'

'I'm breaking this damn thing standing in my way.'

'For God's sake be careful you don't strike me.'

'I've had enough.'

'You haven't had any. If I may suggest. And someone is going to hear you shouting.'

'It's my goddamn castle.'

'Well you are, aren't you. Quite the one. You're behaving just like Jeffrey. And it's most wounding. When a woman offers you her body as I have.'

'You could have been quicker.'

'That wouldn't have been nice. Please why don't you just shut up and lie down here next to me.'

'The shouts are getting louder. They must be up in the northwest turret.'

'Where are we.'

'Mid way between northwest and southwest turrets. But don't count on it.'

'I'm aquiver. It would be so much more suitable if I were fighting off your advances.'

'You would be, honestly. I swear. But you have no idea what goes on here. It's a nightmare. I want this to be a normal castle.'

'You mustn't allow things to get you down. You must turn your head and look the other way.'

'That's exactly what I do and it's always where the next disaster is.'

'Is this nice running my finger very lightly along the underside.'

'Gail it is. It really is but I've got to go. I know by the sound that it's terribly serious. Erconwald never raises his voice.'

'But it's getting hard.'

'Please Gail. I'll come back.'

'O God Mr Clementine, or Clayton or Claw, I'll never get up my nerve like this again.'

'You will.'

'I know I won't. I've led an entirely sheltered life. Do you know what it's like to be raised by a nannie with three under nannies.'

'No. Just with one nannie.'

'Well I can tell you that straight from that to a girl's school there's been little opportunity to know men.'

'I could be back in just a minute if it's nothing serious and then we could talk about this.'

'My breasts are quite good you know.'

'I'm sure they are.'

'How do you know when you haven't felt one. Give me your hand. See.'

'Gail I mean it. I really mean it that I want to come back and feel. But this could be something I'm going to be sued about. I'd only be wretched and not at my best. You wouldn't want that would you.'

'Yes. And there's something I could do. No I couldn't. No I won't. I'm glad I didn't say that.'

'Say what. What were you going to say.'

'No I won't say it. It would be just too humiliating.'

'For God's sake, come on. Tell me. They might be getting closer.'

'Well I could give you money.'

'Could you.'

'Yes.'

'How much.'

'Something quite substantial. If you are in the terrible predicament you say you're in. I would like to help you. Dear me, you are subsiding again.'

'I can't help it. The thought of money gives me a whole new landscape of images. That'll have to go away before it comes up again.'

'That's Jeffrey. That's his voice.'

'O boy.'

'We could be found.'

Clementine stiffening. Along the hair follicles. And down the spine. The voices echo. Rebounding in the courtyard. Up over the battlements. Worrying far out in the night.

Shouted on the loneliness creeping over the dark mountain. And far away along the coast.

'Gail I really think there is something wrong. And to save my own skin I've got to investigate. I'd like to come back and talk about my financial predicament with you.'

'That's all very well. But if I am giving you money. I ought to come first.'

'You will, honestly. But a little later.'

'Do you mean that.'

'Yes.'

'I feel I've failed.'

'Good heavens you're beautiful and rich.'

'You don't understand. Veronica has no money. And for seventeen years she's never had less than forty different men a year. Don't you understand. That's six hundred and eighty men. I've only had my cousin when I was six and he was seven and we didn't know what we were doing. And then Jeffrey was next. That's at best one and a half men.'

'I wish I could help. I really do, Gail. Someone saved my life once. I know what defeat feels like. Here let me wipe your eyes. You're crying.'

'I'm sorry. I have no right to trouble you with my complaints. It's most inconsiderate of me. I thought the morning you came into the Porcelain Room caught in the morning light that you had a most beautiful profile. I realized I could give myself to you. And break my vows to Jeffrey. He's quite literally trampled his own to me. I still worship him though. But he's gone up other women and I don't see why other men should not go up me.'

'I must go. Not up. But out. Each second could be vital. Someone's steps sound very military. Could be Jeffrey.'

'O God I'll wait. What else can I do.'

'Everything's going to be all right.'

'Kiss me. Please.'

Tiptoeing into the hall. A carpet out here underfoot. Stay centre away from the creeping weakness along the walls. Shouts rise up the stairwells. Just stop and take a peek from this room. Where there must be a window. Or a slit for spears and arrows. A lantern down below on the gravel entrance. Shadows of folk. Cold hand encircles the heart. Numb chill of disaster.

Clementine running the length of the corridor. Opening a door and feeling his way down a tightly curving stone stair. Past three floors. Try this door and make way in the direction of the chapel. Nip in for some agreement with God. And then down by the grand staircase. Good lord, what's this. In the vague moonlight. It's vast. Biggest bloody room in the castle. Three chandeliers, a painted ceiling. A ballroom. Could accommodate casual explosions. And make echoes of all the shouts I'm hearing from Macfugger.

'Clementine. For God's sake man. Where the fuck are you.'

At the top of the grand staircase. Over the great hall. Watching a throng of inmates whispering down there. Who might have it planned to all attack at once. And kick the living shit not already curdled right out of me. Lift this sword and shield off the wall. Better to look ridiculous and live than be calm and have fifty boots thudding odoriferously in under the armpits implanting fatal contusions.

Macfugger strutting in the door. Clicking across the tiles of the great hall. It looks like his eyebrows are close together. They say a forty five has the kick of a mule. The stopping power knocks you flying on your back. Much worse than those bullets which go right through. And kills someone else behind. And you can stand there with fingers over the leaks. Macfugger will see his wife's hand prints all over me.

'My God Clementine, there you are. Began to think you were out there too. Gail for God's sake is with them. I can't find her anywhere.'

'What's wrong.'

'They're out there. We've got to save them. Last sign was a waving light. Five minutes ago. Completely vanished. That bull fighting bugger called Bligh out there with my ruddy wife and a boat load of children. On an ebb tide. Every second counts. At five knots it won't be long before they'll be swamped in the open sea.'

Clementine's shield clanking to the floor, one hand grabbing the balustrade. Macfugger catching him by the arm.

'What's wrong.'

'I think it's my heart.'

'Pull yourself together man. This is no ruddy time for your heart to pack up. We've got to save Gail.'

'Yes of course.'

'I may have trod a little on the matrimonial codes in my time but I love the old cow's arse dearly.'

'Yes of course.'

'Don't stand there saying yes of course, we've got to put out after them. We need a boat.'

The beach alive with lights. A bonfire blazing orange on the sand. The lapping of waves ahead. Macfugger, Bloodmourn, Franz and the Baron behind. Down over this path between shadowy trees towards the boathouse. Leaves rustling with a breeze. Gentle. For the time being anyway. On this sheltered hillside. Macfugger your wife's safe back where I left her half undressed on mouldy eiderdowns waiting patiently for me to get back and put it up her. Aren't you too overjoyed by that news to shoot me. And she can chalk up two and a half men. Raise her score while a whole gang of silver voiced kiddies are out in a leaky rowboat. Bloodmourn's stomach at least I know is at ease in heavy seas. Good lord, the Baron is in yachting cap, blazer and white ducks. Instant protocol for all occasions.

The group making their way to the boathouse door. Macfugger unleashing his forty five, blasting off the padlock and rushing down the steps and up the gangway with a lantern. Scrabbling at the lashing across the lifeboats abaft of the funnel. He's military. And at the moment desperately impassioned. Best take matters naval into my hands. While he seems to be peeling back the keel of that small craft.

'Clementine God damn it. You couldn't float a turd across a toilet bowl with these boats.'

'All right Macfugger you mustn't panic.'

'Panic. By God my own flesh and blood is out there. I may have married for money but she's a damn good wife with stacks yet to be inherited.'

'Do you mind if I take over command. It's rather my field. I've had naval training.'

'Don't talk rubbish man, what the hell good's your training. We need a boat.'

'We'll see if this one will go.'

'What. Impossible for God's sake.'

Macfugger's reddened cheeks in the lantern light. Maybe
now's the time to tell him. If he'd get rid of that gun. Your
wife is set to lay for me and steam shovel loads of bullion
my way in return. Ah Franz. Exiting from the wheelhouse,
lips pursed, hair scattered over his head. Those dark steamy
sad eyes.

'Mr Clementine I will go to the engine room. It is possible
that I may be of assistance to you.'

'Yes certainly. Go. And Baron please, do you know how
to fire a cannon. Are you shaking your head yes or no.'

Macfugger one hand on hip, the other tightly in a fist
waving in front of his face. Calm on one side, hysterical
on the other.

'To hell with the cannon. We've got to get airborne out
of here.'

'Macfugger will you please control yourself. The first principle of naval procedure is to get squared away. Bloodmourn
you were in the Navy. What was your rank.'

'Lieutenant commander.'

'I see. I'm outranked. You must assume command.'

Bloodmourn rubbing hands together. A strange smile on
his face. He lifts up his chin where one suddenly imagines
a stiff white collar and a small knotted tie and two black
sleeves sporting two and a half stripes. His voice calm. Here
on the quarter deck. Stand back a little. Let the skipper
speak.

'Thank you Mr Clementine. I know how you all feel
here tonight. You want to get out there as soon as possible.
But putting to sea with one's jib dangling is imprudent. Pull
together, keep on the ball, noses clean, and our mission will
be accomplished. Lieutenant Clementine will be my execu-
tive and chart course. Baron, please take over as officer of the
deck. And Mr Macfugger you're boatswain. Franz below
will be engineer. Dismissed.'

'Will you stop this bloody charade.'

'I'll thank you to keep your trap shut boatswain. And take orders.'

Lapping water against the granite quay and ship side. Franz banging on the pipes below. Captain Bloodmourn calling for azimuth and compass. The sound of an engine. Light flickering on in the wheelhouse. Go down and cry at Franz's feet. Ask forgiveness. For all the mean uncharitable thoughts one has had during the digging of his excavation. He's got the generator. Humming.

'All right Lieutenant. See that we're clear astern.'

'Aye aye Captain.'

Boatswain Macfugger muttering. As the two of us wind a winch handle round and round. The great door of the boathouse rising. Smell of sea and rippling blackness out there. Red glow of the fire on the beach. My hands trembling. Whisper the truth to Macfugger while his are occupied. And get a boot in the jewels.

The deck aflood with light. The Baron rigidly at attention. More clanks and tinkerings on the pipes. A splutter and twin black clouds of smoke bubbling up under the stern. A monstrous trembling shaking the ship. Waters boiling out and heaving in the blackness. A voice over the intercom.

'Now hear this, this is your captain speaking. We have succeeded starting engines. We will be proceeding astern into the bay and when sufficiently into deep water shall make for sea. Cast off all lines. Good luck.'

'Clementine who does he think he is. Only that Gail's life is at stake I'd give him a ruddy piece of my mind. Can you imagine an ex infantry captain through six campaigns, a boatswain. I mean to say I was brevet major. It's simply not on.'

The night clear. Voices coming over the water. We're moving. One port but no starboard light. Whoops. A swell. Distinctly sweeping in from sea. To rock this nice little ship load of friends. Made closer by days of accumulated bitter stratagems playing chess. All put afloat together. Shipmates. Anchors aweigh. Out over the blue black glistening deeps where lay lobster and crab and lurks the great conger.

'Now hear this, this is your captain. We are underweigh

at six knots. Will Lieutenant Clementine please come to the quarterdeck.'

Awfully nice the way things are being run. The Baron taking the breeze head on standing there useless in the bows. Wind whistling in the rigging. Mahogany decks. Little slippery moss here and there. One lonely light across on a black shadowy headland. Sound of waves washing up cliffs on the port side. Walk by the portholes of the saloon. A whole new life opening up. One could just keep going in this thing. If fuel lasts and no leaks are sprung.

'Lieutenant Clementine reporting sir.'

'Take the wheel Lieutenant. Some crests beginning to break about. We're heading into a moderate breeze. I've marked a search area six miles square. It'll be moderate to fresh in open sea. Our speed's cut by the headwind. But by my reckoning we should come upon them at any moment.'

Bloodmourn with a pair of eyeglasses slipped down on his nose. Hands spread out over the chart. Sea spray on the windscreen. A knock on the porthole. The Baron sticking his head in the hatchway.

'Dat's dem. I hear der voices.'

Clementine rushing out to the bow rails. Listening into the dark ahead. Sound of Bligh coming over the water.

'Everyone loosen collars, take anything sharp out of your pockets.'

Macfugger looming up close out of shadows. Huffing and puffing. A life jacket belt draped over each arm.

'Good God Clementine any sign of Gail. That chap thinks he's in an airliner crashlanding. Listen to him.'

'Everyone overboard with all shoes and other personal accessories not of a religious nature. Now catch holt each of you to your oar. Feather the props.'

'Clementine, your man thinks he's airborne. I suggest we approach with caution. He's out of his mind.'

'Now hear this, this is your captain speaking. The boat in distress is forty five degrees on our starboard bow. Stop engines. Will Boatswain Macfugger go below and check the rudder steering. It appears to be jammed.'

'Unless I am addressed by my proper rank I'm not moving.'

A silhouette standing up in the small boat out on the tossing waves. Bligh's shouts echoing across the waters and back from the headlands.

'The occupants of this boat are to submit to my absolute command. Keep your mouths shut. I will do all the talking. All women get forward with the little children. Now the rest of you row. Row you dogs row.'

'Clementine that stupid bastard doesn't even see us. He'll fall out of the boat. And by God he'd better address my wife in a civil fashion.'

'Macfugger tell the captain we're heading past them.'

The yacht sliding through the waters. The wind rising to a fresh breeze. The big diesel pistons thrashing down below. The drive shaft churning. A white wake spreading in the faint moonlight. Swells of ocean rising. As we leave the great dark high headlands of shore. Ahead the new world. Only three thousand miles away.

Bligh's voice fading. Getting louder as the shadow of his little craft rises up on the swells, teeters and goes down out of sight. Leaving his impassioned vowels bouncing on the waves.

'Girls get down on your knees. Anyone with rosaries get them out. And by God pray. Pray.'

'Ah Mr Clementine, dat ist awful out dere. Humanity ist adrift in an open boat.'

'Yes Baron.'

'Permit me, I have not before spoken very much to you. It is only because I see the stark realities you face in your castle which must make you sad. But tonight I would like you to know I am with you in this the greatest sadness of all.'

Clementine stepping back on the bridge. Where Bloodmourn pounds his fist on the binnacle. Shouting down the speaking tube to the engine room.

'Engineer did you hear me, stop engines.'

'I heard you, I cannot stop them.'

'Clementine did you hear that. Our rudder's jammed. We're doing eight knots. On a tide of five we're heading for disaster at thirteen. We're beginning to heel over badly.

The fresh breeze has turned to strong. Check for icebergs.'

The voice of Nails Macfugger shouting from the stern back into the night. Drowned by the wind and crash of the prow into large foam crested waves.

'We'll be back Gail. Don't worry. Hold on.'

Clementine rushing from the wheelhouse up into the bows. Climbing over tattered lines and piles of anchor chain. Can hardly see ahead in the spray. When Franz said he could only increase and not decrease revolutions, Bloodmourn's hand closed clutching tightly over a damp chart. Both of us shit scared ploughing on into the rising blackness ahead. No icebergs but when we run out of fuel we'll be adrift in the steam ship lanes. And be rammed in half.

Back in the wheelhouse. Bloodmourn raging in circles fists hitting at the sides of his head.

'You'd think Lieutenant that with all the rusted pipes and disconnected wires we could slow this tub down. I was about to write some pleasant things in the ship's log before this happened.'

'We'll run out of fuel soon.'

'You think that's funny. While I'm commander of this ship I want no attempts to amuse on my quarter deck. Is that understood.'

'Aye aye Captain.'

'Or else I'll order you below.'

'I'm not feeling very well.'

'Get out on deck and breathe deeply. Shake your head back and forth. Have we brandy aboard.'

'I'll order a search made sir.'

Clementine and the Baron tripping below decks fishing through lockers, between paint cans, pots, dishes and under mattresses. To unearth a bottle. Of clear pure spirit. Just as God made it. Bloodmourn said. As he quaffed a cupful.

'Lieutenant I've got the bows into the weather. But the name of this ship worries me. Novena. In the dictionary here it says nine days devotion for a religious intention. And mine right now is to avoid foundering.'

'Captain we're afloat on the finest teak and mahogany. Just rap the bulkhead. Listen to that. Even the crappers are flushing.'

'You mean you've been taking a shit on my ship when we're at action stations. That's a court martial offence.'

'Bloodmourn. Please. Give the owner of the ship a chance. I mean in an emergency of course one defers to superior experience and rank but if I want to take a shit, I'm not going to go through the chain of command on a god forsaken ocean in peacetime.'

'Do you know what a stetson wrench is.'

'Bloodmourn we're in trouble. Fighting like this on the quarterdeck can only make things worse. Good lord. A roller. Coming. It's fifty feet high.'

Bloodmourn grabbing the wheel. A great black mountain spilling right out of the sky. The good ship Novena heading into this hissing darkness with a deafening thud of bow. Lights out. A roar and crash. Water pouring knee deep through the deck house. Shattering glass. Lights on again. The bow mast sticking into the wheel house. Bloodmourn with a grim lipped smile, water dripping from his face.

'Lieutenant, the steering is functioning again.'

Clementine bent double spewing forth. Hanging his head hands agrip on the window rail.

'Lieutenant this is no time to be seasick. Get a grip on yourself. Straighten up and fly right. If the bilge pumps aren't working I may have to order abandon ship. Engineer, can you hear me.'

'Yes indeed mon cher Captain.'

'Commence bilge pumps.'

'Ah but they are already commenced Captain.'

'Clementine, that Franz, the man's unbelievable. We may be able to hang on. We can lash you to the mast. What there is of it. Only last half an hour in this sea. Bligh and his boat will never have survived that wave.'

'Captain we had better send up flares. The lifeboats what's left of them are tinkling from the davits.'

'Nonsense Lieutenant we have a clipper bow and cruiser spoon stern. I've got the gross register, net register and standard displacement listed right here. If we made it through that wave we can make it through anything. I've still got a few seafaring moves up my sleeve.'

'I'm feeling awfully sick.'

Clementine's mouth opening, his hands entwined. Eyes closed as his throat groaned forth green bile. Huddled arms clutched across his chest. Bloodmourn taking a cup of the white spirit.

'Drink this, it could save you.'

Clementine putting back a cupful. Lifting his head. Sad eyes watching Bloodmourn jumping from the wheel to lockers.

'What are you looking for Bloodmourn.'

'The flag locker. Run up Q.'

'What for.'

'Because if we are swept somewhere into civilization and we are lying unconscious on the deck of this wheelhouse, flying Q means our vessel is healthy and we request permission to hold intercourse with the port.'

Nails Macfugger red hair soaked stumbling into the wheelhouse, catching his breath and slamming the hatch with his shoulder.

'That's ruddy right. And we're ready to put it up every alluring unfaithful wife down every dock side street.'

'Boatswain why aren't you on deck keeping tackle secure.'

'Are you out of your mind. I was nearly washed over board with the Baron.'

'O my God Nails, is the Baron overboard.'

'Well he's not leading a symphony orchestra on deck at the moment I can tell you. And if you take my advice Clementine. This captain friend here of yours is going to get us all drowned.'

'How dare you sir.'

'For God's sake Bloodmourn and Macfugger stop fighting. I think we're foundering. Right now.'

'As captain I order abandon ship.'

'And as owner I order stand fast. Because for one I am not going to go out into that.'

'Lieutenant as your captain I might reflect that you are a little short on seamanship but long on wisdom. I unreservedly withdraw that last command.'

Three gentlemen in the wheelhouse. Macfugger at the tiller. Bloodmourn shouting Mayday into the transmitter. Clementine searching for flares. The little ship crashing on. The radio dead. The stern rising up under passing waves and lurching and shaking as the screws spin free in the air. Take a couple of minutes' silence for the Baron. Who with all his chess defences may be waging one final battle against the deeps. Perhaps the last moment is not the saddest. Mine was when they wouldn't let me be an altar boy. Chose the chap who said he wanted to be close to God. I said I wanted to carry a big candle so I could look great and my aunt could see me. Waltzing on the altar of a sunday.

Wave crests toppling and rolling over. Long patches of foam across the sea. White everywhere with spray. Bloodmourn sneaking the vessel down a trough in a broadside manoeuvre. And turning to take the big seas on the bow. Forty degrees of list. My pockets feel full of creamed spinach. Salt on the lips. Last thing you taste going down into the watery grave. Dying with a dearth of arse. Could have been Veronica's forty first for the year. Missed piece after piece in the castle. Even Gail who was begging for an implant of tool. At the final curtain of water let Macfugger know she was pure and faithful to the last. Safe back on shore. Her husband lost. Out on a savage sea.

The deck awash. Clementine in oilskins. A chorus singing. Beyond the waves rising and falling. Bligh standing in the open boat less than a cable away. A white garment flying from an oar held upright. And good lord. The Baron. Still in yachting cap. Next to Bligh.

Bloodmourn now at the tiller. The good ship Novena rolling and crashing towards the distressed. The Baron falling over. Each time rising anew and coming to the salute. Clementine casting a line across the open water. Barechested Bligh jumping into the waves. Taking the line between his teeth and swimming back to his little choristers soothingly humming. Macfugger amidships straining out over the rails.

'I don't see Gail. Can you Clementine.'
'I'm sure she's all right.'
'She's not in the boat. How can that be all right.'
'Well perhaps it isn't.'
'You're damn right it isn't. I say Gail. Where are you.'

       Dear Nails
       I am way back
       Here
       Totally indiscreet
       With a big dog
       Licking
       My awfully cold
       Feet

13

Midnight that night a little trail of people making their way up the hill from the beach to the Castle Charnel. The lifeboat put out from along the coast taking the lot of us in tow. Breaking two hawsers tugging a fuelless Novena back to the shelter of the bay. The storm still lashing as Bligh signed autographs at the castle door, raindrops creeping through the hairs on his chest. And Macfugger disconsolate and sobbing in the great hall.

I hotfooted it up the stairs in a trail of oilskins. By the ballroom and aloft ascending the circular stone steps. Whispering into each room. Until I came to heavy breathing. And couldn't hear my own. In the shadows two figures entwined on the floor. Through recent sea sick eyes one could just make out the pale moonlit fatless arse of Lead Kindly Light. As it rocked and swayed. Pumping up and down on Lady Macfugger.

The township arrived in carts, in prams and on donkeys. Lanterns swinging. Their faces downcast at the lack of disaster. I was introduced to three tourists, Mr and Mrs Utah, both in big brown shoes and hats. And a bright eyed girl shivering in a tight white dress. All staying at the hotel. They followed the commotion rushing through the town. And sir we'd kinda like to look round the castle when it's daylight out here sometime.

Nails Macfugger roared and bellowed as Lady Macfugger slowly came down the grand staircase. Her hands trembling. Wishing she was only a ghost. As she said. O there you are Jeffrey. And Macfugger's hand grabbed her by the hair dragging her forward across the hall and crashing her through the library doors. During the screams I tried to stop my cheeks from smiling.

And next morning I woke sneezing, hands blistered, arms sore and legs stiff. Charlene leaving my tray without a word. After breakfast came Percival. Said local reporters were in the great hall to get the news. Spread by the lips far and wide. About the brilliant seamanship and bravery of those aboard the Novena. Now gently at anchor in the bay.

'By God sir you're a name overnight in the community. Human durability has been put on the map.'

The Lady Macfugger had both eyes blackened and a lower bicuspid knocked out. Her nose out like a football and her lips bruised and swollen. She sat in the Porcelain Room on a pale green chair in a long purple gown. Just a tiny slender inkling of her splendid ankle showing. Dark glasses over eyes and her nose covered with gauze and bandage. She smiled as I came in with a box of chocolates.

'Very good of you to come and see me all poorly like this.'

Bonaparte shuffling in. Deep growling grunts of apology pouring the absinthe. A cold late morning sunlight through a pink window pane. Mist clearing down the low fields and meadows. Crows cawing through the treetops. Gail's cigarette sending a curling smoke slowly to the ceiling.

'Jeffrey has hardly said ten words to me. I used to sit here an hour now I sit here most of the day. Would you just see that the door's locked please. The motto is don't get caught. And I did the first time. You're the only one I know I can turn to. What should I do.'

'Sit tight. He'll get over it. You'll both feel better the next time he catches you.'

'O God what a thought. He's so consumed I don't think he'll notice the next time. He simply goes berserk. He's done it right out there in the middle of the park. I couldn't see everything with my opera glasses but it was pure frenzy. I sit here quaking and quite sick to my stomach. But why I asked you to come was just to say that I'll keep the part of the bargain I made. How much money do you need.'

Strange apparitions arise. Hope given to heap on the hopelessness. Stand looking upwards at the rising mountain of debt. Just like the barren slopes where Clarence skips with his latest in sexual knowledge. Manufactured constantly below in the Castle Charnel. Where all the faces lurk grinning in the tunnels and corridors. Happy to be a guest. Flattering my beleaguered munificence as they pass me in the halls like a bunch of ungrateful inlaws laden with trays fresh up from the kitchens.

'I don't know how much I owe.'

'Doesn't Percival keep books.'

'No.'

'What about bills.'

'I've never been sent one.'

'You must ask. They'll never send one. It's not considered polite.'

Shotgun blasts echoing out in the park. Lady Macfugger rushing to the window with her opera glass. Little puffs of white smoke. Three figures near a tree. A sigh from Gail's lips. Plonking back on her chair. Replacing her dark spectacles.

'O God it's so tense. I've been thinking of going away. He lies prone in the front hall and with the door open and telescopic sights he shoots neighbours' sheep a mile away who merely stick a head through a fence. He tramps the house at night. The servants are terrified. Even the insurgents are at bay. He's never without a gun. Clicking the safety on and off. Bonaparte takes a ghoulish delight to see him shoot down a chandelier from the ceiling. Any second I expect to find him in here amidst the porcelain. Splintering it with a shower of lead. He likes you. Thinks you're one of the last pure princes of the blood royal. But God help any poacher. He wouldn't stand a chance of saving his life. And Jeffrey waits behind walls. For the defiant ones. He calls them. They humanly manure the vista approaches to the house. Usually balancing their droppings on awkward points of stone. Just to let you know they've been there. In the rose garden or outside the French windows. An ugly little game. Things are bad enough without them being embarrassing as well. The people are quite wretched. Jeffrey's fond of saying one's food tastes better surrounded by poverty. But dear me one's spirit does not soar. Their souls are screaming to get out from their wretched minds and bodies. Jeffrey's one of them himself. Brutal and callous. Submerged under a rather splendid veneer. But I don't want to lose him.'

On the granite steps of Macfugger House between the tall sweating pillars. The green ground dropping away. Down towards trees, great dark leafy mushrooms towering over the grass. A lonely sound of wind. The grey grey clouds cramped in the heavens. Listen for souls. When they sound. Bellowing out in the night. Thudding through ditches. Squeezing out the bitter drops of hate. To scar and sour the soil. Step between them. To kiss goodbye this sad woman on the end of a bandaged nose.

The hairiest of the exprisoners waiting at the wheel of Erconwald's motor parked on the gravel. With tyres on and the engine back in. His voice quiet and charming. Asking what's troubling me. Ask him an answer for a question.

'What advice do you give another man's unfaithful wife.'

'Be unfaithful again, Mr Clementine. It only counts the first time.'

Now with a chauffeur and body guard. Up over the rocky mountain road. Deep gullies gouged by the storm. The afternoon dying. Each clump of golden blossomed gorse a little outpost sheltered coconut perfumed in the barren wastes of endless brown bog. Night comes. Ghosts awake. Out of the watery wild grassy stubbles. Lights along streets. Of another land. Windows yellow with half drawn shades. Look in as you walk by. A man in shirtsleeves reads a newspaper. Leans to take up something in his hand. A wife steams a window cooking. Two children play with trains. A heart needs a haven to go on beating. Sail but a little distance on an outburst of anger. Into calm. Where the sadness stills. And you look for a smile.

Tiny dots of lights aglow. Charnel Castle sitting shadowy above the alley of tree tops. The exprisoner said rain gutters of valuable lead blanket the battlements. Sending the water down spouts into big tanks for the laundry. Where Charlene scrubs what's left of my threadbare underwear. Winter seems always coming instead of going. Lady Macfugger wrote on a slip of paper coloured bright green. Put it in an envelope handed to me and smiled. Said don't open it for a week. All the bruising of her elegant lips. Pounded under a husband's fists.

Percival opening the door. A chair ready in the library at the fire. A decanter of port and dish of biscuits and cheese.

'Ah sir I hope you don't mind, I took a lovely couple and a young woman on a tour of the castle. From the snake pit to the chapel. A Mr and Mrs Utah. They were beside themselves over the dungeons. The grandest thing they'd ever seen. You wouldn't mind now if they joined you for dinner. They have a great interest to see how the gentry lives secluded on their own.'

'I'm not living like gentry, Percival.'

'Tonight you are. I have a pair of old satin pantaloons, black silk hose and ballroom slippers laid out in your chamber. With a cutaway coat and frilled shirt you'll look smashing, and just like your lofty grace. Sure we'll give you a shepherd's crook. We'll put on such a dog they won't know what hit or bit them.'

The dining hall cleaned and polished since the blast. Percival intoning make way for his grace as he preceded me with candelabra down the grand staircase. Guests assembled in the great hall. Mrs L K L in a flowing sari in her sedan chair. Franz surrounding his excavation with linen embroidered screens. Everyone doing their bit. Putlog trumpeted the organ. I carefully parted my hair and brushed my teeth. Splashed disinfectant under the oxsters. Took each slow measured step. To sit once again at the head of the table. And look down at the faces. All dressed fit to kill. Ominously enough.

At Clementine's right, Gloria the girl in the tight white dress. Now in tight lavender. With a great black belt with a great brass buckle. Big brown bright eyes in a square face. Oscar tip toeing widely around Lead Kindly Light. Already turning pages deep in a tome. The Baron nodding to faces up and down the table. Rose sporting a pre glacial feather cape next to Mr Utah in his rimless spectacles. As this girl leans towards me smiling.

'It's wonderful here everything is so rustic.'

'Yes.'

'I'm going to touch you because I've heard you're a prince.'

'I feel like one with you seated there.'

'O hey can you throw a line. But I think the whole place is just wonderful. What's that whistle.'

'A curlew. A long beaked bird. Nests in the fields. Flies by night.'

'O God. A bird.'

'Yes.'

'That's just really terrific. You don't know how lucky you are to live here like this. In a whole great castle so full of history. And even with champagne. You know right away I'm feeling a deep affinity for you. No kidding. It's like this whole world here is a revelation. All these really happy people. They're so real.'

A stream of dark purple wine. Poured. From a decanter. Splashing from the table out of a glass and down on Gloria. With one lifted eyebrow in apology from Charlene. Who handed over a napkin and withdrew.

'I'm sorry, your dress.'

'O no it's all right. She didn't mean it. I'm an heiress. It doesn't matter.'

Avocados down on the train from the capital. Specially imported. A crate of prawns in a crate of ice. Specially selected. Slabs of mutton. Specially sliced. From a sheep recently bleating. Piles of potatoes. Leaves of cabbages. The molar crunched smell of onions. Smilingly devoured by Erconwald and associates engaging Mr and Mrs Utah in a blaze of conversation. As other inmates reach between the sauce boats for condiments. And Gloria sighs.

'Prince it's kind of like everyone is so mature. Right in the arms of nature. The surroundings are so normal. That's the fifth glass of wine I've had. I just want to be here. To concentrate. To experience this freedom. O God let me just hold your hand. Under the table. Fast. O God.'

Gloria bending her head forward. Closing her eyes. Her whole body shivering. Whispering from her lips.

'God. I'm coming. I'm coming. I'm coming.'

'I beg your pardon.'

'Yes. Yes. I'm coming.'

Putlog to my left. Beads of sweat on his face. Eyes popping. His fork into a potato lifting it to his lips. Chewing as he watches Gloria. Grind hips in the seat of her chair, head lolling on her shoulders. Breath gasping from her smiling mouth in a last quiver. A chance here to ask Putlog was his recent tempo andante or larghetto. Better first see if Gloria has slipped a disc or burnt out a cartilage.

'Good lord. Are you all right.'

'I'm wonderful, just so wonderful. O I never want it to finish. It was just wonderful.'

'O maybe you didn't know what happened. I had an orgasm. I have them all the time like that. I guess you people maybe don't have them over here.'

The ladies withdrew. Bligh asked permission to have his confession heard. During a slack moment in the chapel. Mr Utah took off his glasses and polished them in a napkin. Before she left table Gloria said she was from Sandusky. And asked if she could meet me somewhere alone.

Port poured. Bligh recounting the brave exploit of the rescue. And what chance did the human body have out there on the waves. It wouldn't be like wood which could float.

'What do you mean float.'

'I said float.'

'Wood can sink.'

'I said it floats.'

'Well you've said enough then.'

'By God say that just once more.'

I stood. The table stood. Percival announced that his graceful worship would take leave and join them much much later. I slipped out. With a certain breezy freedom about the legs. Heart beating casually. To get to the cloisters.

'Gloria.'

'I'm here. I nearly got lost. I'm just loving all these old stone walls.'

'Good.'

'Gee I hope you understood. Sometimes I just can't control myself. Want to see me do it again. Do you. Just watch. I'll get right down here on the stone. And stretch right out. Can you see me.'

'Yes.'

Gloria extended, arms in a cross. Hair spread behind her. A whiff of meadow on the evening air. Seagulls float by. A beast coughs. And Elmer growls downwind wondering who it is out here. He knows every smell in the castle. More than a few of which are his own.

'Touch me. Just on the arm. O God. Here I go. I'm going. That's it. I'm coming. I'm coming. God forgive me I'm coming.'

The wine stain across her dress. The big black belt and buckle. Stiffly she lies. On these great paving stones. Palms downward. Pressing to hold the world still as she vibrates. Under the architecture. By the fluted pillars. In the damp. In the night and the cool and moonlight.

'O hello. Up there.'

'Hello.'

'Did you see me.'

'Yes.'

'Not as good as the other one. You know I'll tell you something. Usually I don't come that easily at all. But you know what really excites me. A boy with an erection steaming up under his bathing suit. O man, that really explodes me. Would you do that for me. I mean I respect your position. And everything like that. But it isn't too much to ask is it. I mean I don't have to have a beach or sand or anything. Your crazy satin knickers. They explode me. You know let's really be honest with each other. What the hell are you doing here.'

'I beg your pardon.'

'Come on. Don't kid me. We're compatriots. What kind of set up is this. You know I've been around. And this is weird. That dame carried down to dinner in that chair by those guys. I have the feeling you might be a phony. I mean you're out of style. I've been trying to shake off those drips the Utahs. They're out of style too. And those three guys, scientists come up to me and say could they measure my moisture. Creeps. I love flying. I fly all over the world. You know how I feel don't you. You understand.'

'Yes.'

'In just a few hours you're like a friend. Isn't that something. You know, when I close my eyes a whole bunch of guys dance in front of me. Stark naked. That may sound strange to you.'

'Not at all.'

'Nobody knows how an heiress feels. They think o wow you've got all that money. Everything must be wonderful. Well it has been wonderful. But not all of it is wonderful if you know what I mean. Hey have you got somewhere we could go more comfortable. I'd like to go there. Because this stone is really turning my kidneys into ice cubes.'

Clementine climbing behind Gloria. A low slung arse bulging ripely in lavender. Up a ladder leaning against the hay. In under eaves and cobwebbed beams. Sinking down into the dry soft stalks and sweet fumes. Passed a billy goat standing in the courtyard. Only newly arrived out of the blue. Ready to nibble the free pickings between the cobbles.

'This is wonderful. Are you married.'

'No.'

'I don't believe you. But that's all right. Let's leave it like it's your little story. Well I was married. We got estranged right on our wedding night. Hey I'm not keeping you from your guests or anything like that.'

'No, they feel quite at home.'

'O well I guess you would tell me. Anyway it's swell out here. Like the whole world was inside busy counting their money. And you're waiting for them to come out again to start shoving and pushing. And all we have to do is just lie here. Well I told you I had a husband. His father never met my father because my father is dead. But my mother who is alive met his mother and father and they should have been dead. They came in their private railway car, we came in ours. You think that's funny. I'm telling you it was damn serious.'

'Sorry.'

'That's OK. You know what he said to me. Right on our wedding night. Just because I was having orgasms all over the place. He said you dirty filthy human being. I said me. A dirty filthy human being. I said whoa. Wait a minute you jerk. Well right there it all exploded. I relaxed. I rang room service. I just said bring me coffee and sedatives. I guess it might have been asking him to get in the bathing suit. It was too small. He didn't believe what was happening to him. Maybe it was the colours red, brown and blue candy stripes. I used to carry it in my bag to give to guys to put on. Hey wait a minute. Why are you so easy to talk to. And furthermore. Why are you listening. Like you were going to print it. But who cares. This is good. You're good. I can tell. But hey where do you get off with that shit. That spooky scene coming down the staircase. With that nut you call Percival making like it was the last supper. I nearly was going to bust out laughing. Then I thought so what if they believe it. But prince my arse. But wait a minute. That's intolerant. No. That's not nice I said that. I ought to be glad I'm lost like I am in this rainy soggy desert. Hey could I stay here. OK you don't have to answer that yet. You want to hear the rest of my history. I filed for divorce. Wham bam, did my lawyers hit him. Wham bam did his lawyers hit back. Wham bam what a bill he got from my laywers. Six months later I got married again. He was much older. But not eighty. He sold bonds. His grandmother owned a cemetery. He wore narrow ties with little knots when everyone else was wearing them wide with big knots. He was that sort of guy. Marriage lasted three months. He was too old to look good in the bathing suit. After that I tried women. After I tried about sixteen more guys. I carried four different sizes of the bathing suit. Some guys said it wasn't sanitary looking after a while. Funny the guys struggling to get them on, sneaking glances over at me sneaking looks out from under the sheets. Look any time you want to turn me off, just say. I mean just call me a taxi and I'll go back to that creepy town. I only got there anyway because I got on the wrong train at the wrong station. Then just as I'm in bed I thought wow it's the mardi gras. Everyone shouting through the streets. About an ocean liner sunk and hundreds of people adrift in an open boat. It was like a miracle. After I was going out of my mind. Hey I want to come off again. Would you just touch me. Just on the inside of my arm. By the elbow. Yes. There. O man. Hold it. Right there. Just there. I'm going to come.'

Gloria groaning and churning in the hay. Bats flitting in and out. A breeze through an arched ventilation in the wall. Keep us cool. For more mayhem in the castle. When she hands out the bathing suits. Writhing in orgasms sending sparks off the pubic hairs. In a castle chock full of nuts you've got to see that people don't eat each other.

'Let me ask you a question prince. Do you know the town Sandusky.'

'Yes.'

'O God. Do you. I mean don't kid me about a thing like that.'

'Yes I know Sandusky.'

'Wow. You don't know what that town does to me. That word. Sandusky. It was where Hilda was from. I was pretty casual with her. I'd be talking to room service when she was going down on me. We roared around in a sports car. Slept on trains in each other's arms. I had a sugar daddy too. He wasn't like other sugar daddies. He had the biggest pair of balls. But he got ruptured lifting weights in an athletic club. He got scared when I started spending his money. He never knew it could be spent like that. He didn't know the years of practice I had. I'd come back from shopping like I was a supply truck and open his fly with the packages stacked around us and play with him till he was purple in the face. Hilda was trying to blackmail him. His wife was trying to get him certified insane to stop him spending money on me. One day high up he walks out a window. Leaves a note. Four words. It's cheaper this way. O boy to be free of all that. His wife came after the funeral and smeared dog shit all over my apartment. I mean what did she think I was doing, blowing him in his coffin or something. She had five detectives following me. One of them I gave a piece of ass to and stole his wallet. I laugh when I come to out of the way bergs like this. They could be out there crouched behind the wind swept boulders freezing. I have the funniest feeling. Like there is something strange. Like the silence is getting ready to explode.'

'The west's awake.'

'You said it. It's the stink of all the raw onions they're eating around here. I'm just about ready to come off again. Get's a little harder each time. I mean I left my bag back in the castle. If you went and got it and tried on the bathing suit we could have some fun.'

Clementine down the ladder. Out across the cobbles. The billy goat has a goatee. He watches me as I go by. Taking a deep breath. To look up at the bright moonlight splashing over the towering walls. It could be great to get up Gloria.

One tip toes along. To avoid lurking humans. No easy matter making light conversation. Sparkling with little flatteries cast back and forth. Putting lips to chocolate mints. And chewing with a smile. While the dark wines warm through the blood. And one hopes as a host that no guest will suddenly arise foaming at the mouth.

In the shadows. Whoops. Someone ahead. Stop. Adjust testicles. Stand still. Snakepit only a short way down the hall. Not the kind of death one wants. Wish I wore parking lights. Percival said there was an x ray Charlie who could glow in the dark. Downed a dram of mild radium. Had himself x rayed from head to toe. Kept the negatives handy like an atlas for all to see. Ready to discuss any inner part of himself or submit to new surveys if the internal situation changed.

'Ah good person. It is you. It is I Erconwald. Suffer me to send greetings through the darkness. And invite you to take a little of the precious distillate that I hasten back to your guests.'

Clementine taking a swig. Taste of prune juice. Erconwald might have grabbed the wrong bottle in the dark. Could be the lethal laxative. Have the whole castle shitting. Instead of screwing. Moaning instead of groaning. With the runs instead of lust. So sad Erconwald. His lonely life prodding secrets out of the universe. Presented himself on one inclement and chill day. Climbing up the steps of an august society of scientists in the capital. Stood taking his credentials from under various armpits as the rain poured down. To be politely but firmly not received. By all those folk inside gathered together arse deep on the leather cushions. So sure of themselves. With voices pitched high and little letters after their names.

'Erconwald. I'm cracking up.'

'Good person. No. Say not such words.'

'I am. I need to get out. Do you know somewhere I could stay in the capital.'

Under a tapestry on a table in the first state room. Gloria's bag. Awful temptation to look in. And find it full of bathing suits. Give one to Erconwald who promised me an address. And touched my arm gently with sympathy. Wait by the doors of the library. He goes back in again. To where the whole party is cavorting. Look and listen through this massive keyhole. Erconwald handing round a chalice. They're positively gay in there. Without the castle owner Looking pained by ruts across the mahogany. Mr Utah up on my desk kicking around on top of the ledgers. Doing a dance for folk. Drunk as a skunk.

'Me and my Ladyqueen have had our eyes opened to a different way with you folk here. Back home I've often stood out there on my lawn wondering what in tarnation was the need of cutting it. Except the neighbours would grouse. We're just plain folks. I'll take a swig at this here distillate you say puts the gizz back in. But let me tell you a story. We have an oldster living behind us there back home. This one night about three a.m. with the lights on in his bedroom he was shouting at the top of his voice. We thought maybe his house was on fire or a rattler was loose under his bed. Me and Ladyqueen we got up and in our kimonos just as fast as we could we shot over there and busted open his screen door. Well there was old Charlie, I mean we're kids compared to Charlie. He stood there. In the middle of the bedroom with the light blazing on stark as the naked he was born with a bone on nearly tickling his chin. You'd a thought he'd a had a bit of modesty with me and my Mrs standing there. But he just crowed out like he was a rooster. Lookee here Clem and Martha it just come up like this all by itself, ain't it wonderful to see. Wasn't it the truth Ladyqueen. I mean we're taking a page out of your folks' book here and talking real plain like. Now wasn't it the truth Ladyqueen.'

Mr Utah thumbs caught under suspenders. Looking down upon Mrs Utah swaying with a bottle. Mrs L K L with a lorgnette, squinting at these plain folk. A blazing turf fire. Bligh bouncing up and down in a dance routine with Rose. See away in their corner. Just the bent heads of Bloodmourn and the Baron. Engrossed in chess. Miss Ovary waltzes with Putlog. Into and out of sight. Social standards staggering between servants and guests. I've seen the Utahs before. Jumping backwards from the sight of Elmer in our compartment on the train. Both of them here now with flashing rimless spectacles shouting freckle faced in their cups.

'Ain't it right what I'm saying Martha.'

'Well Clem I sure didn't believe my eyes that Charlie would act like that. But I understood it was kind of important in his life to have it up like that, rigid as a post.'

'Now tell 'em Martha, didn't Charlie ask you to feel it for real and didn't you feel it.'

'I felt it all right just like I'm telling you, like a fence post.'

'Now the trouble was just as me and Martha was standing there watching Charlie with his bone, what did I hear but a rattler. These two eyes glittering under Charlie's bureau and a tail sizzling away. Course Charlie woke up the whole neighbourhood and here we was rushing him out of there fast as we could go with the back porch light on. We went through the flower border to get back into my garden at the double. You folks will understand this was kinda a big night for us. Charlie died not more than four months later. And he never did get another bone on.'

'Yes he did Clem.'

'You never told me Martha.'

'Well he showed it to me. You were sleeping and I didn't want to wake you at the time. He told me kind of in secret that if ever he got another bone on, he would switch the outside garage light on and off which comes in to our window and he would stand in his kitchen where we could see him from ours. And there he was, a bone on a mile long and he was smiling and drinking a container of milk. I never did see such a thing as Charlie has.'

'Shut up Martha, that's no kind of talk.'

'Charlie had the biggest thing I ever did see.'

'Now Martha that ain't no way to talk in front of all these good folk.'

Clementine rising from knees. Eyeballs covered in dust blown through the keyhole. Bag hooked over an arm. Feel the way onward. A look of astonishment forever on my face. People always at their best in a memory. And when I've tucked away all these recent months. Look back then on one vast invasion of privacy. Sending castle ghosts running for their lives. Dreamt last night a man passed me on a street corner. Said sir your light tan shoes are unforgivable. I walked six miles in a circle mumbling bitter replies. Woke up. Felt my toes sticking chilled out of the bed. Licked by Elmer. Who leads his own life these days. Chewing cow flop and chasing his tail.

Clementine climbing the ladder to the hay loft. Sounds up there. Gloria in another orgasm. Or doing gymnastics. Owl hoots. Send the rats for cover. Who dat dere. One on top of another. Legs scissored around a pair of small moonlit buttocks. Vibrating like the hammers of hell. That fuck pig of multiplicities. That L K L.

> They take
> Your bacon
> They take
> Your rind
> Go get the bathing suit
> And they screw you
> Blind

14

Bloodmourn picked a speck of fluff from my lapel and smiled. He rubbed hands as the others bowed. The hairy exprisoner drove me up the stony winding road to wait for the train. Coming choo choo out from under the pink grey striped sky. The countryside stilled. A spiral of smoke from Clarence's cottage. The hoof sounds of Tim sweeping away down the centre of the road.

Erconwald gave me five pounds. Folded the big white note away deep in my pocket. And looked at it again as the platforms of the stations swept by. Across lands haunted green and lonely by dark hedges and solitary trees. Man at a gate with a donkey. Woman looks up from a sack in the fields. Arms wave. Hello. Goodbye. To the click clack heading towards a creeping grey horizon.

Smoky shadowy terminus. Weather burnt faces lugging bags tied with straps and strings. Lost eyes staring around the metropolis. A lamp light with a yellow glow on a wet gleaming street. Horse cab at the curb. Take it clip clop along a wall by the river. Turning right up a steep cobbled hillside. Broken windows flickering with firelight. Down a street of bleak darkened commercial houses. In there a shop window full of gentleman's gear. For horses, sheep and shooting. One bank after another. And into that one there with the grey granite pillars. I will go tomorrow with my slip of green paper. From Lady Gail Allouise Trudy Macfugger.

Strange to be all dressed up. For a city. To feel warm under cloth. Albeit the toes are cold. And the eye looks for some warmly lit snuggery. Where waits a plate of cheese and glass of wine. Just stand here at this space between the mahogany partitions. And refreshment slides across the marble.

'And may I have some pickled onions too.'
'Certainly.'
Clementine taking sips of wine and chunks of cheese. Teeth sink through the red soft tang. Such a relief from the hungering around the castle halls. Rid of the many mouths. To privately pay attention to my own. With just a barman on a stool reading the evening newspaper. Turning over the pages. See great black headlines there. If the gentleman would only hold it a bit higher. Ah. Thank you.

DARING RESCUE OF CHOIR AT SEA

Fourteen silver voiced children and their choir master were rescued Tuesday night during a force nine gale. The little ones having set forth with their leader in an open boat as a treat were in difficulties as they were swept by the tide out to sea where many mariners over the years have come to grief off the western coast. Four brave stalwart men led by Commander Bloodmourn and assisted by Brevet Major Macfugger, V.C., M.O.H., Dr Franz Pickle, B.F.B. and the Baron Von Freeze single handedly launched the large motor yacht, Novena, which has been out of commission for some years and set forth to the rescue. The brave gentlemen were staying as the guests of Clementine of The Three Glands, the owner of Charnel Castle who remained behind to alert the lifeboat. As the stout hearted made their way through the treacherous seas with their mast broken and decks awash they refused to turn back when nearly submerged by a monster wave and forged onwards to the distressed boat without heed for their own personal safety.

Bartender turning the page. What a lot of really awful people. Nobody gives a good god damn anymore. About the real truth or anything, just so long as they look good themselves. Elbow you out of the limelight. In shame if possible.

'Bartender, please can I have another glass of wine.'
'And why not.'
Lights softer on the eyes. As wine cheers the spirit. Bartender pours with a smile from the corners of his mouth and twinkling eyes. Could say that was me you read about. I was there. Really with them. Out on the waves. But they cheated me out of the publicity.

Clementine setting off with gladstone bag. Walking up a narrow street of shop windows. To look into this one with medical instruments. A skeleton hanging there in the dark. Faint smell of roasted coffee bean. Whirr of cycles passing on the wooden blocks of the road. Turn left. A high fence and park across the street. Any door now. Will be Erconwald's laboratory.

Clementine pressing a white ceramic button in a round brass circle. Waiting. Pressing again. Folks wrapped in scarves go by. It's late. I'm tight. I'm cold. Let me in. I can easily settle down among the test tubes. Not a sound inside. Drive me out of my own castle. Then give me an address where there's no reply. Stagger back out on the paving stone. Head for an hotel. In damp socks and cold feet. Behind this woman ahead whispering to a cat.

Clementine walking by the dark coated figure. As she leans by the curb coaxing this furry creature across a puddle. With a voice one has heard before. Turning at my footsteps to look up. Gracious me. Veronica.

'Look who's here. In town from his country seat. I was just beginning to feel rather lonely, making friends with this cat. Will you buy me a drink.'

In the corner of a small dim lit crowded bar. Around the corner from a cheese shop. Clementine taking out an orange ten shilling note. To purchase large brandies. As we sit together in a tight corner. Upon this reunion. Just when with the damp bleakness of this town the soul was freezing up. To see a face I know nearly laughing. Gay and gurgling. Free of pox and roller skates. Crossing her legs. Pulling her skirt down on white cold knees. Her strong big fingers around her glass. If the world is empty. The smile of another fills it up.

'I got a positively devastating note from Gail. She was as it's said these days slugged in the kisser by Jeffrey. Poor girl. Jealousy. Almost like my former nasty husband who can scratch but not punch. I was having a séance with an old old friend. And we afforded ourselves the privacy of an hotel. Just as we were rather savouring our quiet retreat who should come raging up the stairs pounding on our door but

Roger. Demanding to find his wife. I had in my altogether to nip outside on the window ledge. Clinging to god knows what. While Roger with too much to drink and exceedingly riled stormed around the room searching everywhere. I was subjected, totally without garments, to the most harrowing experience. A group hooting, jeering and laughing collected in the street below. I shan't forget it but how good to see you. Bygones are bygones. This brandy is quite the saving of me. I was on my way back to my flat. Awfully depressed. I get that way. Going from chemist shop to chemist shop all day. I don't know what these people do for sanitary napkins. I just can't get an order. But now you're here, you must let me put you up.'

'I couldn't impose.'

'I insist. I really do. I only live ten minutes away.'

'Erconwald gave me the address of his laboratory.'

'But my dear boy you could never stay in that zoo.'

'He said there was a cubby hole with a couch.'

'There's an operating table and a dissecting slab.'

'O.'

'You must come home with me.'

'That's very kind.'

'I'm always kind. Have all the scars to show for it. But dear boy. I can't believe it. I'm really so glad to see you. You're so young and well profiled, just as Gail says. Would it be awful of me to ask for another brandy.'

The bar packing tighter and tighter. No room left to stand. Drinks held up to the sides of cheeks. Outside were all the wet empty streets. And bubbling within. The voices smiles and deep throated laughter. Her hair swept back in a flowing curve and falling down around her shoulders. With white scalp in a parting down the middle. Tiny speck of dandruff there.

'I may call you Clayton, mayn't I. Well Clayton. Ha ha. Ho ho. Shall we have a party. Yes. We shall.'

Weaving along the granite pavements. A group of dark figures armed with parcels. Veronica dancing out in front as they follow in her wake. Take up the rear lugging my gladstone bag. Introduced to one hundred sudden friends in the city. Happy and forgiving. Gay and carefree. Offering drink, cigarettes and sympathies. All the days heavy hearted beneath the lead roofed battlements, shivered by dinner blasts, sopping at sea rescues and cold toed in debt. Now swept away warmly by good fellowship.

Up the steps of a terraced green doored tall house. Between pillars and iron black railings. Ascending more steps at the end of a long hall. Round and round landings. To one last at the top. Guests pour in under the eaves. To snug rooms. One leading to another. Patchwork quilts. Vases of flowers. Corks popping. Strife dispersed. And clacking them just beneath her ears Veronica cavorting with castanets.

Gentlemen waltzing. Others wincing. One woman and all these men. Discussing architecture. Sitting on each other's lap. How tall and wide is yours. Hands into flies. Let me see. Tell by tugging and pulling. As one repairs backwards to the kitchen. And stands dithering with the fingertips playing wildly on the lapels. Maybe find some hot milk purring on the stove. Warm me up after a long journey.

'O there you are. You must come out and see Victor do his dance. He contorts in his altogether.'

Clementine with a glass of milk. And a cookie. A naked gentleman against the book case. Gyrating to the click of Veronica's castanets. And blushing shyly at his onlookers. Two chaps one sitting upon the other. They look up from a large scrap book. And back again. Turning with wide smiling eyes the pages. Of suspended perpendicular and horizontal pudenda. One could be back in one's innocent castle. With straightforward serpents, bullfights and Gloria playing her instant orgasm. Where my last instruction to Percival was. When anyone asks again at the castle if the boss is in. Say yes. Deeply. In debt. And does not want to be disturbed.

The floor creaking under the weight of the bodies. Veronica twirling between the upright gentlemen tickling momentarily wherever there waved a tool. Till a fist, appearing through a cream panel of the door and followed by a big black greasy head with the face smiling, stopped the gathering dead.

'How are you all in there.'

A big bellied gentleman entering, a belt across his navel. The rest of his clothing tucked up under his arm. A small spiky penis wagging as he elbowed his way up to Veronica. Planting a big smacking kiss on her cheek.

'How are you Veronica.'

'You did not have to break my door.'

'It was only a friendly act to get into the festivities without frightening you with my sudden appearance all at once. Now for the love of God will you cheer up before there's need of chastisement.'

'You're a horrid dirty person.'

'I am not.'

'You shat on my floor last time you were here. It still smells where I had to clean it up.'

'My good lady I'm too flabbergasted to deny such an outrageous accusation. So I won't. I'll admit it. I did indeed shit on your floor. But only over there in a corner where it was out of the way.'

'Disgusting.'

'Would you have me risk my health using a water closet where the germs are high jumping up at you off the porcelain. Don't be so unhygienic.'

'Will someone please punch him.'

'Madam I am at most times a pacifist but if any man posing as a woman here so much as twitches his prick at me the city corporation will want to know upon what authority demolition of the present premises was carried out.'

'I will not stand for more of your barbarous indecorums.'

'I am madam, to be sure uncombed unlicked untamed unpolished and uncouth but how dare you. How dare you bespeak of me as indecorous when I haven't yet gathered me flesh together for a memorable pose upon a pedestal in the proper posture of saint and scholar. Both of whom no matter how much their piety and erudition had to move their bowels over the centuries.'

'You bowel moved and made a sandwich of it. And put it in our picnic lunch.'

'Madam I am wounded.'

'And one of my dearest friends fainted unwrapping it.'

'I am scourged. Cringe do I now before you on my knees. I deny it. The acccusation is an outright slap in the face of my rarest principles. Your fucking la de da dearest friend as a matter of fact objected to me taking an early morning shit out on the lawn with the bunch of you watching from the terrace like you had a winner in the last furlong.'

'You so much as admit it.'

'Admit. Nonsense. I deny it. And will report you and Lady Macfugger to the society of coprophagers.'

'Get out of my flat. This instant.'

'Not this instant. Not in any bleeding instant as yet unrecorded. Not till I've had me humpful bumfull.'

'Please someone punch him for me. He shat in my hostess's sandwich. Buttered it and put it in our picnic basket. Punch him.'

'Madam I stand here. Stark naked before you with the belt across me navel for the sake of decency. I would wish harm to no man. Nor lady. But where a bowel must move in the cause of justice I have moved it. I was apprenticed to the cobbling trade. Anyone of you here take off a shoe and I'll give you a sole. I crap in the tradition of my ancestors unenfeebled by the pipe and water cistern.'

Veronica holding hands up to her face. The black belted figure grabbing the man of the embarrassed pink cheeks and shaking him by the clavicles.

'And what do you think you're staring at. I'll corrugate your map till it would trip a goat, you cunt faced parrot.'

A figure emerging heavy shouldered into the fray. Stepping between the two naked men and letting loose with a right and left hook that spun the belted figure around once in each direction to fold in a heap on the floor. Hands gathering him up. Flinging him through the door and down the stairs. In a contortion of flapping limbs. Voices descending. As the body was dumped out the granite porched entrance. And I tip toed through a dark bedroom to peer out into the street. Where the white figure lay in the gutter struggling up, a shoe in each hand. Bending unsteadily to push them on the feet. To stand peeing. One hand shaking a raised fist up at the windows, the other squeezing off a few last drops. With a few words of defiance.

'I'll be back.'

Veronica coyly lifting her sweater over her head, unbuttoning three top buttons of her long sleeved underwear, pulling in her belly as it drops around her waist. Clattering the castanets as she weaves along the book cases and out between the playful gentlemen smiling as she sweeps by. Those whose hands were free politely clapping. Two austere elegant guests seated side by side, one's hand on the other's knee.

'Alfred it's so refreshing.'

Clementine with another glass of milk. Veronica cruising close wagging and shaking breasts. Faint night of clear sky. Shadows of mountains beyond the glistening slate roof tops. A small hunched man entering. The Monk Minor. Up from his casino in the cellar. Where roulette balls bounced till dawn. They said when his mother went on holiday he pawned her newly installed plumbing piece by piece to get started. To now move thinly through the gathering giving odds and taking bets on any human or inhuman possibility.

Clementine quietly retreating. Backwards. To stretch wearily out on a bed. Comfort me. To walk lonely into a city desperate. For the warmth of another voice. Asking your name. Thrice Glandular thank you. Or telling you the time of world it is. Half past bedlam. Put a hand up across the eyes. Feel something tugging at the flies. Two heads down there in the dark. One Veronica. Shouting.

'Get away leave him alone.'

'He was perfectly all right till you came.'

'Take your hand off his penis, he's staying here as my guest.'

Veronica shoving the figure out the door. Closing it. Gyrating back through the shadows. Sure footed since the roller skates and parasol. Leans down to smack my face. Softly with her breast mounds. Nicely on each cheek. Bring me back to my senses. Overloaded with the unsublime. More shouts up from the street.

'That tiresome lout. Can you imagine Gail nearly took a

bite. Ruined our whole picnic. Horrid monster. But why waste words on him. Let me get rid of everyone.'

Voices saying goodbye. Feet moving down the hall. Steps down the stairs. Shutters closed. Battened down. Lie here. Not so much in sorrow or self inflicted bitterness. But just ready for another tuesday. To say to everyone. Pardon my disfigurement. Wrought by the constant fear of snake bite blast and bullfight. And a double robbery recently of pieces of arse. One elegant the other low slung. Erconwald somewhere in a notebook has my heat of crystallization. Even the weight of my hopes. Measured by his axiometer. Dream of a world where there are patches of surplus women. Rushing to hand out a lifetime of cool fingers tickling the back. Don't get killed in the rush of men. Undo my laces. Push off my shoes. Hear singing out on the night. Wiggle toes for warmth while Veronica's standing there. With her body. Weaving back and forth. Come I have in from the country. To feel your breasts and taste your arms tightening around my chest. Never know when fifty eight small minded fuckers will appear on the horizon all at once. And begin to behave repugnantly. Where do I keep my feelings. Of ferocious anger. While I make all my pleasant replies. And pray. Dear God withhold the tranquillity no longer from your harassed servant. And please. If you don't help at least one of us soon.

> At the rate
> The world
> Is going
> It will
> Be
> Poor old
> Everybody

15

'Darling do that as soon as you can again. Then I'll put you in my scrapbook.'

White faint dawn. Veronica's hair hangs down. Beads of sweat on her brow. Crouching over me. Wild grin on her face. Sitting up on it pumping and grunting away. Beams across the ceiling. A bird chirping at the bread crumbs on the window sill. Hardly a second's rest through the night. Adding grocery bills. And through the zeros stare up and see her eyes. As she speaks down into mine.

'You are my six hundredth and eighty first man dear boy.'

Horse hooves in the street. Bottles clanking on the steps of these buildings. With big barren cold sprawling rooms. The only warmth tucked up in the attics. Had a dream of Bloodmourn. Rushing up on the bridge of an ocean liner, slapping the captain's face, taking over the ship and ordering stores of champagne and smoked salmon to be broken open on the quoit deck for third class passengers. Woke with Veronica up on top of me again. The hundreds of arms around her. The well ploughed pasture. Plenty deep for sowing. Sheets and blankets make us a little cave. To cavort in. While I write letter after letter to grand aunt. And get back the same reply.

Dear Auntie,
    Please send soon moneys desperately needed to maintain me in the manner to which I must be accustomed or die.
                            Your devoted grand nephew,
                                                Clayton

My dear Nephew,
    Nothing doing, you are on your own.
                            Your devoted grand aunt,
                                                Jezebel

Dear Auntie,

Only need a few thousand to buy livestock and tide me over till I get up on my feet and roar like a lion.

Your devoted grand nephew,

Prince Clayton

My dear Prince Lion Hearted,

Any roars you make will be out of your own lungs.

Your devoted grand aunt,

Jezebel

Stand barefooted on cold linoleum and pee. See down into a mews. From the narrow water closet window. Horses nibbling hay. Thought the whinnies in the night were stray guests caught in ecstasy on the stairs. Heard fists pounding on doors. Then thudding on jaws. Growlings and rantings through the streets. And whimpers near dawn. How to get out of here. While I still have a prick left at all.

'Dear boy aren't you coming back to bed.'

'I thought I might get dressed.'

'I've tired you out.'

'O no I'm all right.'

'I really am awfully sorry. Your walk is quite decrepit. Are you sure you're all right.'

'I think something has happened to me around the groin.'

'I've discerned something quite jolly interesting there. If you wouldn't mind I have my camera here.'

'I'd rather you didn't photograph me.'

'Come come now don't be childish and a mumble grumble. Then I'll make you breakfast.'

Clementine standing in poses various. No spoilsport. Profiled in the flood light. Somehow makes one feel quite saucy. Even with the little there's left. After the lot she's taken. And now walking back and forth surveying. Sticking out her own chest and flexing biceps before each clicking of her camera.

'I should have been born a man you know. It's my overabundance of creative power. Being a woman is simply not enough for me. Dear boy you are quite flaccid. Come come now. Make it big and strong for Veronica.'

'I can't I can hardly stand.'

'O dear what a waste. Let me give it a little tickle and kiss.'

'No please leave it alone.'

'Well that's gratitude. Give you the hospitality of my flat. And the total freedom of my body. I mean are you quite content to stand there and say you can't get it up for a little picture.'

'Yes I am.'

'Well perhaps if you had some breakfast then. Cocoa. And some bacon and eggs. You must think me quite cruel. To insist. But my pictures are culturally meritorious. Of course, ha ha, I have had occasion to sell them. You needn't worry I'm not selling yours. A flaccid penis is only of interest if it can be seen in full erection as well. My boy friends are quite good customers. I'd be starving to death trying to sell sanitary napkins.'

A tiny table set for two. Little bird yellow throated and blue winged joined by another pecking on the window sill. A white bowl with porridge. Veronica sits with strong hands buttering a piece of toast. Kimono open to the navel. Could do worse than have her as house keeper. Be able to mix cement and milk a cow. Arrange flowers in the great hall. Hold exhibitions of her photography in the ballroom. Could be wild. Plead loss of scenic amenity when the county council tries to close it down.

'Will you come back tonight dear boy.'

'Well.'

'You needn't be frightened. I'll leave you quite alone. If you wish. You're so shy. Quite gracefully limbed. We didn't start out so badly. I'm actually quite a good roller skater.'

Clementine heading down the stairs two at a time into the street. Head chilled hair wet. Cycles massing down the roads. A beep beep of an automobile. Early morning smoke from chimneys sweeping grey across the city. A mist over the park. A tram roaring by. Bell clanging. Could just barely get it up after breakfast. Swollen painfully pink. For a portrait.

Clementine passing the glass canopy of this hotel. A holly tree growing up from the basement. Buy a paper from the newsboy. A woman in a shawl with a chill child in her arms. Sitting on the wet pavement. Turn this corner here. Find somewhere for a cup of coffee. Follow the smell of the roasted bean.

'Clayton, Clayton, wait for me.'

Gloria. Zooming out of the hotel. Running down the street. In another clinging dress. And black coat flying open.

'Hey hi.'

'Hi.'

'No kidding am I glad to see you. I mean what happened. You were there on top of me in the hay with that crazy helmet on. I mean you didn't even have to put on the bathing suit. Holy God can you do it. I must have fallen asleep. I was exhausted. But I woke up looking for more. All over the castle. Why didn't you tell me. I had to hire two taxis to get here. They had to go one behind the other. They kept breaking down.'

Clementine holding a door open into an oriental café. Climbing stairs in the bread and cake and coffee smells. Seated at a glass topped table overlooking the street. Black uniformed waitresses bringing white cups. Cream poured from little jugs into the black liquid and rising steam. Hold one's horses for a moment. Slather on the butter balls and nip into a currant bun. Take stock. Sit down. Slap the knee caps back on. Open up the ears. And into the fray.

'Clayton, she tried to shoot me. That Mrs L K L in the crazy chair. We've got to stick together. She's following me up here to shoot me too she said. What did I do to her. Can you tell me. Those people are crazy. They're nuts out of their minds. Do you really think she's going to come up here after me.'

'Yes.'

'O my God. Tell me what I did to her. That's all I'm asking. I never saw her before in my life. I'm only eight months out of college. I don't want to die that way. Couldn't we find a port. To go to together. I mean you're so damn good in the hay. Who knows I might be satisfied. By the way are you rich.'

'In appearances, yes. But in fact, no.'

'Gee that's too bad. But appearances count too. I could be your constant companion. I'm easy to have around. I really mean it. Could you stop her shooting me.'

'No.'

'You mean you wouldn't.'

'I couldn't.'

'Hey come on what kind of guy are you. I'd be shot down.'

'That's right.'

'Well pardon me for minding. What is this a conspiracy. I should have known. By the way you know your feet smell and your shirt was green under the armpits. And you should see a dentist too. And forget what I said. You're no big lover.'

'That wasn't me who was on top of you.'

'O come on now. What are you ashamed.'

'No just avoiding false pretences.'

'Now wait a minute. You mean it wasn't you.'

'No.'

'O boy. You could be right. That's the best yet. I thought you had got smaller suddenly. Hey wow. Who was it. I'm going to underline that one in my diary. Zang bang. That really explodes me. Here I am all the way back in taxi. Even when I'm helping them to put back on the wheels. Thinking of you like my lover. Hey why are we fighting. We're friends.'

Down through the throng on the street. Shopping and cruising. Faces whispering by. Gentlemen with red curly hair and poppy in the buttonhole poised with notebook noting each shoe flapping by untied. Rushing after the culprit with a summons. Sky brightening. Gloria pleased and smiling. Holds my swinging hand. Says we're brothers. And got to stick together. As I head now towards the bank. Watching out for a bullet. That might part chums.

High dome. Long counters. Tiled cool floor. A gentleman says come this way. Gloria sits on a stone bench. Unfolds my newspaper and crosses her tan fleet legs. Lead Kindly

Light gets the arse and gives me friends. Through this little door. Go with the note I didn't open for a week.

Dear Clayton,

If you present this letter to Mr Oboe at the bank on the Green you will hear something to your advantage.

Your friend,
Gail

Mr Oboe sitting with a pencil pressed on its point on a pad of paper. Smilingly standing. Hair parted in the middle. Offering his hand. Collar glistening. Picture of a steam ship behind his head on the wall.

'Lady Macfugger has told me about you your highness. A little short for the moment are you. We'll fix that in a hurry. No trouble about that. Please be seated.'

'Thank you.'

'How do you like it over here. Bit quiet for you I suppose.'

'No it's been quite piquant.'

'Is that so. Well can I on behalf of our bank extend to you our most convenient welcome. I'll just have our Mr Bop fit you out with the necessary cheque books. Large or small size.'

'Large please.'

'Well do feel free to make full use now. Nothing as tiresome for a bank totalling up pittances. Making alterations and additions to your castle are you. Keep you busy. How are you for some ready cash at the moment.'

'Not awfully good.'

'What would you like.'

'Could I have ten.'

'But of course, you can have a hundred if you like.'

'Well a hundred would be fine.'

Bows and smiles out the door. One hates to leave that man. Something about him that makes one feel at ease. Says come back and call any time. Always like to see you. If you're caught short at the races just give us a tinkle and we'll organise a bundle for you in time for the next runners. And do please give Lady Macfugger my regards.

Stand in the sunlight. Hold my face up to the warmth under the sky and squeeze this roll of fresh new notes in the pocket. We all give Lady Macfugger our regards. The clammy hands lift. That go clamping and grabbing on you. Need a barber, a hair wash and manicure. Superficials first and later the inessentials. Dear Gail I now know what Jeffrey means. How could anyone do without you.'

'Gosh you're cheered up.'

'Yes. I am you know.'

'It's nice.'

'Yes. I'm going to have my hair cut.'

'Can I watch.'

'Yes.'

Gloria at Clementine's elbow. Making way down the steps of a likely place. Nice plate glass door with a curtain. An invitation please step in. Grey moustached barber twirling his white cape. Before tucking it around my neck. Standing back. Surveying the subject.

'Now how would you like it sir. The tonsorial art is like conducting a symphony. In the hands of the maestro it's but a few trumpet blasts there around the ears. A bit off the back with a few throbs of the cello. Not so as you'd ever miss it. A little virtuoso of the vibro scalp stimulator as a coda. It'll have the blood forming whirlpools around your every follicle. Madam just find yourself a seat there and be comfortable while we get on with the symphonic variation on a theme that would clip every hair the right length once and for all.'

Clementine sitting wrapped in white. Your maestro commencing with the scissors. A molto adagio lopping off of a cascade of hair from the top. Gloria sucking in her breath with a smile. Her eyes closing. Elbows slowly flapping. Mouth opening. Gasping. Head wagging back against the wall. Magazines falling to the floor. The maestro turning from his podium to look. In the direction of this present prone percussionist.

'Ah God I'll get the hot towels to her. The lady's having an attack of something.'

Maestro opening his cabinet. A bundle of towels falling

out. Gloria sliding down, legs quivering akimbo on the floor. Maestro packing the cotton softness under her head.

'It's a fit she must be having. With the smile of death on her face. We're too late for the doctor. The poor innocent creature. Never knew when her moment had come.'

> Juicy
> In
> The
> Groin
>
> That
> Was
> Her
> Fugue

16

Veronica wore her love bites like gems. When she wasn't wearing anything else. Standing as I watched her scratch under her breasts and snuff out the candle as we went early to bed. Climbing in under the covers. On one more chill rainy evening. After she tried to level out the notches and gaps across my scalp.

'I mean that's simply outrageous to let a barber do that to your hair.'

'He was upset.'

'I don't care what he was. You look institutionalised.'

It was true the maestro had lopped here there and everywhere as his symphony went to pieces. And Gloria arose after her orgasm. Cutting loose with a stream of remarks. Passed to both barbers one just back from coffee. I winced. At the words. You mannerless charmless fuckers. Then she slammed the door. The plate glass splintered on the floor. She said she felt the barber's hand up between her thighs. While she was otherwise engaged.

I stood paying the bill. A round estimation for a nice big broken pane. And for the performance of trembling scissors and hands. Giving the latest and last word in a rough cut. Ten yards away I walked into the snug of a public house. To take stock. Of again being nearly penniless. Over a creamy topped pint of porter. And slab of red cheese. Quaffing a throatful of restoration. As a hand comes quietly down on my shoulder. And the liquid starts into and gets blasted out of. My lungs. In a fine spray of cheese and stout. All over the bar.

'My God Bloodmourn, it's you.'

'I've been looking for you all over town. Now you must

not get upset. At what I am going to tell you. There's been a little fire.'

'O God.'

'There's still a great deal standing.'

'Standing.'

'O yes. Remarkable walls. Although a bit charred still as sound as ever. Plenty of roof left.'

Bloodmourn walked close by my shoulder as I made for the quays. Drawing my attention to comforting bits of architecture. Till we reached the river. Crossed over the bridge. And pounded quickly up the stairs of this dark damp shadowy building. To enter this room once more. Stacked a little higher with papers. The stuffed owl still wide eyed at the window.

'Ah do come in Mr Clementine, Clayton Cleaver Claw, is it not.'

'Claw Cleaver.'

'Ah forgive me. But of course. And your friend. I do not believe I have had the honour.'

'Mr Bloodmourn.'

'I am Mr Thorn. Now. Please. Be seated. Just push the briefs to one side. Now can I be of assistance.'

'The castle has burned down.'

'Good grief.'

'And I want to know if I'm insured.'

'Ah. But of course you would like to know if you are insured. I quite understand. Well let me see now. Insured. That would be a policy wouldn't it. I mean you would be paying premiums and that kind of thing. Monthly, quarterly, biannually. Let me see now. Here in the file. Ah. It's lapsed. You're ruined.'

'Thank you.'

Bloodmourn said the lead melted on a turret top and fell down like rain. Percival and Tim emptied bottles of wine over the conflagration. Confining it to the northwest and holding it back from the great hall where the excavation was still intact. And minerals might yet be found. Bloodmourn was sorry to see me take it the way I did. Because it brought the guests closer together. Running for their lives into each other's arms. And there was much in the way of bravery. Bligh bare chested heaved smouldering mattresses down from the battlements. L K L tippling constantly peed endlessly upon the flames. Helped by Elmer. And Putlog made music with a song.

> Put your nozzle
> Over the portcullis
> Let the urine rain free
> Down on the emerald
> Green the colour chosen
> When god made this land
> For part time sinners
> And full time damned

And I put a hand up to feel my shorn scalp as I lie here safely under Veronica. After a nomadic day. Battered and shattered with tears in the eyes. A house no matter how monstrous barren and insane. Is better unburnt. And Bloodmourn steered me by the elbow. From one dark cave of refreshment to another. Down twisting narrow back steets. Standing shoulder to shoulder. Pint to pint. Looking into the future. Somewhere behind the bottles the other side of the bar. Bloodmourn said he wished people would leave him to his prejudices and stop interfering with his hatreds. That folk were divided into classes. Of cunts, shits, fuckers and dirty bastards. Only the fuckers had any saving graces. And that brotherly understanding was ruining the sense of purpose in the world. Which my hand was nudging up under Veronica's cool breast. Press a nipple against the eye. Wind blows shaking the window. Wait for tomorrow. Head west. On foot. Bloodmourn says a little walk would do us both good. Tramping along beside the road. Looking out over the fields. The weather getting warmer the grass greener. Arrive and see a hillside of smoking remains. Sticking up. As I am into Veronica. While she puts her tongue deeply squirming in my ear. Practising for some little part time proclivity. She later performs. Asked me to wear an apron. So I could make a little tent. Before we went to bed. And she could lift it up and step in. I said another time because some of my castle had burned down.

'You poor boy. How tiresome for you. Just lie there and let me do the work on top.'

Veronica makes strange faces. Rears up backwards with grimaces and grins. Thought any moment she would get out the castanets. Until she did. Clicking them while breasts were wagging. Winding round and round showing a nice bit of rib cage in her more extraordinary gyrations. Trying to frighten me. Into some strange submission. Leaning down again close to my ear. And shouting.

'Glorious.'

'Wow, my ear drums.'

'Sorry dear boy.'

Collapsing sweatily Veronica snoring. Her head on my shoulder as one listens to a sleeping city. Voices below. From the back windows of the gambling den. And floor boards creaking. Somewhere in the next room. Heard a door open and shut. Just after the shout of Veronica's glorious. Concussion made my ears ring. Like the blast at the Charnel. Stayed pounding in my head for days. Veronica gave me a buttered crust before bed. I chewed as she undressed. Food tastes better when two people have an appetite for each other. Just count my balls. Make sure one didn't get bounced up between my lungs. Envy rubbery people who can twist and squirm. Her tongue stuck out as she snorted and sported. Crouching smothering with an abundant tuft of pubic hair. Authority has always been out to stop ecstasy. In case it spreads around. If people get a taste. Then everyone wants it. I hear a sound. A grunt. Another. And the smell of an unholy stink.

'Veronica wake up.'

'What is it.'

'I don't know. But there's a noise. And a terrible smell.'

Veronica crawling over the twinging springs gathering her kimono. Sticking her feet into slippers. Stands sweeping back her hair. Stepping to the door and slowly pulling it open. Switching on the light. To a deep groan and straining grunt.

'O no. Horrid.'

'Will you turn off that fucking light.'

'O horrid.'

'That's only half but it will do you now for decoration.'

'You are abominable. Get out. How did you get in. Get out. You would dare to do such a thing again.'

'The call of nature is periodic madam.'

'Right where you did it before.'

'I am a creature of habit if not comfort.'

'Clayton come and strike him.'

Both hands go down. To pull up the sheets. In this land of ice cold sun. Called upon for courage. When all I want is calm. Back at the Charnel could summon my aide de camp to crust him one on the snout. While Percival delivers an upward shaft to the rear and Elmer takes a taste of his dangling testes.

'Clean that dastardly mess up.'

'Fuck off.'

Veronica must have lunged. On that last note of umbrage. Grunts now between the growls screams and shouts. Toppling items trembling the floor. And one monstrous turbulence shaking the entire house. Her muscles all over her. Sleek and lean. Streaks of grey in her hair. Feet coming up the stairs. Pounding on the door. Now heaving open.

Clementine staring from the bedcovers. As a gentleman wrapped in a thick red dressing gown peers in. Consternation convulsed on his face. Wiping eye glasses in his sleeve. Plaster down over his hair and ears. His finger pointing at me.

'Who are you.'

'Who are you.'

'I'm the owner of this house. That's who I am. And the ceiling underneath has just come down on top of me and my wife in bed. Where is she.'

Clementine shifting a fraction lower in the sheets. Best not to volunteer information. Already being broadcast in cataclysms. Have him come down to my castle for a few days. If you think an avalanche of plaster is tough. And get knocked out by lead raindrops. Smashing on your head in a cauldron of flame.

Landlord trembling in his tracks. Just behind his head is a portrait of an army officer in full regalia. Matching the colour of this enraged gent's garb. Who wonders what to do next. Which better be in a hurry. As he steps through into the adjoining room. Just in time for another floor quivering crash.

Clementine leaping from the bed. Grabbing clothes and sticking limbs into the openings. Pulling on the socks. At the dressing table mirror. Slip on tie. The last of the candle light guttering away. Plunge into shoes. As the shouting commences. Voices raised and raging.

'Get out of my house you filth.'

'Shut up. In a second you won't have a house.'

Peek in before I go. Cruising out into the night. With arse without sleep. In there all gone quiet. Just grunting and groans. Push back the door. Hold my nose. There my God. The three of them. Veronica her hands dug in the landlord's plaster flecked hair. Giving him a woolling as they rolled. Closer to the man of the belt across the belly. Crouched. Taking his shit. With a face so wreathed in concentration.

No one
Could ever
Say
He was
Whimsical

17

Bloodmourn waiting. Without crutches. In the early afternoon. At the mahogany bar. In this high ceilinged public house. Named Cosmos after the universe.

Last night I stumbled down the stairs. Tugging my gladstone bag out the front door. Through a gate in railings. And down some more. Mini Monk or Monk Minor bowed me into his gambling den. Join the skill and repartee he said. Among the famed figures wandering to and fro. And a ballet dancer came on with his big pudenda for the floor show. Each flying leap sending out billows of choking dust. While I plonked down my last chips. Bought with my last cheque. And lost them all.

A curly haired gentleman in a raincoat smiled. Standing near me in sympathy. I nodded and he bowed. He was naked from the knees down. Pawned all his clothes the previous morning for a sure win on a horse. Which beat everything in sight but ran the wrong way on the track. And left him incarcerated in his flat. Till three a.m. when he could get out barefoot without being seen for a walk around town. He asked me if I had a dark pair of shoes I could lend him for a funeral. Where he was certain of a loan.

The smoke thick. Dust swirling. Mini Monk urging guests not to give up. That the odds got better towards dawn. I departed hearing a voice pleading behind a closed door. Give me your body before someone else spoils it.

Climbing up into daylight. Wandering the quays past the moored ships. Arriving after a cup of coffee bleary eyed at the bank. To borrow the fare to get home. Mr Oboe said it was unfortunate my castle burned down. And loans to rebuild or travel were difficult at the moment since yesterday. But perhaps when I'd supplied further and better particulars of the amazing thickness of the walls or the distance to be travelled he would see what he could do. I stood taking my departure backwards.

Now Bloodmourn smiles. He said although no one knew it, it was a holiday the whole world over. He felt it in the bones. And with just a little rummage in his sports jacket he'd find some spare spondulicks. Now in the abyss was the time to spend. Run up credit with abandon. The increased turnover made everyone feel secure. And he rapped on the floor with a cane. And tapped on the bar with a coin.

A grey covering the sky. Between these commercial buildings and banks to walk a haunted road. As it goes West. Bloodmourn a few hurried paces ahead. Tickling himself with his fingers. Skipping in little steps. Waiting at the bottom of a hill. Over which we must climb. Hoping to find on the other side white tables spread with condiments. To go skating over. Carving off slabs of beef sublime.

'Bloodmourn I'm hungry.'

'Clementine. Soon there will be time for that. Give me your blind demeanour and stop all that dementia and doubt.'

Over a cobbled road. A detour down hill past a park, prison and hospital. A railway station. Where the castle goodies from abundant emporiums were loaded on the train. And where Bloodmourn insisted for the sake of light travelling that my gladstone bag go by freight. He is very flat on the back of the head. A big brow. Keeps mumbling pop off into top hole. Everytime he stops in his tracks, to coax me onwards west.

'Come Clementine. It's not far.'

Each public house entered to study the architecture of the bar. And the facial qualities of the inmates. Bloodmourn patiently awaiting my hesitation under the sign, licensed to sell spirits and tobacco to the public. Grinning out a little smile.

'Come Clementine. Once through and back out again fast.'

Three hours to cover one hundred and thirty two yards. Bloodmourn said that's the speed it takes to cut a social swath. And make conviviality with the natives. Get to know their quaint customs. Delight to their carefree buffooneries. Never slouch. Always spin twist and twirl. Laugh at a laugh. Smile at a smile. Accumulate a fact. Show shock at a fiction. In short take a moment to keep calm for a while. And pop. Off. Into top hole. With the utmost devastating rapidity. And stay there. In that lofty glad position.

The last of a bleak red sun sinking. Below pink faint strands of cloud. All strung across the sky. The great gates of a park. Up along a curving road through plantations of trees. A lonely monument sticking high. The darknesses creep. The afternoon dies. Cattle grazing. The two figures following one another along the road. Bloodmourn said the latter day chaps had taught him a lot. Which added to some of the things he already knew. Borrow big lend small. And beat it later. If you have to.

'Clementine I will tell you something. I have a wife and three little children. She is a nice wife. They are good little children. To say I did not regard them fondly would be heresy. Someday I will come to them with an armful of presents. Heaped all over. It may not make them like me. But for a moment at least they'll think I'm big time. I know the pitfalls. I can tell you. You are just starting out. Listen to me. Then you will know.'

Bloodmourn with hands quietly folded across his stomach. Moving along the byway. Tiny lightening steps. Clementine lagging behind. Breaking into a trot. Catching up. Walking briefly at the heels of Bloodmourn. Till he slowly pulled away again. A nervous hurrying figure into the distance.

Ahead low hills. A village and row of houses. Another ochre coloured licensed premises by the side of the road. To catch up Bloodmourn as he waits smiling at the entrance. A pint of plain in his hand.

'You are doing much better Clementine. I see great improvements. Note only the top half of my porter is consumed. Previously I have managed to down a whole pint. Ah you are tired. Are you not.'

'Yes.'

'It will be worth it. There is a lot you have to face on the other side of this land. And you must not be lacking in fortitude. By pressing on. We build up that commodity. Till we have a lot. To waltz through a whole new avalanche of calamities.'

'What do you do for blisters.'

'Change socks. Right to left. Left to right. We are seafaring blokes. But we will make it. Now. Just stand here. Look. See. The highway straight all the way to the horizon.'

Ahead two distant houses. Facing each other across the road. Pass between them in a crossfire of eyes. A figure lurches out. A little dot staggering and weaving.

'It's haunted out there Bloodmourn.'

'That is because there are not enough humans to fill the silence. Just follow me. We go.'

The last glimmer of light. A donkey and a cart outside a thatched roofed pub nestled low between two hills. Unseen till Bloodmourn smiled. And awaited my sore footed limping arrival. Pointing a finger downwards into the dell.

'There now Clementine. A cosy refuge. Come.'

Under a low smoky ceiling. Damp dark interior. A tinted picture of a purple mountain rearing behind a lake. An oil lamp flickering on a mantelpiece. A turf fire smouldering. Man standing at the bar his hand gripped around a dark pint. Battered hat with the rim down over his ears and eyes. I sit on a barrel. Dangle the feet. Wait. A half hour. A woman comes. Pulls the pump, fills the glasses and departs. Bloodmourn giving toast to the gentleman at the bar.

'Good luck.'

'Good luck.'

The dark coated figure draining half his glass. Putting it slowly back on the oak planking. Raising his chin and staring over a right shoulder at a corner of the ceiling. His strange calm chanting voice rising.

'O the captain said to me in great confidence. He said to

me in great awe. I do be hearing the sound of waves he said. Are we still far from shore.'

Bloodmourn staring down upon his entwining fingers. A wind blows smoke down the chimney. A beast moos out on the land. Bloodmourn bowing. Glasses raised and emptied once more. The woman comes in. Pulls the pints and is gone again. I feel my blisters and see blackness out the tiny window. Bloodmourn whispers.

'Clementine this man knows something. It would be madness to go further on the road. And leave wisdom behind.'

'For god's sake hurry up and ask him so we can go.'

Bloodmourn advancing to the bar. Outside a bicycle goes whirring by. A silent toast. Glasses up. The creamy liquid goes down. Man tilting his hat back on his head. Bloodmourn making a greeting.

'Good evening.'

'Good evening sir.'

'It's a nice evening.'

'Tis that sir.'

'It's a fine pint.'

'Tis that sir too. Tis the only thing. I've tried everything else. I took my time over the years. I had a farm there not half a mile away. I was out on a hot day with a scythe in the fields. I went to the hedge and looked down the road. I sold the hay. And came in here to this. Till I'd drunk all the money away. I'd go back then. Be there digging a ditch. And it wouldn't be long till I'd be taking a look down the road. And I sold me field. And came back to this. I took a wife. Tried being a married man. It wasn't a month till I looked down the road again and got rid of her. And came back to this. I sold me stock one by one, bullocks, cows,, pigs and sheep. Sold me every field. And came back to this. Right here on this spot I've sailed the seas. Travelled where there have been lights and people. Seen all the wonders happening up there in the corner of the ceiling. With no need for any other creature save me donkey and cart. Only thing I have left after my horse died. I loved him every bit as much as I love meself. Rode him at night across the fields. As hard as he would go. Mile beyond mile. Under the moon. I rode him and rode him. Till the poor powerful animal fell down dead. And I wept. And I came back to this. A pint of plain is your only man.'

Midnight bells tolling. Bloodmourn buying bottles of stout from the silent woman. Stuffing them in pockets and under armpits. Making ready for the road. While your man of the many pints of plain stepped out and fell lying in a heap on the back of his little cart. And the donkey trotted away up the hill in the dark.

Headlights of a car sweeping across the night. Bloodmourn raising his hand. An automobile stopping. Door opening. Gentleman said step in. I sat in the back. Bloodmourn in the front. Where he could conduct the passing of little pleasantries. As we rolled along. And every mile or so one heard a pop. Might be Bloodmourn going off into top hole. As he twitches nervously in his seat. And the car owner turns to look at him.

At village signposts Bloodmourn said yes we should be pleased to go that way too. The driver talking about the labouring classes. Who were doing better than they deserved these days. He was a salesman of gent's high class undergarments. Happy to be of assistance in aiding two respectable stranded travellers. Another pop. Each louder and getting closer to an explosion. A quiver, the vehicle wavering and wobbling as the gent gets a grip on himself to steer a steady course again. To hopefully find a light somewhere. To see what was going on.

A crossroads. Man waiting asking Bloodmourn cautiously which way did he want to go. Because he wasn't going that way too. Bloodmourn's efforts to look good, fading. His door opening. We pile out along with the flooding liquid. And a cascade of corks. Popped from foaming bottles.

The two vagrant figures by the side of the trail. Gent leaning wide eyed from his automobile in approaching car lights. To grab his door. And slam it shut. Shattering the window. To roar off down the road. Followed by a quiet Bloodmourn murmur.

'You ubiquitous fuckpig.'

Don't you
Ever
Find my face
Familiar
Again

Or I'll
Break yours

18

Bloodmourn soaked in stout. Armpit to ankle. Dripping the universal visceral solvent from knee caps. Undaunted at the side of the road.

The night chilly. A wind in tall poplar trees. By big iron gates to a country house. Lost on these flat lands. Shadow of hedgerows rearing. Sound of mystery across the night. The two transients drain the residue of bottles. Waiting these hours till another car dawns down the highway. Full of gentlemen and ladies. Roaring from a wedding. They said.

Bloodmourn and Clementine invited sitting in the back, a lady each on the lap. The remaining gents in the front dishing out female comfort and hospitality. Of giggling and wiggling crinoline couched arses. Necks entwined with baubles. Sweet perfumes in under the hair. Jostled and bounced. Engine whining. A hand on my hand. To take it up and press across her tit. Thrilled by proximity. Fanned by the sparks. Of laughter, lipstick and smouldering farts. It wasn't me. It was Bloodmourn. Or one of them. Stinking us out.

Windows opened. The ladies clean cut as they were simple. Both with minds like a bank. Asking if we were rich between the kisses. Till the driver's voice was heard.

'That has gone far enough back there.'

The motorist turning to see how far was enough. His friend grabbing the wheel. A bump. A swerve. A flash of light. Branches of trees scratching past the window. The whole caboodle turning up on its side. Wheels spinning and horn honking. Clinging women screaming. My face softly sunk between two breasts. Feel a squeeze on the balls and a muddy ooze creeping over my arm.

Bloodmourn taking command. Ordering the occupants to sit tight. Dishevelled in their garb. He would get help. While they waited. Arse deep in bog. And led me back on the road. To vault a field gate on the other side. Said let's get out of here. At speed. Shoelace deep in cow flop. Across the endless darkness. Through the brambles beyond. To cover our tracks centuries deep in the hinterland.

Bloodmourn digging out a hole in a cock of hay. Both of us crawling in to lie there. Listening. To a cry called out again and again in the distant night.

> Are you suited
> Elsewhere yet
> Speak to me Maggie
> Are you suited
> Elsewhere yet

Till cawing crows brought dawn. And we crept out to daylight on the side of a hill. Surrounded everywhere by fields. A mist across low lands. A sun shining above. A touch of warmth on face and hands. Clothes crusty and stale with stout. Hunger rumbling in the stomach. The feet wet and cold.

'Good morning Clementine. I spy a cottage with a spiral of bacon smoke sneaking into the sky. Breakfast will be soon. Don't you like this countryside. This peace. To pop. Off. If you like. Into top hole.'

Bloodmourn ordering me ahead up the pebbled path under a bower of roses to knock on the door. Peeling whitewashed walls holding up an overhanging thatch. A curtain twitching. All silent inside. Bloodmourn approaching. Rapping once. Raising his voice.

'Hello there. We're weary travellers. Come great distances. It is but the merest slaking of our thirst we seek.'

The wry countenance of Bloodmourn. Brows knitting above the eyes. Knocking once more. Waiting. A chicken scurrying round the corner of the cottage. The honk of a pig. Followed by a shout from Bloodmourn as he unleashed a frenzy of kicks against the door.

'Bring water to us weary travellers out here this instant or I'll break and possibly enter your primitive premises.'

The upper half door opening. An old wizened face shrouded by a head of grey hair. A black shawled woman narrowing eyes to see in the bright light. The two waiting figures. The top half of the door closing. Bloodmourn advancing forward. Drawing back a foot for a kick. As the lower half of the door opens. To pour out three snarling tiny dogs. Sailing open mouthed for the ankles of Bloodmourn and Clementine. As they turn heel. To sprint down the pebbled path and leap one after another the white wooden gate under the bower of roses. To the safety of the road.

'Damn mutt tore a piece out of my grey flannels. Unsporting little old witch.'

'You were kicking her door down.'

'I was merely demonstrating one's urgent thirst.'

Along the smooth surfaced road. Softened by a noon day sun. Bloodmourn taking up a rapid lead. Across the flat sour lands of bog, heather and gorse. The distant white of a cottage over scraggly fields. A heron flapping greyly. A stone bridge and little stream. Where Bloodmourn sits dangling legs. And trout gently weave as they lurk in the shadows.

'Bloodmourn I'm hungry and tired. I wish you wouldn't walk so fast.'

'See. Fish. Right there. A most reliable source of food. Make a hook from a pin. Few threads from a cloth attached to a piece of willow. And bob will be your rudd.'

Sun sinking far faster than yesterday. Bloodmourn dangling his long line of shirt tail threads over the water. One lost cow walked past mooing on the road. Bloodmourn interrupting fishing to stalk her. Attempting to grab a teat between her flashing hooves. For a mouthful of milk.

'Bloodmourn can't we just reach a town and get a meal.'

'We're broke. But the will to live still burns brightly. Just a little spot of colour on this hook. And it will soon be yummies for tummies. Fish are uncontrollably inquisitive you know.'

Light fading. Bloodmourn with a last cast of his willow

branch. As one leans dazed on cold elbows. First whiff of evening chill on a breeze. Bracken rustling. The blood curdling call of a donkey. With a dram of distillate could raise a fever to run raping and plundering the countryside. Start off with this war cry just uttered from Bloodmourn's lips.

'Ahhhhhhhhhh.'

A splash. Bloodmourn chest deep in the water. Wading towards shore. Climbing out over mossy boulders. Silently dripping. As he drags after him his bent wire hook. Up through the dock weed, stinging nettles and tall needle pointed grass. To stand shoeless in mud slathered socks.

At a fork in the road a weary Clementine and a soaked Bloodmourn bore left. To confound the gods. After a long elbow deep oozing dig to find the shoes. And later stand stunned as a series of automobiles passed each driven by a woman smoking a cigarettte. The moment of mirages has set in. Do not ask Bloodmourn did you see that too. In case he has. Then both of us are finished. And need to pray. Please dear god stop us from being incurable. Just wrap us up in warmth and friendship. Make us more remembered than forgotten.

'Clementine. I've read my naval survival book from one end to the other. This terrain is easy. It's the mangrove and coral reef you've got to watch. Th: tundra and the desert. Here food surrounds us. But first a fire.'

Bloodmourn running a stick back and forth in a groove. Many blisters later smoke rising in the tinder. Leaves and twigs gathered. Flames ascending. As night settles. Over this grove of trees just in off the road. And Bloodmourn goes in search of food. As I wait by the orange glow. The strange whirrings. Cyclists steam by. Cloaked in darkness.

Bloodmourn stumbling back to the camp fire with an armful of turnips. Brushing off the caked soil and sinking teeth into the dense spicy fibre. Waiting for the cold substance to bump down the throat and lay coldly curled in the stomach. To the sound of a whistle blown out across the fields. With a strange distant music and glow on the horizon.

'Clementine. That light must be a metropolis. Full of sausages, bacon, tomatoes, arse and eggs. I shall make for it. You wait here.'

'No.'

'But only one of us must risk leaving the camp site. Trust me. I'll be back.'

Stretch out on the damp grass. Turn the body over to toast this side and then the other. One bit gets dry while the other gets wet. Hard to look ahead into the future and see there any golden glorious days. When one first meets a girl. A tall lank smiling well built stranger. Who tiptoes to peek over the edge into your life. And you grab her under the armpits. Drag her down. To lie abed after a bang. Telling life stories. Up at the ceiling. And eating out of each other's hand.

Hear the curses of Bloodmourn making his way over the rough country. Till the eyes close. To sleep. And dream of a board meeting. Grand aunt presiding. Directors trembling. As she goes stepping on their toes. Her big company cranking out the profit. While she sits the rest of the year under an awning. Out of the heat and sun. And I kneel begging her. On the grey boards of the porch. For hot water bottles and thick woollies. To suddenly awake choking in horror. Both hands fighting to get into my mouth. To pull and spit out a toad struggling there. Ghosts and scurrying things everywhere at an elbow. A crack of a branch. Be an irate farmer approaching. To urge me at hay fork point. To get the other side of a ten foot high hedgerow. Fast. Or get punctured.

'It's you Bloodmourn.'

'Yes. And I have with me a most charming young lady. Naomi. We met at the fair. I have a chocolate bar. Six eggs and a piece of cheese. I also won a paper hat. And a little badge. Which says Samson. I must leave you now. To take Naomi home. Her father beats the living shit out of her when she's late. I go with her to explain. Do excuse me once more Clementine.'

'Don't leave me alone.'

'Be brave. I must. Besides Naomi and I are being pursued by the fair owner. I won a prize on his strength machine. A meter operates to say how strong you are. You bang a big button with a great big hammer and if you ring the bell you win a prize. The bell rang. And I was just putting out my hand to take the Samson badge when the entire machine collapsed. Cogs, springs and other yokes and semblances rolled in many directions. The contraption lay in a melted heap before my very eyes. Out of nowhere charged the fair owner. Told him to pop off into top hole. Since he did not do so I availed myself of Naomi's immediate leadership to get me safely across the fields. Now I must look to her good keeping. I wanted so much to see a Mr Sudden Suck at the fair, the human vacuum cleaner before I was so inhospitably driven away.'

Bloodmourn said soon the remnants of the moon would pass on the horizon. And keep me company. I watched the two shadows cross into the darkness over the field. I eased the raw unboiled contents of two eggs down the throat. Followed by chunks of cheese. I wore the paper hat. And pinned on the strength badge won by Bloodmourn. Gets one's courage up again to face the dark. And keep the mouth shut to leaping toads.

Shivering at dawn. Over the grey warm embers of the fire. Bloodmourn's jacket across my shoulders. But no Bloodmourn. Birds singing. In the sky's cold grey emptiness. Joints stiff. Rise up. Look for water. To drink and splash over the face.

Clementine moving high footed across the wet grass. Wearing the cabbage green crêpe paper hat. Bloodmourn's footprints. Go this way. Down rather deeply into this ditch. And gouges over there where the struggle must have commenced to drag Naomi up the other side. Bloodmourn a good faithful friend. Came in the night to cover me with his coat. Sort of man who forges on when remarks of ridicule resound around. While people are easily thrilled these days. He takes his light relief from heavy drinking. Makes no rush back to civilisation. Quite happy to be slogging cold, wet and hungry across the endless fields.

A grove of willow trees. Sound of flowing water. A stream. Babbling over boulders. Pools surrounded by rushes. Stop here to take a pee. Help a plant along. To rear up green out of this dark soft soil. And my god, what's that. A pair of knees and legs in the air. Stilled. Where a slayer may have struck. Some poor creature. Down.

Clementine, heart pounding. Approaching. With penis wagging pee. To see. Good lord. Bloodmourn. Where the death vapours enrapture him. Upon her pale and prone. Taking perhaps what she may have refused easily to give in life. The constant hazard of this land journey warping him into the sort who would get up on his grandmother in her coffin. Knocking the gas out of her. With feverish prodding. Unmindful and vicious in his lust.

Thank god. Her legs are moving. She's alive. Under Bloodmourn. Two bodies enamoured. That smart operator screwing among the cat-tails. On this morning. When you stand scratching your head. Asking. In one's own orgasm of discomfort. As you see so many others busily enjoying themselves.

Where were
You
When the brains
Were passed
Out

I was
Taking
A pee
All over
Me foot

19

At a point on the side of a rocky outcrop of mountain. The sun mid high in the early afternoon. Bloodmourn with his Samson badge on the lapel smiled and pointed. To the blue sea. Trembling whitely along the crooked shore.

On this road. Not now many miles away from the castle. Four days from where we commenced. To creep stumble and run. As the crow flies in a hundred different directions. Almost trampled sleeping by a stallion in the dark. And nearly gored by a bull. Bloodmourn invited to fight fairly in a field. And the bloody beast unfairly barely missed killing us both.

Naomi fed us in a shed behind her cottage. While her father screamed murder searching miles of countryside. Platefuls of umber rashers stretched beneath a heap of sunny fried eggs. Swimming in a sweet jelly of fat. Mounds of bread and yellow butter. Mugs of steamy milky tea. Served with a smile and delighted signals back and forth. Between Naomi and Bloodmourn. Who could speak fluently to the deaf and dumb.

A great black car humming round the mountain side. Bloodmourn flattening his lapels checking his flies and sticking up his thumb. A uniformed chauffeur in the front compartment. And something white seated in the back. Which lets out a scream of recognition.

'Holy cow I've been looking for you guys all over.'

A face last seen rolling on the floor of a barber shop. Way way back to town. Now ensconced on fuzzy white upholstery. And wrapped in white woolly tweeds. Over a powder blue dress. As she reaches two handed to grab us.

Hugging and squeezing. A hand in each of our laps. Held as she sits between us like a queen. And says Cuthbert drive on.

The train puffing by twelve hours late. Or twelve hours early. High up across the trellis bridge. Swaying over a silver stream spilling down the mountain side. The sky ablaze in sunset. The fields darkening. The motor car humming by low walls and past a pub. In the distance down the sloping green hills the faint sandy crescent of the beach. And beyond the grey massive roof of the boathouse. And above. Charnel Castle. Still standing ghostly on the hillside.

The great front iron gates ajar. A face pulling back from a window. Gloria dancing doorwards over the pebbles. Charred mattresses and bedsprings, tables, chests and chairs stacked against the castle walls. Withered and scorched ivy on a stone turret. Big black nosed Elmer jumping up barking and wagging tail. Percival paintbrush in hand smiling and saluting on the front steps. Nods his head.

'Welcome home sir. I do be replacing this bit of varnish on the front door. Scratched off by a rowdy group of interlopers attempting to gain entry. The bunch of them down from the capital. Telling me there was rumoured a party raging here. One of them with a roulette wheel under the arm. Said he would lay on a bit of gambling for the guests. I told him I'd lay a latch key on his skull and it wouldn't be to improve his good health.'

The Baron in his cutaway coat and striped trousers bowing and clicking heels at the library door. One averted eyes passing the excavation. Could not miss the scaffolding. And a door marked danger keep out. Thing to do is keep moving. Fast. The mind on things far in the future. When the soot smell would fade. And all the guests will go away. Somewhere else for satisfaction. Ask each of them. What kind of rapture are you looking for. That keeps you here. Searching.

Up the grand staircase. Along the familiar corridors. Feel one is being watched. From doorways and apertures. Lower and clang shut the iron barrier of the Octagonal room. Still intact. Neat and clean. Smoking jacket laid out. A piece of soap on the washstand. Letters on the bedside table. Sit down to open one.

Dear Sir,

Certain particulars have come to our attention and we are, the four of us related by marriage at this office, bewildered by the damaging quality of the scurrilous contempt and cavalier ridicule to which our client has been subjected by the brazen publication in charcoal scrawled on the interior walls of your castle. Referring to our client as follows.

> Everybody knows she blows
> The gas meter reader
> And says between sucks
> I don't normally do this
> With my dentures removed

The above legend has been duly photographed and our client refutes such statement utterly and we call upon you to reveal the name of the meter reader as well as the number of cubic feet recorded of gas consumed at the time of the above alleged act. Further may we make quite clear to you sir, that not one of us is standing here wondering what to do next. We close reminding you of our previous grievances and the satisfaction we require without delay.

Yours faithfully
Bottomless Diddle Blameworthy
and Dawn.

Clementine sitting on the side of the bed. Nice greeting to be waiting when you get home. Rush back a rebuttal of such moral magnitude as to make them quake feverishly and sustain injury jumping towards tomes containing the appropriate precedents. Upon which to muster an unwieldy defence.

Dear Sirs,

A cameraman long stationed unseen in the window across the road from your office will be pleased to acquaint you with last tuesday's tasty sequence. To wit. One medium closeup of three of you, obviously senior partners attempting to strum a banjo with your client's engorged nipple while you held her engripped. I am of the bald opinion that your fourth partner although pretending otherwise was making gestures at your client's rear quarters while balanced on a bundle of letters where he most certainly was wondering what to do next. Socially none of you stand a chance.

Clementine
Of The Three Glands

Clayton Claw stretching back on the bed to rest. In shoes and clothes. The habit of discomfort. Not a toilet seat seen across the countryside. Nor a mirror to record a glimpse of one's appearance. Bloodmourn said he had the god granted right to steal. If no one was looking. But there were heads behind twitching curtains and figures nipping in and out of doorways as we passed through a town. Lined with dying dreams in each shop window. Of how to make a pound hand over fist. Before enrolling with the institute of destitution. Could go on sleeping now. Till the last hour of dying. Where I've been before. Praying it hurts less than living. While you live. And it always pains more. In that big hollow silence. Waiting lonely. A glowing fear in the eyes. As the soul seeps away. When my father was knocked out for the count. He was sitting in his club. An old drab big windowed house behind a little lawn and an iron picket fence on the wide main street the middle of town. He reared up lunch time out of his leather chair. Other members thought he was about to sock someone and got scarce. And came tip toeing back to find him face down dead. Spread out on the morning newspaper his nose pressing against the prices of grain. That was my pop. Who only consummated the most urgent of dirty deals. Those with the biggest and fastest profit. Told me standing on the carpet. Clayton look everyone straight in the eye. Try to scare the shit out of him. And if it doesn't work, smile and firmly shake hands. Then kick the shit out of him. That was my pop. So strong he could twist the neck of a bull or tear a fire escape off the side of a house. One upon which I was trying to retreat. I was momentarily saved by a ball of lightning. Came crackling out of the sky exploding just above pop's head. I said back at him. There. Let's see you knock god around the place. But he was up again. Breaking a plank over his knee. As I looked desperately for my usual small aperture through which to disappear. And I thought I was imagining things. The luck of a bolt of current out of the sky. To incinerate dad. But when the punches were raining down on my ribs. I smelled his scorched hair. That was my pop. Who gave my mother me.

And that evening the middle of spring. The first night of my return. Came a clang at the door. A voice. Erconwald. Asking to enter. Tell him about my father. And perhaps he would tell me about his. Might be a story so sad. Could make a whole nation break down in tears. He stands eyes shining. White collar of a summer shirt out over his lapels.

'Ah good evening good person. It is so nice to see you once again. I trust your trip to the capital was calm and wonderful. And that your return is not too troubled by the scars of the conflagration. For which I extend my most melancholy condolences. It was entirely my fault. I was administering a hot foot to L K L and measuring the pain when he ran out of control into the tower. We have patched up and cleared away where possible. I come now to say goodbye. Reluctantly I must leave.'

'Are the mambas going.'

'They are packed. Our motor is full with petrol. Tyres at their proper pressure.'

'Erconwald. I'm sorry to see you go.'

'Putlog has tuned your organ. Franz has his mineral samples. Of which we hope to send you good news. Should any collapse occur in the mine shaft you have but to let us know.'

'Thank you.'

'The Baron with your permission should like to stay a short while longer. He has found a gramophone and collection of records to which he would like to listen.'

On that sad evening I raised my head from the pillow. Casting an eye across bed tapestries and the mouldering mahoganies. My satin pantaloons and silk hose over the back of a chair. To watch the gentle retreat of this man.

Who said, that though the pestilences devastate and the earth quake, the stately ruins of Castle Charnel would astonish those who came after. Despite the stains of bespattered gore. Left by Bligh. Who enfeebled the L K Ls. With injuries inflicted in your absence. The three locked an hour in combat in the chapel breaking the pews. Bligh leaving Two Backsides Contorted. Who now lay prostrate abed together reciting a litany of legal steps. One prays they will proceed softly. So that the morrows come with hues anew bursting with gladness upon the eyes. And good person you are of splendid mercy. Of kindness never failed. As a young child of three I could multiply two factors and take the cube root of the result in a micro second. Now I go to attend to the death mask of my recently deceased mother during the repose of her remains. I will always answer, good person should you ever cry out. Comfort me.

At dawn from an upper window in the hall I looked down upon the departure. Franz locking a great strap over the bonnet of the motor. Putlog stacking cases on the roof. Hands waved from windows. And down the hill they go. And up over the little stone bridge. And out of sight in the trees of the demesne.

I took suppers before my bedroom fire. Cabbage soup, boiled nettles and potatoes. Credit getting squeezed up at the shop. Voices of discontent heard. About the large amounts owed. But no bill was sent to avoid giving offence. Percival said he was a happy enough shop keeper up there on the hillside behind his counter. Sleeves rolled up over the ledger. His bald head with a big pair of rosy cheeks that used to smile as he rushed in with the latest order. Now they paled and he was very slow to stack up the bacon. Nearly weeping as Percival staggered away under the load. Pausing in the shop doorway to whisper about the latest signs of zinc lead and radium down the mine shaft.

Bloodmourn stood by in the present nervousness. Taking time off from his chess battles with the Baron to nip out of doorways along the corridor bowing and smiling. Said Clementine keep the engines of the good ship Charnel churning. Only a matter of time before the shore of plenty turned up. Meanwhile he was always available on deck to heap new complications when necessary on any misunderstanding. Which came quite soon. With the sound of a motor throbbing up the hill as it did all those months ago. To disgorge again onion eaters. Who had got only as far as the pub. Where an unholy bash raged for three days. While Erconwald went further to the capital on the train to take a death mask of his mother.

Castle inmates short cutted back and forth across the fields to stick out their necks awhile. In the dark throbbing public house interior. Called the Loop Hole. Pushing Mr and Mrs Utah in wheel chairs. So that they too could get toasted in the furnace of blasphemy. And lose a few grey hairs in the maws of discontent. The exprisoners now guarding Gloria. About whom L K L screamed that she was a fuck laid on like hot water in the pipes for anyone able to turn a tap. And that he had already taken a bath.

And the pair of Lead Kindly Lights gave me unfriendly looks as both were perambulated for afternoon outings along the upper hall by Ena and Imelda in white lacy caps to whom they had given large boxes of cream chocolates. Everyone now migrated southerly away from the charred northern rooms. And early one morning Erconwald stood silently in the sunshine streaming through the great hall dome. Binoculars to his eyes as he watched birds nesting in the plaster flamboyancies above the ceiling cornices. Said there were three rare species. Anyone of whom could bomb one with bird shit. And one did just as Erconwald announced that Gloria and he were engaged to be married.

Charlene mornings when I reached for her pulled away. And huffed and said what did I take her for. Since I could hardly take anybody for anything I waited till tea time. When one was more robust. As she backed in with her tray. After a pleasantly solemn afternoon planning my suicide. To take place at dawn on an ocean liner. The moment least objectionable to one's fellow passengers. When most are busy up each other and too exhausted to mind a little sadness over breakfast. If they have the energy to eat at all. Must not be too early in the voyage to depress everyone for the rest of the trip. At four a.m. plunge over the rails at the stern. On the night of the fancy dress ball. Just when everyone got to know each other. Well enough for a little discord to set in. But before the deep dislike began. With the blossom of friendship.

'What's the matter Charlene.'

'Nothing's the matter.'

'You're angry.'

'I'm not.'

'You are.'

'What if I am. Why should you want to know. When you've ignored me over all these weeks. I'm only a servant. Ordered around by everyone in this place. I'm fed up with it. And I'm leaving. I only waited till you got back to tell you so. It's not that I'm not content to keep my place. But you let the gang of them sponge, steal, cheat you and nearly burn the place down. The shenanigans that went on here after you were gone would make the devil himself blush. Every night the same. I was chased in fear of my life. If they weren't pestering me in the kitchen they were one after the other pounding on my bedroom door drunk to get in. Percival lugging the wine non stop to them. The first course wouldn't be down before half of them would be up fighting. The plates of food flung all over the place. I'm not saying I didn't have a good laugh now and again. When Mrs L K L went after that Gloria off with her husband. The two of them sacrilegiously in behind the organ pipes of the chapel. Have your tea before it gets cold.'

Swallows zooming out across the sky. Scooping up midges, moths and butterflies. A honk from pigs Tim is rearing in a barn. Grinding down everything they get their mouths to. Crunching apples, crushing berries and tearing through cabbage leaves. Tails tightly curled up on their backs. Eating with such purity of demeanour. To get fat.

'I'm sorry you had difficulties Charlene.'

'It was nothing as to what some others had. One afternoon didn't a pleasant lady and gentleman real swank with walking sticks arrive just asking about the historic site. And they themselves were a sight soon enough. It started with just a comment on a painting. One of them ones on the dining room wall. I wouldn't know what he meant but Franz called them cultural impostors. Seated to dinner they were. And this L K L takes down the two paintings and calmly as you please he crashes one over the man's head and another over the lady. Leaving the two of them speechless sitting with their faces sticking out from the portraits. Can you imagine. Your property. Wrecked on a pair of strangers you didn't even invite by a gang of spongers you can't get rid of. Then didn't the visitors lift off the paintings and go on eating their food as if not a thing had happened. That's the thing with this place, you can do what you like to anyone but not one of them will get up and leave. Except Percival. And he's taken leave of his senses. Referring to you as his royal highness and to himself as maître d'hôtel. An hour he was teaching me pronounce it. Waltzing into the kitchens. Standing up on an old crate like he was directing an army of slaves. Calling me the sauce cook. As if we had a fish cook, meat cook and a veg cook. I gave him the back side of a ladle as the soup cook. It missed him because when I swung he was falling off the crate drunk. You're just too good hearted. Everyone is taking advantage of you. I was saving some nice little bits of ham for your return. Had it ready to hide away. I went to relieve myself and got back and it was gone every scrap. But tonight I have hidden a nice bit of fish. Not one of them will find. Swimming it is in the rain barrel in the courtyard. Would you like it fried in a bit of butter.'

Percival setting a table for dinner in the octagonal room. Wine coasters, decanters and candelabra. The turf fire blazing in the grate dancing on his monocle. He said he'd been delving into science in the library. And that the milky way was the road by which the dead travel to heaven. Stepping from star to star.

'Sure sir I know more than any one of them. Gave that Franz a dose of scientific data that had him gasping in his tracks. So desperate was he I let him have the definition of an amputon. He didn't have the faintest idea it was an electron without armpits. There he was standing dumbfounded in his sandals in the great hall ready to go down in history as an eegit. I told him I didn't like his aeronautics one bit. The likes of him are still paying their respects to the flat earth society. I am myself of course a member of the society for the prevention of clocks recording time. What I wouldn't do to him in the glare of public opinion. I'd mesmerize him first with the facts and then reduce him to academic nudity in his socks.'

'Have we any clean napkins.'

'Ah there's been such a call lately on the linen sir. Before it can be washed I find it's got to be re-used first.'

'The wine.'

'Ah the wine. There's been a call on that too sir. You've never seen the likes of the capacity of this crowd for madeira, hock and claret.'

'I want locks put on the linen, the silver, the wine, the larder.'

'Your highness go no further. Haven't I been wanting to do that all the while. But there isn't a lock in the place.'

'Use nails.'

'Nails sir wouldn't stop this bunch. Even before their appetites get the better of them they're wielding crow bars to get their hands on things. Haven't I caught them L K Ls time and again trying to get off with an heirloom. Sir it's the bad manners. If it wasn't for that Erconwald the lack of manners would send the lot of us jumping out the monk's tunnel into the jaws of the great conger. A light is badly needed in the moral darkness. Castle ghosts are hiding in shame. But now sir listen. I have it in a nutshell. Introduce expertise to the running of the castle. Of a morning collect a tariff from the occupants of every room. Why not look forward rather than backward sir. It's a hotel we're running.'

A steaming tureen. Charlene's fish in sauce. Served by Percival assisted by Oscar wearing a cap because he was jumping up hitting his head with fright. Along the servants' passages. And now a white wine poured. Good moments like this. Warmed by flames and tastiness. As the night begins. Out on a wild coast. Where the sheep shelter against the stone walls. Sea swells hissing up cliff sides. And exploding in caves to send overland bubbles of creamy white spray. Long necked birds perched on the rocks. Black feathers washed by the sad grey waves. Touch a golden wine to the lips. Ease down the buttery fish. Surrounded by all these choosy little courtesies.

Clementine eating his sweet of cream smothered butterscotch pudding. With news that the mob had descended again from the pub and were braying outside the walls. Percival telling them to go away. That the master was at vespers and could not be disturbed.

'Sir it's that one with the roulette wheel. Said he'd give you some of the rake off.'

'Tell him to come back tomorrow. There's going to be a ball.'

'You don't mean to say sir.'

'I want the ballroom opened. And lashings of everything laid on.'

'Sir I knew all the time you'd strike the right note. But that bunch when finished emptying the bottles would drink the darkness out of a cave.'

'I want you to get an invitation to the Macfuggers.'

'It's action stations sir. I could get the Novena flying flags and have it moored with lights out in the bay.'

'Just the ballroom.'

'Aye aye. Would we care to get some publicity sir. You'd want to be pretty nippy now to keep up a proper image. With the likes of the sort prancing in the limelight these days. Ah I'm telling you the enchantment is going to be to your liking. Leave it to me. The priest to hear confessions in the chapel ahead of time. Start off spiritually fresh. Nothing like a new sin committed when you're forgiven of the old. Have you ever confessed sir.'

'No.'

'Do you a power of good. You've been in a pessimistic state. A confession clears up the past in one go. Lays the future at your feet flat as a pancake you'd dance over and roll up and eat. I've never been happier in me life before. Even with this bunch we've got beating the daylights out of one another. But hasn't it always cleared the air and led to a meeting of the minds as soon as they could lift their heads up off the carpet. I'll admit sometimes you'd ask for a bit of solitude to move the bowels in peace. Which is no longer the case in any field up there beyond where every one of them poisonous snakes has got away below the pub.'

Percival brings port. Lain quietly waiting for lips for forty years. Stretch out in the chair bathed with red fire glow. The slowly pounding sea. Cold draughts blowing up between the floor boards. Grand aunt must have planned to freeze me out of the world. When they couldn't kill me in the hospital. Good to sit for a change in one's own castle eating the lion's share. Swallowing this purple sweet sustenance. When summer comes can lie out on the grass. Let the ticks suck my blood. After all the mambas are killed. The world will explode in green again. If only I can be there waiting. Having over the years abided by my little commandments. Thou shalt not pick nose, nor fart loudly in another's proximity, nor within another's sight play too robustly with the privates. Nor stick the prick where it is not wanted. Just a little belching is to be allowed. Not to end up being the man folk show their children. To say don't grow up dilapidated like him. Bloodmourn knows some secret. Keeps him undaunted. Franz has his water clock. A buoyant brass bowl with a tiny hole in the bottom. Floats in a pail of liquid. Gauge the aqueous atoms passing through the hole as it sinks. None of the three trust the modern watch. Erconwald a stickler for the column sundial. Putlog for wheatstone's solar chronometer. Rose said they once beat the shit out of each other over the right time. Wielding their various clocks. On a street corner of the park near their laboratory in the capital. Franz flinging his portable pail of water in Erconwald and Putlog's faces. When the argument was settled another fight commenced a block later as to the nature of the earth's core. A random substance suggested brought colour to the cheeks of some onlookers. As the other two shouted and gesticulated at a silent Erconwald. None of them ever without a pocket sundial with polar pin to adjust to suit any latitude. Know the time and direction in which to follow a theory. And Erconwald that evening attired in boots pushing a wheelbarrow with a lantern illuminating a geographical graph of semi-precious minerals. The three engrossed in experiment were melancholic. But before they were finished they would be selling daylight to the world.

Charlene collecting tray. Stands with her moist sparkling eyes. Arms held out. Sleeves of a green sweater pushed up on her pale strong wrists. Her nose a neat white rudder on her face. Steer her near. With flattery and affection. Before one more heavy hearted day has landed.

'The fish was excellent and the pudding a delight.'

'It's just the work of a nobody.'

'Put the tray down.'

'Why. What's the use of me getting upset thinking you might have something to do with me when you could be gone tomorrow and I'd be left mumbling to myself.'

'Put down the tray. Please.'

'I'll do as I'm told. But that won't change a thing.'

'We're having a ball. I want you to come as a guest.'

'I'd be jeered out of the kitchens and sent cowering down into the dungeons by the rest of them. They'd be striped purple in the face with jealousy. It isn't that I wouldn't like to come as a guest but I could be there anyway.'

'It's going to be a house warming.'

'You'd hardly need that after the burnings and blastings.'

Charlene lowering the tray to the table. And scraping up a finger full of whipped cream and butterscotch pudding. Sucking it into her mouth. Sits on the edge of the bed as she licks her lips. Curls on her head glistening in the candle-light. The whiteness of her wrists where it fades into the red of her hands. Muscle across the smooth corner of her jaw twitching. And a vein below on her throat throbbing. The blue eyed strength of her with a body like a bird.

'Your highness would you ever lower the iron door. It's not that I'm suspicious but you just never know in this place whose ears are getting a mindful. And to tell you the truth there's never a time I pass that coffin room down the steps there when I'm not thinking something might come out at me dead or alive and either worse than the other.'

Clementine lowering the portal. With squeaks and the clank of chain. Lifting across iron bars. Turning bolts. To step back through the ante room. Bolt the servants' door. Fortified against the world. To see her sitting in the light. Of one candle on the table. The wax smoke smell of the others blown out. Her sweater in her lap. Two more at her feet on the floor. One yellow one pink. A garment draped from her waist over her hips. Her breast silhouetted in the light. Count the thin shadows of three ribs below. Her fists clenched tight. Her knees knocking. Who dat dere. The west's awake tonight.'

'Wow.'

'In case you've seen a lot of women. I thought I'd show you what I had.'

Clayton Claw Cleaver slowly rising on tiptoe. To see what one could see flat footed. Swallowing saliva by the bucket. Her shoulders arched forward. Always thought they were so big. Now they're small. Without the sweaters. Folded wings. Tips of breasts dipping and tipping. As she leans. And bows her head. Which she chopped off a chicken. In one almighty swipe. When I retreated some paces backwards from the splashing blood. Relieved by her smile. Death all over the place. Rats fuming under floorboards. Hear night cries from seagulls perched on the ramparts. Bloodmourn said on the trip cross country that he frequently needed a change of human beings. To vary the flavour of the treacheries. Charlene can milk forty cows at a sitting. Sinewy muscles flex in her arms. Sits waiting her hands atremble. Biting her lips. If Elmer had a mate I could breed more of him and live surrounded by faithful man eating dogs. No one likes a growling monster breathing heavily rushing at you in the dark. Teeth flashing if there's moonlight. Sound of fangs gnashing if there isn't. Descend now upon one of my loyal staff. Like that man with his prow of a ship crossing the waters down Rose's flooded flat. A moment remembered by mariners everywhere. With jib booms jutting. This is what I look like under sail. As she sits there ready for my vessel sailing into port.

'Charlene why are you shaking.'

'Because I'm scared. Because you might throw me out when you've finished with me. And I don't want to go. I kissed you the time of the blast when I had your head in my hands. I was thrilled the first moment you came into the kitchens. I was at me wits' end with despair. Not knowing where to find this or that. Or what was expected of me. Thought there'd be some mad old red nosed landowner with a big stick and gaiters ready to jump out at me and beat me within an inch of my life.'

Clementine standing trousers dropped around the ankles. In last month's underwear. Never know I had a haberdasher once. Just up the concrete street from aunt's big corporation. All the drawers, shirts and socks spread out tied up in ribbons behind two shiny windows. Always met with a smile of devastating courtesy. When stepping in out of the lunchtime window watchers. Ah Mr Clementine, how are you for socks. Fine. But just now I'm in a bad way with castles. I liked that man. Fervently selling shirts. There when needed. To comfort me. With his confidential whisper, this is what they're wearing now. I'd try to be calm. And not shout out for god's sake give me some. To stun the guys at the office. Who had no mercy if they caught you a fraction out of style. Passing me with side glances at the water cooler. Where I'd have a think over a paper cup. About why the clock had such a slow struggle to move the hands around to quitting time. When I could go thronging with thousands of others to the train. That never stopped at a crossroads. Where there's nothing but night and day. Of winds, mist and rain. And another gull's cry. As Charlene charges. Tugging at my clothes. Tearing off her own. Hands digging in my hair. Teeth sinking in my neck. A randy hearted tigress roaring up from the kitchens. Hold tight to her hard handy bumps of arse. Spin together down on the bed. Crawling up on me pushing a breast smothering on my face. Where goes a mariner. On this stormy sailing. Avoiding ship wreck in wet dreams. Grab tendons stretched under her armpits. Flourishing with hair. Musty and steamy scented. Chewing at my ears. Biting down along my throat.

Feel I've been dug up out of last winter's leaves. A root shining ripe and white. Get it into her. Veins and all. Between the soft liquids swelling. As the words rush out of her mouth. Your highness I would give up God for you. Not that he's ever given me anything but a kick in the teeth. But wherever you look there's some kind of trouble. You'd wonder how does a mother's love last that a child takes away. Mine's been just a little knot tied up in me ready to burst. Like tonight. When I can't control or help myself. And it would be no relief to know that everyone has these worries. That have denied me beautiful fingernails. Chewed as they've been with distress. That thing of yours up me is like a blessing from on high. The light of a sacred candle I'm telling you. Scares away all me mountainous horrors. You were struck with that Lady Macfugger. The thought of it gives me heartburn. Maybe I'm not socially up to scratch. But I defy her to enjoy your tool more. They'll never make me marry a dirty old man with his hands all over me. And not one of his own teeth to keep his jaw from shutting up over his nose. That's what they do with us here in the country. They farrow you fat every year like a pig. Till you get swept away with the sorrow. Of the screaming children growing up around your knees. Ah there in your eyes. I see soft things. Doves and the like of that flying. I'm a woman but the contemplation of babies in my belly makes me vomit. Unless it had a father like you. I was the smartest young girl in the district. With just a lot of hard calluses on my hands and heels to show for it. And if you had nothing further to do with me. You'd be right. I could go away content with your juice up inside. But what you need is a wife. That shook you. Forget I mentioned it. It's not a safe subject. Like the lady visitor in the town who made an observation in the pub about the weather thinking it harmless enough among the touchy customers. Said it was a rainy day and had her nose broken for it. That's all it is, cantankerousness.

Charlene swinging her head spreading her hair. All over her shoulders. Gallant frisky girl. Her chest flushed red. Taste of salty sweat on her skin. Whispered she was a fiery fuck. While she said mind your tongue or I'll give you a wallop for your impudence, provided you give me more of another gallop. For our pleasures. Over this grand night ahead. Heard tell you could do it sitting on a stool. Get up on it like you would a saddle. Let's try it like that. When you think a moment, there's much more to living than fuchsia, grass and granite. Heard tell it could be kissed. And I'll have a taste of that too.

Musty mouldering smells on my palms. Tainted from the damp upholstery. Sitting as she sits on top of it her legs crossing my lap. So many times in this life when you can throw a thoroughly wasted tantrum. Or fuck. Or let evil thwartings rise up so big they blind and make you prisoner. Till you can't walk nor talk. Charlene said she laughed a moment when she lost her virginity. When the man who owned the shops said in confidence. That his wife when he was up on her read the deaths in the evening newspaper over his shoulder where she held it open behind his back. He got so used to it he'd ask her who was shaking hands with God today. And nothing now for me to see behind Charlene as we just look behind each other. Where I can't believe the wall has begun to move. But it has. Creaking slowly open. Right there where once there was a panel. And now there's an opening door. And standing there. As Charlene and I clutch each other naked. Is Bloodmourn. Festooned in cobwebs and dust. In yachting cap and trousers and his Samson badge. A lantern held high. Deflecting his face in view of our modesty. To make that remark.

'I beg your pardon.'

And
Does one
Say
It's given
In this delicate
Moment
Of despair

20

As suddenly as he had come. Bloodmourn disappeared that night. Falling backwards down a flight of stairs behind him that he'd just climbed up. Said he found the passage exploring his bedroom wall when he thought he heard sounds in there.

In my portable copper bath steamed up with bubbles I lay basking. As Oscar lugged the pails of hot water. And with a tin of Gloria's talcum powder Bloodmourn came in. This time under the suspended iron door. Bathing the night of the ball. While confessions were being heard in the chapel. And in robes of state dug out by Percival, Bloodmourn sat on the stool. Held out wrists from the ermine cuffs and surveyed his fingernails. And his hands shook.

'Clementine you've got to marry that girl.'

'I beg your pardon.'

'I insist upon it. The engagement must be announced at once. You must give your solemn undertaking that you will do this. And end your reckless bachelorhood of wanton lust instantly. I will be best man of course.'

Bloodmourn's smile. Says he dearly loves his own wife and children. Making an appointment each year for a photographer to snap them seated together to show that they were a little family united. His lips widen whitely over his teeth as he takes his leave. He thought he might try confession in the chapel. Under great strain these days in the chess battle with the Baron, who was winning in the recent campaign fourteen games to seven. Who said now to Bloodmourn's moves. If dat's so den dis is so.

From an ancient armoury in a windowless vault beneath the cloisters. Six small cannons were rolled out and lugged upstairs to give a military air to the ballroom. Holly leaves with berries strung up on walls and pilasters. Blazing fires lit under the carved marble mantelpieces. Emblazoned with the arms of Clementine. Candle light gleaming and sparkling through the crystal chandeliers. Ina and Imelda with plates of goodies. As Tim and Oscar ferry wine from the caves and Percival chalks off the dangerous areas of the floor.

Turning into the chapel I saw Mini Monk with a group of assistants carry his roulette wheel along the hallway. He said the percentage rake off could be substantial. With the doors open to all comers. For a floor show Padrick could do the trick with his tool. While Rose reaches high c in an octave of her choosing. And Putlog will pound the organ with an anniversary waltz. Danced by Mr and Mrs Utah.

Two bowed figures in the front row of the chapel. Flowers on the altar rail, the marble balustrade polished gleaming. A stone confessional, gargoyles of spitting devils sticking from the cornices. A painted screen behind which the sinner kneels. As I kneel to watch the rays of light stream in the narrow windows behind the altar, throwing soft shadows on the cold white stone walls. Hear larks chirping and voices in the confessional. One of which is Bligh's.

'I committed an impure act father.'

'What was that. What did you say.'

'I committed an impure act.'

'I can't hear you. Speak up.'

'I committed an impure act.'

'That's better. Was it alone or with others.'

'With others. But I also did alone.'

'How many times did you commit the impure act alone.'

'Six.'

'And with others.'

'It was a night of impurity father. I couldn't help myself.'

'What do you mean by that.'

'It started before midnight and ended at dawn.'

'What on earth were you doing.'

'I beg your pardon father.'

'You heard me, what on earth were you doing.'

'For Jesus' sake father not so loud.'

'Don't you dare you dirty cur invoke the name of the saviour in this confessional.'

'I'm only after forgiveness father. It's not nice to be called a cur. And I have a business to watch after.'

'O you have have you. After your night of impurity. Is she married or single this creature victim of your carnal appetite.'

'I wouldn't know how to answer that.'

'Did you pick up with a woman of the streets. Do you want to be diseased in body as well as in mind.'

'To tell you the truth father I just want to get me absolution and get out of here. I'm only a visitor to the place.'

'Well I've heard plenty of tales in this confessional before from better people than yourself and if you had the time to sin you'll have the time now to confess.'

'Father there might be people listening will you give me the absolution. I'm a business man.'

'Business man, what difference do you think that makes to me. You dirty thing you. You should be ashamed of yourself. Spending your profits on whoredom when the lord has a kingdom in need of income. Dirty.'

'Father the church owns plenty.'

'And we need it with the likes of you coming in here to this confessional demanding absolution for a night of lust.'

'I spent the night with a man.'

'You what.'

'A man.'

'Well now that's an entirely different cauldron of octopus altogether.'

'Thank you father.'

'Close your mouth you eegit, thank me, how dare you presume such a tactic. Where were you educated.'

'In the capital.'

'Keep your dirty city habits to yourself then and not bring them out here among these poor innocent people. What business are you in.'

'I can't tell you that father.'

'By God you will or I'll come out of this confessional and drive you from the sanctity of this chapel.'

265

'Well I am as you might say in the brewing trade.'

'Scandalous that you should behave then as you've done with a good business of that nature.'

'Well recently I've expanded into electrical appliances.'

'Dear God you might have guessed it. Are you a practising homosexual.'

'No no, I'm only learning.'

'Do you know how your lord looks on such behaviour. He despises it. You're the sort who would be watching down there on the beach of a summer evening bare bottomed little boys disrobing to attire themselves in bathing costumes while their fresh gleaming cheeks shone in the sunlight.'

'I've not been down there on the beach father. Except to launch some little kiddies for a boat ride after a choir recital.'

'So you're the one. Took those innocents out there on the high seas where they nearly lost their lives.'

'Ah father for God's sake will you give me a chance to remain obscure. For the moment at least. And when I run for political office I'll let you know.'

'Don't you despise yourself.'

'A little bit father.'

'You should be ashamed.'

'I am. A whole lot.'

'You sullied yourself. Insulted God. Threw in his face a mess of filth. God who loves you. Who has given you a good business.'

'Yes father.'

'Beg his forgiveness, go to him now, lay your heart at his feet.'

'Yes father.'

'And when the temptation comes again to consort with men ask him to give you strength to resist. And if this is not possible try not to let heinousness continue till dawn. Are you with me. What on earth are you doing.'

'Sorry father, it's tomorrow's first race, the three thirty, there's a bookmaker taking bets at the castle ball tonight.'

'Well I'll give you a tip for that.'

'I fancy Incorrigible to win.'

'Not a bit of it, put your money on Unborn Son.'

'Thank you father.'

'Now say the rosary six times, put a pound in the poor box.'

'It'd be stolen by the inmates in a second here father.'

'Give it to me then.'

'Put it on Unborn Son.'

'That's enough of that kind of a suggestion.'

'Sorry father.'

'Make a novena to steer you from any temptation in the future. And god willing try to direct your thoughts to the purity of the blessed virgin. Remember that simplicity, candour and artlessness are the hallmarks of a noble nature. Let the current of deep faith sweep you into the arms of our lady.'

'Watch that now father.'

'Yes perhaps that's not the proper expression.'

'I'll say not.'

'Go then and sin no more.'

'Right you are. Are you coming to the ball father.'

'I don't think I've been invited.'

'Well you are now.'

'Thank you.'

'Thank you father.'

Bligh head bowed, his grey jacket stretched tight by his enormous shoulders and thick neck, slowly approaches the altar and kneels. As Clementine retreats smartly into the shadows. And emerges in a doorway of the ballroom. Mini Monk standing under a chandelier hunched over a table. Taking a few practice flicks of the little steel ball zooming and clattering around the spinning wheel.

'I think your majesty you'll be very happy with this wee caper tonight. You'll have a nice little cut of the pie. Your premises I don't mind saying are most suitable. You wouldn't be interested would you in a more permanent use. As you might say for a casino. I mean I know you would not care to enter trade or that kind of thing. Just a discreet little operation. With only the very best people.

None of your yobs and yobos. Strictly the better sort of type. I am personally acquainted with a clientele of the calibre of Major Macfugger and Lady Macfugger. The major likes a little pot luck on the wheel of fortune. Ah speak of the devil. Major.'

'I say there Mini Monk you wretched little mole tunnelling into people's fortunes. By God Clementine you're not half having a little soirée. Just got your invitation. Thought I'd come early. Been in a bit of a funk you know. Badly need a bash. Caught my woman taking another's horn. Threw me back a bit. Man doesn't like his mare having a stray poke. Very shoddy. Simply not on. But by jove, you're looking the part. The Clementine. I'd say we'll give the women in the bed more fornicators as well as delphiniums tonight. Send a lot of your cunts straight back to sea level.'

Major Macfugger in a three cornered hat and long pink swallow tailed coat. Lacy frills at his throat. Black pantaloons with shiny leather codpiece and white hose stretched tightly on Nails' solid legs. Hanging between his sky blue faced lapels a crystal locket enclosing a splinter of the true cross. As he tapped a bull whip against the tip of his gleaming slipper.

'By God Clementine the wenches will get due discharge of the usual local impulses of country gentlemen on this night or I stand here unjustified like a stiff prick without balls.'

Macfugger raising his bull whip overhead. Mini Monk and Clementine ducking as the long lash curled down the ballroom where it cut a candle in half with a bang.

'I mean to say haven't lost my touch. Keeps a party from getting out of hand. Some chap want to prang the missus and we might make a little sliced cucumber out of his cock.'

Clementine carefully and slowly folding hands together. Wouldn't want that around the neck. Who knows what Lady Macfugger might have said in her sleep. Begging me to get up her. And then groaning that I was. Take comfort she's a lady of principle. Not the sort to whisper the name, address and number of testes of a lover. To the hubby. Just to fuss things up a bit.

'Yes Clementine by God, just let me catch the chap. I'll make his arse hole hoot in fear because his neck will be splashing blood like a fountain.'

'Excuse me major, just must see to a few things. Please, do help yourself to a drink.'

Clementine striding quickly down the hall. Past all these bed, dressing and ante rooms. At the top of the grand staircase. Looking down. People taking off their coats. And my God. Lady Macfugger. Must find out if she's squealed. About our harmless little innocent attempt. To play temporary husband and wife. Percival lifting a white fur wrap from her shoulders. Ermine everywhere. Even round my own neck and wrists. Makes one feel one can make a decision. Amazing what a little costume does for the spirit.

'Gail, how good to see you.'

'How good to see you Clayton. I am sorry about my bank getting cold feet. They take such a short sighted view. Especially if you cloud it with a little bad news. By the way what are all those men doing assembling out in front of the castle. They look like troops.'

Clementine rushing up the grand stair followed by a stately white gowned Lady Macfugger red flushes where the black was round her eyes. Both stopping along the hall to peer out a window in the lowering dusk. Colonel Macdurex standing in front of a band of men abreast row after row. An evening mist tumbling over their heads. Just push this window open a bit. To hear.

'All right men. Company A and B take the north rear. F Company are already in position in the orchard cloisters and mountain meadows. C Company will take possession of the wine cellars. D Company will remain in position. Myself and adjutants will enter the front. Two rapid shots fired is the signal that resistance has been encountered and you all know what to do. Synchronize watches. Proceed now to your previously assigned objectives. Up the republic.'

Weapons bulging under their raincoats, Macdurex standing mid hall with his command. Nodding his head as Clementine approaches. Percival peeking from the doorway under stair. Three exprisoners emerging from the state room sten guns levelled. Infiltrators had us occupied the whole time. Not even a chance to make a ceremonial boom from the cannons. Lady Macfugger just behind me a little to my left. Her eyebrows raised. Group of guests I've never seen before appear to be biting their fingernails. Watching this bloodless victory.

'Good evening Mr Clementine, as you can see the time has come. It's only a matter now of determining whether you want us to embroider easter lilies in your lapels by sten gun or offer no resistance to my troops carrying out their authorized commands. We have you surrounded and have achieved complete isolation of this area with a road block at the bridge. All coaxial cables have been severed. Now with fourteen minor explosions courteously effected or four major blasts rudely implemented Charnel Castle symbol of oppression would be no more. It means little to us whether we are obliged to effect completion of the mission by using the former or the latter.'

'Colonel.'

'Commandant.'

'Commandant I'd rather if you and your troops just made yourselves at home and joined the ball I'm giving tonight.'

'A little irregular but I take it that you do not intend to offer resistance.'

'No.'

'Adjutant, call off the air support immediately.'

'Yes sir.'

'Good God, Commandant were you going to bomb us.'

'No need to be alarmed. It would have only been a little bit of softening up. Loosen the mortar around the stones as you might say. With a few near misses. Just some explosive chucked from our corps of hot air balloons.'

A military march thundering from the library where the Baron sits listening to the gramophone. Tears pouring down his cheeks. Little bit of dried egg yoke on his silver tie. Franz in a white coat, a book open across his lap. Looks up as I come in and back down again as I go out. To stroll along the hall. Where a group of kids stand each holding each other's hand.

'Hello kids. Who's the spokesman. Are you little girl, you're the biggest.'

'These are my brothers and sisters. Charlene who works here is our big sister.'

'Ah. Well welcome. Now you kids just go in that door there. The stairway goes up around in a circle. Go out the first door you come to then follow the crowd. There'll be a lot of good things on the tables to eat. Help yourselves.'

Clementine descending into the cellars. A monstrous rat stops looks and gambols across the tunnel crossroads. At the great range Charlene sweating over the pots and vats. Her two swelling ripe globes of arse. Which both my palms deliciously itch to clutch. And now touch. With heart pounding, breath heaving. As soon as I lay eyes on her. To hear her tuneful voice. As she turns around with a smile.

'You want something don't you.'

'Yes.'

'Can't you see I'm cooking.'

'Leave it.'

'All right.'

Clementine behind Charlene both hands on her cheeks as she mounts the stairs. In the shadows looking backwards delightedly over her shoulder. Must make this fast. Just as Gloria does. Bang bang bang. Charlene licking her lips as we go left through this room with sacks of potatoes. A big beetle squashed under foot. Percival said they were biting the inmates at night. Sinking into legs and thighs with pincers that stung from both head and tail. To leave guests covered with big red weals in the morning. Nowhere safe left in this castle. Any wall might open up and a bunch of turbaned merchants selling rugs descend. So far the insects are on my side.

Clementine in this dark musty storage room. Sweeping

aside court regalia to lift Charlene up by her rear acorns and stick her on it. Get it over fast so she can get back to the cooking. And I can say wow holy cow sooner. And do it again later after the ball. One avoided noticing Rose in the library. Seated with a whole branch of bananas nearly devoured, a stack of skins on the nearby floor. First she was. To blow me in the castle. And warn of the insurgents. Pity they couldn't have knocked off a few of the guests before the surrender. Especially those who drunkenly attempted to eat the embroidered bowls of fruit out of the tapestries. And chewed on shreds instead. Last night I had a dream of the hospital. Where they put two scalpel cuts in a cross over my heart. I heard drums. Saw men with a tiny coffin. Carrying a child. A sorrow too big to hold. And Charlene with all her little brothers and sisters. Born babies could come teeming out of her. Nine months after this cardinal sin. Committed between master and servant. Erconwald seen wandering with Gloria as she wore the death mask of his mother. Keep it all in the family. And suggest a midnight cruise for everybody. Ocean going. With the engines boiling up the dark water. Just how it was when Bloodmourn and I were coming over. Leaving a wake of flat white streaked water marbled green. Each day dawning on that wide open sea. Taking me further away from a grave. Which closes slowly as each thing steps out of your life. Leaving you with what's left of yours. Like one cold thanksgiving day. When the wind came down the streets and shivered one's trousers below the knees. I sat waiting in aunt's chauffeured car. When fingers tapped at the window. Which I lowered and heard a voice ask for money. That he was starving. That he had come out of hospital. That he was a college graduate and an engineer. I shook my head no. And saw him slowly raise his hand in a wave goodbye and his face swing back and forth in despair. He reeled away down the street sick and dying. I called him back. He wasn't lying. And I knew because both of us were going the same way. Helpless and hopeless. All hostility extinguished in the eyes. When someone's got to shout. Loud and clear. And straight down from the stars. Don't

for Christ's sake commit your soul. Into the master's hands
yet you eegit. It will make you think you're in your prime.

> If you
> Wait
> Till you've had
> One more
> Fuck
> Sublime

21

Charlene invited to the ball above said she wanted to stay below. Where she groaned. As I roared. And shook. In our glad throbbing frenzy. I held her by the arse and she clung round my neck. Smashing cobwebs. Knocking mushrooms off the walls with her outstretched legs. As the rats scurried by.

From the musty private dark we left to watch the night fall over the sea. Out the mouth of the monk's tunnel. The black rising waves. A fading crescent of moon. Spring tides thundering waters up against the cliffs. Down where the mollusca cling. And the long tail of the great conger waves. While the huge mouth waits gloating fish eyed in the deep.

Folk collecting in the great hall of Charnel Castle. Where Franz stood costumed as a pirate in the doorway of his mine shaft. Said drilling was still proceeding. In a hole at forty five degrees inclination to the southwest. Through weakly mineralized rock. That would soon strike it rich. And would I like to buy a share. Of my own mine. Just printed. And hot off Erconwald's press.

Percival rushing by. Arms laden with pillows. For folk's bottoms on all the hard ballroom chairs. His big hands and blackened fingernails. Sweat across his brow. Said he'd never seen the like of such an evening. That Mick the strong man had come and was up there balancing a cart wheel on his nose.

'By God your highness it's the last word. You've never seen such a gathering in your life. They're laying bets on the roulette wheel like you'd put hammers into the heads of your inlaws. Commandant Macdurex is now this very moment ready to send fireworks off the battlements. One casualty so far. A champagne cork got your man an insurgent right between the eyes. Knocked him down and gave his hair a rinse. He's claiming war wounds. But your grace you'd better close your cloak. I think your cod piece is missing.'

'O my goodness.'

'Ah on a night like tonight your worship a little item like that showing would not be out of place.'

'What are you suggesting Percival.'

'Well I wouldn't want to give offence but I'd say before the night's over we'll see bottoms up and tops down. Like absurdities are the stuff sir, of great philosophies so too is mixed company the manure for flowering pleasures. Are you right.'

'Are you right Percival.'

'Beg your pardon sir, I shouldn't get so familiar but I wouldn't want you to miss anything in the way of sport. Haven't you had months of troubles. Fissures everywhere in the lead on the roof. Water flowing unwanted down the walls. It's what saved us in the fire. You could see the very flame shrinking back.'

The front portals wide open. Breeze blowing in the sounds of chatter and voices in the forecourt. Hulking man in tattered sweater, blotches of grease on his tiny brow. Great hawk nose between his close set blazing eyes. Standing with another. Shorter fatter rounder. Good grief the man last seen belt around the navel squatted for a shit in Veronica's attic room. While she, brave naked creature that she was, wrestled with the landlord.

These two. They waddle forward. Shoe tongues curled up from their muddy footwear. Eyes darting to the few remaining instruments of war hanging on the wall. And come walking up to me. Their trousers bagged out like balloons.

'Me name's Evil. His name is Bad. Together we are called Fucking Bad Evil. Do you understand me now. That's us. Where's the libation.'

'It's above in the ballroom.'

'I'll take you into my present confidence. Just let me whisper you this. You've never met the likes of us before.

And you'll be fucking thankful not to do so again. Never done a thing in me life to be proud of. And I've never felt in better health. I get me kicks pulling the life savings out of the hands of sick old widows. The only job I ever had was to measure corpses for their coffins heading for the crematorium. I'd measure them all a foot too short. They have to break the legs to fit them in. There would be them with the knees sticking up as they ride towards the flames. I'll tell you it gave the bereaved a sight they'll never forget. I'm villainous and mean. If you want anybody to have his neck broken. Just give me the word. My friend here is famous for his filthy habits. Overnight he can produce squalor that would sicken even the likes of me.'

The Fucking Bad Evil climbed together up the grand stairs. As Percival comes running up. A candelabra in one hand, nodding upwards where the two F B Es stand looking down.

'Sir I don't like the look of them one bit. Chancers the pair of them. Crawled up from out of the ditch somewhere.'

More faces pouring in. The entire hunt rumoured on horseback with hounds crossing the mountains and heading this way. Word travels far and fast over the countryside. And right to the gates of the capital. Where everyone must know there's a bash raging here. For there stands Mr Oboe from the bank. And judging by the nature of the curl in her hair. That's his wife. Tall blonde twinkle eyed and friendly. A cigarette holder in her hand. Short fur wrap over her shoulders.

'Your highness I would like you to meet my wife. I thought I'd look your place over. And see what we could do for you. Fire damage seems limited. My immediate impression is that a lot could be accomplished by the cutting down of overheads. What's that there.'

'The mine shaft.'

'You don't say. Is there something down there.'

'My engineer Dr Franz Pickle BFB says there is adequate evidence of mineralization sufficient for mining.'

'I dare say my directors will not say ho hum when they hear of this.'

'I hope not.'

'Your highness we mustn't keep you from your other guests. But I'll have a chat with your engineer if you don't mind.'

Amazing what a party will do. Besides running up one monstrous bill and cleaning one out of drink forever. Folk get to see the grandiose scheme of things close up. And with a greedy imagination the distant prospect can look great. Sometimes a little of my pop comes out in me. He said the whole world was a bazaar. And just to make it more exciting the prices were different for everybody.

Mr and Mrs Utah got up all over with a festoonery of ostrich feathers. Given to them by that changed man Erconwald. Now with another miniature death mask hanging from his neck. Plus a stop watch to time Gloria's orgasms as she wears the dead expression of his mother. The two of them wandering arm in arm as Erconwald former herbivore wolfed down chunks of raw meat Gloria threw up in the air for him to catch in his mouth. And for the first time I heard Erconwald laugh.

Putlog arriving with two fiddlers and a spoon player in tow and a gentleman with a portable table of bottles into the top of which he blew. The little group assembled by a faded mirror in the ballroom. Putlog with a piece of willow branch conducting the band through some light footed airs. And Mick the strong man with Charlene's brothers and sisters as three sit clinging to each of his outstretched arms.

Mini Monk taking bets. Donning sun glasses and giving little twitches of his shoulders and head with each spin of the wheel. An assistant pale eyed and thin with black hair greased back on his head. Lady Macfugger seated her platinum mesh evening bag next to a mountainous stack of chips. She smiles up at Bligh who must have had a joke with her dressed as he was in a uniform from the castle fire department.

The Lead Kindly Lights make a grand entrance. Using the double ballroom doors. She in the sedan chair a military guard of insurgents on either side. Followed by

Himself of The Backside Contorted adorned as a leprechaun. Carrying a large volume of illustrated architecture. Folk wander staring at the tapestries and paintings. Spouts of champagne gushing at the ceiling. From the hands of the militia who said it was essential to shake the bottle. And from the taller of the Fucking Bad Evil lurking in the distant corner came a shout.

'Give the women in the bed more rigidity.'

Clementine wearing his silver crown of filigree surveying his guests. Passing now to and fro like thirsty cattle on a large desert. Drives away for a moment the doom of the morrow. Which comes pressing on throbbing temples of the brain. As light floods the room with the very last of the candles. Spiced with incense. A man there in a light brown coat. And striped red bow tie. His smooth round cheeks and sandy hair. Eating a canapé. As he smiles to himself. Sees me. And heads over.

'Do you mind if I come over and talk to you. I've never been to a fancy dress ball before. My name's Steve. But nobody talks to me. I just tagged along when a whole gang of people suddenly downed their drinks and poured out of a pub. I guess you were invited I thought I'd retire in this country. It's quaint. But I get awful homesick. Every morning I just sit and imagine myself doing exactly the same thing I did all the years I worked back at the office. Taking my bus, buying the newspaper. Having a cup of coffee on the ferry and sometimes a hot dog crossing the bay. It was just three hundred and eighty six steps across the park. from the ferry slip to the office. I still count them every morning. See myself going up on the elevator. Saying good morning to the guys. I hear their voices as if I was still back at my desk. I try to talk to the embassy staff over here but I never get very far before they seem to want to get rid of me and talk to somebody else. You're one of the first people I've met who has just stood there listening. And you know what. Since you've been so patient I'm not going to bother you one second more. And thanks.'

Steve retreating sadly with his social triumph. Moving along towards the roulette wheel whirring away. Could have told him how I stand sometimes talking to the guys back at the office. Mostly spouting unpleasantly sarcastic things to them. All flat arsed and big stomached with the years of sitting larding on the seniority. Should have cabled them an invitation. You are all carnally invited for a last cavort in the Charnel. Before the joint is put up for sale. As a most attractive large estate. Set in gently mountainous countryside. A fine pre christian castle with later additions all in keeping with the original. Astonishing unspoilt views without and within. Complete with antique furnishings, staff, and varied guests. To be seen strictly at viewer's risk and by appointment only.

The gathering enlarging with arrivals by the minute. Clementine climbing lonely to the rampart of the gate tower. To stand under a clear sky slowly opening from the west. Big bright stars on this moonless night. Air clear moist and cool. Stare up at the blazing sparkling heavens and all worldly wrong doing vanishes. Till you look down again. And hear a voice high pitched and cultured straying out of the night.

'I will not rat. I absolutely will never rat. Unless I absolutely have to.'

Breeze makes the eyes water. A group of farmers standing watching the lighted windows. Too shy to enter the cattle market inside. Full of parlour games. Percival has raised my flag to fly through the night. But time now after this breather to descend back to the ballroom. And find a man raising his château filled bottle high and standing on a chair to maintain.

'I will not be defamed.'

'What will you be.'

'I will be exhumed.'

'And what next begorra.'

'I will be thrilled.'

'And what next for land sakes.'

'I will be excommunicated.'

Commandant Macdurex approaching Clementine for a chat. Glass in hand. Unlike his troops who dispensed with preliminary pourings.

'Ah Mr Clementine I'm watching the boys. I wouldn't want to see a breakdown in discipline. I hope you don't mind but you are my prisoner of war.'

'What.'

'No need for alarm now. I mean to say there will be no incarceration. None of that. I'd be reduced in rank if my superiors ever got wind of what's going on here. Profligacy without profundity but with lots of poteen. Awaiting shall we say the ripeness necessary to squeeze the grapes of beauty. Are you with me.'

'I hope so.'

'The high command are having their portraits painted together back in the capital at this moment. I wouldn't want them to be in receipt of a bad communiqué from the battle front. To put a look of displeasure on their faces recorded for all time. As full as some of them are with the smartology. But now there are two of your fellows here, deserters and betrayers to the cause. And before the night's out we're going to hang them by the bollocks from the towers up there above. The dirty filthy pair of them. Are you with me. Last night we had a successful blast with no political motive but by God it levelled the place anyway. And let the saints be with us in future tactical exploits. Up the republic.'

Figures jigging on the floor. Fiddlers playing to beat the band. Elmer sitting on haunches loosing long yowls and howls. As the guests shrink back. And a man crouches behind a chair with a revolver drawn. Now advancing on hands and knees upon some objective further down the ballroom. And looking up dresses on the way. His face florid. His crouching posture playful. As the commandant surveys the cherubs, clouds and painted pastures on the ceiling and circles round to keep me between himself and Elmer.

'It's a fine place you have here Mr Clementine. If I wasn't running a tank division it would suit me with a few beasts grazing and a cow milking. Here I am with a bunch of them after ministerial posts when the new regime takes over. Private limousines, free liquor and telephone calls. And if they weren't god fearing you might even say free women. To tell you the truth my orders were to turn the lot of you out onto the landscape. But as you displayed hospitality instead of resistance what right thinking man would be churlish enough to do that. You'll be recommended as a man of cultivation in my report back to headquarters. Sure you've laid out the fermented beverages without stint. What could be more humane or law abiding. Or by god patriotic. Now intelligence tells me that at the other end of the room there is a gentleman as has arrived completely coloured black. Now my men have never set eyes on one before. And maybe we could have a view of him if he's still here in the daylight. For me own satisfaction I'd like to know if his more intimate parts are darkened too. Many are the little mysteries in life that still bedevil me.'

Clementine craning neck to see over and between the heads. To a rotund man of dark complexion grinning whitely from his round face. His person aflow in tweeds. Moving this way. A bright orange tie in a large knot on a deep red shirt. And suede boots over which his trouser cuffs generously drape. A retinue of colourfully attired white attendants following him. As he speaks in languorous tones. A gathering of ladies and Charlene's little brothers and sisters pressing near as he pauses to examine tapestries close up. His attendants holding back the crowd. If any more of them push past Percival's chalk line, your Ebony Nibs will be a floor or two below white with dust and debris.

'Will you look at that now Mr Clementine. A man he has holding a platter at the ready at his elbow piled with a plentitude of your fried chicken. And him taking a nibble as the fancy grips him. By God it's a lesson to us with our backward ways.'

'Commandant please let me introduce you to a friend of mine, Major Macfugger.'

'What. What's that. Where. Where is he.'

'Over there.'

'By God I'll have him under arrest.'

'Now Commandant he is after all my guest.'

'Well it's not that I would want to be spiteful. But when hasn't a man concerned with dignified manners not been enforced upon occasion to employ instant justice when some of your niceties had to become scarce.'

Macfugger from his elegant regalia putting forth his hand upon introduction. As Macdurex takes it sheepishly and nods his head. Clementine shifting slowly away as their conversation blossomed concerning the proper manner in which to take a fortified height held in strength with mortars and bren guns.

The evening developing nicely. The victuals being swept off the plates, lobster, oysters, shrimps, jugged hare and roast pigeon. Imelda, Oscar and Percival ferrying the delicate meat pastes, goodies and salmon delights. Stand here as everyone beams at me. Bravely smile back. Even Elmer who gulped down the one and only pheasant tries to lick my face. A fright he gave me this morning as I bent disrobed over my wash bowl slapping up the lathers. And he put in from behind a bumping cold nose investigating against my testiculars. And I thought it was a mamba.

'Sir sir.'

'What is it Percival.'

'We've run out of candles. Not to mention the curry, fruit, shortbread and anchovy. The wicks are going out one by one. Hear the hounds. The hunt will be here any minute. With us plunging into blackness by the second. And there be a lot of people around tonight that might do in the dark what they wouldn't do in the light.'

A roar out in the hall. A gasp of ladies and the gathering parting. A man, a potato sack over his head, two holes cut for a pair of wild eyes, comes charging in with a hedge hook in his hand. Scattering guests in the last flickers of light. The high pitched screams and low growling shouts arising.

'The roulette's a fraud.'

'Down with frugality.'

'Give the woman in the bed a plutocrat.'

'By God I'll puncture your aqueous humour.'

'Who did that.'

'Stop thief my udometer's been stolen.'

'Take your hand out of my mouth.'

'God sir, listen to them. This is it. That's Padrick in the sack. That fearsome scourge of the countryside would drive a team of horses over you laughing while he made a juice of your guts. And by God hasn't he got his sheep and lambs with him. Listen to the bleating. Hear them out there roaring down the halls. We're already destroyed this night and it will be worse if the hounds get in the castle. Where are you your majesty. I've lost me monocle.'

The crack of Macfugger's whip. Four revolver shots. And I am distantly here cowering between a pair of finely carved post medieval gilt wood console tables. The commandant shouting. All troops rendezvous. In the flickering firelight the beastly bombast continues. The band playing on. Grab this bottle of champagne out of this poor momentarily stunned guest's hand. As his mouth drops further open and speaks to the priest next to him.

'Forgive them father for they know not what they do.'

'I've been forgiving them all night and it's time now I had a rest if you don't mind.'

Clementine putting the bottle to his lips. Draining the foaming grape liquid. Just as one last candle reawakened on a chandelier and finally flickered out. Time to head for the routes of escape. Whoops. Back down. Something whistling overhead. And smashing. O my god I can tell by the impact. That the showering pieces are Meissen. Scattering everywhere in the bitterness unbelievable. The silhouette of the Baron. Standing in the doorway.

'Someone hast peed upon die turntable of der gramophone. In die middle of der fifth symphony. Vere is he. I will kill him.'

A collapse of floor boards. Thinning shadows along the east wall. Enough writs will be pouring in to keep the fires raging in the grates. Bloodmourn. The unmistakable flat backed shadow of his head. A bottle upended over his mouth. Looks so at home in his court attire. Could have begun a kingdom. Swarming with serfs. What's this.

Nudging fat lump of wool. A lamb. Thinking I'm its mother. Giving me a case of the shudders. When only looking for udders. As the voices in the wilderness roar.

'You adventist. I'll fix you. Or I'm not Lead Kindly Light of the Partial Previous Paroxysm for nothing.'

'Take your filthy hands off my solicitor.'

'It's your wife I'm after.'

'Give us your truffles and we'll give you a taste of our fucking bad evil.'

A tiny man arms outstretched standing on a chair. Pleading out over the milling heads. With a voice of moderation in the cataclysm.

'Will the misfits among you speak up and be conducted to safety. Those with religious training please assist survivors. Let the children out. I beg of you.'

'If you'll take his colossus why not try my proboscis as well.'

'Up the republic.'

The little lamb between Clementine's knees bleating for its mother. Who will be somewhere butting among the guests. As the hounds bay and hooves clatter down in the forecourt. Peaceful it was back in that hospital bed slowly dying. Waiting till the sheets were pulled up over my face. Just before lunch I would have been quietly rolled away. Slid into the refrigerator. Cold and still. With all the others. Stacked up and beaten. To whisper in the gates of heaven. I'm here. And thank you for having me.

Clementine suddenly crownless cowering further in under the table. Only moments ago on the verge of the best of health. The carnage at least is much as usual. Vituperative visitors up to their elbows in misunderstanding and distress. People adore not paying for the damage that's done. Trampling sauce boats and graceful tureens. Kicking a portable silver egg boiler to pieces. Making sure none of us capture a moment of pastoral peace. Like the kind you find in the front halls of embassies. Where I dreamt I wandered last night. Desperate for decorum. Among the sweet breathed staff in their gleaming shirtsleeves and glazed smooth brown eyes. Two had blue. Oozing ease and relaxa-

tion. As they sat in their spotless cubicles. The right angles
of grey. Cool stiffness everywhere. White printed forms between their pink long fingers. I came to ask them please.
Would you endow my castle for posterity. And they said.
Now sir. Just gaze here on the small print and questions.
Did you wear white socks from your last abode to your most
recent destination. And have you in the last five years been
a mother fucker, cocksucker or any variation thereof.
Please fill in and sign. We like to have a friendly record.
In case you get murdered out there in the lonely countryside. Folk will want to know if you were solvent before you
died. And that your tightfisted grand aunt was your next of
kin. The embassy so calm. With the same kind of cunts
who nudged me to my doom back at the office. And now
I see them all grinning behind their glasses to make me
raise my right hand and say. I do solemnly swear I deserve
what the whole goddamn bunch of you are trying to do to
me.

With a gilt crest emblazoned sauce boat on the head,
Clementine crawling past a rosewood couch where someone
was getting theirs. One underneath and one on top. Just
take a peek. To see who's gasping and kicking in the air.
Whoops. It's Gloria. Gladly supple and supine, death mask
and all. Covered by the tweedy dark complexioned gentleman. Having his fill at her oasis. Get past that sorrow. Of
poor Erconwald. Just a few more feet to the double door.
Out of this hostile hootenanny. Where a grateful voice
asks.

'What pale hand touches me with tenderness.'

'It's fucking well not mine I can tell you.'

North along the corridor. Elmer charging after the thundering hooves of sheep and lambs. As I step back out of
the stampede. Into the narrow entrance and down the spiral
stone stairs. Stop here against the cold wall to catch my
breath. How will I ever recline. Saved in bath waters laced
with scent. Unleashing wisdoms to soothe the mind. To
make peace now to have ass later. Charlene where are you.
Pink and mild of tit. Two flowers alive. Waving on your
bosom. Nestle up against your skin. Before any more

glooms gather. Or members of the hunt with hounds come crashing through. And cries of I've been goosed rise. Or the motto of my forbears is sounded for the last time.

> Be
> Without bitterness
> Be
> Without gall
> And you'll
> Be
> Completely
> Without
> Fuck all

22

A barren dawn. After the ball. Reared up strange. Creeping east. Across the wild dark heathers. A pale purple light rising. Warming Macfugger's pastures beyond the mountains. And turning pink the chill mist over the sea.

Charlene lay down deep under the mountain of covers behind the bed tapestries drawn. A tiny naked friend. Into whom as she lay sobbing I pushed my pole. And planted a seed. With my handy gardening tool.

Last night Commander Macdurex crushed a message in my fist. Not to be read till morning. And on the stained crumpled sheet a poem.

> Deep down
> In that derry
> The ball last night
> Was merry
> The dance
> They did
> Was for
> Two legs
> Because the third
> Was sticking out
> A mile
> For balance

In a hushed household this morning Percival made breakfast. Stood at the bed pouring my coffee and said there was no sign of Charlene. And that the ballroom had the greatest collection of nervous wrecks around which a civilized man ever had to manoeuvre. Only for the exits being guarded by the insurgents one bunch would have got away with a valuable piece of statuary. But the commandant stepped in and said the artistic fitting would be a handy feature for state banquets in the new regime.

Touches of dark green now on the hillsides. That rise up brown and purple in the evening. After a long day lying delectably abed. To get up now and dress. Go collect my gladstone bag due to arrive on the train.

Clementine in long leather great coat walking alone with Elmer. Up the stony winding road. Pheasants chattering somewhere beyond the fuchsia in the briars and laurels. Seagulls back there in the turrets looming of Charnel Castle. From which last night the banker Mr Oboe and his wife fled. As the hunt on horseback went pounding in. Watched at the gates by the shy farmers laughing behind their big hands. Macfugger challenged to a duel a man accusing him that his name was originally Macfuggerborn. And Nails with his bull whip wrapped a lash around the poor chap's ankles and upended him on his arse, saying it was true but no one was going to suggest thereby that he was a born fugger. Then he took a flying leap to the roof of his state coach. And with whip snapping and reins shivering thundered off four horsed down the road shouting.

'Where's my unfaithful wife I want to fuck her.'

At these crossroads. Great grey clouds pass. Leave a sky lonely dark and blue. The same ancient cold chill in my feet. Elmer sniffing and spreading his legs lady like to pee. Found Erconwald last night seated in a corner darkness of the library. Hands folded in his lap. In the light of the glowing turf embers his face awet with tears. The Baron and Bloodmourn nearby across the chess table with a jeroboam of port. On the verge of checkmate. The veins standing out blue and throbbing from Bloodmourn's temples. And as I crossed the great hall in the dawn I saw Franz fixing a new sign to the mine shaft door.

CLOSED FOR REPAIRS

The last light of sun. Sinking at the edge of the sea. Hear the whistle of the train. Puffing and passing over what must now be mamba meadows. Give Clarence something to hop from behind the boulders.

'Good evening.'

The antiquarian standing smiling. As Clementine spins around. Elmer wagging his long grey tail. This man's ash plant tapping the toe of his shoe sticking out from the same bespattered spats. His brown fedora rim low over his eyes. Collar up at his throat. As I squeak out a greeting. Surprised once again from the rear.

'Good evening.'

'I see you and your fine big dog are waiting for the train.'

'Yes.'

'Well I won't disturb your peace while you do anything as important as that. But I'm glad hear tell you've settled nicely in the castle. It's a comfort knowing there's someone out there beyond keeping the loneliness at bay. God bless you this night.'

'Thank you.'

The train chugging to a stop. A salute from the driver giving me an urgent message to be delivered to Dr Franz Pickle. And Micko off the goods van greeting one warmly and handing down my bag. Together with parcels of coffee beans, barmbracks and crystallized ginger for the castle.

The train click clacking down the track. A fading echoing hoot. The arrival of unpaid for goods cheers the heart. Give me energy to go on thinking how to afford it all. And now with burdens ashoulder. Walk this pebbly road. Where a curlew flies up from the land. Its long sad whistle could be a call to another hooley starting in the castle. Awakening bodies hungry for entwinements. Don't you dare slip me your peninsula. Not while I'm panting anyway.

Walk now over this little bridge. Where the brook tumbles under. And grey speckled trout speed for cover. Franz's mother may have died. Or he's found gold in the castle. The road here starts up. Between the trees of the demesne. Out there far away the rest of the world has gone modern. With whole new jumping generations. And holy hell is the only thing we have up to date here. To make the stars bark. When the west's awake. Over the cliffs and roaring sea. Where the moon hides and weeps at night.

And
The weary
Wind
Bewilders
Me

Also in Penguins

THE GINGER MAN

J. P. Donleavy

In the person of *The Ginger Man*, Sebastian Dangerfield, Donleavy created one of the most outrageous scoundrels in contemporary fiction, a whoring, boozing young wastrel who sponges off his friends and beats his wife and girl friends. Donleavy then turns the moral universe on its head by making the reader love Dangerfield for his killer instinct, flamboyant charm, wit, flashing generosity – and above all for his wild, fierce, two-handed grab for every precious second of life – *Time Magazine*

No one who encounters him will forget Sebastian Dangerfield – *New York Herald Tribune*

First published in Paris in 1955. An expurgated edition appeared in England in 1956 and in the United States in 1958. The complete and unexpurgated edition was brought out in England in 1963 and in the United States in 1965.

Also in Penguins

MEET MY MAKER THE MAD MOLECULE

J. P. Donleavy

In this book of short pieces Donleavy has given us the lyric poems to go with his epics. They are almost all elegies – sad songs of decayed hope, bitter little jitter-buggings of an exasperated soul, with barracuda bites of lacerating humour to bring blood-red into the grey of fate. These stories and sketches move between Europe and America, New York and Dublin and London. America is always the spoiled Paradise, the land of curdled milk and maggoty honey. The place that used to get you in the end, but that now does it in the beginning – *Newsweek*

The stories are swift, imaginative, beautiful, and funny, and no contemporary writer is better than J. P. Donleavy at his best – *The New Yorker*

A collection of short stories and sketches which were published between 1954 and 1964 in leading English and American papers and magazines. First published in book form in the United States in 1964, England 1965.

Also in Penguins

THE SADDEST SUMMER OF SAMUEL S

J. P. Donleavy

In this short novel J. P. Donleavy writes of the tiny
battle waged for survival of the spirit in bedrooms and
hearts the world over. Samuel S, hero of lonely
principles, holds out in his bereft lighthouse in Vienna.
Abigail, an American college girl on the prowl in
Europe, drawn by the beacon of this strange outpost,
seeks in her own emancipation the seduction of Samuel
S, the last of the world's solemn failures.

'Mr Donleavy manages to be funny about so much that
one would have thought nobody could be funny about
again – sole drunkenness, hangovers, American
expatriates and tourists, and cross-talk from the
psychiatric couch' – *The New Yorker*

A first-rate comedy of the saddest sort – *New York
Times*

A haunting story, touchingly and outrageously told –
Boston Sunday Globe

First published in the United States in 1966 and
England 1967.

Also in Penguins

A SINGULAR MAN

J. P. Donleavy

His giant mausoleum abuilding, George Smith, the mysterious man of money, lives in a world rampant with mischief, of chiselers and cheats. Having side-stepped slowly away down the little alleys of success he tiptoes through a luxurious, lonely life between a dictatorial Negress housekeeper and two secretaries, one of which, Sally Tomson, the gay wild and willing beauty, he falls in love with.

George Smith is such a man as Manhattan's subway millions have dreamed of being – *Time Magazine*

A masterpiece of writing about love – *National Observer*

One of the strangest, loneliest and unluckiest figures in modern fiction. *A Singular Man* with its pathetically loveable hero, its bawdy humour, its insane atmosphere, is an utterly irresistible broth of a book – *Daily Telegraph*

First published in the United States in 1963 and England 1964.

Also available

The Beastly Beatitudes of Balthazar B

MORE ABOUT PENGUINS

Penguinews, which appears every month, contains details of all the new books issued by Penguins as they are published. From time to time it is supplemented by *Penguins in Print*, which is a complete list of all available books published by Penguins. (There are well over three thousand of these.)

A specimen copy of *Penguinews* will be sent to you free on request, and you can become a subscriber for the price of the postage. For a year's issues (including the complete lists) please send 30p if you live in the United Kingdom, or 60p if you live elsewhere. Just write to Dept EP, Penguin Books Ltd, Harmondsworth, Middlesex, enclosing a cheque or postal order, and your name will be added to the mailing list.

Note: *Penguinews* and *Penguins in Print* are not available in the U.S.A. or Canada